Science without religion is lame.
Religion without science is blind.

Albert Einstein

ACKNOWLEDGMENTS

In no particular order, I'd like to thank Elaine Mills for her increasingly professional editing work and for keeping an eye on the competition for me. Darrell Mills, for lending me his technical expertise and in anticipation of his continued marketing effort. My wife, Kim, for all her insight and effort, but mostly for tolerating the occasional panic attacks that I think grip all novelists on their second try. Laura Liner, for providing the soundtrack. Robert Gottlieb and Matt Bialer at William Morris, for their enthusiasm and hard work. And finally, John Silbersack, Caitlin Blasdell and the rest of the gang at HarperCollins, for all the amazing things they've done for me.

I

A TRAGIC HEART ATTACK AT THE TENDER YOUNG age of fifteen and a half, Jennifer Davis thought. That's what the headlines would say tomorrow.

She stood up on her pedals, but had to sit down again when the back wheel of her mountain bike lost traction. Less than halfway up the last climb of the race, her lungs already felt like they were full of hot tar. Worse, she could hear the unmistakable crunch of tires closing in on her from behind.

Jennifer glanced back over her shoulder, ignoring the flaring color of the sunset as the light filtered through the Phoenix smog, and focused on the face of the rider behind her.

The good news was that he looked like he was in bad shape. His mouth was wide open and, despite the dry cold of the desert, the sweat was literally streaming off his nose.

The bad news was that she felt like he looked.

The angle of the hill eased off a bit and Jennifer stood up again. This time her tire held and she was able to accelerate slightly, struggling to stay out front.

The panting behind her grew louder as the rider began to close the distance between them. Jennifer grudgingly eased her bike right to allow a lane for him to pass, and then dropped her head and pedaled with everything she had.

About twenty-five yards from the crest of the hill, when he was only inches behind, he gave up. She heard a gasped obscenity and the unmistakable click of gears as he downshifted.

Jennifer remained standing, in case it was a trick or he got a second wind, but when she looked back again, he was off his bike, pushing it slowly up the hill.

At the top of the climb, Jennifer leaned forward and rested her arms against her handlebars. A small but enthusiastic crowd lined the narrow trail, and she coasted carefully through them.

She could see her parents threading their way through the throng as she passed under the checkered banner that announced the finish line. When her father jogged up alongside her, she draped an arm around his shoulders and used him as a crutch as she slid off her bike and fell to the ground.

"Great job, Jen! I thought that guy was going to get you on the hill!" She closed her eyes and listened as her father picked up her bike and rolled it off the track.

"Honey? Are you all right?"

Jennifer opened her eyes and looked into the plump face of her mother hovering over her. "Fine, Mom. No problem." She turned to her father. "How'd I do, Dad?"

"Fourth place, looks like to me. Just out of the money."

Jennifer let out a low groan as she stood and began pushing her way through the crowd, shaking various hands and stopping briefly to talk and laugh with friends and other racers.

"We've got a surprise for you, honey," her father

said as they broke free of the crowd and headed for the parking lot. Jennifer slowed and then stopped. Her father just wasn't the no-specific-occasion gift-giving type. Surprises were usually a bad thing. Her eyes followed his outstretched index finger to a white Ford Explorer in the parking lot. Three people stood next to it. Two of the three were waving.

"Oh Dad. You didn't."

"What? The Taylors have really been looking forward to seeing you race."

Her mother smiled. "They really have, honey."

The Taylors had lived two doors down from them for as long as Jennifer could remember. And for as long as she could remember, they and her parents had been conspiring to get her together with Billy, the Taylors' football-playing, cheerleader-chasing, Budweiser-swilling moron of a son.

As they neared the parking lot, Mrs. Taylor rushed up to Jennifer with her arms flung wide. She thought better of the big hug she had undoubtedly been planning when she saw the amount of mud caked on Jennifer's jersey. Instead, she adjusted an imaginary flaw in her rather tall hair and opted for a distant peck on the cheek. "Wow, that was really impressive, Jennifer. Very exciting." She turned to her semicatatonic son. "Wasn't it, Billy?" He snapped out of his stupor long enough to generate a weak smile.

There was a short lull in the conversation while everyone waited to see if he would actually speak. When it became obvious that he wouldn't, her father said, "We thought we'd go out and grab some dinner before we drive back to Flagstaff. What do you think, Jen?"

"Are you kidding? Look at me!" Jennifer took off her helmet and held her arms out to give him a better view. She was spattered head to toe in mud. A gash above her knee, suffered on the first downhill of the race, was still oozing blood. And to top it off, her hair had taken on the shape of her helmet.

Her father didn't look impressed. "We'll just tell them you were in a mountain bike race. They'll understand."

She assumed that "they" referred to the maitre d' of a really, really snooty restaurant, who would look at her like she was a homeless person and then grudgingly get them a table because her father was the largest car dealer in Arizona.

Jennifer sighed and walked over to her parents' Cadillac. Leaning into the open window, she pulled out a small backpack containing a change of underwear, a pair of shorts, and a sweatshirt.

"I'll be back in a minute," she said, walking toward a white van with SPECIALIZED painted in red across the side.

"That work?" Jennifer asked the young man sitting on a lawn chair in front of the van. He put down the hopelessly misshapen wheel he had been contemplating and picked up the end of the hose lying next to him.

"Sure, Jen. You want to spray off your bike?"

"My parents want to go out for dinner."

He examined her carefully and fished a beer out of the cooler next to his chair. "It's gonna be pretty cold."

She tossed her pack through the window of his van and waved him on. "Do it."

"Okay, now I'm ready," Jennifer said, wearing her clean clothes and drying her hair with a heavily stained towel her friend with the van had loaned her. She bent forward and shook out her damp, unnaturally blonde hair. "Hey, Billy. None of this grease is coming off in my hair, is it?"

Her question had the desired effect. Billy looked appalled.

"Well, I thought it was a very nice dinner."

Jennifer rolled her eyes.

"Watch the road, honey," her mother cautioned. "They'll deduct points on your driver's test."

Jennifer reached over and turned the volume of the radio all the way down. "Mom, Billy and I have known each other our whole lives. He's a jerk. And he thinks I'm a jerk. My history teacher says that most people faced with a common enemy, in this case you guys, develop at least a teeny bit of a friendship. You'll notice we haven't."

Her mother's chins drooped. "They're such a nice family, I don't see why you're so resistant . . ."

Jennifer craned her neck and looked at her father, who had retreated to the far corner of the back seat. "Help me out here, Dad."

He ignored her and continued to peruse the road map lying in his lap, apparently oblivious to the fact that they were half a mile from home.

Jennifer turned back before her mother could get on her about her driving again. "Try to follow me here, Mom. Billy likes the cheerleader type. Girls with long red nails who can squeal at just the right pitch when he makes a touchdown. Besides, I *have* a boyfriend. And he hasn't been lobotomized."

Jennifer flipped on the blinker and turned the car into their driveway. She sped along the winding drive and escaped the car before her mother could start in again.

As she pulled her bike off the top of the car, she tried to ignore the cold and her mother's pouting form walking toward the house. It looked like the guilt was going to get pretty thick tonight.

Jennifer wheeled her bike into the open garage and leaned it against the wall. "You want me to pull the car in, Mom?" she yelled at the open door that led to the kitchen.

No answer. Yeah, this was going to be one serious guilt trip, she thought, jogging up a short flight of stairs and stopping at the door. The lights inside the house were still off. "Did we blow another fuse? Dad? Do you want me to check the box?"

"Run, Jennifer!"

She froze at the sound of her father's strangled voice. The rhythm and force of her heartbeat increased until she could almost hear it in the silence following his shout.

She took the last step into the house hesitantly and edged up to the washing machine so she could see into the kitchen. "Dad?"

It took a moment for her eyes to adjust from the glare of the bare bulbs in the garage to the gloom of the kitchen, but the moonlight streaming though the windows above the sink created enough colorless contrast to see what was happening.

A man in a dark suit was dragging her mother toward the living room. His hand was clamped over her mouth and his thumb and index finger pinched her nose shut.

Jennifer resisted the urge to run to her mother and pry the man's hands from her face. Instead, she retreated, almost falling backward down the steps. When she reached out to steady herself, her eyes finally found her father. He was pinned against the kitchen counter by a similarly dressed man. The combination of a thick forearm pressed against his throat and a gun pushed into his cheek had silenced him.

Everything in her told her to stay and fight, but she knew that would be stupid. There was nothing she could do. She had to go for help.

She spun around and cleared the stairs leading into the garage in one jump. The keys were still in the car.

She didn't see the hand as it reached out from behind her father's tool bench and grabbed her by the back of her sweatshirt; she only felt the shirt go tight across her chest and her feet skid out from under her. She would have fallen on her back, except a powerful arm had snaked around her waist. An instant later, the hand that had been tangled in her sweatshirt moved to her face and clamped over her mouth and nose.

She thrashed wildly when her air was cut off, surprising her captor with her strength and throwing them both against the wall. She grabbed at his arm, finally getting her fingers behind something that felt like a thick metal bracelet.

It was hopeless. Panic and lack of air were making her groggy, and she felt herself weakening as she fought back the blank whiteness encroaching on her peripheral vision. It took only a moment for the man to regain his balance and lift her off her feet, robbing her of what little leverage she had.

Making one last effort, she grabbed for the door-jamb as she was carried into the house. Her strength had left her, though, and her sweaty fingers slid ineffectually along the wall.

"Stop!"

Jennifer heard the shout—a woman's voice—but had no idea where it came from. The fingers around her nose loosened and she felt her feet connect with the ground, though the man's arm remained tight around her waist and his hand was still clamped on her mouth. She took in a deep breath through her nose and felt the oxygenated blood begin to clear her head.

A woman stepped out from behind the shadow of the refrigerator, prompting the man holding her to loosen his grip a bit more and allow her to take another deep breath as she watched the woman approach.

She was probably three inches shorter than Jennifer's five-nine, with a boyish haircut—short and parted on the side. Her skin must have been very pale, because it just glowed the color of the moonlight bathing the room.

The woman stopped about a foot away and reached out. Jennifer jerked her head back, but it just bounced off the chest of the man holding her.

"You must be very still and very quiet," the woman said, running a hand through Jennifer's hair.

Jennifer let out a quiet squeal, muffled by the hand still clamped over her mouth. She tried to look into the woman's eyes to see if there was anything there that could tell her what was happening, but they just looked black.

The woman moved to her right slightly, letting the moonlight hit her fully in the face. "Look at me, Jennifer. You will be quiet, won't you?"

Her voice was smooth and soft, but her newly illuminated eyes looked cold and cruel. Jennifer wanted to scream when the man's hand slid from her mouth, but she found herself transfixed by the woman's stare.

"That's better," the woman said, letting her fingers fall from Jennifer's hair and slide down her arm, finally closing them around Jennifer's wrist. "Come with me. There's something I want you to see."

She pulled Jennifer from the arms holding her and toward the living room. Jennifer wanted to break away, to run for help, but she was afraid. Not of the man who had captured her or the ones who had subdued her parents, but of this small, pale woman and what her eyes told Jennifer she was capable of.

She allowed herself to be led to a small loveseat situated on the far wall of the living room. The light was better there, thanks to two skylights and the large windows that surrounded the room.

Jennifer sat down on the sofa that she had spent so many nights on—watching TV, doing homework, talking on the phone. But now her eyes were locked on her parents and the men holding them at gunpoint at the other end of the room. The woman's hand slid from her wrist and Jennifer watched her walk through the moonlight to her parents and begin speaking quietly to them. Jennifer leaned forward to try and hear what was being said, but a strong hand grasped her shoulder and pulled her back.

She watched them for what seemed like forever. The shadows made it difficult to read their expressions, but she could see the tension slowly falling from her parents' bodies. Her father was the first to peel his back off the wall, followed closely by her mother, who stepped forward, put her arms around the small woman, and began to sob. The muffled sound coming from her throat was a strange combination of deep sorrow and joy that Jennifer had only heard once before—when a close family friend had died after a long and painful bout with bone cancer.

Jennifer relaxed slightly. The cruelty she had seen in the woman and that had caused a nauseous feeling of hopelessness to form in the pit of her stomach must have been a trick of light and darkness. Her parents recognized her. Maybe they'd known her for years. Perhaps the woman was afraid, too. Perhaps she was here because she needed their help.

When the man standing next to her father reached out and offered him his gun, Jennifer let out a deep sigh of relief. Certainly killers and rapists weren't in the habit of arming their victims. Maybe she and her family were in some kind of danger and these people were here to protect them?

Her father wiped at his eyes with his sleeve as he took the gun. Jennifer watched as he weighed it uncomfortably, then pointed it at the back of her mother's head and pulled the trigger.

For a moment she felt like she was sitting in a dark theater watching a movie. The crack of the pistol, her mother's body jerking forward, the black fluid momentarily backlit and then silently painting the wall.

Jennifer threw herself forward, trying to escape the sofa, but the man behind her had anticipated this and jerked her back again. The room started to spin and she felt her stomach tighten into a sickening knot as she struggled against the hands that held her in place.

"Daddy!" she screamed as her father tucked the gun under his chin.

Her shout seemed to pull him from his trance, and he hesitated for a moment. "I know this is hard, honey. But you don't belong just to us. You never belonged just to us."

The gun sounded again and the window behind her father cracked from top to bottom, leaving a spiderweb prism as he collapsed to the ground.

She felt all the strength go out of her. She slumped forward and turned away from the scene in front of her. For a moment, it felt as though she had forgotten how to breathe. Her mind seemed to shut down everything as it tried to process what had just happened.

Her parents had both been only children and her grandparents had been dead for years. In an instant she had gone from being one-third of a happy family to being completely alone. It must be a dream. A nightmare. It must be.

She didn't see the woman approach, and barely noticed when she knelt in front of her. Jennifer saw the dull flash of the syringe in the woman's hand and felt herself being pushed face down into the soft cushions. A hand slid beneath her stomach, unbuttoned her shorts, and pulled them and her underwear down. There was the sharp jab of the needle and an unnatural heat flooding her body. Then there was nothing.

2

"PUTTING'S NOT GOLF," MARK BEAMON SAID, finally nudging his ball the last three inches to the hole. "Guess that'd be, uh, seven?"

"Try eight," the man with the scorecard said. "If you didn't swing so hard, you wouldn't have to try to improve your game with creative math."

Beamon hiked up his red-and-green-checked pants and dunked his hand into the cup. "I don't think you appreciate the subtle genius of my game, Dave."

"Oh, but I do, Mark. That genius is the reason I haven't had to pay for a drink at the clubhouse since you moved to Arizona." He nodded toward a tall, squarely built man standing at the edge of the green. "You're up, Jake."

Beamon slid his putter into his bag and dropped into the driver's seat of the cart to watch Jacob Layman, his new boss, putt. It was an easy shot and Beamon tried to will it in, but the ball broke right and missed by a good three inches.

Another brilliant plan shot to hell, he thought as he watched a flush grow slowly out of the man's polo shirt.

Layman was apparently from a "good" Virginia family—whatever that meant. He'd attended the right prep schools and had enjoyed a successful, if not exceptional, career in the FBI.

Because of this, and despite the fact that he wasn't exactly a barrel of laughs, Layman had risen to a respectable height in Arizona's social circles. It was a position that, through incessant name-dropping, he never let anyone forget.

Enter Mark Beamon, an overweight and poorly dressed product of the Texas public school system. Favorite pastime: drinking and eating too much at parties, then insulting the guests.

But Beamon had spent his career riding herd over some of the FBI's most complicated and visible cases. His face had been on TV, in magazines, and all over local newspapers. It was the kind of career that made you powerful friends.

Despite his somewhat intentional lack of social graces and the fact that he'd only moved to Arizona a month ago, Beamon had already been befriended by some of the most powerful people in the state. Suddenly he was what his secretary called an "A" party guest.

Initially, Beamon had accepted his new stature with good humor. Why not? Sure, the people could be a little phony and dangerously boring, but the food was good and the booze was free. He'd started to rethink things, though, when he'd noticed a rapid cooling in Layman's attitude toward him.

At first he'd thought his new boss had found out that some of his people were bypassing him and coming to directly to Beamon for advice on tough cases—a practice Beamon strongly discouraged. But then it became clear that it didn't have anything to do with the job. He just felt that Beamon had overstepped his natural-born social status.

And so here they were.

A few years ago, he would have ignored the situation and eventually paid for his refusal to play the game. But now he was the new, improved Mark Beamon. He'd cut his smoking in half, taken up a sport, made a valiant and modestly successful attempt to replace bourbon with beer, and promised himself that he would suffer no more concussions from beating his head against the Bureau's political brick wall.

Today's golf excursion included the mayor of Flagstaff and the star of a Fox crime drama filmed in Tucson, neither of whom had been particularly excited by Beamon's insistence that his new boss round out the foursome.

And now Layman was having what was probably the worst game of his life.

Beamon twisted around and tossed his empty beer can in the cooler bungee-corded to the back of the cart, then pulled out a full one and popped the top. "Make it up on the next one, Jake," he said as his boss slammed his putter into his bag and slumped into the seat next to him.

Somehow it didn't look like Layman was going to remember this as the peace offering he had intended.

Beamon jumped on the accelerator and hurtled down the cart path, ignoring the cold wind penetrating his golf shirt and trying to forget that the man sitting next to him was probably trying to figure out a way to work the word "asshole" into his next performance appraisal.

When they arrived at the next hole, Beamon

grabbed his driver and went to stand at the tee, leaving Layman to sulk in the cart. As their partners pulled up, the unmistakable chirping of a beeper started in earnest. Layman looked down at his hip and the mayor toward his bag, but Beamon was already holding his up like a trophy. "Mine."

He dropped his driver, walked back to the cart, and began digging through his bag for his cell phone. With a little luck, terrorists had taken a stadium full of college students hostage. Otherwise, he was probably going to have to shoot himself in the foot to get out of the last six holes.

3

EXCEPT FOR THE ODD GOLF TRIP TO PHOENIX, the reality of Arizona just wasn't living up to the fantasy.

Mark Beamon unconsciously lifted his feet as his car plowed through a six-inch-deep snowdrift that washed up under the chassis and lifted the vehicle off the ground. Fortunately, the drift wasn't much wider than it was deep, and he managed to correct a minor fishtail and keep control.

"Goddammit!" he said to the empty car. "It's not supposed to snow in Arizona!"

He had been the Assistant Special Agent in Charge, ASAC, of the FBI's Flagstaff office for about a month. And in that month he'd learned something. It *did* snow in Arizona. Hell, it blizzarded in Arizona. The pictures he'd seen on TV of a guy sipping a margarita in the shade of a twenty-foot-high cactus had probably been taken in California. Or maybe the southern tip of Saudi Arabia. Still, all in all, he had to admit that it wasn't a bad gig—he finally had his own office to run and he had some good kids working for him. Now if he could just keep from screwing it up.

Beamon slowed the car to a crawl and flipped on the interior light. The high-end houses in this Flagstaff neighborhood weren't visible from the road, hidden by dense pine forests and the four-foot snowbanks piled up on either side of the quiet street. According to the directions he'd scribbled on the back of a blank scorecard, though, he wanted to take the next turn.

He aimed the car at a narrow break in the snowbank to his right and started up a long winding drive. He knew he was in the right place when he crested a small hill and saw the tops of the snow-covered trees fading from red to blue and then back again.

It took only a few moments to come upon the source of the light show—two police cruisers wedged between three unmarked cars in the driveway of a large log home.

He grabbed a piece of gum from the package sitting next to him on the passenger seat and shoved it in his mouth next to the two in there already. He'd read somewhere that your sense of smell was supposed to go as you got older, but he hadn't been so lucky. There was something about the stench of day-old blood that made him more nauseous every year. Gum was his latest attempt at a remedy.

Beamon slid his vehicle to a stop and stepped out, feeling the cold air penetrate his sweater and thin golf pants. He'd come directly from the course, a two-and-a-half-hour drive that rose thousands of feet from the mild red desert of Phoenix to the snow-covered forests of Flagstaff.

Beamon waved at two approaching policemen and ducked into the back seat of his car. He pulled out his newly purchased goose-down parka and slipped it on.

At the party celebrating his promotion and transfer to Arizona—and after no less than eight bourbons—he had donned all of his winter clothes at once and performed an elaborate striptease on his friend's dining room table. His wool overcoat had been the first article to be thrown into the cheering crowd. In retrospect, probably not such a great idea.

"Can we help you, sir?" one of the two troopers said, taking a sip from a styrofoam cup. His next breath came out like thick steam.

"Maybe." Beamon held up his right arm, displaying a large price tag hanging from the bright red sleeve of his new jacket. "Either of you guys have scissors?"

The cop with the coffee pointed back down the half-mile-long driveway. "Sir, this is a police matter. I suggest you get back in your—"

"Mark!"

Chet Michaels danced through a tangle of police line tape and deep snow as he made his way down from the house. "It's okay, guys. This is my boss."

The two cops mumbled an apology and started back toward their squad car.

"Sorry to drag you away from your golf game, Mark, but I thought you'd want to see this."

At twenty-five, Chet Michaels had come into the Bureau as one of its youngest agents—an honor he'd earned by graduating from college at nineteen and passing his CPA test on the first try. By all reports, he'd also been one hell of an athlete—a wrestler—but it was a tough mental image to conjure up. The combination of his carrot-red hair and the bumper crop of freckles across the bridge of his nose made him look about as threatening as a cantaloupe.

Beamon took off his plaid golf cap and was going to toss it back into the car, but thought better of it. The sun had dropped behind the mountains and the stars were starting to appear in the deep blue of the sky. It was going to be another cold one.

"Believe me when I tell you that this is the bright spot in my day, Chet," Beamon said, motioning toward the house and letting the young agent lead.

A yellow rope cordoned off the steps climbing to the front door, forcing them to skirt around through a deep snowbank. Beamon was still wearing his golf spikes—great for traction but a little weak in the warmth department.

"Don't think you're gonna get much in the way of footprints, Chet," Beamon observed, trying unsuccessfully to stay in the depressions made by the feet of the people who had gone before him. "It hasn't snowed for a couple of days and it looks like a football team's run up and down these steps ten times."

"You're probably right, but we thought we'd bring in some people to look at it anyway."

Beamon shrugged as he stepped through the front door and into the house. It wasn't much warmer inside than out, so he tucked the price tag into his sleeve and watched Michaels cross the entryway at a slow run and disappear through a set of hand-carved double doors to the left.

All that energy, Beamon thought, shaking his head. He tried to remember the excitement that had gripped him on his first big case, but the feeling was gone. He could recall the details like it was yesterday, filed away in his mind for future reference, but the emotional charge of being twenty-odd years old and out to save the world had shorted out a long time ago.

Beamon reached into the collar of his sweater and pulled out a pair of reading glasses from his shirt pocket. They fogged up instantly, so he let them dangle from his hand as he looked around the entryway.

The walls were constructed of large logs, probably almost a foot and a half in diameter. They'd been haphazardly stained a deep natural brown, giving them a casual worn look that complimented the flagstone floor. An elk-antler chandelier provided a soft light from above that was periodically overpowered by camera flashes emanating from the next room.

Beamon walked across a faded Navajo rug and stopped in front of a small antique table. It was covered with photographs of every size and shape conceivable, each with a simple frame of either gold or silver.

His glasses still hadn't quite cleared, so he hung them around his neck and bent forward, bringing his nose to within a few inches of the pictures.

It looked like sort of a family history. The photos in back were all faded black-and-whites, their subjects uniformly dressed in well-starched suits or dresses with petticoats, and all staring out from the frames with the same stern expression.

Beamon took a step back and jumped forward in time. He picked up the eight-by-ten photo on the edge of the table and brought it up close to his face.

He recognized the man in the tan sweater as Eric Davis. They'd met briefly at a cocktail party a few weeks ago. Beamon didn't remember meeting the tall, heavyset woman standing at his side but guessed that she was his wife.

Beamon's eyes wandered down to the girl sitting in the leaves in front of the couple. The blonde of her hair was the product of a calculatedly obvious dye job, contrasting with the dark, uneven tan of an athlete. There was a slight glint on her left nostril that Beamon guessed was a nose ring.

She was a pretty little thing, probably sixteen or seventeen—though that was really just a wild guess. By design, he really hadn't spent much time around children.

"Mark, I keep losing you. They're in here!" Michaels said, reappearing suddenly in the doorway to the living room.

"All right, all right," Beamon said, putting the picture back on the table. He turned toward the young agent. "Lead on. I'll stay with you this time. Promise."

He followed Michaels into a large, roughly octagonal room surrounded by windows that must have been fifteen feet high. The ceiling rose and disappeared into shadow at the top of an enormous log pillar that, until tonight, would have been the focal point of the room. Beamon shoved his hands into the pockets of his parka and looked down at the new focal point.

Michaels stood next to the two bodies with the proud expression of a sculptor showing off his most recent work. "We assume that these are the remains of Eric and Patricia Davis. The maid who found them IDed them from their build and clothes. Obviously, she can't be a hundred percent sure, though."

Beamon nodded, letting his gaze linger for a moment on the shattered head loosely connected to the body of a plump woman in a thick off-white sweater. He crouched down, careful not to dip the end of his new coat in the puddle of curdling blood at his feet.

It didn't look like their faces had been damaged by the bullet impacts, but the dried blood and brain tissue clinging to their skin had subtly distorted their features. Beamon wouldn't swear to the fact that they were the couple in the picture, but it was probably a pretty good guess.

"Mr. Davis was forty-four years old, Mrs. Davis was forty," Michaels started, reading off a small pad of paper he had pulled from his pocket. "Apparently Mr. Davis owned a number of car dealerships."

"Biggest dealer in Arizona," Beamon said.

"Excuse me?"

"Someone told me he was the biggest dealer in Arizona. I met him at a party a couple of weeks ago. Briefly." Beamon stood and carefully stepped over the puddle of blood at his feet. The plastic spikes on the bottoms of his golf shoes that had served him so well in the snow were proving to be a little treacherous on the polished oak floor. He crouched down again and examined the scene from a slightly different angle.

The Mrs. looked like she'd gotten it in the back of the head. The blood had pooled and dried, leaving something that looked like a large scab over her hair. Beamon couldn't see if there was an exit wound because of the body's position.

Eric Davis's body was a little more perplexing. Based on its condition and the pattern of the splattered blood, it looked like he'd taken his bullet right under the chin. Beamon pointed to the broken window. "Did the bullet break that window? It looks like it should have gone straight up."

"Oh, I think it did. Looks like a piece of Mr. Davis's skull broke the window."

"Lovely," Beamon said, standing up and shoving another piece of gum in his mouth. "What about the girl?"

"Jennifer Davis is fifteen years old. Blonde. Tall—about five-eight or -nine. According to one of the neighbors we talked to, she was competing in a bike race near Phoenix yesterday afternoon. They— the neighbors—were down there watching the race and went out to dinner with them afterward. The Davises would have returned here around ten o'clock."

Beamon flopped down on the sofa and stuffed a fifth stick of gum in his mouth. "So what happened here, Chet?" he slurred.

The young agent looked confident. He'd obviously learned enough about Beamon in their month working together to know the question was coming and to prepare an answer.

"They were waiting for them."

"Who?"

"The perpetrators."

"Why?"

"The garage door's still open and the Davises' car is outside. I figure it this way. The perpetrators get dropped off by an accomplice who takes the car they came in and drives around the neighborhood."

"Why doesn't he just park it?" Beamon broke in.

"The Davises would have been suspicious if there was a strange car in their driveway. And you can't park on the street 'cause of the snow."

Beamon raised his eyebrows and rocked his head back and forth in a calculated effort to make the young agent nervous. Michaels was probably right, but he needed to learn to work under pressure. Besides, what was the fun of being king if you couldn't torture your subjects occasionally?

"Okay, Chet. Go on."

His body language had its intended effect, and Michaels started to sound a little hesitant. "Uh, yeah. So, anyway, they—the Davises—come in through the garage and are ambushed in the kitchen."

"I see." Beamon stood up and walked through the open French doors that led to the kitchen. There was a light haze of fingerprint dust in the air and a man in a blue suit was hunched over the sink, working furiously with a soft brush.

Beamon pointed to a picture lying in a halo of glass on the floor, then rapped on the kitchen table, which had been pushed haphazardly against the wall. A broken dish lay at the base of the refrigerator.

"I'd say the hypothesis that the Davises met our friends in here is a reasonable one," Beamon agreed.

Michaels picked up where he had left off, looking relieved. "Okay, so they all reconvene to the living room, where the perpetrators line Mr. and Mrs. Davis up against the wall and execute them. Then they call their accomplice on their cell phone and have him pick them up."

Beamon peeked through the pantry/mudroom and out through the open door to the garage. "What if it was a car they recognized? Someone they knew?"

"Excuse me?"

"The Davises pull up and someone they know is in their driveway. They all chat while Jennifer takes her bike off the top of the car and then one of them pulls a gun. They come through the garage into the kitchen, and Mr. Davis makes a grab for the gun. There's a struggle that he ultimately loses. They drag them into the living room and shoot them."

The young agent's face fell and he stared at his shoes. "I guess that's possible . . ."

"How 'bout this?" Beamon continued. "Mr. and Mrs. Davis come inside while Jennifer takes her bike off the car. She's too young to drive, so she can't pull the car in, and her mom and pop aren't anxious to go back out in the cold, so they put it off for a while. In the meantime, our perpetrators just drive up and knock on the front door."

Michaels looked up from his shoes. "But then why would the struggle have taken place in the kitchen? It's not between the front door and the living room."

"Maybe they were being forced to prepare omelets against their will." Beamon broke into a smile and backhanded Michaels in the chest. "Your theory's best, bud. You just shouldn't be so damn sure about it. Keep an open mind." Beamon paused. "But not so open your brain falls out, right?"

The bright beam of headlights washed through the windows of the living room, prompting Michaels to lean through the kitchen door. "That must be the coroner."

Beamon nodded. "Go ahead and give him the tour. Oh, one more thing. Get someone to walk around the outside of the house with a flashlight and look for footprints. This could be nothing more than a botched robbery attempt, and if the little girl was an athlete she might have made a break for the woods. She'll freeze her ass off if she's out there lost."

The huge wad of gum in Beamon's mouth was starting to make his jaw ache and he could feel that the smell of the bodies was about to break through his makeshift spearmint barrier. Time for plan B.

He stepped over the latent print guy, who had sunk from the counter to the lower cabinets, and pushed hard on the door at the back of the kitchen. It scraped against the snow and ice on the deck, stopping dead after moving about a foot. Beamon looked dejectedly at the small gap, then down at his bulging waistline. It wouldn't be easy, but then, what in his life ever was? He grabbed the edge of the counter and the doorjamb and forced himself through the opening.

It was a beautiful spot. Large pines filtered the starlight, giving the clean white snow an ethereal glow. There was no wind, and the muffled sounds of the investigation that managed to filter through the broken window in the living room were almost completely swallowed up by the forest.

Beamon retrieved a bag of tobacco and papers from his jacket and began rolling a cigarette. The cold numbed his fingertips, making the process even more arduous than normal.

"What are you doing?"

Beamon jumped, dropping the half-rolled cigarette in the snow and almost losing his balance. Steadying himself against the house, he looked in the direction of the voice.

Less than ten feet away, a small Hispanic woman, wrapped in a thick wool blanket, sat in a lawn chair. She leaned forward and pulled her knees closer to her chest. "What were you doing there? Aren't you a policeman?"

He looked down at himself and chuckled. With the green and red pants and the new parka, he must look like a giant Christmas ornament rolling a joint. "My doctor told me I have to give up cigarettes, so I started rolling my own. It's such a pain, I smoke half as much."

The woman's hand appeared from behind the blanket and pointed toward the scattered tobacco at Beamon's feet. "But those don't have a filter. They're probably twice as bad."

Beamon thought about that for a moment. "No such thing as a perfect plan."

He walked toward her and held out his hand. "I'm Mark Beamon. I work with the FBI. I didn't know anyone was out here."

She took his hand. "Carlotta Juarez. I am the Davises' maid . . . was the Davises' maid."

"Your hand feels like ice, Carlotta. Would you like to go inside?"

She shook her head.

"How about a car? You could go sit in my car and run the heater."

"No, I like it out here."

Beamon leaned against the house and followed her gaze toward a grove of aspen glowing pink in the starlight. "Are you all right?"

Out of the corner of his eye, he could see her turn back toward him. "I came here from Bogotá. I've seen so many horrible things."

Beamon nodded and was silent for almost a minute.

"How long have you worked for the Davises?" he said finally.

"Eight years."

"Do you live here at the house?"

"No. In town with my husband and five sons. I come every day, though."

Beamon slipped his hands under his armpits. "Five sons? That must be a handful."

"Sometimes."

"Have you had a chance to walk through the house, Carlotta? Does it look like anything's missing?"

"Nothing that I could see." She paused. "Only Jennifer."

Beamon looked up at the stars. "Tell me about her."

"She's a wonderful girl. Bright, kind, thoughtful." Her voice trailed away. "How could someone do this?"

He ignored the question, having asked himself that same thing at crime scenes all over the country and never coming up with a good answer. "Does she have a boyfriend?"

"Jamie Dolan. He's a senior at Jennifer's high school."

"Anything unusual going on lately, Carlotta? Strange phone calls? People you didn't know coming over?"

She shook her head.

"How about between Jennifer and her parents? Were they angry at her for something? Maybe they didn't like her boyfriend?"

"Mrs. Davis always wanted Jennifer to see their neighbor's son Bill. But I don't think she disliked Jamie."

Beamon peeled his back from the frozen side of the house. "I appreciate your help, Carlotta. Oh, and I apologize in advance for the people who are going to ask you all the same questions." He turned and began tugging at the door to the kitchen. "Don't freeze out here, okay?"

A couple of brief, but harrowing, expeditions into his sister's room decades ago had given Beamon his only image of a teenage girl's natural habitat. Apparently it was hopelessly outdated.

The wall of dolls and full-sized poster of Shaun Cassidy that he halfway expected to find had been replaced by bicycle parts hanging from the ceiling and posters of what looked like young homeless men. A closer inspection of the posters revealed that they were music groups with names like Gas Huffer and Mudhoney.

Beamon wandered across the room, stepping over the clothes and towels strewn across the floor, occasionally pausing to look into a drawer or box. Nothing leapt out at him as particularly significant so he ducked into the attached bathroom. The counter was covered with various tubes and vials that, as a lifelong bachelor, he found completely baffling. He stepped over the cord of a blow dryer and pulled a few blonde hairs out of the sink. Wrapping them up in a length of toilet paper, he headed back downstairs.

"I'm out of here, Chet!" Beamon yelled from the front door.

Michaels jogged out of the living room and caught Beamon shuffling around the roped-off area on the front porch.

"You're not staying?" He sounded shocked that anyone would choose to spend an evening at home when presented with the opportunity to hang around a house full of blood and death.

Beamon waved his hand dismissively as he cleared the cordoned-off area and made a beeline for his car. "You seem to have it under control, Chet. Call me at home if you run into any really earth-shattering problems. I'm not available for little glitches and snafus 'til tomorrow morning, though. Right?"

4

BEAMON MADE IT THROUGH THE DOOR OF THE FBI's Flagstaff office just as the wall fell.

He saw the expressions of the young agents crammed into the small room converge on resigned annoyance as they covered their coffee cups and computer keyboards. A white cloud of plaster dust enveloped two men in coveralls and billowed slowly across the room.

Beamon stepped over a pile of acoustic tiles and headed for his office, shaking his head. Director Calahan didn't take defeat lightly. When he had finally been shamed into giving Beamon a management position, he'd been overcome with another one of the flashes of complete idiocy that had become the hallmark of his tenure at the Bureau.

He'd decided to take a small resident agency, expand it enough to make it look good to the press, and put Beamon in charge. In the director's mind, giving Beamon the somewhat imaginary title of ASAC-Flagstaff would make him a laughingstock. And as an added benefit, it would separate Beamon from his old cohort Laura Vilechi before he could bring her over to the dark side.

Unfortunately, the expansion of the office was going to cost taxpayers hundreds of thousands of dollars and leave quite a few agents who owned homes in Phoenix with a long and utterly pointless commute. Welcome to the FBI.

"Think we should rename the office Jericho, D.?" Beamon said, ignoring the door to his outer office and walking through a gap in the newly framed wall.

His secretary stood and followed him as he passed by her and went straight for the coffeemaker next to his desk.

"You need one, D.?" Beamon asked, dumping a couple of teaspoons of sugar into his cup.

"No thanks. How went the golf game?"

Beamon flopped into the worn leather chair behind his desk. "Jake shot like a four hundred or something."

His secretary grimaced.

"And that was for twelve holes. I took off before they teed up the thirteenth."

"You know what they say, Mark. The best-laid plans . . ."

He threw his hands up in a gesture of frustration and grabbed the neatly folded newspaper off his desk.

"Two things, Mark. First, you still need to review and sign off on this year's pro forma budget. It's past due."

Beamon pretended not to hear. He hadn't yet built up the willpower to wade through that ocean of paper.

"Second, Chet Michaels has been walking by every five minutes or so for the last hour. He looks like he's going to burst. Should I send him in?"

"Ten minutes, D. Hold him off for ten minutes.

Give me a chance to at least skim the newspaper and get a little caffeine into my system. And I promise I'll go through your budget at home tonight."

She nodded and started back for her desk.

"Hey, D.?"

She stopped and turned back toward him, her sharp, youthful features melting into a sly smile.

Since Beamon's first day in Flagstaff, his secretary had steadfastly refused to tell him her given first name, preferring to be called by her first initial. Of course, he could have looked in her personnel file, but what would be the fun of that?

"I was listening to this Johnny Cash song on the way to work today . . ."

She shook her head sadly. "Good try, Mark. But it's not Delia."

"The old saying is wrong," Beamon said, poking an index finger into the open newspaper spread across his desk. "Kill all the journalists."

From his position at the door to the office, Chet Michaels took it that his boss's sacred and absolutely inviolable ten minutes were up.

"Look at this headline," Beamon said. "'FBI Baffled by Double Murder/Kidnapping.' Shit."

"You aren't?" Michaels said as he sat down in one of the three chairs lined up in front of Beamon's desk.

"There are a few things that baffle me, Chet. Serial killers? Occasionally. Women? More often than not." Beamon looked down at the stained concrete floor of his office. "Why they ripped up my old carpet when the new one isn't due for another couple of weeks? Definitely haven't figured that one out.

But kidnappings? No way. At worst I'm briefly perplexed."

Michaels laced his hands across his stomach and leaned back in his chair. "Well, they were probably talking about me, then. If you've got this thing figured out, I could really use some help."

Beamon spun the paper around so Michaels could see it and slapped his palm on a picture of Jennifer Davis. "Voilà."

"What?"

"What do you mean, 'What?' She did it."

Michaels' bright red eyebrows rose. "The little girl?"

"Honestly, Chet. Sometimes your lack of cynicism disgusts me. Answer me this: Why do people kidnap?"

"I dunno. Lots of reasons, I guess."

"No. There are only three. Financial benefit, blackmail, or you want the kid. Of course, each of those categories has a subheading or two."

Michaels remained silent as Beamon took a slug from his coffee cup. "Okay, Chet, let's start with number three—you want the kid. Why?"

"Uh, ransom?"

Beamon shook his head. "Ransom fits in under financial benefit. No, most often you want the kid because you're a parent that didn't get legal custody. Now, Jennifer's a little old for that kind of nonsense—no one wants to steal a kid they're going to have to put through college in a couple of years. Besides, weren't the Davises still on their first marriage?"

Michaels glanced at the blue file lying in his lap, but didn't open it. "I think so."

"That brings us to subheading number two. You're some crazy pervert. What do you think? Pervert?"

Michaels's eyes scrunched up for a moment. "I doubt it. The facts don't support the theory that one lone person did this. Sex offenders don't usually work in teams."

"I'll buy that," Beamon agreed. "Besides, you told me that this girl races bikes. If I were your garden-variety weirdo, I'd just snag her when she's all alone on some trail in the woods."

Beamon batted away a thick cable hanging from his ceiling and put his feet on his desk. "So, moving right along. Category number two— blackmail. What do you think of that theory."

"Can't blackmail a dead person."

"'Nuff said. Number one, then. Financial benefit. Ransom?"

"Not very practical at this point."

Beamon grinned. "To say the least. So who benefits from this thing?"

Michaels leaned forward in his chair and braced his elbows against his knees. "I know what you want me to say, Mark. That Jennifer lined her parents up and shot them so she'd inherit all their money. That she's gonna show up in a few days with some crazy story about the whole thing." He shook his head. "Doesn't feel right to me."

Beamon pointed again to the picture of Jennifer in the paper. "Are you kidding? Look at her!"

Michaels laughed and picked up the paper for a closer inspection. "Come on, Mark. My girlfriend's got a nose ring. Couple of tattoos, too. Doesn't mean anything. It's just, you know, fashion." A wide grin spread across the young agent's face. "Your parents probably said you looked subversive when you came in with a bunch of grease in your hair and your cigarettes rolled up in the sleeve of your T-shirt."

Beamon rolled his eyes. "I'm only forty-three, you little bastard." He paused for a moment and watched two men in the outer office trying to lift a scaffold over a group of file cabinets. "Okay, it's not a great theory," he admitted. "But it's the best one I can come up with. Could be that this was a botched robbery. The perps had just arrived—didn't have time to take anything—and the Davises came home. They shoot them, then decide to take the girl for some fun and games."

Michaels perked up a bit. "That sounds possible."

"I don't know. A house that you can't see from the street—you'd have to be watching it. No sign of forced entry would suggest they're pros. If the Davises had gone to this race and five miles into their trip remembered they left the iron on and come back, I'd say we've got a great theory. But they were gone all fucking day. All our friends had to do was slip in after the maid left at five and they'd have had time to clean the place out and watch a ball game on the Davises' big-screen TV."

Somewhere in the office, a table saw started.

"When are we gonna get a report on the physical evidence and autopsy?" Beamon shouted over the roar of the saw.

"Should start trickling in tomorrow," Michaels yelled back.

"Okay. Keep thinking about it, Chet. We've missed something, and I'm briefly perplexed as to what it is."

Michaels stood and turned to leave.

"Oh, and Chet! Tell that guy out there that if he doesn't shut that saw off, I'm gonna use it to remove his foot."

5

A WAVE OF HEAT WASHED ACROSS JENNIFER Davis, instantly covering her in tiny beads of sweat. She kicked the covers off the bed, and for a moment the cool air meeting her damp skin eased the nausea that had gripped her since she woke up.

And how long ago had that been? An hour? Two?

The comforting glow of the clock on her nightstand and the gentle creaking of her house as the immense logs dried and settled were gone. Everything was gone. There was no blue-white glow from the snowdrifts beneath her window, no light filtering in from under the door. Just a dizzying blackness.

Jennifer felt another surge of heat overtake her and she rolled on her side, clenching her teeth and struggling to not throw up.

The memories returned slowly, retracing themselves in her mind over and over again until she could see faceless black-and-white outlines moving purposefully across the background of her home. She could feel the strong arms holding her and the adrenaline-surge panic as her air was cut off by a hand damp with perspiration.

It didn't take long for the outlines to sharpen and collect color and sound. The pale woman with dark eyes kneeling in front of her. The shadows crisscrossing her father's face as he raised the gun to his wife's head. The crack of the pistol and the strangely insignificant jerk of her mother's head before she fell, doll-like, to the ground.

No. It couldn't have happened. It was just bad dreams. She must have been coming down with a bug before the race and the effort and dehydration had played tricks on her in her sleep.

She reached out for the lamp beside her bed, but her hand just hung uselessly in the empty air, confirming what she already knew but hadn't been able to fully face. She wasn't in her room. She had no idea where she was.

She tried to stifle it, but the long mournful cry still escaped as she tried to stem the tide of memories projecting themselves onto the darkness that surrounded her.

Her father's image appeared a few feet away, pressing the barrel of the gun under his chin and speaking his final, meaningless words to her. Then her mind replayed the sting of the syringe as it broke her skin and turned the room to quivering mush and then finally to nothing. She felt a tear make its way across the bridge of her nose and down her cheek. Then another. And another. Once she started to cry, her sobbing just grew in intensity, melding with her nausea and leaving her choking and coughing uncontrollably.

She went on like that until the muscles in her stomach and sides exhausted themselves and her mind decided it had had enough and let her drift off into unconsciousness.

When she awoke again, her head still hurt and her throat was painfully dry, but the nausea was gone. The image of her parents' death began creeping back into her mind, but she pushed it off into the emotional numbness that was quickly overtaking her.

"Hello?"

Her voice was little more than a harsh whisper, but it seemed impossibly loud in the darkness and silence that surrounded her.

She waited for some reply, some indication that she wasn't completely alone in the world, but there was nothing.

She cleared her throat painfully. "Is anyone there?"

Louder this time, but still weak. She sounded like a frightened little girl, even to herself.

She sat up slowly and swung her feet onto the cold floor. The blood rushed from her head and she had to bend forward at the waist for a moment to keep from passing out. After a few seconds, she raised her head and slid off the bed.

She tried to crawl but the bruises and cuts on her knees were too painful against the hard floor and she was forced to turn over and slide on her butt until her back reached a wall.

Feeling along it, she finally came to the smooth wood of a doorjamb. She used the doorknob to steady herself and struggled to her feet. It took only a few moments to find the light switch.

She covered her eyes with one hand and flipped the switch with the other. The flare of light worked its way between her fingers as she pulled them slowly away from her face.

When she finally opened her eyes, she fell against the wall and screamed.

A black-clad woman sat motionless in a chair less than a foot from where Jennifer had slept. The woman's head turned slowly toward her as Jennifer backed into the far corner of the room and sank to the floor. The brief surge of adrenaline overloaded her weakened system and her breath came in short, useless gasps as the woman stood and moved across the room.

The pounding of her heart seemed to be robbing her of her strength. Her arms felt impossibly heavy as she raised them in front of her face.

The woman paused and looked down at her, then opened the door and disappeared through it without a word.

Jennifer listened to the latch on the door click shut as she crumpled to her side on the hard tile and struggled to even out her breathing.

It had been the same woman. The one who had driven her parents crazy. The one who had drugged her.

Why had she been sitting there in the darkness? Why hadn't she answered?

Jennifer crawled sobbing toward the door and flipped the light switch. It was better that way, she thought as the darkness closed in on her. Better to see nothing.

6

"YOU ALL RIGHT?" MARK BEAMON YELLED. The brand-new window at the front of his office had gone almost completely opaque with white paint. A smear the size of the painter's back was transparent enough to allow him to see the collapsed scaffold and two slightly dazed construction workers on the other side.

Beamon crossed his office and stood in the open door. The men involved in this latest of a recent string of construction disasters looked more or less unharmed. Unfortunately, that wasn't true of the two freshly painted PCs and three freshly painted FBI agents that had been sitting a little too close.

He sighed quietly, remembering that it was now *his* job to get the Three Stooges Contracting Company to pay up for the damaged computers and business suits.

He pointed at Chet Michaels and reminded himself that he'd been bucking to get into management for years. In the future, he'd be more careful what he wished for.

"I've got the new stuff on the Davis case," Michaels said, walking carefully across the paint-splattered floor with a large box in his hands and a blue folder under his arm. "I take it you're ready?"

Beamon settled back into his chair as one of the

painters attacked the floor in front of his office with a mop. "Yeah. Have a seat."

The young agent dropped the box next to his chair and flipped the file folder open on his lap. "We got the initial background stuff on the Davises."

"And?"

"They're actually not Jennifer's real parents. She was adopted."

"Shit, really?" Beamon snapped his fingers. "That's it, then. Reason number three, subcategory one."

"Huh?"

"Come on, Chet, we talked about this yesterday. What's reason number three for kidnapping someone?"

"Uh, ransom?"

Beamon frowned. "That's reason one. Try again."

"Oh, wait a minute. It's 'cause you want the girl."

"Or whoever. And *why* do you want the girl?"

"Uh, I thought that one was 'cause you were divorced and didn't get custody."

"Precisely. Adoption's just a variation on that theme. Find the biological parents and you find the girl." Beamon lifted his mug in a salute to his own deductive genius and took a sip of the hot coffee.

"We already found the parents, Mark. They're dead. Died in a fire years ago."

Beamon tried not to let his disappointment show. "Oh. Back to Jennifer, then."

Michaels flipped a page in the file. "So far, we're not finding any real problems at the Davises.

The neighbors and friends we've talked to have told us that Jennifer was pretty well adjusted and that there were no significant problems in her relationship with her parents. She's an excellent student, athletic, and well liked—if not exactly popular. As you mentioned, she's a little alternative. Oh, and a pretty good mountain bike racer."

Beamon tapped his front teeth with the nail of his index finger. "The maid told me that maybe Jennifer's mother wasn't crazy about her boyfriend. Was she putting pressure on Jennifer to get rid of him? Love tends to rank right up there with money as a motive for murder."

"Don't think so in this case, Mark. I did get that Mrs. Davis would have liked her to get together with their best friends' son, but that had been going on for a long time and I think she probably knew it was never going to go anywhere."

Beamon interrupted him. "Why not? What makes you say that?"

"I met the kid—Billy's his name. Not a match made in heaven, believe me."

Beamon remained silent, prompting him to continue.

"I went through Jennifer's room with a fine-toothed comb, Mark. She listens to Naked Raygun, reads Kerouac and Burroughs. Rebuilds suspension forks. This guy her mother liked for her was dumb as a post. Pure generic high school football player."

Beamon gave a short laugh and shook his head. "God, you make me feel old, Chet. I have absolutely no idea what you just said."

"Would you care for a translation?"

Beamon held up his hand. "How about I just take your word for it. What about the boyfriend she *did* like?"

"Jamie Dolan. Haven't talked to him yet; I'm going this afternoon. Preliminarily, though, he doesn't look great as a suspect. He's a drummer in a band and was apparently playing that night. I think there are going to be a lot of witnesses nailing him down between way before ten P.M. 'til about three A.M. I don't think there was any way he could have sneaked out between sets, but maybe he could have slipped out of his house early in the morning. I'll know more later."

Beamon looked across his office at the man smearing paint around on his window with a rag. "I have to wonder about that. The Davises were attacked in the living room in the same clothes they'd been seen in at dinner, right? He'd have had to roust them out of bed, get them to put on their clothes, and bring them downstairs before he shot them. Maybe he's that clever, I don't know. Does he have access to a gun?"

"No gun registered to his mother, but who knows?"

"What about the Davises?"

"No gun registered and none of their friends we talked to know of any."

"Shit," Beamon said, tapping out a complex rhythm on his desk with his knuckles. "You're not going to make this easy on me, are you, Chet? Physical evidence?"

"So far, we don't have anything in the way of prints or fibers and the autopsy report's still pend-

STORMING HEAVEN   47

ing. Didn't get anything from phone records. There was no sign of forced entry or robbery. Oh, and Jennifer had a credit card. Last used . . ." He flipped a couple of pages in the folder. "Middle of last month. We're watching for any new usage."

Beamon leaned across his desk. "What's in the box?"

"Oh, we finally got into the Davises' safe." He dropped the folder and hefted the box onto his lap.

"So, what have we won?"

Michaels grabbed a red velvet bag with a ribbon tied around the top and let it dangle from his hand. "A bag of gold and diamond jewelry. Good for evening, or feeding a thousand homeless people for a month."

"Commie."

The young agent affected a hurt expression and dropped the bag on Beamon's desk. "Passports for all three of them, roughly four thousand dollars in cash, a few stock certificates, Mr. Davis's college transcript, the financial statements of the corporation that owns Mr. Davis's car dealerships . . ."

"How do those look? Maybe he was borrowing from the wrong sort?"

"They look pretty strong, actually. Of course they could be bogus."

Beamon screwed up his face. "Maybe. But why keep fakes in your own safe? Partners?"

Michaels shook his head. "He owned the whole thing, one hundred percent."

"Uh-huh. Go on."

"Lessee. Birth certificates for all three, and a copy of the Davises' irrevocable trust."

"What's that say?"

"We've got a lawyer going over it, but I read a lot of these when I was an accountant. It pretty much says that Jennifer gets it all. She's got to attain a certain age and there are provisions for her living and school expenses until that time, as well as some other stuff, but that's the gist of it."

"What if she dies?"

"The whole estate turns into a charitable foundation. No specific charities or people are named."

Beamon leaned back in his chair and folded his hands across his stomach. He sat there for almost a minute, with Michaels watching his face carefully.

"I don't know, Chet. I keep coming back to Jennifer and Jamie. We've got a young couple in love, a mother who doesn't like the boyfriend, and a pretty favorable trust here. What time are you leaving to meet with this kid?"

"Around noon. I'm going to the high school to talk to him and all her friends."

"Set Jamie up for the first interview. I assume you don't mind if I join you."

"Not at all."

7

BEAMON GAZED DEJECTEDLY AT THE LOW-slung yellow brick building as Michaels eased into a parking space next to an overflowing bike rack.

If memory served, the seventies was not one of the most economically sound periods in American history. And if that was true, it must be one of the great mysteries why all public buildings looked like they were built during that decade.

". . . So this kid's pretty bright . . ."

The flat roof of the school had gotten piled with snow and Beamon watched a tall black man walk carefully to the edge and begin to stab at a particularly large cornice with a shovel.

"Mark! Are you listening to me?"

Beamon pressed the release on his seatbelt and let it snap back toward the door. "Sorry, Chet. I was somewhere else. What were you saying?"

"Jamie Dolan. He's seventeen, a senior this year. Extremely intelligent—fifteen eighty on his SATs . . ."

"Is that good?"

"Uh, yeah. To put it in perspective, eight hundred is average. Sixteen hundred's perfect."

"Uh huh."

"So anyway, Jamie's parents split up when he was ten. Apparently his father had a drinking problem and was pretty abusive. Now Jamie lives with his mother in a trailer park about ten miles from here. He works at a local video club to help make ends meet. His mother's a waitress."

Beamon sighed. Sounded like an okay kid. Strong enough to rise above the less than full deck life had dealt him. Had he become impatient? Wanted it all now?

"You okay, Mark?"

"Yeah."

"I talked on the phone with a couple of his teachers and they pretty much all described him the same way. Very bright. Mature beyond his years. Not crazy about authority figures."

Beamon pushed the car door open and grabbed hold of the luggage rack to keep his feet from skidding out from under him as he got out. He knew how he was going to have to play this and was already starting to feel the guilt and regret creeping up on him. Despite the large neon sign in his head pointing to Jennifer and Jamie as the Davises' murderers, his intuition was telling him that that sign might be pointing in the wrong direction.

The problem was that he couldn't figure out if that gut reaction was the result of their innocence, or the fact that he just didn't want to believe they were guilty. There was just no satisfaction in nailing two love-crazed teenagers. Instead of making you feel like you'd won, it just made it feel like everyone had lost.

"Okay, Chet. Let's get this over with," Beamon said as he half-walked, half-slid across a wide puddle of ice to a patch of snow that would get him to the door.

The school didn't look a hell of a lot better inside than out. The walls were painted a uniform faded orange, broken only by an occasional mural, painted with a childlike sensibility that pegged it as the work of the student body. The halls were empty and the doors lining them were all closed. Prompted by a sign that read OFFICE, Beamon turned down a hall to his right and walked through the first door he came to.

The woman behind the tall counter jumped up from behind her desk and looked at Beamon with mild expectation. "Can I help you?"

"I hope so," Beamon said, digging into his jacket and pulling out his credentials. "I'm Special Agent Mark Beamon and this is Special Agent Chet Michaels. We were told we could use one of your conference rooms to talk with a few of your students?"

She looked down at the counter sadly. "I read all about it, but I still can't believe it. Mr. and Mrs. Davis were such nice people. And Jennifer . . . Do you have any leads?"

"We're doing everything we can," Beamon answered, anxious to get this over with and escape the vaguely musty-smelling building before he started having high school flashbacks. "I'm sorry, but I'm running a little tight on time . . ."

She spun on her heel and disappeared through a door behind her. A moment later she reappeared with a sturdy-looking gray-haired woman in a tweed suit.

"Mr. Beamon. I'm the principal here. Louise Darren."

"Nice to meet you, Ms. Darren. This is my associate, Chet Michaels."

As they shook hands, she motioned toward the door behind her. "Jamie and his mother are already in my office. You're welcome to use it to talk to them."

Beamon looked at the cheap hollow-core door that she had indicated, and its proximity to the outer office. "I appreciate that, but I wouldn't want to put you out of your office. Also, it might be more convenient if we could find something with a bit more privacy?"

She thought for a moment and then pointed down a narrow hall with walls papered in various announcements and lists. "There's a room we don't really use anymore down at the end of the hall. It's kind of full of junk, though."

Beamon smiled. "No problem. You should see my office."

"Right though here, Jamie," Beamon said, opening the door to the abandoned office and stepping aside. There was a dusty old desk piled high with papers and old books centered in the room. Chairs were plentiful, but most had been stacked against the walls.

"Why don't you and Chet grab us a few chairs and I'll be back in a minute." Beamon put his hand lightly on Jamie's mother's shoulder before she could enter. He closed the door quietly, leaving Chet and Jamie to rearrange the office.

"I'd like to speak with you for just a moment, if I could . . . Ms. Dolan is it?"

She shook her head. "Rodrigues. I went back to my maiden name when I was divorced."

"Excuse me—Ms. Rodrigues."

She looked up at him with deep concern that bordered on fear. It didn't seem to be an expression specific to the situation—just the generic powerlessness many poor Hispanics seemed to feel when faced with white male law enforcement officials.

And he was about to use that unfortunate feeling of powerlessness to the absolute hilt. What a guy.

"Would you mind terribly if we spoke to Jamie alone? Sometimes having a parent in the room makes kids nervous. You know how they are. It's really important that Jamie be relaxed so that he doesn't forget anything that might allow us to help Jennifer. I've been doing this for a lot of years and I can tell you that the smallest detail can be critical." He spoke—lied—slowly. Ms. Rodrigues's English was less than perfect.

Beamon pointed back down the hall toward the outer office. "Why don't you have a seat out there? We won't be long."

As she walked slowly away from him, Beamon told himself for the thousandth time that sometimes the end justified the means. He actually did believe that, it was just that he'd never run into a situation that he was dead sure qualified.

"Sorry about the wait, Jamie," he said, striding through the door and closing it tightly behind him. "Your mom's decided to wait for you outside."

"Okay."

Beamon took the chair across from the boy and looked him over carefully. His features were generally Caucasian, though he'd obviously inherited his skin and hair color from his mother. His eyes were a light brown that seemed to fade to dark green and then back again as he moved. His clothes were mostly black or dark gray and had that secondhand look that kids seemed to strive for these days— though based on what Chet had told him earlier, it was probably more of an economic necessity for him than an obsession with fashion.

"I guess you haven't found Jennifer yet," the boy said in a tired voice that carried an emotional maturity that should have been impossible at his age.

Beamon shook his head but didn't answer.

"Uh, do you know who did it?"

Beamon's silent stare was having the desired effect. What little calm the boy had entered with was starting to fray.

"Other than you? Nope."

The boy's eyes widened for a moment and he opened his mouth to say something, but checked himself. It was a moment before he finally spoke. "Why would I want to kidnap Jennifer? She was already my girlfriend. Ask anyone. We never even fought, hardly."

Beamon cocked his head. "I don't think you kidnapped her, Jamie. I think you and Jennifer were in this together. I think you finished your little concert and went home. Then I think you sneaked out of the house and took the car to Jennifer's, where you blew her parents' brains all over the living room. Then you took Jennifer somewhere where it would be a pain in the ass for me to find her and went home."

Beamon watched his young opponent carefully. The boy was trembling, but his eyes were clear and he was obviously carefully considering Beamon's words. He had to admire the kid—he'd had grown men face down on the table sobbing for less.

Jamie took a deep, shaky breath. "I read that Mr. and Mrs. Davis were found in the clothes they'd had on that day. No way I could have made it to their house before four in the morning—I got a hundred people I don't even know that'd swear to that. They'd have to sleep in their clothes."

Beamon shrugged. "I hear you got fifteen-eighty on your SATs, Jamie. I have to say I'd be a little disappointed if you'd just shot 'em in bed. No, Jennifer would have known exactly what they were wearing and you'd force them to get dressed and come downstairs. My compliments. Not terribly creative, but not bad for a minor. I mean, at least you didn't shoot the clock to establish a phony time of death, you know?"

Jamie ran a hand through his long black hair, dislodging the sweat from his hairline. Beamon watched as it ran down his face.

"Maybe this wasn't such a good idea. Maybe my mom should—"

Beamon cut him off. "If you're old enough to shoot two human beings in the face, I think you're old enough to talk to us without your mommy, don't you?"

"Why? Why would I kill them?" Jamie said in a pleading voice. "I didn't have anything against the Davises. I mean, what good would it do me that it'd be worth risking my whole life?"

Beamon leaned back in his chair and scraped an imaginary speck of dirt from under his thumbnail. "Oh, come on, Jamie. Don't insult my intelligence. Patricia Davis was not exactly shot in the ass with you. In fact, I think she had someone else in mind for Jennifer. Seems to me like a win-win proposition for you. You get rid of Patty and Jennifer miraculously escapes from her kidnappers a few weeks later. Just in time to pick up her inheritance."

"No!" Jamie protested. "Mrs. Davis liked me. That thing with Billy had been going on for years. Jennifer wasn't interested."

"That's not what I hear, son. What I hear is that she was putting a lot of pressure on Jennifer. That she hated you. She apparently thought that Jennifer could do better than a . . ." Beamon paused imperceptibly, choking a bit on the phrase, "half-spic living in a trailer park."

Jaime's face flashed with anger. "Fuck you, man." He jumped to his feet and pushed a book lying on the desk in front of him as hard as he could, but Beamon stopped it easily before it hit him in the chest.

"Sit down," Beamon ordered, raising his voice for the first time in the "interview." The boy glared at him, his breath coming like he'd just run a race.

"I won't tell you again. Sit."

Jamie looked over at Michaels, whose wide-eyed stare seemed frozen to his face, and then sank back into the chair.

"Look, Jamie. You're underage. You love Jennifer. Maybe she even talked you into this? Been there. It's hard to say no to the woman you love. You start talking to me right now and I'll do everything I can to make things go easy for you. At this point, I think we can keep this in Juvenile—keep you from being tried as an adult." Beamon dropped the front legs of his chair to the floor loudly. "You keep fucking with me, though, and I'm going to make it my mission to get you. You're a smart kid. You go look up some articles on me in the library. You'll find that the people who come up against me end up in prison for the rest of their lives. Or dead."

Tears clouded the boy's eyes for the first time. "I didn't do it, man. Don't you think I want her back? Don't you?"

He ran past them and out the door, slamming it behind him. Beamon didn't bother to stop him.

"Jesus, Mark." Michaels said in a loud whisper that sounded a bit panicked. "You just threatened to kill that kid!"

"Did I?" Beamon pinched the bridge of his nose and tried to shake the feeling that he'd have made a hell of a Gestapo agent. Ripping into a seventeen-year-old kid with a history of abuse—and who was probably lying awake at night imagining his girlfriend being raped in the back of a van or something—was right up there with clubbing baby seals on the fun meter. There were times when he really hated this job.

"So what do you think, Mark?"

Beamon sighed. "I got a bad feeling about that kid."

"Really? You think he did it?"

Beamon shook his head. "No, that would be a good feeling. It'd mean I found our man—boy— and was on the verge of finding Jennifer. I'm afraid that he didn't do it. And if that's true, I don't have a fucking clue where that little girl is."

8

MARK BEAMON SLAMMED HIS FOOT AGAINST the brake pedal and slid into a stand of snow-covered pines. The impact, slow as it was, knocked the snow off the trees and buried the front of his car. Apparently the snow-driving learning curve wasn't real steep for Texans. At least not this one.

The condominium complex that had been his home for the past month sparkled as the beams of widely spaced floodlights bounced off ice clinging to the sides of the buildings. It had been the first place his realtor had taken him. The FBI had relocated him more times than he could remember—in fact, someone had recently pointed out that he might be closing in on the record. And with that many moves under his belt, the monotonous chore of looking for housing had become almost physically painful.

Of course, he had no one to blame for his career as the FBI's itinerant lawman but himself. There was always some new office anxious to take on the man heralded as the best investigative mind in the Bureau. And there was always an office just as anxious to get rid of the man heralded as the biggest pain in the ass in the Bureau.

But that was the old Mark Beamon. He was the new, vastly improved Mark Beamon. He stepped from the car and kicked his front tire. Satisfied that he'd be able to get out the next morning, he started along one of the meticulously shoveled brick walkways that connected the forty units with the main office, frozen swimming pool, and each other.

Each building was configured with two units upstairs and two downstairs, and all faced out onto expanses of grass, trees, and flowers—or at least that's what he'd been told. Any landscaping that existed had been long buried when he'd arrived in January.

He slowed his pace a bit as his building came into view. As expected, Chet Michaels was sitting at the bottom of the stairs that led up to Beamon's condo. He had undoubtedly been there for exactly fifty minutes—Beamon was supposed to have met him there forty-five minutes ago and Michaels was always precisely five minutes early for every appointment. That wasn't the problem. The problem was the little girl who was unsuccessfully trying to catch the snowballs he was gently tossing to her. And the disaster was the auburn-haired woman in electric blue mittens handing him a steaming cup of something or other.

"Chet! You're early," Beamon called. "I said seven o'clock."

Michaels stood and brushed the snow off the back of his jeans as he approached. "You said six, Mark." He pointed to Beamon's right hand. "You wrote it on the back of your hand."

"Oh, yeah. So I did. Sorry." He turned to the woman standing next to Michaels. "Thanks for keeping him from freezing."

Carrie Johnstone smiled slyly and crouched down next to her daughter. "What do we do when Mr. Beamon gets home, Emory?"

The little girl ran at him and latched onto his leg. "Hi, Mr. Beamon," she slurred through a less than full complement of teeth.

"I'm trying to get Mark to relate to children," Carrie explained as Beamon tried to extract his leg from Emory's grip. "It's shaping up to be one of the greatest challenges of my career, but I think I'm wearing him down."

"What do you do, Carrie?" Michaels said.

"I'm a psychiatrist."

"Really? A psychiatrist? Wow." Michaels handed her back the barely touched cup of coffee and started up the steps toward Beamon's condo. About halfway up he paused and turned around. "You know, Doc, those of us who work for Mark would appreciate anything you could do for him. I'm sure I could take up a collection at the office to cover any fee."

Beamon glared at the young agent, who said, "Thanks for the coffee," and disappeared up the steps.

"Before you go up, Mark, could I talk to you?" Carrie said, suddenly looking a little nervous.

"Uh, sure. CHET!"

The young agent peeked over the railing at him and narrowly avoided being hit in the face by Beamon's keys. "Go on in. I'll be up in a second."

Carrie looked at him with a hint of disapproval registering in her expression. "You know, you really shouldn't leave your employees out on the steps to freeze, Mark. I tried to get him to come inside, but he wouldn't. Thought you'd be mad."

Beamon frowned. Michaels had obviously been busy using that Howdy Doody face to drum up sympathy from Carrie and make him look like an ogre. He'd have to remember to make his life a living hell for the next week or so.

"Couldn't be helped."

There was a brief lull in the conversation as Carrie reached one of her mitten-covered hands into her coat and pulled out an envelope. "I, uh, got this invitation to go to a wedding on Saturday and it says Carrie Johnstone and guest." She held it out as though he'd require proof. "Anyway, it's probably going to be pretty nice. I was wondering if you might want to go?"

He felt his eyebrows start to rise, but managed to stop them before they got too far from their normal resting position. He had met Carrie the day he'd moved in and had been instantly taken with her. She was intelligent, funny, and had a sarcastic edge that, while admittedly underdeveloped, showed real potential. He'd spent the last month trying to figure out a clever excuse to spend some time with her, but so far his normally devious mind had been a blank.

"Are you asking me on a date?" he said, a hint of a smile playing at his lips.

"Uh, I don't know if I'd call it a date. I just thought it'd be . . . fun."

He nodded thoughtfully and crouched down to bring himself eye-level with her daughter. "What do you think, Emory? Should I go on a non-date with your mother? Or should I insist on full date status?"

Emory looked at him blankly and then giggled and squealed. "Date!"

Beamon looked back up at Carrie. "Your daughter seems to think I deserve all the rights and privileges afforded a full-blooded date."

Carrie's expression turned severe, but he could tell she was trying not to laugh. "We'll have to talk about what you consider 'full rights and privileges,' but I'm willing to compromise. I'd consider an honorary title."

"I can live with that."

Beamon knocked the snow off his boots with a couple of violent kicks to the doorjamb and dropped his coat on the floor. Things were starting to look up. Of course, he still had no idea as to the whereabouts of the elusive Jennifer Davis, but he had managed to get a date with Carrie without having to go through the torture of actually asking. Not every day you got something for nothing.

"Okay, Chet, what've you got for me?"

Michaels leaned back into the sofa and put his feet on the large box that contained Beamon's coffee table. "She's really cool. Pretty, too. And a doctor." He rubbed at his bright red chin. "I think she likes you."

Beamon opened his refrigerator and pulled out two beers. "You'd better be talking about Jennifer Davis." He popped the tops off the bottles and walked around to Michaels.

"I was talking about Carrie."

Beamon sat down in a chair facing the sofa and

took a long pull from his beer. "So what I'm hearing you saying, Chet, is that you don't actually want to keep your job."

The young agent smirked and pulled two folders out of the open knapsack at his feet. He pointed to one of them. "Autopsy." Then the other. "Jennifer's real parents. Which one do you want to start with?"

Beamon polished off his beer with one more healthy gulp and started toward the kitchen for a refill. "I'm pretty sure the cause of death was their brains leaving their heads at the speed of sound, so why don't we start with the parents."

"Good choice. We've started to get in the info you wanted on Jennifer's real parents. James and Carol Passal. James was a grocery store manager in Portland, Oregon—Carol was a full-time mother, as near as we can tell. Both were killed in a fire that destroyed their home when Jennifer was two years old."

"Where was Jennifer?"

"They found her wandering around on the lawn."

"She was outside playing when the fire started?"

Michaels shook his head. "The fire started around midnight."

"Midnight, huh. What caused it?"

"The report's pretty cryptic. They ruled out foul play, but I'm not sure how, since they don't give a cause. Also, no one seems to have ever figured out how Jennifer got onto the lawn."

"Interesting."

"Oh, it gets way better than that. James had a

brother. He lived in Salem 'til he left town under a black cloud."

"And that cloud was . . ."

"Kidnapping category number three. Suspicion of child molestation."

Beamon fell back into the chair with his fresh beer. "Now that really *is* interesting. Was Jennifer involved?"

"It's possible, but I can't say for sure. The police investigated briefly, but when David took off, I guess they never got anything concrete enough to warrant bringing him back."

"Where is he now?"

"I think near Kanab, Utah."

"Where?"

"It's on the southern border of the state. Not that far from here, actually. I'm still trying to get a specific address, but the sheriff there said that Passal just lives up in the hills—pretty much keeps to himself."

"We need to find him, Chet. Now."

"I've called the guys that cover that area, they—"

Beamon pointed at the young agent, cutting him off. "That's fine, Chet, but the buck stops here. I expect to be face to face with this guy, like, tomorrow. Understood?"

Michaels looked down at the floor and nodded.

"Okay," Beamon said. "If you run into any problems, call me here or beep me. I'm available twenty-four hours a day for this. Now what else do you have for me?"

Michaels didn't seem to want to speak.

"Come on, Chet. Out with it."

"We can't seem to figure out who Carol Passal was."

"What, did Social Security lose her maiden name?"

Michaels grabbed his beer off the box/coffee table in front of him. "No, we found her maiden name no problem. We also found another identity prior to that. We're still trying peel back the layers and get at the original."

"Really? You're telling me that she purposefully changed her identity?"

He nodded.

"Only one reason to do that—you don't want to be found," Beamon said. "Check the database for any outstanding warrants on someone fitting her description. Maybe she was running from the law. Check with the IRS, too. People just hate paying their taxes. Otherwise, keep after it. Could be she was trying to get away from a psycho ex-husband or something. Anything else?"

Michaels shook his head and scribbled Beamon's instructions on the back of the folder.

"Okay, then. Hit me with the autopsy report. Just the highlights—it's getting late."

"Both Mr. and Mrs. Davis were shot with the same forty-five, Mrs. Davis in the right side of the back of her head and Mr. Davis under the chin. There were minor contusions around Mrs. Davis's mouth and nose that would suggest that someone pretty strong had grabbed her." He put his hand over his mouth and pinched his nose shut with his thumb and index finger to illustrate the point.

"Various contusions and a few fresh cuts were found on Mr. Davis, also suggesting a struggle."

Beamon nodded. "We saw the aftermath of all that in the kitchen."

"Yeah. Uh, no evidence that either of them was tied at any time, no evidence that either body was moved postmortem."

"Time of death?"

"They're putting it between eight P.M. and three A.M."

"That's kind of broad. The window?"

"Yeah. They had to make some assumptions about how fast the room cooled off after the window was broken."

Beamon nodded. "So based on what we have from the neighbors, between ten and three."

"Yeah. It would have been tight, but I don't think we can completely rule out the boyfriend based on the physical evidence."

"Yeah," Beamon sighed. "But I have to admit that I'm having a hard time creating a scenario that includes the kind of struggle you're describing if it was just him and Jennifer. That would mean, what? Jennifer held her mother while Jamie fought with her father? The struggle took place at two different times? There were more kids involved? I don't know." Beamon jumped up out of his chair and clapped his hands, startling the young agent a bit. "Okay, Chet. Get out of here. It's Friday night and that girl with the tattoos you like so much probably wants to be taken to dinner."

"I'm okay, Mark. If you want to, you know, drink a few beers and bat around some ideas . . ."

Beamon ignored the hopeful look on Michaels's face and pointed at the door as he made his way back to the refrigerator. He still had three more beers to put away before he reached his recently self-imposed limit of five per day. "Thanks, Chet, but you should go out and have a good time tonight, because this weekend you're going to be doing what?"

"Finding David Passal," Michaels mumbled as he gathered up his folders and headed for the door. "Oh, Mark. I took a message for you this afternoon from the lab. It's on your desk, but it said something like, 'A year's worth of hair, no drugs.' Does that make any sense?"

"Yeah, thanks," Beamon said, dropping onto the sofa as Michaels pulled the door shut behind him.

With his foot, Beamon snagged the coat he'd thrown on the floor and retrieved a tobacco pouch from the breast pocket. The message meant that the hair he'd retrieved from Jennifer Davis's sink—a year's growth—showed no narcotic residue. She was clean.

What was he missing? he wondered as he tapped tobacco into a paper wrapper.

What would someone want with Jennifer Davis? What good was she with her parents dead? Every time he came up with a plausible answer, there were two or three facts to refute it.

He finished rolling the cigarette and looked at it longingly for a few moments. No smoking in the house. It was another one of his new and ironclad rules. That rule, combined with the rather majestic local weather, had been instrumental in reducing his smoking from a two packs a day to five or six of these hand-rolled jobs.

He looked over at his front door. It was rattling slightly as the frigid wind outside battered it. Beamon laid the cigarette on his stomach and decided that gazing at it and drinking a few more beers would have to satisfy his vices for the night.

9

BEAMON SHUFFLED THROUGH THE TEETER-
ing stack of personnel files on his sofa, finally
finding the one he was looking for in the middle.
He gave it a quick jerk and watched the rest of the
pile destabilize and topple onto the floor of his living room.

He kicked them over toward the wall and wondered for the hundredth time if he really had what
it took to run an office. He'd spent the last weeks
trying to get around to familiarizing himself with
the backgrounds of his new staff—something that
should have been a simple task. D. gave him the
files and he just had to flip through them. Why
then, two weeks later, were they strewn across his
floor, unread?

The answer was as obvious as it was unsettling:
He owed a great deal of his success to date to his
ability to ignore the noise around him and focus all
his attention on one task. A wonderful quality in an
investigator. A shitty quality in a manager.

As he saw it, he'd already proven that he made
an impossible subordinate. So it was time to get his
ass in gear and prove that he made one hell of a
good boss. Otherwise, he had serious problems.

Beamon leaned forward and picked up his
glasses. Perching them on his nose, he flipped open

the folder in his lap and tried to concentrate on the picture of the young man stapled to the inside cover.

He was a second office agent—talented, diligent, hard-working. That is, until about a month ago when his wife ran off with the pool guy. Beamon had initially thought that this was an elaborate joke, created to welcome him to the world of management. But it turned out that she actually did. The goddamn pool guy.

And now, as the new Assistant Special Agent in Charge–Flagstaff, this was *his* problem. He had to figure out a way to straighten this kid out before he did or didn't do something that would permanently fuck up his career. The question was, how? Tell him to cowboy up? Walk it off? No, wait—how about, "There are a lot of fish in the sea?"

Christ.

Beamon dropped the folder on the couch and let the Jennifer Davis problem creep back into his mind. While he was sitting around worrying about the sexual trysts of his staff's spouses, her clock was ticking. The statistics on this kind of disappearance were clear—every day she was missing, his chances of finding her alive got cut in half.

"I'm sorry, I was expecting Mark Beamon. What can I do for you?" Carrie Johnstone said, stepping back to better take in the full impact of what stood before her.

Beamon tugged uncomfortably at the lapel of his suit. The silky-smooth wool felt strange beneath his fingers. "C'mon, Carrie. Give me a break. I feel weird enough as it is."

"Weird?" she said, motioning for him to come inside. "Why would you feel weird? You look fantastic! I don't think I've ever seen you in a suit that fit you and didn't have holes in it."

Beamon nodded self-consciously. "It was a gift. I mean, it's a great suit, but it makes me look like I mugged a European tourist."

She reached around the back of his neck and yanked his collar up. "Hugo Boss? Someone gave you a Hugo Boss suit?"

"Yeah. A mob boss in New York, actually."

"I see," Carrie said as she sat down at a small writing desk in the living room and started scribbling on a Post-it note. "Should I be concerned that my tax dollars are paying the salary of an FBI agent who receives expensive gifts from organized crime?"

"Probably."

Her dress was a deep maroon that seemed to change color magically as she moved. High-quality silk, Beamon knew—he'd become something of an expert at identifying different fabrics on an investigation involving a bomb planted in a clothing-filled suitcase.

What was important, though, was that it clung to her body perfectly. Not too tight, but suggestive in all the right places. Her auburn hair swayed slightly as she wrote, revealing brief glimpses of the smooth skin of her back.

She looked much younger than she did in the business suits and heavy sweaters Beamon normally saw her in. He made a mental note to try to devise a clever way of ferreting out her age over the course of the evening.

"When did you start wearing glasses, Mark?" Carrie asked without looking up.

"I got them a few months ago, but I don't wear them much. Having kind of a hard time getting used to them."

Carrie finished what she was writing and looked down a hall to her left. "Stacey! We're leaving now. I left some instructions on the stuff in the oven and my cell phone number in case there are any problems. Don't call me unless it's an emergency, okay, hon? I'm going to be in a church."

Beamon heard a muffled reply and Carrie, apparently satisfied, grabbed her purse and slid an arm into his.

"Why?"

"Why what?" Beamon said, having a little trouble holding onto coherent thoughts as she brushed against him.

"Why are you having a hard time getting used to them? I think they look very distinguished."

"Oh, it's not the glasses per se, it's more the clarity. I'm not sure I didn't like the world better with softer edges." Beamon reached out and opened the door for her. "By the way, have I mentioned how incredibly beautiful you look tonight?"

"No, you hadn't, actually."

"Well, it's because I was trying to find a more artistic way of phrasing it."

She smiled as they walked out into the silence of the snow-covered courtyard. "I think most women would settle for 'incredibly beautiful.'"

- - -

Beamon had read somewhere that the construction of a church pew was actually an art of some subtlety. The craftsman had to strike a perfect balance between intense discomfort—so your less fervent worshippers wouldn't fall asleep—and ergonomics, so the truly devout wouldn't suffer crippling back and neck injuries.

Fully an hour into a ceremony that didn't seem to be in any danger of wrapping up, Beamon managed to find a position that briefly relieved the pressure on his spine. Permanent damage might yet be avoided.

His chiropractic distress momentarily eased, Beamon was able to turn his attention back to the ceremony, which he had to admit had been very educational.

He knew criminally little about the fledgling Church of the Evolution and its leader Albert Kneiss, especially considering that it was headquartered right in the middle of his new back yard. It was the fastest-growing religion in the world and it was unpopular with the German government. Other than that, his knowledge consisted of a bunch of unconnected factoids.

There was really no excuse for his ignorance. The Kneissians had brought countless jobs to the area, built hospitals, schools, and museums. Beamon seemed to remember reading somewhere that their numbers had swelled to over eleven million members worldwide, and their influence over the Flagstaff area, and Arizona in general, continued to expand.

He turned to Carrie to ask her a question about the progress of the ceremony, or more accurately when the hell it would be over, but she seemed to be lost in the thoughts she was scribbling into the notebook on her lap. He sighed quietly and looked around him.

The cathedral surrounding them had been only recently completed, but the architecture and carefully chosen materials gave it a look of permanence usually reserved for buildings hundreds of years old. The complex grid of arches supporting the ceiling were hewn of a light wood and tipped with ornate geometric carvings that dangled into space like stalactites. That touch of vaguely Scandinavian informality was countered by the heavy stone of the walls—a few of which had water running down their mossy faces into marble pools.

Despite its size, the church was packed. With few exceptions, the congregation had that well turned out but unimaginative way of dressing and impeccable grooming that the world had come to associate with followers of Kneiss.

At the altar, the bride and groom were passing their hands ceremoniously through the flame of an ornate candle held by a pious-looking man spouting some mumbo-jumbo about purification.

Beamon looked over at Carrie, who was still scribbling furiously, and decided to interrupt her. He had never been much for long religious spectacles. By now, even God had to be about ready for a couple of stiff drinks and a cocktail weenie.

"Nice ceremony," he whispered.

She looked up from her pad and smiled.

"Uh, about how much longer do they generally go on?"

"Don't really know, Mark. I've never been to one of these."

"Really? You mean you're not . . ."

"A Kneissian? No."

Beamon nodded silently but decided to exercise a little more of his curiosity while he had her talking. "What's that you keep writing?"

She looked around conspiratorially and leaned so close that he could feel her lips brush against his ear. "I'm doing a study on how religious affiliation can influence various psychoses. I don't really know that much about this faith, and I thought this would be helpful."

Beamon let that process for a moment.

"Lucky you knew a Kneissian who happened to be getting married this weekend," he said hopefully.

Her expression went blank for a moment.

"We're crashing this wedding, aren't we, Carrie?"

"'Crashing' is such an ugly w—"

The congregation stood and the sound of rustling clothes and dropping Bibles drowned out the rest of Carrie's sentence.

Beamon smiled politely and waved at the young couple as they walked elatedly down the aisle, followed by their attendants. He leaned over to Carrie again. "They make such a nice couple. And what a beautiful wedding. I can't wait for the reception."

"I wasn't really planning on going to the reception," Carrie said. "I think that might be pushing it."

"Are you kidding? There's no way I'm sitting through an," he looked at his watch, "hour-and-twenty-minute wedding ceremony and not going to the reception."

"I thought maybe I'd take you out to dinner instead," she said, starting to sound a bit apprehensive.

Beamon shook his head. "Wouldn't be much of a substitute, would it?"

Now this *was* fun. Already it had completely made up for that endless ceremony.

The conference room of the Radisson, lined with balloons and paper streamers for the occasion, had been set up with countless small round tables, each surrounded by tipsy wedding revelers. The band at the other end of the room had just started and the table where he and Carrie sat had been abandoned at the first chords of "Louie Louie."

Beamon swirled a shrimp in a blob of cream cheese and popped it in his mouth. One thing he had to say about the Kneissians—they could really throw a party. Great food, and enormous open bar with only top-shelf stuff, and man, were they friendly. At a minimum, twenty-five people had approached them and struck up a conversation. And thankfully, due either to the nice suit and glasses he was wearing, or the dim light and booze, not a single person had recognized him as the man who had been recently besieged by the press over Jennifer Davis's disappearance.

Of course, his anonymity had been helped along by the fact that he told everyone who approached him that he was hard of hearing and really only Carrie's date. She was the one intimately acquainted with the bride.

Thus had started a rather long and painful

evening for Carrie Johnstone. She'd delighted Beamon for the last hour with a string of confused lies and brief outbursts of nervous laughter as she discussed the bride from childhood to present.

The blue-haired woman who had been chatting with Carrie through a smile that looked like it was held in place by fishhooks finally straightened up, waved a good-bye to Beamon, and began weaving though the crowd toward the bar.

"Shrimp?" Beamon said, holding a cream-cheese-doused shellfish in Carrie's general direction.

"I'm going to get you for this, Mark. I don't know how. And I'm not sure when. But I will."

Beamon slipped into his most innocent smile. "You've just spent an hour conversing with your test subjects, Carrie. I thought you'd be thanking me."

She held out her hand and scowled. "Give me the shrimp."

She popped it in her mouth, then sucked down half the glass of wine in front of her.

"C'mon, Carrie. You can't tell me this hasn't been even more productive than the ceremony. I've learned volumes just sitting here. As venues for people-watching, wedding receptions are right up there with . . ." He was about to say "strip bars," but caught himself. "Uh, public parks."

She took another gulp of her wine. "Well, what *I've* learned is that *you* can't be trusted. I assume from my conversations that you've been telling people that you're just my date and that you don't know anybody here."

"Uh, I think I used the words toy boy, actually. Oh, and there was that deafness thing."

"Right, a few people mentioned your little hearing problem. You'll be happy to know that I told them it was the result of untreated syphilis."

That probably explained the strange looks on the faces of a few of the people Carrie had spoken to and their furtive glances in his direction.

"Touché," he said, surprised at the depth of the relief he felt when her face broke into a beautiful smile. He'd had no idea how she would take his little prank. Some women seemed so perfect, but then you found out that they couldn't laugh at themselves.

Beamon scooted his chair closer to her and looked around to make sure no one was within earshot. "Serves you right. Getting the head of the FBI's local office to aid and abet you in crashing a wedding. At least tell me what the paper you're writing is about."

"It's about the way religion affects people's mental health." Beamon could hear the excitement creep into her voice as she started to explain her work. Another mark in the Carrie Johnston plus column. He loved people who were passionate about something. Didn't really matter what.

"How do you mean?"

"Well, if you believe very strongly in any particular religion, that dogma is going to affect your perceptions and therefore your mental outlook. Let's compare a very devout Muslim woman with a devout Kneissian woman. Now, many Muslims have very strong beliefs that keep women as sort of second-class citizens. This might create, for instance, problems with self-esteem."

Beamon thought about that for a moment.

Seemed to make sense. "And the Kneissian woman?"

"Well, the Kneissians are at the other end of the spectrum. They are almost completely lacking in institutional chauvinism. On the other hand, they are very focused on financial and political success. So a Kneissian woman might have self-esteem problems just as severe, but they would relate to, say, a lack of success in her job."

"I'll buy that."

"Obviously, that's an oversimplified example. Here's a better one. How old do you think the bride and groom are?"

Beamon shrugged. "I have no idea. They looked like kids to me, but then, so does half my staff."

"I'd guess that they were just out of high school. For some reason, Kneissians get married very young and have an extremely high divorce rate."

Beamon nodded thoughtfully. "Recruitment."

"Excuse me?"

"That's why they marry early and get divorced," he said. "Recruitment."

"I don't think I follow you."

Beamon grabbed another shrimp. "What's the purpose of religion?"

"That's a pretty complicated question. To make people feel less alone?"

Beamon scowled. "No. That's the purpose of God. The purpose of a religion is simply to force everyone into its way of thinking."

"Why, Mark. You're a cynic. I never would have guessed."

Beamon ignored the jibe. "Seriously. The Church of the Evolution doesn't miss many opportunities to tell you it's the fastest-growing religion in the world. How do you think they achieved that?"

She pushed a dirty plate out of her way and leaned against the table. "I think they've created a pretty attractive belief system that fills a lot—" The expression on Beamon's face made her stop. "You're going to tell me that I'm overthinking again, aren't you?"

He smiled and nodded furiously. "They're growing faster than any other religion 'cause they've been more scientific about recruitment. Take our young couple today. Let's assume a perfect scenario for the church. The boy was, I don't know . . . Buddhist. He converted in order to marry the girl, who was Kneissian. They have a couple of kids and get divorced, say five years from now. Our groom likes the church and decides to stay. They're both single for a few years, then he finds a nice Baptist he wants to marry and she converts. Same thing happens to our bride, but maybe she converts a Protestant. Both new couples have two more kids. How many new Kneissians have we just created?"

Carrie counted on her fingers. "Uh, nine?"

"Sounds about right."

She held her glass up in salute and took another sip of her wine. "I have to say, Mark, that's got to be the most malignant piece of deductive reasoning I've ever heard."

"Thank you. Are you ready to take me to dinner?"

She folded her arms across her chest and gave him a stern look. "That offer was *instead* of the reception, not in addition to. Besides—you have to have eaten a hundred shrimp already."

The way her eyes crinkled at the edges when she smiled really was dazzling. The truth was, he really wasn't hungry—and the shrimp and cream cheese he'd eaten had definitely not been on the new and improved Mark Beamon diet—but he didn't want the evening to end just yet. "Yeah, but they weren't very good."

The silk of her dress gathered and dispersed the dim light of the room hypnotically as she stood. "Okay, Mark. You win. Since you seem to have elevated cynicism to the level of a religion, I think I might be able to write the check off on my taxes."

10

"HELLO?" BEAMON CALLED INTO THE EMPTY reception area of the Kane County, Utah, sheriff's office. No answer.

He leaned his head into the half-open window centered in the wall. "Hello! Anyone home? I'm Mark Beamon from the FBI."

There was a moment of silence, then a disembodied voice. "Wait in the conference room."

Beamon stepped back and scanned the missing persons posters taped haphazardly to the glass. Jennifer Davis smiled out from one of them, posing self-consciously alongside a bicycle with a big red bow on the seat. The other lost souls had similarly cheerful expressions and stood with jumping dogs, new motorcycles, and loved ones, oblivious to their current plights.

Those frozen images were all that was left of most of them, Beamon knew. Few would ever be found, and most of the ones who were would be discovered because some lost hiker tripped over one of their sun-bleached bones.

"This is it," Chet Michaels said, pointing to an open door in the hall to Beamon's left and breaking him out of his trance.

They waited in the large conference room for almost twenty minutes before the sheriff finally strutted in, flanked by two deputies.

That was probably a bad sign. It was Sunday afternoon and all he needed was directions to David Passal's place. He could have just taken them over the phone, but it was his practice to meet the locals before he started prowling around their jurisdiction.

One of the deputies hopped up on the counter running along the edge of the room and tapped his hand rhythmically on the edge of the sink next to him. The other just leaned against the wall next to the door and tried to look as imposing as possible.

"You Beamon?" the sheriff said, standing near the end of the conference table and looking them over carefully.

Beamon had decided to make this trip a casual-dress affair. He was wearing an old pair of jeans and a pair of cowboy boots that hadn't seen his feet since his days as a firearms instructor to the Nevada police. No point rushing into Kanab looking like a cross between an IRS agent and a funeral director. Made people uncomfortable.

"Yeah. Call me Mark." Beamon considered standing and offering his hand but instead just motioned to his right. "I think you spoke to Chet yesterday."

The sheriff nodded curtly. He had that impossible build that seemed so common in rural America. His face, arms, and legs were lean—thin, almost—but he had a great expanse of a belly that had wrestled his gray-tan shirttail out of his pants and was now covering up the ornate tooling on his leather gunbelt.

"What do you FBI boys want with Dave Passal?"

Beamon wasn't anxious to stand around posturing with the locals, but he didn't really have a choice.

He had no idea how to find Passal, and you never knew when you'd be desperately in need of some quick firepower.

"Would you know where we could find him?"

"Nope. He don't come into town much. Could be anywhere."

His backup snorted quietly.

"David's Jennifer Davis's uncle. Her only living blood relative," Beamon said. "I thought he might know something that could help me."

The sheriff—who still hadn't introduced himself—tried not to let his surprise show. "You think maybe Dave might have been involved?"

Beamon put on a bored expression. "Drive all that way to kidnap a girl he hadn't seen or spoken to in twelve years? I doubt it." Not exactly the truth, but he had no idea if the sheriff was Passal's hunting partner, brother-in-law, or best friend.

"We had a bank robbery here awhile back," the sheriff started. "Teller got killed. Nice kid. Bunch of your boys came up from Salt Lake. Started givin' half the town the rubber hose treatment. You know what they found in the end?

"Actually, I have no idea," Beamon said.

"Nothin'. Turned my town upside down and inside out, then they just packed up their stuff and left."

"Look, Sheriff . . . ?"

"Parkinson."

"Sheriff Parkinson. It's just me and Chet here. We want to see if this guy knows anything, then we plan to ride off into the sunset. With a little luck, we're talking *tonight's* sunset."

Parkinson nodded silently. Suspicion was still etched clearly across his face, but the hostility seemed to be fading a bit.

"Don't see much of Dave, but I reckon he's still up there."

"Up there?" Michaels prompted excitedly.

The sheriff raised his hand lazily and pointed in a generally eastward direction. "Got a place up in the hills about an hour outside of town. Doesn't come down much. Just to get supplies every now and again."

"Could you give us directions on how to get there?"

"Why don't I just send a couple of my boys up there with you." He looked into the innocent face of Chet Michaels. "I'd hate to see the paperwork if I let a couple of you FBI boys get your asses shot off."

Michaels leaned forward over the table. "So you think he's armed?"

Beamon winced and Parkinson's deputies giggled.

"Hell yeah, he's armed, son. Probably kills most of what he eats. That and he always struck me as one of those paranoid types. You know, thinks there's a Russian behind every tree. I doubt he gets many visitors and I reckon he likes it that way."

Beamon sighed quietly. If Passal was involved, the last thing he needed was a couple of the sheriff's lackeys standing around siding with the man. They'd be there all week. "I appreciate the offer, Sheriff, but I don't really think it's necessary. We aren't after Passal, we just want to talk to him for a few minutes and then we're gone."

The sheriff looked strangely pleased that Beamon had declined his offer. Probably curious to see what Passal would do to the city slickers from Flagstaff. "Your call," he said with a condescending shrug of his shoulders.

Beamon managed to open the car door about a foot before the wind blew it shut again. Chet Michaels's quiet laughter was silenced when his door was torn from his hand with the sound of bending metal.

"You mind? I'm still making payments on this thing," Beamon said, putting his shoulder into the door and successfully escaping the car before the wind blew it shut again.

They'd stopped just as the road crested a hill and disappeared into the darkening sky. In the near distance Beamon could see a column of smoke rise above the dense pine forest and then suddenly disperse in the swirling wind.

Better to finish this trip on foot, try to get close to Passal before he had a chance to dust off his grenade launcher.

"Okay, Chet, here we go. Why don't you walk up the road and knock on the door. See if anyone's home."

The young agent looked apprehensive. "What're you going to be doing?"

"I was going to sit in the car and have a smoke. It's freezing out here." Beamon smiled. "Relax. I'll be right behind you. I'm going to walk up through the trees here. Just in case."

Michaels reached for his gun, but Beamon stopped him. "Think friendly, Chet. Just going up there to borrow a cup of venison jerky, right? No need for anyone to get upset."

Michaels reluctantly flipped his sweater back over the butt of his gun and looked up at the road, trying to gauge the distance to the fading column of smoke.

"Wait about three minutes, then get moving, okay, Chet?" Beamon could feel the cold penetrating his parka and wanted to get moving before he started to get sluggish. "No, on second thought, give me about ten minutes. I think I'm going to take it easy." Michaels nodded as Beamon slid his new glasses onto his nose and pulled out his .357.

It was slow going. Utah's drought year and constant sun had kept the roads and endless miles of sagebrush relatively clear, but in the shadows of the trees, the snow and ice had accumulated. Beamon concentrated on every step, scanning the ground carefully and occasionally bypassing an area where the shadows had grown too deep to see well. He guessed he was about halfway to the source of the smoke they'd seen earlier when he saw the fading sun glint off something he'd hoped not to find.

A thin piece of fishing line about three inches from the ground blocked his path. It spanned about four feet between a small sapling and a dense tangle of sagebrush.

Beamon knelt down, ignoring the jagged edges of frozen pine needles beneath his knees, and leaned forward until his ear was almost to the ground. He gently pushed away a dead branch and exposed a simple but undoubtedly efficient mechanism involving a gas can and a road flare.

He stood and stepped carefully over the fishing line, scanning the ground for secondary trip wires.

The darkness was coming fast as the sun dipped behind a butte to the west. Beamon knew he was moving too quickly, but according to his watch, Michaels had been making his way up the road for almost a minute now. And sending him in alone to face down a man who obviously had no qualms about setting trespassers on fire would definitely take him out of the running for manager of the year.

Two minutes and one more trip wire later, Beamon could see the faded white of a trailer through the woods. He stopped just before the edge of the clearing and hovered behind a deformed pine.

It was about what he'd expected. The single-wide looked like it had been patched together with plywood and duct tape, and the only thing holding the roof on was a mismatched collection of old tires piled two high across the front edge.

The only other building visible was about twenty-five yards away and looked to be entirely constructed of old wooden signs. The low hum emanating from it and the cable snaking between it and the trailer suggested that it housed a generator. No way to get power run this far north of the middle of nowhere.

Beamon scanned the clearing as Michaels walked stiffly around the corner and started toward the trailer. Nothing. Just the wind blowing half-frozen dust and intermittent snowflakes through the air.

Michaels was almost to the door when Beamon saw one of the tires on top of the trailer move out of sync with the wind. He raised his gun too late and watched helplessly as a man in camouflage pants and a black sweatshirt jumped from the roof and landed on a very surprised Chet Michaels.

The force of the impact upended the makeshift staircase that Michaels had been standing on, and both men went down hard. Beamon jumped up from his crouched position and was about to run to Michaels's aid when the man he assumed was David Passal dragged the young agent to his feet and pushed a pistol into his neck.

Outstanding.

"What do you want?" Passal yelled, jerking back and forth on the back of Michael's sweater for no apparent reason.

Beamon was still one of the best pistol shots in the FBI, but this one just wasn't doable. It was a good twenty yards in a stiff wind. Couple that with the fact that Michaels was flopping around like a rag doll and it would have been fifty-fifty for Annie Oakley.

"I haven't told nobody nothing! You said you'd leave me alone!" Passal pulled his pistol from Michaels's neck and used the sight to scan the treeline.

With the gun no longer trained on Michaels, Beamon felt his heart rate notch higher. It was time to do something. Walking out of the trees probably wasn't a great call. Passal looked pretty agitated and would almost certainly shoot him.

Beamon turned his gaze from Passal and focused on Michaels. The fear he expected to find on the young agent's face hadn't materialized. As near as Beamon could tell from this distance, his young associate's current mood was hovering somewhere between irritated and mildly pissed off.

Passal's eyes were darting back and forth wildly. "Come out. Do it! Come out where I can see you. I'll kill him before you can do me!"

The situation wasn't improving and it didn't look like it was going to. Beamon aimed his gun a couple of feet wide of Passal's ear, took a deep breath. Hopefully this was where he was going to find out how a guy who looked like Howdy Doody became a champion collegiate wrestler.

He squeezed the trigger and the bullet smashed through the front window of the trailer, prompting Passal to duck away from the shower of glass.

And that was all the time Michaels needed. With one hand he grabbed the gun and with the other he lifted Passal's right leg off the ground and tipped him over onto his back.

When Beamon finally ran up to them, Passal's pistol was lying in the dirt and Michaels had the man's limbs so twisted and tangled up that he looked like a contortionist. A contortionist in considerable pain.

Beamon picked up the gun, flipped the safety, and stuck it in his waistband. "You had me worried there for a second, Chet."

Michaels gave one last subtle twist of his hips that made Passal cry out in pain and then pulled him to his feet. "Sorry. I wasn't looking for him on the roof."

"It was my fault. I had the wide view."

Passal tried to back away, but Beamon grabbed him by the front of his shirt.

"What do you want?" the man said in a terrified voice. "I did what you asked! Leave me alone!"

Beamon moved his hand to Passal's throat and slammed him against the trailer. "That's not what we hear, David. We hear you've been talking to people you shouldn't."

Out of the corner of his eye, Beamon could see Michaels's confused expression. Not exactly an FBI-approved interrogation technique, but he had no idea who Passal thought they were and his curiosity was getting the better of him.

Beamon squeezed the man's neck a little harder. Just enough to make his point, but not so hard that the man couldn't answer him. Passal grabbed his wrist and Beamon tensed his arm to keep the man under control. Instead of trying to pull his hand away, though, Passal became momentarily confused, finally pushing the sleeve of Beamon's parka up to the middle of his forearm.

"Who the fuck are you guys?" Passal said, the fear draining from his face in a matter of seconds.

Beamon released him and stepped back, wondering what the hell had just happened. He produced his credentials from the inside pocket of his coat.

"FBI!?" Passal said. "What the fuck do you want? Get off my property!"

"We just want to talk to you for a few minutes. We'd already be gone if you hadn't decided to do your Superman impression from the roof."

Passal grunted and looked over at Michaels.

"Who did you think we were?" Beamon asked.

"I don't have to say anything to you, man," Passal said, starting to shiver. The wind was obviously cutting through his sweatshirt as if it weren't there.

Beamon kicked the stairs back upright and took a step toward Passal's trailer. "It's been a good five minutes since I felt my toes, Dave. Why don't you invite us in?" He balanced his way up the rickety steps and through the front door of the trailer. It wasn't much warmer inside than it was out. The cold wind streaming through the window Beamon's bullet had shattered was starting to overpower the old iron wood-burning stove in the corner.

Beamon walked the length of the small trailer examining the makeshift shelves lining the walls and the large cans of fruits and vegetables stacked on them. Other than that, there were some skins drying on 2x4s and a bed in the corner. The only weapon he found was an unloaded shotgun, unless he counted the hatchet lying on an empty paint can.

"Come on up, Dave. It's cold out there," Beamon said, sliding both the shotgun and the hatchet under the bed and out of reach

Passal walked up to the door and paused as though he was entering a house he'd never seen before. Beamon motioned to one of two chairs around a formica-covered card table and stuffed a couple of split logs into the stove. When the flames reached a more satisfying height and intensity, he turned back to Michaels, who was standing in the doorway. "Why don't you go have a look around while we talk. Stay out of the woods, though— booby traps. Just around the trailer and generator house. Carefully."

"Hey, he can't do that!" Passal said as Michaels disappeared through the door.

Beamon sat down across the table from him. "He just did."

While the trailer was just about what Beamon had imagined, Passal himself wasn't. Despite his threadbare clothes and less than cosmopolitan surroundings, he was alert, and his hair was reasonably well kept—not the long scraggly locks or military cut that people who chose this type of life normally favored. The eyes that had a few minutes ago flashed with paranoia and fear had settled into the calm apprehension of a thinking man.

Beamon considered his plan of attack carefully. "I'd like to talk to you about your niece."

"My what?"

"Your niece. Jennifer?"

Passal's expression softened for a moment. "Haven't thought about her in a long time. She was two last time I saw her. Couldn't be much more than fourteen now."

"Almost sixteen, actually."

Passal nodded thoughtfully. "What's the FBI want with a fifteen-year-old girl?"

"To find her. She was kidnapped a few days back. The couple who adopted her were both shot in the head. Hell of a mess."

The muscles in the man's jaw rippled subtly as his teeth clenched. "So you thought maybe the child molester did it. Fuck you."

"Don't know who did it, Dave. Thought you might be able to help me. Maybe your brother or your sister-in-law might have had some enemies. Any ideas?"

"They're both dead," Passal said. "Any enemies they had ought to be satisfied with that, don't you think?"

"You tell me."

Passal's quiet apprehension seemed to be slowly evolving into full-fledged nervousness. "No. No enemies."

"You're sure."

"Yeah. I'm sure."

"What can you tell me about your sister-in-law?"

"What do you mean?"

"It sounds kind of strange, but we're having a hard time figuring out who she was. Looks like she might have changed her name a few times, moved around a bit. Would you know anything about that?"

"No."

Beamon pulled a pouch of tobacco from his pocket and began slowly rolling a cigarette. "Maybe you remember where she was from? Did she ever mention any family?"

"No."

Passal knew something, but his fixed stare and the set of his jaw told Beamon that he wasn't going to succumb to any classroom interrogation techniques. Beamon considered taking him in, but decided that it would be pointless and possibly dangerous. If the man did have Jennifer stashed around here somewhere, she'd likely die without him tending her. Goddamn cold in Utah at night.

Beamon lit the cigarette and mulled over his options. They were all bad. All he could do was move as quickly as possible and hope that luck was with him. He stood abruptly, prompting Passal to scoot back in his chair.

"Okay, then, sorry to have bothered you. Is there any way we can reach you if we come up with something that might jog your memory?"

Passal looked down at the table. "You won't."

Beamon paused for a moment just outside the door. "Must get kind of lonely up here sometimes. Don't know if I could do it."

Passal turned a tired face toward him. "Maybe you'll get a chance to find out. There's an empty lot about a mile down the creek. I'll save it for you."

Beamon cocked his head and opened his mouth to speak, but then thought better of it. He'd get what Passal knew. He just needed a little leverage.

"Okay, Chet, we're out of here," Beamon called.

Michaels was walking with comic slowness through the sagebrush west of Passal's trailer, his eyes locked on the ground.

"Anything?" Beamon asked as Michaels retraced his steps and came alongside him on the road.

"That shack over there is the only other building. There's a snowmobile and a generator in it and that's about it. I looked under the trailer—it's up on a bunch of cinderblocks cemented together. Nothing but some old lumber. How 'bout you?"

"He knows something, but he sure doesn't want to tell me what it is."

"So you think he's involved?"

"Either that or he has an idea who is. I don't know. This one's throwing me."

Beamon looked up at the stars coming to life in the darkening sky and pulled his parka close around his neck. "You hear the weather forecast for tonight?"

"Yeah. The wind's supposed to die down. Other than that, clear and cold."

"Good flying weather."

"You're going to fly back to Flagstaff?"

The sound of pounding drifted up behind them on the wind. Michaels jerked around, but Beamon just kept walking. Passal patching his broken window. "No, we're going to stick around."

"And watch Passal?"

"And improve our relationship with the sheriff."

"But what if he's got her? He might be planning on getting rid of her right now!"

"It's possible," Beamon said hesitantly, trying to fight back the memories of his most spectacular failure. "But if we bring in a bunch of people to watch him, he'd know it. Hell, we couldn't even sneak up on him today."

It had been years ago in the heat of a southern Texas summer. He had brought in no less than ten agents to watch and occasionally harass Bill Meyers, his primary suspect in the kidnapping of a ten-year-old girl from El Paso.

A few weeks later he'd found the girl tied up in a pit about a mile from Meyers's house. The memory of how she looked, staring up at him, her skin turning black and her swollen tongue prying her mouth open, was still painfully vivid.

It seemed that Meyers had stopped bringing the girl food and water when Beamon's men started watching him. According to the local coroner, the little girl's death had been extremely unpleasant.

II

"Okay, so I'm still behind the tree. I thought I caught the guy solid through his car window, but I'm not sure, right? And I'm not too happy about having to stick my head out 'cause the tree next to me doesn't have any bark left from this asshole's machine gun."

Beamon kicked an empty chair across the floor to demonstrate the tree's relative position. "I had to do something, though, you know?"

The man was an artist, there was just no denying it. Sheriff John Parkinson and three of his deputies sat literally on the edges of the seats surrounding the torn-up old wood table, transfixed by Mark Beamon's manic way of telling a story.

Chet Michaels leaned back, took another sip from the Budweiser he'd been nursing for the last hour, and watched his boss's face intently. There was nothing in his expression or tone that would indicate that he was anything more than some good-old-boy cop from Texas. No trace of the reportedly off-the-scale IQ, the pressure of the press's impossible expectations and constant scrutiny, the endless distractions that came hand-in-hand with running an office. The little girl who was most likely dead or dying somewhere.

But those things were there—he'd seen them. Sometimes when Beamon didn't think anyone was looking, he'd suck the right side of his lower lip between his teeth and fix his eyes on the nearest wall. In those brief moments, he seemed like a completely different person.

Michaels took another tiny sip of his beer and continued to study Beamon's performance. In the two days that they'd been in Kanab, local law enforcement's attitude toward them had gone from mild suspicion to near-worship. He would never be able to pull that off. You just had to be born with that kind of charisma.

"I must have waited there for five minutes," Beamon continued, barely pausing to breathe. "Listening for the guy to get out of the car. Nothing. Finally I take a quick look. Shit, you can't even see into the goddamn car anymore 'cause of the blood all over the windows. Looks like he exploded in there, you know?"

The glassy-eyed cops grinned in unison.

"So I go up to it. No mistaking it, the guy's dead. I open the door and he kind of flops down face first on the back seat. Anyway, I grab him by the hair— he's got this really long hair—to pull the body out." Beamon paused dramatically. "Pulled his head clean off. Shotgun blast had caught him right in the neck."

The cops were silent for a moment and then burst out laughing. Sheriff Parkinson pounded drunkenly on the table with a closed fist.

"True story," Beamon said, leaning back and polishing off his beer. "Puked all over my shoes. Had to write a full report to get the Bureau to buy me a new—"

The sound of his beeper going off stopped Beamon in mid-sentence. "Whoops, that's us, John. I think our fax is coming through."

Parkinson pointed to the empty beers in front of Beamon. "One more quick one for the road?"

"Thanks, but no," Beamon said. "We've got to move."

"You boys still coming by the house for dinner?"

Michaels grimaced. He'd hoped Parkinson's invitation had been hypothetical.

"Hell yeah," Beamon said. "It isn't often I get a home-cooked meal. Six o'clock, right?"

"What *is* this?" Chet Michaels said, spreading the slick fax paper out on the bedspread in the hotel room he and Beamon had been sharing for the last two nights.

Beamon double-checked that his gun was loaded and began digging through his suitcase for a heavier sweater. "Think about it, Chet. Try to understand the psyche of your average backwoods paranoid."

Michaels looked down again at what seemed to be a bad fax of a photograph that hadn't turned out. He flipped it upside down. Still nothing. "I think it must have gotten screwed up in the fax, Mark. It's just dark with a few light splotches."

Beamon ignored him. "As I was saying, the psyche of the backwoods paranoid. When the Red hordes—or more likely the ATF—come over the hills and surround 'em, their trailer sure as hell isn't going to save them. What do they do?"

"Head for the hills?"

"Hell, no. That'd be un-American. They go for their bomb shelters."

Beamon slid an arm though the sleeve of the sweater he'd turned up and pointed to the photograph. "I got turned on to these things years ago when I was looking for another girl, a little younger than Jennifer. What you're looking at is an aerial photo of Passal's spread taken with heat-sensitive cameras. Tell me what you see."

Michaels studied the fax for a few more moments, then pointed to a roughly rectangular off-white splotch centered on it. "That must be the trailer. You can see the stove here in the middle."

"That'd be my take on it."

"This little thing here must be that shack where the generator was running."

"Uh-huh."

Michael's finger traced along the edge of the photo, stopping on another anomaly in the dark gray background of the photograph. "What's that?"

"That's where the ground isn't being heated by the sun. It would seem to indicate that there's something under there that's not under the rest of the area."

Michaels brought the fax up close to his face. "What do you think it is?" he said excitedly.

"I'm hoping for Jennifer Davis, but I doubt I'm that lucky."

12

JENNIFER STIRRED, BUT DIDN'T OPEN HER
eyes. She rolled to her back, kicked the sheets off,
and breathed deeply. Bright light filtered through her
eyelids, and for a moment she imagined that they
had become transparent. Through them she could
see the pine ceiling of her home and the enormous
wrought-iron chandelier that hung above her bed.

This was it. It had to be. Today she would finally
wake up from the nightmare. Today she'd be home.
Jennifer took a final deep breath and opened her
eyes.

The glare off the stark white ceiling blinded her,
just as it had the last five times she had played out
this elaborate ritual. She threw her forearm over her
eyes, rolled on her side, and began to cry quietly.

Why was this happening? Had she done something wrong? Maybe she was sick—and this was a
hospital. The horrible dreams were just part of the
illness. High fever could cause those things—she'd
seen it on TV. And that's why she was alone. She was
contagious. Quarantined.

She would think about that for a time, as she
did every "morning" in the windowless room.
When she had once again convinced herself of the
plausibility of this explanation, she would rise and
walk slowly to the doorless bathroom at the other

side of the room, splash water on her face, and stare at the empty wall above the sink.

Finally, she would look down at herself. At the short white T-shirt and cotton panties that were the only clothes provided for her. At the unnaturally pale hue her skin had taken on.

She would let her fingers trace the outlines of the fading green-brown bruises that had adorned her body in various configurations since she had taken up mountain biking. Then she would return to the twin bed and sit with her back against the wall and stare at the empty room, eventually sinking to the mattress and into something that felt more like a trance than sleep. When she awoke, there would be a plate of food, a towel, and a clean T-shirt and pair of underpants by the door.

She had no idea how long she'd been alone in this room. The difference between day and night was just a flick of a light switch and there had been no sounds emanating from behind the heavy wooden door that led to . . . where?

Sometimes the feeling that she was caught in a cube in the middle of an empty desert plain overwhelmed her. She would become panicked that one day the person silently depositing her meals would lose interest and she would die alone and hungry, never knowing what had happened to her and to her family. Or worse, that the meals would continue to silently appear forever, leaving her to drown in loneliness and confusion.

At first the quiet clink of metal against metal didn't sound real. Just another trick played by her mind. When it came again, though, she struggled back to a sitting position. The heavy knob on the door jiggled almost imperceptibly.

It was real.

She pressed her back against the wall and drew her knees to her chest, feeling the numbness and despair that had become oddly comforting in their familiarity wash away in a flood of adrenaline.

Could it be her father? Of course, it must be. He'd finally come for her. It had all been a fever-induced dream. And now she was better.

The door opened slowly as Jennifer slid to the edge of the bed and began to stand, wanting nothing more than to be folded in her dad's arms and to be told that she was okay now and going home.

"Jennifer."

She fell back onto the bed, legs pedaling desperately in the tangle of sheets until her back slammed against the wall. It was her. The woman who had made her father go crazy. The woman who had been sitting at the edge of her bed staring into the dark while she slept.

Jennifer kicked at the air weakly in an effort to keep the woman away, to no effect. She easily caught one of Jennifer's ankles and threw her legs to the side.

"Be still," the woman said, grabbing the back of her hair. Out of the corner of her eye, Jennifer saw a man with a thick black mustache pull the door closed, leaving them alone.

Jennifer could feel the woman's eyes boring into her and tried to turn away, but the woman's grip on her hair kept her head immobile. "No, you look at me, Jennifer. Look at me."

Jennifer wanted to push her away, but she felt

weak, confused. Like she was floating in a current that was impossible to fight.

"Do you know what's happened?" the woman said.

Jennifer opened her mouth, but she hadn't spoken in so long and she was so afraid, her throat felt paralyzed.

"Do you know what's happened?"

"I don't know," Jennifer got out.

"Yes you do. Tell me."

The images of her parents' death that seemed to have finally begun to fade suddenly returned to her with devastating clarity. "My parents," she stammered. "They're . . . gone."

"That's right, Jennifer. They're dead. And you know how, don't you. Tell me how."

Jennifer threw her arms over her face and felt the tears begin to flow down her temples. "No," she sobbed. "No, don't make me."

The woman pulled Jennifer's arms away from her face and tightened her grip on her hair.

"How did it happen, Jennifer?"

"He killed her . . . then he killed himself. What did you do to them? What did you do to my parents?"

She felt the woman slide her hand under her T-shirt and gently caress the skin on her stomach from her navel to just beneath her breasts. Jennifer tried to move away, but the powerful hand tangled in her hair held her fast. "They weren't your parents, dear. You know that. Don't you?"

"They were," Jennifer heard herself say. "They loved me just as much as if I was their real daughter."

"That's what you were supposed to think, Jennifer," the woman said, shaking her head with something that looked like sadness. "It's what I told them to make you believe."

"You're lying!"

The edges of the woman's mouth curled up almost imperceptibly. "Then why didn't your father use the gun I gave him to save you?"

Jennifer closed her eyes so tight she could see dull streaks of imaginary light streaking across the insides of her eyelids. "He would have . . . he wanted . . ." Her voice trailed off. Why hadn't he? Why hadn't he saved her?"

"He didn't save you because you weren't really his child. I gave you to them and told them to take care of you until it was time for you to come back to me. That's all."

The woman's hand slid from underneath her shirt and into her hand. Jennifer heard her stand and felt a gentle pull. She allowed herself to be led into the bathroom.

"I'm the only one who loves you now, Jennifer. I'm the one who takes care of you," the woman said, reaching into the small shower and turning on the water. She tested the temperature and then turned back to Jennifer, who was standing immobile on the cold tile floor. Jennifer didn't resist as the woman pulled her T-shirt over her head and then dropped to her knees and slid her panties down her legs.

She stepped silently into the hot shower, trying to fight off the distorted image of her parents' shattered bodies swirling around her in the thick steam. She closed her eyes again as she felt the woman begin to run a soapy washcloth along her wet skin, trying to let her mind retreat into the past. She surrounded herself with the memory of her last race, her friend spraying the mud off her with a hose, the look on her parents' faces as she toweled her hair with the old grease rag.

"I want to go home," she said so quietly that the sound was almost completely swallowed up by the running water.

The woman dropped the washrag into the bottom of the shower and ran a soapy hand slowly down Jennifer's back. "You are home, dear."

13

THE STOVE WAS PRETTY MUCH COLD.

Beamon stuck his hands into the open grate and tried to warm them on the few remaining coals glowing dimly through a blanket of ash. The cans lining the walls around him had gone pale white with a thin layer of frost. The door had been wide open when they'd arrived.

Beamon dropped to his knees and looked under the bed. The shotgun and hatchet he'd put under it were gone.

"You got anything, Chet?" Beamon yelled, walking down the steps and back into the blinding light of a heatless sun.

Michaels threw open the door to the generator house, gun stretched out in front of him. He poked his head into it, lowered his gun, and turned back toward Beamon. "Nothing."

"Now, where the hell did he get off to?" Beamon said.

Michaels walked slowly toward him, scanning the clearing. "Do you think he just headed into the hills? His truck's still here."

Beamon shook his head. It had been a bad call. He should have been watching. "I don't know. Let's see that fax again."

Despite the clarity of the heat signature on the photograph, it was difficult to judge distances with any real precision. Beamon made his best guess as to the location of the possible underground chamber and he and Michaels began kicking through debris-scattered underbrush in a less than scientific pattern to find the entrance.

"Are you sure that blob on the picture is something underground?" Michaels said, dropping to his knees and peering under an unusually thick stand of thistles.

"I'm starting to wonder." Beamon kicked a rotted piece of plywood. It flew into the air and was sent careening across the clearing by a strong gust of wind. "It feels right."

Beamon tried to jam his toe under an old sign lying flat on the ground in front of him, but it wouldn't budge. Thinking that it was perhaps stuck in the ground frost, he crouched down and felt around the edges. Along the back, the rough surface of peeling paint was broken intermittently by the oily metal of hinges.

"Chet. Over here."

Michaels jogged up and looked down at the old sign. "You think this is it?"

Beamon nodded.

"You think he might be in there?"

"Don't know. His truck's still here, and it looks like most of his stuff's still in the trailer. But then, why let the stove die down and leave the door open?"

Beamon took a step back and pulled his gun from his jacket. "Mr. Passal! David!" he yelled at the plywood sign at his feet. "It's Mark Beamon with the FBI. I have a few more questions for you. Why don't you come on up and we can talk."

Michaels scanned the treeline nervously. Out in the open like this he couldn't shake the feeling that there was a set of crosshairs tickling the back of his neck.

"Dave! Come on! Let's go!" Beamon shouted, giving the makeshift trapdoor a hard kick.

Nothing. Why couldn't anything ever be simple?

"You ready, Chet?"

Michaels jerked his head in the affirmative and aimed his gun at the sign.

"Don't shoot my foot off, now," Beamon said, finding a place where he could work the toe of his boot under the edge of the plywood.

"Okay, Dave. Come on out," Beamon said, kicking the trapdoor open and inching forward with his gun aimed into the hole.

No answer.

Beamon lay down on his stomach and slid slowly forward until his head was almost even with the edge. He shook off the mental picture of Passal sitting down there with that damn shotgun and burst forward, shoving his gun hand into the hole. It wasn't shot off, so he poked his head in and swept his eyes back and forth, scanning for movement.

"You okay, Mark?" Michaels said nervously. "Is he in there?"

Beamon pulled back, letting a little more light into the hole and slowing the rush of blood to his head. "Yeah, he's in here. But he's seen better days."

One of David Passal's legs was resting on the bottom of the ladder that led into the hole, bent at an unnatural angle. It looked as though it had been snapped when he'd fallen, caught between the 2x4s that made up the rungs.

Passal's head was resting in a wide puddle of blood that was beginning to form little white ice crystals across the top. Beamon adjusted himself so that the sunlight could fall directly on the man's face. His skin was a less than healthy shade of blue and his eyes were frozen wide open.

"What've you got, Mark?"

"He doesn't look like he's got much to say."

"What?"

"Looks like he fell down the ladder, hit his head, and froze," Beamon said, pulling his lighter from his pocket. He flicked the wheel and the flame sparked to life, improving visibility only marginally.

The hole was probably only about ten feet square and maybe six and a half feet deep. The clay walls still showed the marks of the shovel that had created them behind wooden shelves.

Beamon got to his knees and slid into the hole, careful not to disturb Passal's snapped leg.

The shelves were a sturdier version of the ones in Passal's trailer, probably providing structural support as well as storage space. They were covered with neatly stacked cans of meat and vegetables. Large bags of sugar and flour were propped in the corner.

Beamon leaned over and confirmed his diagnosis. Passal was definitely dead.

The stack of old lumber he'd landed on had a number of nails sticking out of it. Unfortunately, one of them had lined up nicely with the back of his head.

The guns Beamon knew he would find were piled on a wide shelf to his left. He stepped closer and examined the black body of an M-16 through the thick, clear plastic bag it was stored in.

This was all he'd been looking for—he'd never really believed that Passal had the girl, only that he knew something that could help. The threat of being brought up on an illegal weapons charge would have gone a long way toward convincing him to open up.

"You all right in there, Mark?" Michaels called into the hole.

"Yeah, fine," Beamon said, sitting down next to the corpse.

"You coming up?"

"In a minute. I need to think."

He sat with his back against the cold dirt wall for almost ten, his eyes wandering from Passal to the ladder and back again. The man must have come down it a thousand times—he stored food down here. Why did he decide to fall today? What was different about today than all those other days? Only one thing he could think of. The FBI was poking around asking questions.

Sheriff John Parkinson pulled his head from the hole and rocked to his feet using his vast stomach as a fulcrum. "Yeah, that's dead, all right. You say he hit a nail?"

Beamon nodded and looked around him. The sheriff's men had cordoned off the clearing—not that this was exactly a high-traffic area—and were all standing around shifting their weight from one foot to the other in an effort to stave off the cold of the approaching night.

"Right in the back of the head," Beamon said. "Bad goddamn luck."

"Accidents happen out here, Mark. You get a little ice on the ladder. Or maybe you have a few too many snorts before you come out here. And then you're dead."

"You're probably right." Beamon clapped him on the back as they started toward the line of cars blocking the narrow dirt road. "But to be sure, I'm going to have a few guys come up and take a look."

Parkinson didn't look excited by the prospect.

"Me and Chet, though, we've got to get out of here," Beamon continued. "I'd appreciate it if you and your boys'd look after things till my guys get here."

"Sure, Mark, whatever you need."

"Okay, then. You've got my card. If any of our people start being a pain in your ass, use it."

14

JENNIFER DAVIS STOOD IN THE MIDDLE OF THE
room, bunching the light cotton of the pants she'd
been given in her still-damp fists. She was strangely
transfixed by the sight of the open door and the simple hallway on the other side of it. Transfixed and terrified.

All the little things that made up her life had
disappeared overnight. Everything she knew—all
that was familiar now—was in this room. What
would she find outside of it?

"I . . . I can't," Jennifer said, her voice quivering
slightly.

The woman's eyes flared as she strode across the
room and put her hand on the back of Jennifer's
neck. "There are people who want to hurt you, Jennifer. I'm going to do everything I can to stop them,
but you have to help me."

"Yes, but I'm afraid. I . . ."

The woman was behind her now. She couldn't
see her anymore, but felt an arm slide around her
stomach and pull her close. "I'm taking you to
someone, Jennifer. He's going to talk to you, ask you
questions. When he does, you will answer simply
and directly. Before you speak, though, I want you
to look at him very carefully. To see how weak he is.
He can't protect you, Jennifer, only I can. But only if

you follow my instructions very carefully. Do you understand?"

She didn't understand. She didn't understand anything anymore. Was this woman telling the truth? Every time Jennifer felt her touch or looked into her eyes, she felt hopeless and afraid.

Her head began to throb dully, making thought even more impossible. "I . . ."

The pressure around her stomach increased, silencing her.

"Do you understand?" the woman repeated quietly.

Jennifer fought back the tears that she felt coming and nodded.

Unlike hers, the room she was taken to was enormous—so far across that you'd have to shout to be heard by someone on the other side. The ceiling was more than thirty feet high, with heavy-looking moldings around the top. Three of the walls were blank, but the fourth had tall, heavily tinted windows that filtered the light from outside into long, jagged shadows.

It was daytime, Jennifer realized as the woman steered her toward the far wall, where there was a small bed surrounded by light gray medical machines. They stopped a few feet from the side of the bed and Jennifer looked down at its occupant.

Was he dead? His closed eyes had sunk so deep that she could see the outline of the round holes in his skull. The color of his skin wasn't much different from the color of the machines humming around him, except that it was occasionally broken by bright

red sores or the spidery tracks of broken blood ves-
sels. Long tufts of white hair still clung at random to
the rice-paper-thin skin of his scalp.

The woman's hand dropped from the back of
Jennifer's neck, and she took a syringe from a stain-
less steel tray next to the bed. Jennifer took an involuntary step backward but realized it wasn't for her as
the woman inserted it into an IV tube taped to the
man's forearm.

Jennifer watched the man's face as the sound resonating from the heart monitor turned erratic and
then fell back into a livelier pattern. His eyelids flut-
tered slightly and then opened into a blank stare. He
stayed that way for almost a minute until, finally, his
head lolled over and his gaze settled on Jennifer.

"Don't be afraid," he breathed through cracked
and peeling lips. "Come."

His left hand turned palm up and edged to the
side of the bed, but she didn't move. A moment
later, the woman's hand took its place on the back of
her neck again, and she felt herself being pushed
forward.

"Please. I won't hurt you," he said. His voice had
strengthened a bit, but was still almost completely
lost in the expanse of the room and the humming of
the machines surrounding them.

The pressure on her neck increased, and she
reached out and placed her hand in his. It felt like a
cold bag full of chicken bones.

"I'm so glad you're here."

Jennifer struggled to overcome her fear and
forced herself to look into the old man's eyes. She
was surprised at what she found there. A strange

spark, dimmed by time for sure, but still there. An incredible depth of emotion. Kindness. Strength. Suffering.

"This must be so hard for you," he said. "To have to leave your parents and come here; everything so unfamiliar. You'll understand soon, though. You'll understand everything." He looked at the woman standing behind her. "Listen to Sara and the others. They have so much to teach you. I wish I could do more, but I'm so tired."

His voice was losing what little strength it had had a few moments before. Jennifer leaned forward, unconsciously squeezing his hand.

"Sara," the old man said, turning his head toward the woman behind him. "I want to talk to you and the others. It must be soon."

Jennifer tried to move away as the woman— Sara, he'd called her—stepped closer to the bed, but the old man's hand tightened around hers and she was afraid she'd hurt him if she pulled away. .

"Of course," Sara said. "As soon as I can."

"She's your responsibility now, Sara. You have to teach her."

15

MARK BEAMON TURNED THE KEY IN THE LOCK and pushed the icy door to his condo with his shoulder. It flexed slightly but held fast as a faint ringing on the other side became audible.

He stepped back and gave it a short kick. Not the full-on door kick that had made his Quantico instructor so proud, but enough to shatter the thin film of ice gleaming in the complex's floodlights and allow him to throw open the door and run for the phone.

"Beamon," he said, mouth not yet within optimal range of the handset.

"Mark? It's Trace."

Trace Fontain ran the FBI's lab and had reluctantly agreed, as a personal favor, to go to Utah and supervise the extraction of Passal's body.

"Trace! How are you feeling?" The Utah winter probably had Fontain's bronchitis well on its way to full-blown pneumonia by now, Beamon thought with a pang of guilt.

"Not so good. I think this could be turning into pneumonia." He coughed loudly into the phone, and Beamon felt the pang turn into a twinge at the sound of Fontain's inhaler.

"I'm really sorry, Trace. Couldn't be helped. I've got this little girl missing out here and I can't seem to put the facts together so they make any sense. I needed the best."

Another fit of coughing. The rattle in his lungs sounded like static over the phone. "I'd hold off on the flattery till you hear what I've got to say."

"What've you got?"

"You're going to be pissed."

"Come on, Trace. You have to have something."

"I don't know what happened here."

Beamon pried off his snow-covered boots and grabbed a beer out of the fridge. "What is it exactly that you don't know?"

"Well, I don't know whether your Mr. Passal was murdered or whether it was an accident. And I don't know for sure whether Jennifer Davis was ever here."

"Let's start with the first one. Why isn't it murder?"

"I didn't say it wasn't. I put a couple of mattresses on the ground and pushed one of the local cops down the ladder about twenty times. Figured out how you could do it—one guy behind the ladder grabs his foot and pulls it through the rungs, the other grabs his face and the shoulder of his jacket and pulls him down onto the nail. Once you got the technique down, it wasn't too hard."

"Wouldn't there be contusions on Passal's face or stretched material on his jacket, then?"

"Don't think so." Cough. "The victim is in the air, so the attacker's got all the leverage. Wouldn't really have to exert much force. Besides, Passal was wearing one of those heavy wool hunting jackets. I don't think it would be possible to stretch it with your hand."

"So it's possible that it was murder, but likely it was an accident."

"That's the way my report's going to look."

"Moving on, then. What about Jennifer?"

"We've gone over the trailer, the generator house, and the pit with a fine-toothed comb and we've got nothing."

"Nothing?"

"Well, we'll run it up more thoroughly when we get back, but I brought some equipment along and I doubt the main lab's gonna tell me anything different. No blonde hairs at all. Hell, we haven't found *any* that don't look like they came directly from Passal's head. Or some game animal."

"He was apparently kind of a hermit," Beamon said.

"That would explain it. With very few exceptions, we've eyeballed all fibers as belonging to stuff in his closet."

"And the exceptions?"

"They look old. Probably stuff he got rid of. In any event, I seriously doubt we're going to find any matches in the wardrobe of a fifteen-year-old girl."

"Prints?"

"We found two sets that weren't his on the formica table in the trailer and one set on the doorknob. They're in pretty good shape, and . . ."

Beamon finished his thought. "They're mine and Chet's."

"That'd be my guess. We'll confirm when we get back."

A knock at the door startled Beamon, breaking his concentration. "Trace, could you hold that thought for a minute? Someone's here."

Beamon walked through the snow melting on

his carpet in his stocking feet and pulled the door open. Carrie Johnstone stood on the other side, haphazardly dressed in a down jacket, boots, and light cotton pants. Emory stood next to her, similarly dressed, except pajama bottoms substituted for the cotton pants.

Carrie looked at the phone in Beamon's hand and then at the cord stretched out across the room. "I'm sorry, Mark," she whispered. "I didn't know you were on the phone."

"No problem. I won't be much longer. Come on in."

A strained look crossed her normally cheerful face. "Actually, I came to ask a favor. One of my patients called and is having . . . some problems. There's no one to stay with Emory and I was wondering . . . well, could you watch her for a while?"

Beamon looked down at the little girl, whose face was turned up toward him. She smiled and waved at him.

He pulled the phone off his chest and up to his mouth. "One more second, Trace. I'll be right with you."

He took it as a positive sign that Carrie was willing to trust him with her daughter, but what the hell did he know about children? "Uh, Carrie, I'd be happy to in theory, but I really don't know much about taking care of a four-year-old girl."

"I'm almost five," Emory reminded him.

He looked down at her and laughed. Hell, how hard could it be? You feed them, let them watch a little TV, then put them to bed. Right?

"Almost five?" he said, stepping out of the way

and providing her a clear path into the condo. "In that case, come on in." Emory ran past him and dove onto his couch.

"It's an hour 'til her bedtime, Mark," Carrie said, looking relieved. "She's already eaten and brushed her teeth—won't be any trouble at all." She gave her daughter a stern, motherly look. "Will you, honey?"

"Uh-uh," Emory replied convincingly, punching buttons at random on the TV remote control.

"Thanks, Mark. I'll be back as soon as I can," Carrie said, already heading for the snow-covered steps.

He leaned out the door. "Take your time. No problem."

By the time Beamon had closed the door and walked back to the kitchen, Emory had found the ON button and was surfing through the channels at breakneck speed.

"Sorry, Trace. Minor emergency. Where were we?"

"Nowhere."

"Oh, yeah. Right."

"Anyway," Fontain continued, "I examined Passal's body to see if there were any scratches or injuries that might suggest he participated in a rape. Nothing."

"He could have tied her up before he r—" Beamon looked over at Emory, who was bouncing up and down on her rear in the soft cushions of the sofa. "Before he, you know . . ."

There was a confused silence over the phone for a moment. "Before he raped her, Mark?"

"Yeah. Before that."

"The only comfortable place to do that looks

like the bed in the trailer. No marks on the bedposts or fibers that might have been left by a rope. We did find a rope in the generator shed that had a lot of blood on it, but my guess is that we're going to find out it was deer or elk or something. The good news is, it doesn't look like this guy's taken a shower in weeks, so if he has come into contact with Jennifer, we'll be able to tell you."

"But you're not hopeful."

"I just don't think she was here, Mark."

"Yeah. Shit. Listen, Trace. I want you to get the locals to widen the search of the area. And bring in that heat photography plane to go over the area again. Passal's been running around the backcountry there for years. He could have her stashed a ways out from his property. I think you're right, but let's be sure, okay?"

"Then can I go home?"

"Then you can come home."

Beamon hung up the phone and leaned over the counter. "Hey, Emory. Give you a cookie if you flip it to channel seven for a while."

She craned her neck around and pushed herself up high enough to see over the back of the sofa. "What's seven?"

"The news."

"Yechy," she said, crinkling up her nose.

Damn. He figured the cookie ploy would be foolproof. What was he going to do now?

"*The Tick*'s on," she said hopefully.

"I'd, uh, kind of rather watch the news for a few minutes."

She shrugged and flipped the channel to seven without another word.

Beamon smiled. That wasn't so hard. This could be fun. One cookie for the news, one for going to bed, and he'd still have enough to put him in a sugar coma while he awaited Carrie's speedy return.

"You want milk, too?" he asked.

Emory flipped over on the sofa so all he could see was her feet sticking up over the back. "Mom says I can't eat cookies."

"Can't eat cookies?" He lowered his voice. "A food Nazi, huh? I should have guessed." Beamon grabbed his beer and took a seat in the chair next to the sofa. The newscast was just starting.

"What's a Nazi?"

He stopped the beer a few inches from his mouth. It probably wouldn't take Carrie long to figure out who had been working on her daughter's vocabulary. "Nazi? I didn't say Nazi."

Emory was about to continue her line of questioning when the local news anchor saved him.

"Mark Beamon refused to comment on the FBI's ongoing investigation into the kidnapping of Jennifer Davis . . ."

Emory, her attention momentarily diverted, flipped over and scooted forward so that she was half on the box containing his coffee table and half on the sofa. She squealed excitedly when the screen went from the newsroom to a group of reporters mobbing Beamon as he fought to get through the front door of his office building.

"That's you! You're on TV!"

"That's me."

"Mommy was on TV once, too, but it was really boring," she said excitedly.

The screen cut back to the anchor, framed by a large photograph of the building housing the FBI's Flagstaff office. Beamon's head sank into his hands as the man began quoting an unnamed source regarding the possibility of a white slavery ring operating in the Flagstaff area. The office building background faded artistically into a picture of Jennifer Davis's young body stuffed into a black halter top and skin-tight biking shorts as the newscaster related a sordid tale of wealthy Arabs and their penchant for spunky young blondes.

Beamon groaned quietly. It wasn't enough for them that a fifteen-year-old girl was missing and possibly dead. No, there had to be some sex in there somewhere to loosen up the advertisers' check-writing hands.

He looked over at Emory and pointed to the TV. "You don't believe anything you see on this thing, do you?"

She looked at him like he was crazy. "Sure."

16

"HEY, D. HOW ARE YOU THIS UNGODLY morning?" Beamon said, knocking his umbrella on the floor and leaving a ring of slush in front of his secretary's desk.

"I'm fine. How was Utah?" Her voice sounded tentative.

"Weird. Something wrong?"

"Well, I've got good news and I've got bad news."

Beamon grimaced. D. hated to deliver bad news, so she always dreamed up something inconsequentially positive to try to cheer him up. "Bad news first, please."

"I couldn't hold her off anymore."

Beamon leaned over and peeked through the open door of his office. There was a tall blonde hairdo growing from the back of one of the chairs in front of his desk.

"I assume that the hair belongs to Nell Taylor."

She nodded. "Sorry."

Nell and her husband Tom owned the house two doors down from the now defunct Davis family. She had taken it upon herself to use her considerable financial resources to lead a civilian search for the missing girl and her kidnappers.

She seemed to have made it her life's pursuit to see that Jennifer's face was plastered across nearly every city, town, and crossroad in the U.S. She'd hired a virtual army of private investigators that were at this minute running around Flagstaff like the Keystone Kops. And man, did she like to talk to the press.

"I gotta know, D.," Beamon said. "What's the good news?"

His secretary flipped his calendar around on her desk and jabbed at it. "You had two hours open this morning. I told her you had fifteen minutes."

Beamon entered his office with a wide smile. "Mrs. Taylor! I'm so glad we're finally able to get our schedules to dovetail."

The hair turned and rose from behind the high-backed chair. When the pudgy face supporting it appeared, Beamon held out his hand.

"I appreciate you taking the time to meet with me, Mr. Beamon." Her tone was cold.

Beamon dropped his coat and umbrella next to his desk and walked to the percolating coffee pot at the other end of the office. "Can I tempt you with a cup, Mrs. Taylor?"

"No, thank you."

"I was in a small town in Utah a couple of days ago and there was a poster with Jennifer's picture on it in the window of the sheriff's office," Beamon said, sitting down in the chair next to her. He took a tentative sip from the steaming cup in his hand. "I assume it was one of yours. Quite an accomplishment to get that kind of coverage so quickly."

The compliment seemed to go unnoticed. Or at least unacknowledged.

"What is it that I can do for you, ma'am?"

She smoothed an imaginary wrinkle from her gray business suit and then folded her hands neatly on the manila envelope in her lap. "I wanted to discuss the direction you're taking in this investigation, Mr. Beamon."

"Mark, please."

She ignored him. "We have some concerns."

"We?"

"The Jennifer Davis Recovery Foundation."

"The Jennifer Davis Recovery Foundation," Beamon repeated. "Of course you do. And what exactly are they?"

She cleared her throat. "Did you see the local news broadcast last night? Channel seven?"

Beamon thought for a moment. "I did, actually, yes."

"What are we going to do about it?"

Beamon tried his most winning smile. "Well, Mrs. Taylor, as much as I'd like to, I can't just go around shooting reporters."

The look of impatience etched across her face deepened. "Mr. Beamon, you may think this is all very funny, but I know Jennifer Davis. She's a wonderful girl . . ." She paused for a moment and seemed to be switching back to her mental script. "We are very disturbed that Jennifer, right now, may be suffering the worst kind of . . . abuse at the hands of Arab terrorists while the FBI is harassing and threatening an innocent seventeen-year-old boy."

Could this case get any worse? Beamon wondered. It wasn't bad enough that he didn't have a single reasonable suspect and hadn't been able to dream up even a farfetched motive that fit the facts, but now a woman with a beehive was telling him how to conduct an investigation. There used to be some goddamn dignity in being an FBI agent.

"I assume you're speaking of Jamie Dolan," he said.

She nodded in a single jerky motion. Her hairdo flexed perilously.

"You have to understand, Mrs. Taylor, that the FBI doesn't just follow one line of investigation. Just because we talked with Jamie doesn't mean that we aren't pursuing many other leads. We have to cover all the bases."

She looked like she had something to say, but Beamon continued before she could get anything out.

"I have to tell you, though, for the record, that I've seen nothing to suggest that there is anything even remotely resembling a white slavery ring operating in the Flagstaff area. In fact, if you look at the data, there have been relatively few unsolved abductions of girls and women who would be . . ." He was going to say "salable," but thought better of it. "That would fit the profile. Frankly, I don't know where they got that story. I'm guessing that it's a complete fabrication."

She picked up the envelope from her lap and handed it to Beamon. "I hired a psychic to look into this matter, Mr. Beamon. She's one of the best in the field. It was she who uncovered the Arab connection."

The Arab connection. It sounded so terribly official. Beamon shook off the image of a woman with a handkerchief on her head looking into a crystal ball. "I appreciate the information, Mrs. Taylor. I'll have my people review it right away."

Beamon waved to Michaels, who had been hovering outside his window for the last five minutes. "Before you leave, Mrs. Taylor, there is someone I'd like you to meet. This is Chet Michaels. He's working with me on this investigation."

She stood and took his hand.

"Nice to meet you, Mrs. Taylor," Michaels said with a hint of recognition in his voice.

"My pleasure."

"Mrs. Taylor is the head of the Jennifer Davis Recovery Fund."

"Foundation," she corrected.

"I'm sorry, foundation. Chet here's up on all the details of the case, Mrs. Taylor. And he's probably much easier to get in touch with than I am. If you have any questions or concerns, please feel free to give him a call."

She granted them one more of her jerky little nods and the two FBI agents watched her walk proudly from the room.

"Thanks a lot, Mark. I have a feeling I'm going to be spending a lot of time on the phone with that woman."

Beamon handed Michaels the envelope she'd given him and settled into the chair behind his desk. "Better you than me, son. When you get a few minutes, look over the stuff in that envelope. My guess is she's going to quiz you on it when she calls this afternoon. Now, what have you got for me on Passal?"

"I haven't talked with the guys in Utah yet . . ." Michaels said.

"I have. Inconclusive on all counts. No evidence that Jennifer was there and nothing pointing in any particular direction on his death."

"We had a mechanic go over Passal's truck," Michaels said. "The thing looks like it has a top speed of thirty miles an hour and it gushes black smoke."

"Any record of him renting a car?"

"None. We circulated his name and description to all the agencies in the area. Nothing. Preliminarily, a check of signatures on rental contracts for the time period we're looking at doesn't match his handwriting. The guy didn't even have a credit card."

"Figure out what roads he could have taken to Flagstaff and call the state cops. See if anyone remembers seeing a pickup like his crawling along the highway billowing smoke," Beamon said, then leaned back in his chair and began tapping out a rhythm on the desk with his pen.

"What're you thinking, Mark?"

"Wondering. Based on my conversation with Passal, I'd be willing to bet that he knew more than he was telling us. But what did he know? Who did he think we were when we got there and how did he suddenly figure out that we weren't them? And last, why the hell did he pick this week to go to that big trailer park in the sky?"

"You think maybe he wasn't involved directly, but knew something and was killed for it?"

Beamon shrugged. "I think it's possible. I mean, we go and talk to him and suddenly he falls off a ladder he's been down a thousand times before? You see, Chet, there are only a few reasons people die—"

"Wait a minute. Let me write this down. I can't keep up with all your lists."

"What lists?"

"Why you kidnap, why you die . . ."

Beamon chuckled. "I didn't realize I had so many. Tell you what, though. This one's easy. You give it to me. There are four."

Michaels chewed on his eraser. "Okay. Murder, accident, natural causes." Pause. "And, uh, um . . ."

"Suicide."

"Right. Suicide."

"For the sake of argument, let's rule out natural causes. It's possible, of course, but kind of boring."

"Uh, he had a nail in the back of his head, Mark. Doesn't that kind of automatically rule out natural causes?"

"No. What if the autopsy finds that he had a heart attack on the way down that ladder? Dead before he hit the ground?"

Michaels looked at his shoes. "You're right."

"Where was I? . . . Oh, yeah. Suicide. I like suicide from a motivational standpoint—FBI's on to him, so he kills himself. But the logistics of throwing yourself backward off a ladder onto a nail are pretty complex. You'd probably die of tetanus before you hit the thing right. So that leaves accident and murder. And accident seems like just too much of a goddamn coincidence to me."

Beamon stopped tapping his pencil and pointed to the blue folder that Michaels had put on the desk when he'd come in. "Okay, enough mental mastur-bation. What's in the folder?"

Michaels grinned and picked it up. "This is really going to destroy your day, Mark. We finally tracked down Jennifer's mother's real identity. She'd changed her name illegally four times before she was married—each time relocating geographically."

"Did you check to see if she was wanted?"

"Yup. But she wasn't."

"So who was she?"

Michaels paused dramatically. "Her name was Carol Kneiss."

Beamon raised his eyebrows. "As in nice day or as in our local messiah?"

"As in our local messiah. You're going to love this—Carol was his daughter. Jennifer's his grand-daughter."

Beamon stared over the young agent's shoulder and watched through his window as two workmen sorted through a thick stalk of brightly colored wires dangling from the ceiling.

"So, what do you think, Mark? Is there a con-nection?"

Beamon let out a deep breath and turned his palms up. "Shit, I have no idea. Don't know that much about the Kneissians. They serve good food at weddings." Beamon pointed across the desk at Michaels. "You're from Tucson. You must know some-thing."

Michaels pursed his lips thoughtfully. "I remem-ber all the publicity when they chose Flagstaff as a base—I was in junior high or something. There was a real uproar from the born-agains. Blasphemous cult. Satanists—you know, same thing they say about everyone. But it seems like as soon as the Christians got on a roll, they suddenly shut up. Decided that keeping Kneiss out of Arizona would be un-Christian, I guess. Since then, the Kneissians have bought up half of Arizona and three-quarters of Flagstaff. And then, I suppose you know about Kneiss's ascension."

Beamon rolled his eyes. There was no way to live in Flagstaff and not hear about that at least once a day. "This is the year that Kneiss is going to take his seat at the right hand of God. On Good Friday, right? Translation: They can't keep the old fart alive any longer. He must be, what? About a hundred and fifty?"

Michaels shrugged. "He's pretty old. I don't think he's been seen in public for years."

"Does Kneiss have any living relatives other than Jennifer?"

"Not as far as I can tell."

Beamon downed the last of the lukewarm coffee in his cup and walked across the office to get a refill. "I don't know, Chet. It's worth following up on, though. What if some Kneissian zealot found out about Jennifer? Kneiss has scheduled his own death for a month from now and this guy goes nuts. Can't handle it. Figures Jennifer's the next best thing."

"You never know," Michaels said enthusiastically. "Religion can get people to do things they'd never normally do."

"Tell you what, Chet. Why don't you *quietly* gather some information on the church? Just stuff available publicly, no inquiries. See if we can put a scenario together that makes sense." Beamon wiped up a small spill with his last paper towel as Michaels stood and gathered up his folders. "Oh, and Chet? Let's not talk about this with anyone just yet. If the papers get hold of this I'll have every weirdo in Arizona camped out on my front lawn."

17

BEAMON SWUNG HIS CAR INTO A LOVINGLY shoveled driveway next to an old but well-maintained Ford Explorer. Almost a half-hour late, he hurried toward the small white house, patting his pockets to confirm that he had brought his pad and pen. The door opened before he had a chance to knock.

"Mark Beamon. How was it that I knew you'd be late?"

He'd only met Marjorie Dunham once, years ago—at a retirement party for a mutual friend—but she hadn't changed a bit. Her light brown hair was still cut straight and off the shoulder and her face was almost completely unlined. If he remembered her right, the smooth skin was probably the result of breaking into a smile only about once a year.

"I'm from Texas," Beamon said, trying to sound apologetic. "Haven't learned to maneuver in the Arizona arctic zone yet."

"Uh-huh. Well, come in before you freeze."

Beamon used a boulder next to the door to kick the snow off his boots and stepped into the modest entryway of her home. A moment later, two labradors pounced on him.

"They like you," Marjorie said. "Most guests, they just rip their throats out."

Beamon rubbed the two dogs' heads vigorously

and padded off behind the woman in stocking feet. The labs followed along right behind him, having identified him as an easy mark for a good head scratch.

"Have a seat," Marjorie said, pointing to a worn sofa against the wall and pulling a rather uncomfortable-looking chair up to face him.

The dogs curled up at his feet as he sank into the old couch and looked around the cluttered but obviously well-organized den.

"So I hear you've already managed to turn my old office completely upside down," she said.

Beamon sighed and shook his head. Until about a month and a half ago, Marjorie had been the supervisor of the FBI's Flagstaff office. When she'd retired, they'd turned it into a bogus ASAC position and thrown it to him as a bone. "Not me. Layman and the director are behind that. At first I thought they were just trying to make my getting an office look respectable—but now I think they're trying to kill me with paint fumes."

"I wouldn't put it past them," she said humorlessly. "So what can I do for you? I know you can't be having problems figuring out my filing system."

"No, D. seems to be pretty much on top of things. Actually, I wanted to talk to you about the Church of the Evolution."

"Really. What are you doing with the Church?"

Beamon had thought long and hard about how to answer that question on the drive over. "Nothing very interesting. We've got a lead on a guy who might be embezzling from them. When I started digging into it I found out how completely ignorant

I am about the church and I figured you could help me out. You were here, what? Five years?"

"Six. I would have thought you'd be wrapped up in this Jennifer Davis thing," she said, obviously probing for gossip.

"Oh, I am. But with the church as politically connected as they are around here, I can't exactly ignore their problems."

"Well, that's probably wise. What *do* you know about the church?"

"I'm embarrassed to say almost nothing."

"Do you know any of the church's followers?"

"Don't think so."

Beamon didn't really see that he had much in common with the Kneissians. He found their fresh-scrubbed optimism and well-pressed look a little irritating, if the truth were to be known. The human equivalent of Wonder Bread.

"So you don't even know what its members believe?"

He shrugged. "That this Kneiss guy is God and he's going to die next month and rule over heaven or something?"

"Hardly," Marjorie said. "The premise of the religion is that every two thousand years God sends a messenger to earth to teach humanity about Him and His will."

"And Albert Kneiss is that messenger?"

She nodded. "Each messenger was at one time human and is chosen to serve God for some period of time before he or she is sent to his or her reward. The—call him an archangel if you like—that appears to us now as Albert Kneiss also appeared two thousand years ago as Jesus. Before that he had other names, but no record has survived of his prior incarnations beyond a few mentions in the Kneissian Bible."

Beamon rubbed the back of one of her dogs with his foot, trying to digest what Marjorie had told him. "So God sends Kneiss down here and he writes another Bible. Isn't that redundant? What's wrong with the one he wrote two thousand years ago?"

"That's a little more complicated." She looked thoughtful for a moment. "Let me see how I can explain this clearly . . . okay. It's really just a matter of context. We," she pointed to herself and then Beamon, "as humans are still too limited to truly understand the mind of God."

"I'll buy that."

"But we're not as limited as the people Jesus taught two thousand years ago," she continued. "That is to say, as a group, we're more enlightened than they were."

"I'd argue that point," Beamon said.

"Let me rephrase. We know more than they did—about ourselves and the world around us."

"Okay, you've got me hooked again."

"So when the archangel that we now know as Kneiss appeared as Jesus, he had to put the teachings of God into the current context. And that, uh, dumbing down of God's message is what has created all the paradoxes and inaccuracies in the regular version of the Bible."

Beamon's rubbed his chin. "Okay, yeah. It works on the principle that you can't explain the Big Bang to people who think flatulence is caused by evil spirits crawling up their behinds."

Marjorie let a rare smile pass her lips, but it disappeared too quickly to cause wrinkles. "I've never heard it expressed quite that way, but you're exactly right."

"And so now Jesus has reappeared as Albert Kneiss," Beamon started. "And he's rewritten the Bible to take into account what we've learned in the last two thousand years."

"Precisely. The spirit of Kneiss's version of the Bible isn't that different from the traditional Bible. But the way it's laid out and the way it embraces current scientific, psychological and sociological thinking is radically different."

"It's pretty far flung now, isn't it?" Beamon said.

"The church? Very much so. It's increased its membership geometrically in the last decade or so. It's up to around eleven million members now. Something like that."

"Pretty impressive," Beamon said.

She leaned forward in her chair. "Unprecedented, really. It seems that there are a lot of Christians out there who are having trouble with the obvious inaccuracies in the traditional Bible. Kneiss's message—that God wasn't wrong, we were just too dumb for Him to tell us the whole truth—has proved to be very attractive."

"And are we watching them?" Beamon asked.

"We meaning the FBI? No. Why would we?"

There was no reason, Beamon knew. It was just that he had always been a little suspicious of large religious machines. Organizations bigoted by definition and full of millions of people whose motivations were very strong and, to him, very murky. "Remember a few years back when we busted those people at the IRS for browsing through people's returns?" Beamon said. "Weren't they Kneissians? Did we ever follow up?"

She shook her head. "Three of the four convicted were members of the church. But what if three of the four had been Catholic? Would we have gone after the Vatican?"

"I might have," Beamon responded.

"Well, *we* didn't. Very dangerous politically in a country that was founded on the principle of religious freedom."

"What about the Germans?" Beamon asked. He'd read numerous articles about Germany's persecution of the Kneissians. It seemed that having an organization as rich and powerful as the CotE operating independently within its borders wasn't sitting well with its government.

"The Germans, for some reason, have become very paranoid about the church and blatantly persecute its members. It's very disturbing—the parallels between their treatment of the Jews during the war and the Kneissians now."

"Would you know anyone, maybe at the German embassy, that I could call? I'd be interested in what they have to say."

She shook her head. "I don't know. Obviously, the Germans' treatment of the church has been a public relations nightmare for them in the States. I doubt you'd find many of their officials interested in talking."

"You're probably right." Beamon glanced at his

watch and wrestled himself out of the sofa. "I've got to run, Marjorie. I really appreciate your time." He breathed in deeply. "It smells like your dinner's about ready."

She rose from her seat and took his hand. "I was going to ask you to stay for dinner. My husband makes a wonderful veal parmesan."

"I'd love to, but I can't. You won't be surprised to hear that I'm already late for my next meeting."

"No, I guess I wouldn't be. Be careful driving now."

Beamon started out of the den but paused at the door, suddenly realizing that in their entire conversation, she had never used the word "they" when speaking about the church. He turned back to face her. "One other thing, Marjorie. Are you a member of the Church of the Evolution?"

She hesitated, crouching down and stroking her two dogs simultaneously. "Yes. Yes, I am."

18

IT WAS NIGHTTIME. THE TALL WINDOWS surrounding the room looked dead. Black streaks against the stark white of the walls.

Just inside the door, Sara stopped and knelt down beside her. "There's something I have to tell you, Jennifer. Are you listening?"

Jennifer nodded silently, her eyes moving to the machines grouped around the small bed and then to the old man lying motionless there.

"Do you know who he is?" Sara asked.

"No."

"His name is Albert Kneiss. You recognize the name, don't you?"

She did, but hearing it just added to the confusion that had continued to weaken her. She tried to concentrate, to process what she knew about Kneiss and his church. She'd lived in Flagstaff for most of her life; many of her friends—some of her best friends—were Kneissians.

"Yes," she said finally.

"Good. That's good, Jennifer." Sara took her hand and gently caressed it. Jennifer's mind told her that this woman was a liar—that she wanted to hurt her—but she couldn't pull away. She was so lonely and Sara was all she had. In the little room that had become her universe, Jennifer was beginning to have trouble distinguishing minutes from hours and hours from days. Sara's visits were becoming one of the only things that reminded her that time moved on and that there was a world outside.

"I know it's hard for you, staying in that room all alone," Sara said, seeming to read her mind. "But it's very dangerous for you right now and it's the best way for me to protect you. You understand that, don't you? You understand that I just want to keep you safe?"

"Yes," Jennifer mumbled, still trying to overcome the effects of her captivity and think clearly. What did this woman want? And why was she about to speak again with a man many people she knew thought was God?

Sara stood and steered Jennifer to the bedside of the old man. His breathing was even more labored than she remembered, each gasp punctuated by the quiet click of a machine next to him, making it obvious it was no longer a completely biological act.

Jennifer stood immobile as Sara inserted a syringe into the clear tube running into his arm. She watched the operation for a moment and then let her eyes wander from machine to machine, finally letting them fall on the papers taped to the back of the heart monitor. They were calendar pages.

Jennifer felt a weak rush of adrenaline as she shuffled silently to her right. Sara was completely absorbed in what she was doing, all her concentration locked on the old man's face. The two pages of the calendar became readable as she took one more small step. They were for February and March.

She leaned forward at the waist, afraid to move

any closer, and scanned the writing in the small squares, searching for anything that would tell her where she was and why. But it was only medication and cleaning schedules.

Jennifer took a step closer to the heart monitor as it stuttered and began to increase in tempo. The small clock built into the display read Thursday, February 27, 7:32 P.M.

Jennifer moved back to her original position, feeling a brief sense of elation at her small triumph, followed closely by a deadening sensation of despair. She had been there a week and a half.

The random fluttering of the old man's eyes became more purposeful and Jennifer turned her full attention to him, watching the gray mask come to life as his eyes opened and cleared.

He took a few shallow but conscious breaths and once again reached out to offer his hand.

"Jennifer. You don't know the peace the sight of you brings me."

This time she moved toward him without prompting and slid her hand into his. Despite everything— the memories of her parents' death, her loneliness and confusion—Jennifer felt a sense of calm spread through her as she looked into the ancient face.

The old man's head rose almost imperceptibly from the pillow as he looked around the room. "Where are the others?"

Sara knelt next to the bed and put a hand gently on his shoulder. "There was a storm, Albert. No one can travel."

The deep lines in the old man's face rearranged themselves into an expression of deep thought for a moment. "Perhaps it would be best to wait, then. They all must hear. They all must understand."

Sara's hand moved from the old man's shoulder to his nearly bare scalp. "I don't think we can wait any longer. You're becoming so weak. If what you have to say is important, you should say it now."

"Sara. My Sara," he said, smiling weakly and then looking back at Jennifer, who was standing transfixed, waiting for him to speak. She was finally going to find out what had happened to her. She could feel it.

"You're right, of course," he said. "It doesn't matter. You've done more to deliver my message than I ever could have hoped. I'll ask you to help me one more time."

She kissed his cheek and moved away from them. As she passed by, though, she brushed against Jennifer in a way that suggested that she would be watching her closely.

"You know who I am, don't you, Jennifer?"

She nodded slowly. "You're Albert Kneiss. People think you were sent here by God."

Another weak smile. "That's right. God did send me here. To teach and make people better understand Him. And themselves."

She concentrated on the face of the old man in front of her, breathing in the strong scent of dust and antiseptic cleaner that seemed to emanate from him. "You don't look like an angel," she heard herself say.

He breathed out audibly. The laugh of a man too weak to laugh. "No, I don't suppose I do."

Kneiss moved his free hand to a worn leather

book lying next to him. "Take this. It's yours now."

Jennifer sat down on the edge of the bed and leaned across the old man, gently sliding the book from under his hand. She'd seen it many times before. On TV, in local bookstores, in the hands of her friends and neighbors. The gold letters on the front had been almost completely worn away by time but were still legible.

THE HOLY BIBLE
Kneiss Edition

Jennifer opened it and turned a few of the cracked and yellowed pages. Each was cluttered with notes scrawled through the margins in an elegant hand that must have been his.

"You probably didn't know that I had a daughter, did you, Jennifer?"

She looked up from the book.

"Her name was Carol."

"Carol," Jennifer repeated quietly, as she carefully closed his Bible.

"And she, in turn, had a daughter," the old man continued. "That daughter is you."

Jennifer stood and backed slowly away from the bed, pulling her hand from his and letting the book fall to the floor.

Kneiss reached out to her again, but she just moved farther away. She had always been told that her real parents were dead and that she had no blood relatives. But she could see now that it had just been another lie. Her whole life was just one stacked on another. And now it was all coming down around her.

"When my daughter and her husband died— you were very young then—I wanted to bring you here. To raise you myself, in the church. To prepare you." He looked past her at Sara. "Sara convinced me that it would be a mistake. That trying to bring you up surrounded by people who knew who you were and what you would become would be impossible. Seeing you now, I know she was right. She so often is."

Jennifer glanced back at Sara as the old man continued. "Eric and Patricia Davis were two of my most devoted followers. And they were childless. We decided that it would be best for you to develop naturally on your own. Without my influence or the influence of the church."

"Why?" Jennifer stammered. "Why did you do this to me?"

"I know this is hard, Jennifer, but my time here is almost over. You understand that, don't you? That I have only a short time left here?"

She nodded dumbly. He was supposed to die on Good Friday, just like Jesus. Everyone knew that.

"Well, when I'm gone, the church will be yours to lead."

19

"YOU'RE EITHER GOING TO HAVE TO START getting here on time or give me a key," Chet Michaels said. "I'm numb from the waist down."

Beamon adjusted the gym bag thrown over his shoulder into a marginally more comfortable position as the young agent peeled himself from the steps.

Today had been his first session with the personal trainer he had hired, and his first attempt at real exercise since his unheralded but pivotal benchwarming position on his high school football team.

This regime of self-improvement was starting to get to him. Nicotine withdrawal, booze with no burn, and now a set of quivering leg muscles that probably wouldn't propel him the rest of the way to his front door. He wondered if all healthy people felt like crap and were just good liars.

"You been working out?" Michaels said. "Feels great, doesn't it? Get out of the office and sweat off your stress?"

Beamon threw his gym bag at the young agent. "Shut up and carry that up the stairs for me."

Michaels grinned and bounded up the icy stairs two at a time as Beamon tested the first step with his foot and grabbed the handrail.

"You all right, Mark?" Michaels said, his head appearing over the railing above him

God, how he hated that kid.

Beamon could feel Michaels's eyes on him as he waddled across the living room to the fridge.

"I forgot it was your first day with that personal trainer. How'd it go? I love—"

Beamon looked up from the two beers he was hovering over and gave Michaels a glare that prompted him to change the subject.

"Man, I could have used a hot cup of coffee tonight. Your neighbor decided not to take pity on me, I guess."

Beamon dropped into the sofa and pushed one of the bottles toward Michaels, who was pulling a folder out of the small backpack that had been slung over his shoulder.

"She's visiting her mother."

Michaels' eyebrows rose slightly. "Really? When's she coming back?"

"Don't know," Beamon lied. In truth, he knew she'd be back the day after tomorrow. And if he'd regained full use of his legs by then, he intended to take his newly buffed physique over to her door and ask her out on a proper date. "Let's go, Chet. I just want to have a couple of beers and go to bed."

"If you're tired, I could just—"

"Nah, you're here and I'm going to D.C. Sunday. Won't be back till Monday afternoon."

"What're you doing there?"

"Budget meeting," Beamon lied.

The truth was that he was scheduled for another in a string of pointless hearings relating to a case he'd wrapped up almost six months ago. When a group of well-organized vigilantes had decided to end America's drug problem by poisoning the narcotics supply, one of their early victims had, unfortunately, been the son of a powerful senator. The hearings, ostensibly begun to ensure that America's hospitals would never again be flooded with thousands of dying addicts, had now degenerated into a forum for Senator James Mirth to allocate the blame for his son's death. Blame that, by all reports, rested firmly on his shoulders.

Michaels looked a little uncomfortable as he held out a thin stack of paper.

Beamon eased himself forward and took it. The pages consisted of a few copied articles on the Church of the Evolution from various newspapers and magazines.

"I'm underwhelmed," Beamon said. "Where's the rest of it?"

"There is no rest right now. I *am* working on getting some more, though."

Beamon scanned a copy of a *Wall Street Journal* story describing the phenomenal investment performance and financial strength of the church, then flipped through the remaining articles. Most related to the persecution of the church by the German government.

"Come on, Chet. You're telling me that an organization with eleven million members," he flipped back to the *Journal* article, "bringing in ten billion dollars a year, has had a whopping seven articles written about it—five of which are about its activities abroad? I don't think so."

Michaels seemed to have anticipated Beamon's skepticism. "I went through the academic index at

the library and searched for the Church of the Evolution, Albert Kneiss, God, organized religion, cults,
you name it."

"And this is all you found?"

Michaels shook his head. "Not exactly. It's true
that there hasn't been much written on the church
considering its size . . ." He pulled out another piece
of printer paper from his bag and laid it in front of
Beamon. "But this is probably why."

The page was full of titles of articles printed
directly off an index. Most related to libel suits filed
against various media companies. The list included
such names as ABC, the *New York Times,* and
Newsweek.

"Okay," Beamon said. "This is more the type of
thing I was looking for. Where's the text to those
articles?"

"Gone."

"Gone?"

"I went to three different libraries. When you go
back into the old newspaper and magazine issues,
the pages that these articles appear on are missing. If
it's on microfilm, the microfilm is missing. I've
ordered copies directly from the publishers, but it's
going to take some time to get them."

Beamon took a long pull from his beer. "I guess
when you have eleven million devoted followers,
there isn't much reason to leave negative articles
lying around where the public might stumble onto
them."

Michaels nodded. "Yeah. Notice how most of
the articles I *could* find relate to the Germans?"

"Makes perfect sense," Beamon said. "America

was founded on the concept of free religion. The hatred of religious persecution is in our genes. If I was running the church, I'd milk this Germany thing for everything it's worth."

The phone rang as Beamon drained the last of his beer. He held the empty bottle out toward Michaels and motioned toward the kitchen.

Michaels took the empty, walked over to the phone and picked it up.

"Hold on a second," he said and handed it to Beamon, who pointed to the refrigerator in an effort to get another beer without having to make an attempt at getting out of the chair.

"Hello?"

"Mark? Jake Layman."

"What can I do for you, Jake?" Beamon said tentatively. His new boss had certainly never called him at home. Hell, they hadn't even spoken since that unfortunate round of golf.

"I wanted to talk to you about the Jennifer Davis case, Mark. A very disturbing memo came across my desk today."

Beamon heard the unmistakable sound of air escaping from the neck of a beer bottle and he held his hand up over his head.

"Disturbing how, Jake?"

"It says that you've been looking into the Church of the Evolution in relation to the case."

Beamon was a bit surprised. "Who wrote the memo?"

"I don't think that's important, Mark. What is important is whether or not it's accurate."

Beamon felt the cold glass of a beer bottle hit

his hand and watched Michaels walk around him and sit down. "I am following up on Jennifer's family connections. As near as I can tell, Albert Kneiss is her only surviving biological relative—her grandfather."

There was silence over the phone for a few moments. "I'm not sure how that's relevant to the investigation, Mark."

That didn't surprise him. Layman probably didn't understand how gasoline was relevant to his car starting in the morning.

"Probably isn't," Beamon said. "But on the other hand, you never know. With Kneiss scheduled to bop off to heaven next month, maybe some nut wants his own personal messiah. Maybe Kneiss has made enemies in his business dealings. Hell, maybe the church—"

"Look, Mark," Layman interrupted. "I know it's got to be tough for you going from D.C. to a little post in Flagstaff, but this is where you landed and you're going to have to adjust. We're dealing with a pedophile or a botched robbery here. Not a religious conspiracy. Are you going to be able to keep your eye on the ball? Because there's a lot of media coverage on this thing and we can't afford a fumble."

Beamon covered the receiver and took a deep breath. The old Mark Beamon would point out that his conviction rate in kidnapping cases was the best in the Bureau and at least three times Layman's. But the new Mark Beamon was going to handle this situation with the well-balanced mix of calm dignity and bald-faced lies that it demanded. "Just trying to be thorough, Jake."

"Hey, and I appreciate that, Mark. I know you're doing the best you can out there. But we have to look at the big picture. After Waco and Ruby Ridge, we're not ready for the press to start in on us again. Don't embarrass the Bureau, right, buddy?"

"Yeah. You're right, Jake. Sure."

"So you're on the team, then?" Layman said.

Beamon frowned. One more sports cliché and he was going to drive down to Phoenix and beat Layman to death with a hockey stick. "Yeah, Jake. I'm on the team."

"All right. Good. I knew I could count on you."

Beamon hung up the phone and turned to Michaels. "What else you got for me?"

"Was that Layman?"

"Mmm-hmmm."

"He doesn't like the church angle?"

"Not excited about it, no."

"Are we going to get off it?"

"As far as I'm concerned, we're really not on it. Just following up all the angles." Beamon paused. "Having said that, when we're looking into stuff that's church-related, we probably shouldn't wave flags and blow horns. Okay?"

Michaels nodded.

"Now where were we?"

"The fact that there isn't much info on the church."

Beamon leaned forward in the chair, ignoring the pain in his lower back. "What about an exposé? Some ex-Kneissian who was pissed off about not getting God's personal phone number or something and wrote a book?"

Michaels flipped another piece of paper from his knapsack and let it spin through the air and onto the cardboard box serving as a coffee table. "*The Betrayal of a Messiah: Albert Kneiss and His Church*. By Ernest Willard."

"I knew you wouldn't let me down, Chet. Where is it?"

"What?"

"The book."

"It's been out of print for years. Publisher's out of business. I called over a hundred libraries and probably fifty stores dealing in rare books and came up empty-handed. Even the Library of Congress has managed to lose their copy."

"Great. What about the author?"

"Looked in all the regular places. Nothing. I managed to track down his agent, but she says she hasn't heard from him in years. I'll keep digging."

Michaels stood and began slipping on his jacket. "Beyond that, we're still following up Passal's known acquaintances and anyone who might have had an infatuation with Jennifer, and we've expanded our investigation of local sex offenders to neighboring states."

"You in a hurry?"

"Told my girlfriend I'd meet her at the brewpub for a beer at eight-thirty. You want to come? It's a really fun place." He pointed at the bottle in Beamon's hand. "And their beer beats the hell out of that swill."

Beamon shook his head. "I like this swill. Thanks anyway, but I think I'm just going to spend some time with my couch tonight." His legs had continued to stiffen during their conversation. Hopefully, a few beers would loosen them up enough to get him to the bedroom.

"I'll see you in the morning, Mark."

"Right," Beamon said, punching the ON button on the TV remote and then surfing through the channels until he landed on the Church of the Evolution's cable access channel.

Albert Kneiss was wandering benignly across a gloomy stage talking about God's plan for humanity. "August 1969" was printed in the bottom corner of the screen.

Despite the poor quality of the tape, the image of Kneiss moving smoothly along the elevated stage and the sound of his powerful voice resonating through the static was strangely hypnotic. Even to an old agnostic like him.

20

NONE OF THIS WOULD EXIST WITHOUT HER. None of it.

Sara Renslier stood silently in the middle of the small chapel that had been built into the expansive compound housing the room where Albert Kneiss was spending his final days on earth.

She stared through the moonlight penetrating the large skylights overhead and at the ten-foot-high cross glowing dully above the altar. Even that was hers. A symbol she had created for people to rally around. Its design, with its stylized head and footboard, was close enough to the standard cross to be comfortable to the world's powerful Christian population, but different enough not to alienate the more significant number of non-Christians. She ran her hands down the bottom of the cross and over the smooth stone of the altar, thinking back to her earliest memories of God.

She had been immersed in the Catholic Church almost from the day she was born—Catholic schools, mass two days a week, confession once a month. She could still remember how she'd felt at her first communion, awed by the ancient ritual and air of the supernatural that had swirled around her in the cold of the cathedral.

She'd chosen a college close to home, unwilling to leave her parish for the four years it would take to complete a business degree—instead becoming even more involved in the church. By the end of her first year, she had joined most of the local Catholic organizations and was attending mass almost daily.

It was during that time that she'd begun to see weaknesses in the Catholic machine. Much of the dogma that ruled the actions of the church seemed hopelessly mired in civilization's distant and superstitious past. The aging priests whom she had always seen as spiritually superior to the rest of humanity began to look out of touch and reckless in the direction they'd chosen for their church.

As her studies progressed, she'd become fascinated with the idea of adapting the increasingly scientific theories of business and marketing to the management of a religious organization. She chose that as the subject of her senior thesis, writing an elaborate analysis of the mistakes made by the world's major religions and creating a blueprint—in hindsight, more of a rough sketch—of how to steer a church to a position of dominance. Her professor, a young man whose ponytail and round wire-rimmed glasses made him almost indistinguishable from the student body, had given her an A⁺. Next to the grade, written in a bold scrawl, was one word. *"Terrifying."*

Shortly after her graduation, she had gathered up the courage to meet with her priest and present her ideas. She'd argued that the Catholic Church was allowing itself to be slowly stripped of its power—that it had become self-indulgent and no longer provided a service that people needed or wanted.

He had listened politely for almost an hour but had heard nothing. Sara remembered falling silent as he began a passionless and disjointed speech about God's will and the wisdom of the Vatican. Later, when she'd defended her position, he had accused her of vanity and a lack of faith.

Vanity and a lack of faith! Had it been vanity to want to save her church from the backward-thinking old men destroying it? Had it been a lack of faith to want to use the gifts God had given humanity to effectively carry out His will?

Sara sat down on the cold marble steps leading to the altar, remembering the pain she had felt as she walked from the priest's office, and her single-minded determination to have her ideas heard. Over the next few months, she sent literally hundreds of letters to the church's leadership and lay organizations. Each contained a clear explanation of her ideas and a plea for reform.

She'd received very few letters back, mostly from people she knew or had met briefly at church functions. Their responses were all the same—full of carefully chosen words, caution, and fear.

Finally, almost a year after she had met with her local priest, a different kind of letter arrived at her small apartment. It was handwritten on the elegant stationery of the bishop and granted her an audience.

She'd gone prepared to make her argument for change, but when she'd arrived, she discovered that the intimate exchange of ideas she had hoped for was not what had been planned. There were five of them, dressed in the formal robes that hadn't changed in six hundred years. In front of each man was a copy of her senior thesis—a document that she had enclosed with many of the letters she had sent.

It didn't take long for it to become obvious that they weren't there to listen. They were there to punish. They'd spoken angrily, reading highlighted lines from her thesis out of context and accusing her of atheism. In the end, they had made vague intimations about excommunication and implied that if she were to confess her sins then and there, God would forgive her.

She'd walked out without a word. A few weeks later, she had moved across the country and taken a job in a small accounting firm in upstate New York. It was there that she had become obsessed with the study of religion, and it was there that she had lost her faith. Contemporary religions, she had found, were nothing more than a collage of earlier and more primitive beliefs pieced together by the ruling class as a convenient way to control its subjects. The considered infliction of fear and hope, it turned out, was infinitely more effective than the infliction of pain and death.

As time went on, she had become entrenched in her atheism, beginning to look down on the faithful as desperate and weak. They knew that the childish concept of God was a lie created to keep them docile but hadn't the courage to accept that and go out into the world alone. No, they found it easier to wrap themselves in the ridiculous paradoxes of the Bible and books like it, and to ignore the truth.

She had moved quickly through the ranks of her firm, spending impossibly long hours in the office and continuing her education through courses at night. The owner, a small, weak man of limited ability, had continued to heap more and more responsibility on her.

It had been a little after seven o'clock, in the summer of 1975, when he had dragged a box full of loose notebook paper and receipts to her desk and sat down with the grave expression that he always seemed to wear at the office.

They had never spoken about religion, but it was common knowledge that he was involved with an esoteric little cult centered near Lake Placid. At the time, she hadn't known much about the fledgling church or its leader, Albert Kneiss, beyond the fact that he claimed to be a reincarnation of Jesus.

She had reluctantly accepted her boss's invitation to a "presentation" that Kneiss was making at a small auditorium nearby, as well as his request that she take over as shepherd of the church's paltry accounts.

That night had changed everything.

The less than half-full auditorium had smelled vaguely of marijuana when they walked through the curtains at the back. She and her boss—she couldn't remember his name, though she thought she'd read that he'd died recently—settled into a couple of folding chairs just as the lights dimmed and Albert Kneiss wandered onto the stage.

His long white hair had seemed to move on its own as he slowly paced in front of them, speaking in a low, patient tone. Despite the poor acoustics of the auditorium, his voice didn't fade as it floated to the back where they sat.

It had been far from the bizarre and pointless evening she had steeled herself for. The self-absorbed megalomaniac that she had expected to appear and ramble incoherently instead delivered a message that stripped away the superstition and compromise from Christianity, leaving a simple and elegant melding of God and science.

This man, with his penetrating charisma and beautifully constructed theology, seemed to have created something with almost unlimited appeal. His ideas had the potential to spread like wildfire through the hearts of the myriad people who wanted desperately to believe in something but also wanted that something to reflect the world they lived in and not the world of their distant ancestors.

She remembered taking a paperback copy of Kneiss's Bible from a poorly groomed young man at the auditorium's exit and walking out into the cold night somewhat dazed. Albert Kneiss had done something that she had never considered. He had taken the philosophy she had applied to religious organizations and used it to reinvent God.

Over the following year, her boss had happily diverted her non-church-related clients to other accountants at the firm until she was, in essence, working for Kneiss's organization full-time. As she dug deeper and deeper into the workings of the church, she began to tailor the ideas she had developed to fit the infinitely more flexible and forward-thinking Church of the Evolution.

When she had finally presented her ideas to the seven Elders who controlled the church, she'd found their minds just as closed as the priests who had threatened her with excommunication. At first she'd thought that their disinterest stemmed from the fact that she was not actually a follower of Kneiss, so in 1976 she joined his church. Her conversion, though, did nothing to penetrate the wall the Elders had built around themselves.

She could still remember, down to the last smell and sound, the day almost twenty years ago when she had opened the door to her apartment and found herself face-to-face with Albert Kneiss—the man some believed to be the returned Jesus.

He accepted a cup of tea and told her that he had been instructed by God to come to her and hear her ideas on the future of His church. She remembered how still he sat and the passive expression on his face as she described her theories on building a contemporary church. But, like her priest, he didn't really seem to be listening. When she finally fell silent, he stood and walked toward the door of her apartment. He didn't close it behind him, and she heard him speak as he disappeared down the hall. "You'll lead my church into the next century, Sara."

It had taken months to break down the barriers the Elders created to try to make her look incompetent. What she had found when she finally penetrated the deepest layers of the church's management had horrified her. The financial reports the Elders had been providing her were completely fictitious. It was an organization teetering on the brink of bankruptcy, led by a group of ineffectual, bickering asses, all jockeying for the attention of their messiah.

When she reported to Albert what she had

found, he had just smiled calmly and told her that he would no longer be involved in the management of the church. That his God had directed him to focus on making people understand. The church was hers to run as she saw fit.

She hadn't believed him at first, but when he sat passively by as she disbanded the existing group of Elders and replaced them with volunteers experienced in practical areas such as finance, psychology, and marketing, she'd begun to feel the power and potential of her position. That had been the true first day of the Church of the Evolution.

At that time, the church had been made up of about twenty-five thousand loosely connected members, largely confined to the northeastern U.S. And now, as the sun continued to set on Catholicism, her church had swelled to millions of members and was growing faster than any other in the world. The priests should have listened.

Sara stood and turned back toward the altar. She had created this church from nothing and now Albert was trying to take it from her. She had always known that this day would come, that before he died he would make one last desperately sentimental act. And she had been preparing for that act ever since she'd become aware of Jennifer's existence.

Over the years, she had systematically isolated Albert until his wishes and hers were indistinguishable to the church's members and leadership. It had been a simple matter, really. Albert preferred quiet reflection and needed time alone to exercise his genius for devising ever-new ways to enthrall the public with his message.

What she hadn't anticipated was that he would, for the first time in a decade, call a meeting of all the Elders instead of passing along his wishes through her. It was at that meeting that he had announced Jennifer's existence to the others and ordered Sara to bring her to the compound.

At that point she'd had no choice but to comply. Her power at the church was nearly absolute, but not so unshakeable that she could ignore Albert's wishes with impunity.

She had come here that night full of rage and panic. Slowly, though, she'd come upon a way to keep control of the church that she had built. She had set her plan in motion when she convinced Eric and Patricia Davis that it was Albert's wish that they ascend to heaven before him. She had chosen them for their blind fanaticism and she had chosen well.

Witnessing her parents' death had thrown Jennifer into a state of confusion and pain that Sara had been able to amplify and use to keep control of the girl. With that control, the problem of Jennifer's existence and Albert's ambiguous speech about her to the Elders could be solved simply and finally. When Albert and his granddaughter were gone, the church would be free to grow in size and influence. And she would grow with it.

21

"YOUR TIMING WAS MOST FORTUITOUS, MARK," Hans Volker said, slowing his boat of a BMW to a crawl and slipping it expertly through the thick crowd of people milling about in the street. "The Church of the Evolution is expecting over half a million people to attend this rally. Quite extraordinary, really—they only began planning it three weeks ago."

Despite the dreary skies and intermittent rain, it looked like that estimate would prove low. From their position near the Capitol Building, only occasional flashes of asphalt and grass were visible beneath the flowing carpet of well-dressed humanity.

Beamon had sicced his secretary on the German embassy last week, figuring it would take her at least a few days to coax someone into meeting with him while he was in D.C. subjecting himself to another fiery Senate inquisition. He'd been more than a little surprised when, two minutes into her first attempt, she'd connected him with Volker—the German government's U.S. watchdog in all things church-related. He'd been even more surprised when Volker not only agreed to meet with him, but also offered to personally pick him up from the airport.

"I really appreciate you taking the time to meet with me on such short notice, Hans."

Volker waved his hand dismissively. "It is I who should thank you. I have been meaning to contact you since you took your post in Flagstaff. I had hoped to cultivate a better relationship with you than with your predecessor, Ms. Dunham."

"You knew Marjorie?"

"Oh, yes, I'm afraid so. I had a number of conversations and meetings with her relating to our concerns about the church. This was a number of years ago, of course, before I discovered that she was a member and just using me to gather intelligence for Albert Kneiss. As I'm sure you can imagine, our relationship cooled after that."

"I guess I can see how it would," Beamon said, remembering his conversation with Marjorie Dunham and her insistence that the German would be unwilling to talk with him. He turned and looked through the tinted windows, noting the glares that they were getting from the people around them. He wasn't sure if the problem was that theirs was the only car moving on the pedestrian-choked street or if it was that they were driving a car manufactured in Germany.

"So all this is for you, Hans? I mean, I'd read that Kneiss was upset about your government's policies, but this looks more like pissed off than upset." Beamon said.

"Pissed off? Oh, yes, absolutely. The church has been very vocal in their criticism of Germany's treatment of the church's followers and I'm afraid they've found a willing audience in the American public." He paused for a moment. "I assume that you are aware of our disagreements with Kneiss's church?"

"Aware, yes. Knowledgeable about, no. I under-stand that Kneissians can't hold public office and are barred from a bunch of other sensitive positions in the German government. I think someone told me that they're denied positions that might allow them to influence young people, too—teachers, day care workers, that kind of thing."

"That's all true," Volker said.

"Seems like I also heard that if a church member owns a business, the fact that they're Kneissian has to be disclosed on their letterhead and business cards."

Volker tapped his brake to avoid bumping a man who had lifted the car's windshield wiper and shoved a bright yellow flyer under it. The text of the flyer was impossible to read, but the heading GESTAPO TACTICS was clearly legible through the windshield.

"And how do you feel about those policies, Mark?"

"I don't see any reason to lie to you. I think it all sounds very familiar."

Volker nodded. "The church has been very effi-cient in distributing propaganda comparing our policies to the Nazis' treatment of the Jews during the war. It's ironic, really. Our actions have been fueled by a fear of what happened to the Jews in our country. That the Kneissians' organization could incite their German followers."

Volker slowed the car again, this time rolling to a stop in front of an angry-looking group of young people who were obviously blocking their path on purpose.

Beamon watched as they talked urgently amongst themselves, building their courage and finally directing their shouts toward the car. It was impossible to hear exactly what they were saying through the two-ton piece of German engineering, but Beamon wasn't having a hard time catching the gist. "You know, Hans, I appreciate the tour, but it might be time we backed on out of here. I thought the dirty looks we were getting were about your car, but it may go beyond that."

"Hm?" Volker said, apparently completely unconcerned. "No, you're quite right, Mark. I'm sure they recognize my car. The church keeps its members very well informed."

Beamon twisted around and looked out the rear window at the crowd that had closed in behind them. "I've got to tell you, Hans, I've been an FBI agent long enough to learn more than I ever wanted to about this kind of group dynamics. If one of those kids gets fired up enough to so much as throw a spitball at us, the others are going to tear this car apart and then do the same thing to us."

Volker laughed quietly and inched the car forward. Miraculously, the crowd parted. "I'm afraid that you don't understand the Kneissians, Mark. They would never perpetrate any kind of overt public act against me—or against anyone, for that matter. That could generate negative publicity. No, they prefer to work in the dark. To use intimidation."

Volker took his diplomatic immunity out for a spin, jumping two wheels up on the sidewalk and heading toward the center of activity. "Let me give you an example. A few years ago, my son was being consistently singled out for harassment at his school by a particular instructor—to the point that the woman was warned and finally let go. Prior to this, her credentials were spotless. Her superiors apologized profusely to me, but were baffled by her behavior."

"I take it you weren't."

Volker shook his head. "It's my understanding that she took a position in a private school owned by the Kneissians within a few weeks. At first it surprised me that a woman who clearly loved children would attack my child to get at me, but as I learned more about the Kneissians I began to understand how dangerous their beliefs and organization really are."

"I don't know, Hans," Beamon said, rolling down the window and pulling the flyer from under the wiper. "This just isn't all that new. How long has religion been prompting people to attack non-believers? 'I can see into the mind of God and you—Hindu, Muslim, Jew, whoever—can't. Therefore, I am good and you are evil, irrelevant, or damned.'"

"Do you have a copy of Kneiss's Bible, Mark?"

Beamon shook his head.

"I suggest you read it. You'll see that the Kneissians look to the future—not to the past, as do most religions. This is what makes them so dangerous. By discarding many of the traditions of older faiths, they've been able to gain a great deal of power too quickly. And that forced us—the German government—to slow down their growth before they were able to begin imposing their bigotry on others."

Beamon frowned deeply. He'd heard a saying once—that you could tell a bad man from a good one not by his actions but only his intent. He'd thought long and hard about it and wasn't sure if he agreed. Religious persecution was just too easy to justify.

Volker stopped the car and set the brake. "The Kneissians are starting to use their great membership and wealth to indulge their organizational paranoia. To crush those they perceive to be their enemies and to spy on those who might exert some control over them. I suspect that they are very interested in you, Mark. They are quite concerned with America's enforcement agencies—FBI, CIA, IRS, NSA—and you, as the head of the FBI's Flagstaff office, probably top their list. I assure you that they are quite ruthless. But clever at keeping themselves from the media."

Volker opened his door a few inches, letting in the buzz of the enormous crowd and the sound of intermittent feedback as a PA system was tested. "It might surprise you to know that we have to sweep the phones at the embassy and my home on a daily basis. On three separate occasions we have found listening devices. Once the police apprehended a man placing one of them. He was a member of Kneiss's church."

"Are we getting out?" Beamon said, as Volker pushed the door the rest of the way open and stepped from the car. The German poked his head back in and pointed behind him at a large stage set up at the end of the Mall. "I thought it would be easier for you to hear the speaker. And that perhaps you would like to, uh, mingle a bit. I assure you there's no danger."

Somehow the assurance of one slightly effeminate European surrounded by half a million people who thought he was spitting in the face of their god didn't make Beamon feel all that warm and fuzzy. But what the hell—he hadn't incited a riot since college. "I guess whatever happens to me happens to you first," he said, stepping from the car.

Volker smiled and began to talk loudly over the drone of the crowd, ignoring the hostile looks of the people within earshot. "I and my wife are routinely followed—the church makes no effort to hide it, hoping, I imagine, to intimidate me. Men I've worked with in Germany have suffered even more. One had a number of rather graphic photographs of him and his mistress sent to his wife, another was elaborately framed for a crime which he had nothing to do with."

Beamon had heard quiet whisperings of the church wielding their power a bit unethically, but he'd never seen any proof. As much as he liked to believe the worst of organized religion, without corroboration, he'd always assumed that it was just mudslinging by rival faiths jealous of the Kneissians' success.

Beamon let Volker hook an arm though his but didn't move when the German tried to pull him away from the car and toward the stage. "I'd rather not have to shoot my way out of here, Hans. As much as I appreciate the effort, I'd be just as happy finishing this conversation over a cup of coffee at your office."

Volker tugged insistently on his arm. "Please don't worry, Mark. I personally guarantee your safety."

Beamon stood his ground for a moment and then gave up and allowed himself to be led through the crush of people. "What can you tell me about Albert Kneiss?"

"A fascinating figure," Volker shouted over a deafening round of applause. A man in a dark suit had just walked on the stage and everyone seemed happy to see him. "Born Christmas Day 1913 to a devout Christian preacher. You're aware that it is believed that Kneiss will ascend to heaven—die—on Good Friday this year?"

"Yeah. Born on Christmas, dead on Good Friday. Just like Jesus."

Volker nodded. "Interestingly, Kneiss did not immediately follow his father into the spiritual, but studied anthropology and later became a professor at the University of Chicago. He was quite brilliant, but his theories were extremely radical for the time. One—that a number of different species of humans inhabited the earth at the same time—has only recently been adopted. Unfortunately, his approach to anthropology was too much for the university, and he was eventually let go—a laughingstock in the world of science."

Volker stopped next to a small knot of people in blue polo shirts identifying their home parish as Spokane, Washington. Between them, they held a large banner reading FREEDOM TO WORSHIP.

"This should do, don't you think?" Volker said, looking up at the man on the stage and gauging their distance. "You probably recognize Senator Tompkins from Massachusetts."

Now that he looked more carefully, Beamon

did recognize him. Tompkins had taken a leadership role in criticizing Germany's policies toward the church. It was impossible not to see him posturing in the media for the benefit of religious freedom at least once a week.

"Now what was it you were saying about Kneiss?"

"Oh, I'm sorry. Soon after his removal from the university, his wife succumbed to cancer, leaving him with an infant daughter. He disappeared from the eyes of history for a number of years around this time. Eventually he reappeared in upstate New York with his Bible, transformed into God's messenger on earth."

"So he just combined his two areas of expertise—theology, which he learned from his father, and science, which was his chosen profession."

"One would assume."

"If he was born in 1913 he's in his late eighties now. Is he still in control of the church?"

Volker shrugged. "I think it's unlikely. There's a group of seven Elders who operate the church. A woman named Sara Renslier controls the group." He pointed toward the stage. "See the rather petite woman with short dark hair sitting at the back?"

Beamon nodded.

"That's her. It was her appointment some twenty-five years ago that was the turning point for Kneiss and his followers. A formidable woman. She will certainly become the unequivocal head of the organization when Kneiss dies."

Beamon pulled a pad from his pocket and struggled to overcome the jostling of the people around him and write the name down. "But if he dies on Good Friday, shouldn't he be resurrected on Easter like he was last time?"

Volker chuckled. "That would be quite a trick, wouldn't it? But the answer, of course, is no. The Kneissians do not believe that the resurrection of Jesus had any real significance. Nothing more than the last in a long list of what they consider banal parlor tricks that Jesus—Kneiss—was forced to perform to gain credibility in a hopelessly superstitious time."

"And he's been doing this since the dawn of humanity—popping in every two thousand years to update the current thinking?"

Volker rose onto his toes to get a better view as two men shook hands on stage. "You really should make it a point to read their Bible, Mark. But the answer to your question is no. They believe that at some time in the distant past, the entity we now know as Kneiss was chosen by God to take the place of the prior messenger, who had gone on to his reward. And one day another messenger will be chosen to replace Kneiss."

The booming voice of Senator Joseph Tompkins resonated over the PA system, and Volker had to raise his voice another notch to be heard. "This issue has become quite a boon for the senator, don't you think? The church strongly encourages its members to contribute to his campaign fund every year, and what American doesn't hold the issue of religious freedom close to his heart?"

22

BEAMON PULLED THE NOTEPAD OUT OF ITS paper sack and stuck it to the inside of his windshield with the suction cup on the back. Damn Volker was making him paranoid.

He groaned quietly as he forced his still-sore legs to jog through the snow toward the office of his condo complex. The light was still on, and Beamon could see that the property manager was stuffing papers into a large leather briefcase in preparation for calling it a day. He tossed a half-smoked cigarette—his first of the day—into a snowbank and slipped through the door.

"Tina! How goes it?"

She flashed him that broad smile full of straight white teeth that always seemed to take the chill off. She was such a cute little thing, just out of college and surrounded by the healthy glow that seemed specific to the inhabitants of America's mountainous middle section.

"Mr. Beamon! What brings you out in this weather?"

"I was wondering if you could help me with a little information."

"Have you been smoking?" she said, sniffing at the air.

"Just one," Beamon said proudly, electing not to volunteer that he'd been in either Hans Volker's car, the J. Edgar Hoover Building, or an airplane since eight that morning. All locales under the ruthless control of the smoking Nazis.

She looked at him with mock severity. "I'll let it go. But just this once. You absolutely must quit. Okay?"

He gave a noncommittal nod.

"Okay. Now, what can I do for you?"

"I need some information on a few of the renters here."

"Which ones?"

Beamon ran his finger along the full-color map of the complex taped to the counter. "Anyone from buildings A, C, F, or H."

"That's a lot of people," she said, obviously anxious to leave for the day.

"Let me narrow it down. I'm not interested in any leases signed before I got here, so just people who moved in January fifteenth or later. And I'm not interested in anything shorter-term than, say, a month."

"Well, you're in luck," she said, turning and crouching down next to a cardboard box on the floor. "I hate filing and tend to put it off forever." She pulled out a stack of folders and began sorting through them, tossing a few on the counter but dropping most back in the box. When she was finished, she neatened the stack of five folders lying on the counter and centered them in front of her. "These are all the ones signed in January and February for those buildings." She flipped open each folder and threw three of them back in the box. "These two are the only ones that aren't short-term."

Beamon opened the first one. A family of four had signed a one-year lease. The second was a single male. Robert Andrews. Also a year. Beamon ran his finger down to the "employment" line. It simply read "self."

"Could I get copies of these, Tina?"

"Sure." She looked at him slyly. "Fugitives from the law?"

Beamon laughed. "Nah. Just haven't hit them up for the FBI raffle yet."

As usual, the phone was ringing when he stepped through the door, leaving him no time to take off his shoes. There was a visible trail of mud and water emerging on his carpet.

"Yeah. Hello," he said, grabbing the phone

"Mark! It's Chet. Man, I've been trying to reach you all day! I thought you were supposed to be back at two."

"It was a more elaborate trip than I bargained for. What's up?"

"Hey, have I ever told you about that friend I have at the coroner's office? Susan Moorland? You know, the girl I went to school with."

Beamon thought for a moment, but his brain was already in shutdown mode. He just wanted to get into his beer rations and then into bed. "Sure," he lied. "Seems like you've mentioned her."

"Well, she called me this morning. Apparently she helped do the work on Jennifer Davis's parents when they came in. She wants to talk to us about it."

Beamon peeled off his parka and cradled the phone with his shoulder. "I've read the report, Chet—

and we both saw the bodies. If she wants to make an amendment, that's what fax machines are for."

"She didn't do the report, Mark. Her boss did. And she disagrees with his conclusions—strongly, judging from her phone call. I guess he's normally pretty receptive to what she has to say, but this time he freaked out when she contradicted him. I can pretty much guarantee she isn't going to put anything in writing."

Beamon sighed. "Let me guess. She wants me to haul my ass out there in the middle of the night and stand around in a refrigerator with a bunch of corpses."

"Uh, yeah. Tonight, actually. I know how you feel about morgues, but she's got the bodies there still and she can't keep losing their paperwork forever. Come on, Mark—meet you at the back door at nine? Please?"

Beamon rubbed at his eyes. He was dying to say no. Michaels and his little friend had undoubtedly tripped over a molehill and built it into a mountain while he was in D.C. But he knew that the kid would be devastated if he passed. "All right. You win. Nine o'clock. Anything else?"

"Uh, I don't think so. No, wait. I got the stuff you wanted on Jennifer's adoption. Nothing very interesting—quick and easy. She was only at the foster home for a couple of days when the Davises started paperwork."

Beamon perked up a bit. "Really? Now, how does that work? Is it like buying a car? When the foster home gets in something they think you'd like they give you a call?"

Michaels laughed. "You make it sound so . . . cheap. I don't know if that's how it usually works, but it's not the way it went in this case. The Davises hadn't ever tried to adopt before."

Beamon nodded into the phone. "The ever-present impulse purchaser."

"You're a sick man, Mark. I don't know why I hang out with you."

"I sign your paychecks."

23

BEAMON STAMPED HIS FEET LOUDLY ON the icy concrete and thrust his hands deeper into the pockets of his parka. The mercury was down around zero, but on the bright side, the cold was keeping any strange smells from escaping the dumpster they were using as a windblock. No telling what those creepy coroners threw in there.

"Jesus Christ, Chet," Beamon said, staring at the firmly locked side door to the newly constructed Flagstaff morgue. "If I knew we were going to spend a couple of hours out here I would have brought along a couple of Huskies and some firewood."

Michaels put his finger to his lips, but Beamon refused to take the hint. He'd lost the feeling in his toes five minutes ago. "You know, Chet, they might let us in the front door, since I am, well, *the goddamn head of the FBI here.*"

"I told you, Mark," Michaels said in an exaggerated whisper. "Susan's really going out on a limb here. She already wrote a contradictory report and her boss went nuts and threw it in the shredder. If he knew she'd called us she'd probably lose her job."

"Uh-huh," Beamon growled as he dug Robert Andrews's lease agreement out of his pocket and handed it to Michaels. "Get me what you can on this guy, Chet. Nothing fancy, just a quickie."

Michaels tried to read it, but the dim glow provided by the ice-covered lamp above the door made it impossible. He stuffed it in his coat. "What is it?"

"Probably nothing. A guy leasing a condo near mine. Oh, see if you can get some background on a Sara Renslier. Apparently she runs Kneiss's church. Again, nothing fa—"

The metal on metal sound of a deadbolt sliding back, followed by a blast of warm air, interrupted him. He squeezed past a slightly startled young woman without a word and into the relative warmth of the building.

"Mark Beamon," he said quietly, holding out his hand. She took it as Michaels slipped through the doorway and closed it behind him.

"I'm sorry you had to wait out there," she said, already starting down the hall. "Some of the people in the office decided to stay late. Follow me, and please be as quiet as possible."

The initial warmth Beamon had felt seemed to fade as they hurried deeper into the building—though he assumed it was just his imagination. With all the cigarettes, straight bourbons, and chili dogs he'd consumed in his lifetime, morgues tended to put a little too much perspective on things.

The woman in front of him stopped short as the hall came to a T, and Beamon watched as she poked her head around the corner and peered down the hall. She was small—no more than five-three—with long dark hair tied in a ponytail that was pinned under the top strap of the green apron she wore. Something about her reminded him of Carrie. Maybe it was the purposeful stride, or . . .

"We're going to go left here, Mr. Beamon. It's possible that the night watchman could come by. If you hear him, just duck into one of the rooms."

As she moved out into the hall, Beamon leaned in close to Michaels. "I'm having real dignity problems with this, Chet."

The young agent grinned silently back at him and tiptoed out into the hall at Susan's "all clear" signal. He looked like he was having the time of his life. Real cops-and-robbers stuff.

Fortunately, the rest of their journey was a bit less cloak-and-dagger, and in three minutes Susan was locking the door to the examination room behind them.

"All right. We made it!" Michaels gushed.

Susan took a deep breath and let it out loudly. "Sorry about the melodrama, guys. But this could get me in a lot of trouble."

Beamon hopped up onto the hard slab of the examining table and scanned the grid of metal doors covering the wall to his left. "We appreciate the risk you took, Susan," he said without enthusiasm. She couldn't possibly have been more than a year out of college. This was starting to look like an exhausting waste of time. "What have you got for us?"

She walked over to the wall of drawers and pulled out two of them, then unzipped the bags containing the bodies of Eric and Patricia Davis. From his position on the table, Beamon could see the blood-matted hair dried to their scalps and black stitching left by the coroner.

He stuffed a piece of gum in his mouth as Michaels approached the bodies and looked down at them. To his credit, the young agent managed to look somber and to stifle the cry of "cool!" that Beamon could tell was trying to bubble to the surface.

"I believe that the autopsy report you read was colored by the facts of the case," Susan said.

"How so?" Michaels said, still struggling to sound the calm professional. Beamon picked up a styrofoam head off the table next to him. It had what looked a bit like a shish kebab skewer stuck all the way through it, beginning under the chin.

"*I* think we should just have the bodies dropped off and be left to our own conclusions," Susan explained. "Having the facts of the case just creates preconceived ideas about cause of death."

Beamon looked back at the two pieced-together corpses, then at the young professionals hovering over them. "Are you going to tell me that the cause of death wasn't gunshot wounds, Susan?"

She shook her head. "No, it was definitely gunshot. But I think there are some pretty surprising indications about the gunman that didn't make it to the report."

"You have my undivided attention, my dear," Beamon said, hoping she'd move things along. He had just realized that he'd been going nonstop for almost twenty-two hours.

Susan walked over to a large chalkboard on the wall and pointed to a drawing depicting two stick figures. One was aiming a crudely rendered handgun at the other. There was a dotted line drawn from the gun through the victim's head.

"From what I can piece together," she tapped

the board, "this is what happened to Patricia Davis." Beamon shrugged and nodded.

"Now, as you probably noticed from the autopsy report, Mr. Davis was only five-eight, and Mrs. Davis was taller—five-ten. Now, judging from the powder burns on the side of Mrs. Davis's head, we can infer that the gun was approximately one foot three inches from her head when it was fired. Based on this and the angle of the bullet's trajectory, we can calculate that the killer had a shoulder height of four feet eight inches."

Beamon scowled and jumped off the table. He picked up a piece of chalk and continued the dotted line through the killer depicted on the board and drew another stick figure, shorter and farther away. "Come on, Susan, that powder burn stuff is voodoo. You could be off six inches one way or another. It could have been a shorter guy farther away, or a taller guy closer."

She looked indignant. "I believe that my calculations are quite precise, Mr. Beamon. But even if I'm off your six inches, I think we can be fairly confident that the perpetrator was shorter than Mrs. Davis."

Beamon looked into her face and, seeing the steady stare and the set of her jaw, sat back down on the table, scratching the back of his head. "Okay, Susan. I'll give you that one. Why? Because I have no idea where you're going with this."

She gave him a polite smile and picked up the styrofoam head that he had been playing with earlier. "This shows the angle of the bullet that killed Mr. Davis."

She pulled a rather realistic-looking plastic pistol out of one of the pockets of her apron and handed it to Michaels. "Okay, Chet. I want you to shoot me, just like this." She pulled a matching skewer out of her apron pocket and held it up to her head, mimicking the angle of the one in the styrofoam facsimile.

Michaels stood in front of her and stuck the plastic gun under her chin. Because of their height differential, he couldn't get anywhere close to the almost vertical bullet trajectory. Instead, the gun was aimed at a severe angle that would have sent the bullet out of the back of her head.

She stepped up on a small overturned crate that she had obviously put there for the purpose. "This makes me roughly Mr. Davis's height." The angle moved closer, but was still significantly off.

Normally, Beamon would have had to laugh at the sight of a tiny young woman holding a shish-kebab skewer to her head and being held at plastic gunpoint by a guy who looked like Richie Cunningham from *Happy Days*. But he was starting to get interested despite himself.

Michaels bent his wrist unnaturally but still wasn't able to get the angle right before the butt of the gun hit Susan in the chest. He stepped back for a moment and circled around her. Holding the gun under her chin from behind put it at the correct angle.

Susan jumped down from the box. "Exactly what I came up with, Chet. It seems to me that the killer would have had to be standing behind Mr. Davis in order to produce the correct bullet trajectory. I think you'll agree that you wouldn't want to be standing that close behind him when the top of his head came off."

Michaels nodded vigorously.

"Are you starting to get interested yet, Mr. Beamon?"

"Mark, please." He shrugged. "Interested might be too strong a word. Intrigued, maybe. For now, call me mildly attentive."

She gave him a sly look and walked over to the two corpses protruding from the wall. "Come on over, Mark. I'd like you to look at something."

Beamon jumped off his perch and walked slowly toward the corpses as Susan picked up Mr. Davis's right hand and held it out toward him. She pointed to the pale skin between the dead man's thumb and index finger. "See these parallel scratches here?"

Beamon pulled his glasses from his pocket and put them on. The scratches were small, but obvious when pointed out. He nodded.

"They precisely match the slide on a forty-five."

She pulled out a tape measure from the seemingly inexhaustible pocket of her apron and ran it from Mr. Davis's feet to his shoulder. The tape read four feet eight inches.

Beamon smiled. "Uh-huh."

"Hold on, I've got one more thing." She rushed into the attached office and came back with a diagram of a man standing slightly sideways aiming a gun directly out of the picture. There were various splotches drawn onto the man's body in red. Each had a line going from it to some writing at the edge of the sheet. Beamon had no idea what it meant.

"I did some tests on the bloodstains on Mr. Davis. Many of them matched Mrs. Davis's blood type. This diagram shows those findings. I think you'll agree that the pattern is intriguing. Her blood is most prevalent on Mr. Davis's right hand in the pattern that's shown there."

"Now we're getting into some serious voodoo," Beamon said.

She nodded her agreement. "There are other explanations. I really just did this test to see if it refuted the overall hypothesis."

Michaels looked at the diagram with a confused expression. "I guess I'm just dumb, you guys. What overall hypothesis are we talking about?"

Beamon took a deep breath of stale, antiseptic air. "It seems that your friend here thinks Mr. Davis killed his wife and then committed suicide."

"What? No way!"

"Why not?" Susan said confidently.

"Because it's nuts, Susan. It doesn't even come close to fitting into what we know."

Beamon ignored the heated debate that started between them and picked up Eric Davis's cold hand again. He hoped that on further inspection he could come up with a more plausible explanation for the marks. He couldn't.

24

SARA RENSLIER LOOKED DOWN AT THE shriveled form of Albert Kneiss and then to the tank that fed his nearly paralyzed lungs oxygen. The room was almost completely dark. The large windows had turned to mirrors, vibrating with the low howl of the storm battering the world outside. Only the light from the heart monitor made it possible to see, casting a flickering glow over the bed and the man lying in it.

She watched silently as the shadows cast across his face shifted and his eyes opened. "Sara?"

She reached out and touched the old man's cool, dry forehead. He looked so small now, the charisma that had made him such a powerful tool almost completely lost in his withered body.

"Don't speak, Albert," she said, running her hand along his scalp and through the few remaining tufts of hair clinging to it. She felt Kneiss's eyes on her as she pulled a syringe from her pocket and removed the plastic cap covering the tip of the needle.

"What is it, Sara?" he whispered as she slid the needle into his IV tube.

In the semidarkness, she couldn't see the fluid from the syringe make its way down the tube toward his arm, but she knew that it had reached his bloodstream when the slow rhythm of the heart monitor began to shudder and the old man began to jerk weakly. His right arm came to life, reaching for the IV needle taped into his veins, but Sara held it firmly in place.

"What . . . what are you doing?" he said, clawing pathetically against the back of her hand.

She knelt down and leaned in close to him. "The church has outgrown its living prophet, Albert. I need one now who can appear to its children in times of trouble. One that can appear to them on their deathbeds."

The stimulant she had injected into Kneiss cleared his eyes as it began to overload what was left of the systems in his broken body. "What are you doing to me?" he repeated in a stronger voice.

"You've never understood, have you, Albert? You've never been able to grasp what the church has become. What I've made it." A thin smile crossed her lips as she watched the old man struggle to control his ragged breathing enough to speak. "What could have possibly made you think I'd let you take it away from me?"

"What are you saying, Sara? You . . . you've been my most devoted pupil. You helped Jennifer. After my daughter died. You knew that she—"

"How can you be so naïve, Albert? Your daughter didn't die. I killed her. She would have poisoned Jennifer against the church—made her useless to me."

Kneiss's heart rate notched higher. "No. No, you couldn't have. You believe. I gave you my trust. My love."

Sara gripped his arm tighter until she could feel

the slight movement of the IV needle as it vibrated with the old man's heartbeat. "I know you did, Albert. And I gave you what you most wanted—an audience." A tear ran down his nearly paralyzed cheek and she wiped it away with her thumb. "I thought I needed Jennifer—that someday I might have to use her to help me maintain control of the church. But I already have control, don't I? You gave it to me. She can only cause problems now, Albert. Confuse my followers."

Kneiss was finding it increasingly difficult to speak. "You can't. The others—they know about her. They won't let you harm . . ."

"You still don't understand, do you, Albert? You're dying. Right now. Not on Good Friday. Now. What does that mean?"

He just stared up at her with that supernatural expression of pain and despair that had sucked in so many. The rock she'd built her church on.

"You know, don't you, Albert? It's in your Bible. Your brilliant Bible. If you die before Good Friday, your time as God's Messenger is done." She smiled. "And I've helped Him choose your successor."

Kneiss's hand closed on hers again, but she couldn't tell if it was intentional or just the final random firing of his dying nerve endings. "No. Sara, you don't know what you're doing. There's still time for you to stop this."

"It's your fault, Albert. If you had just slipped away quietly like you were supposed to, none of this would have to happen. But you didn't, did you?"

"Not her, Sara," he gasped. "Please."

She felt his hand fall away from hers and his

eyes fix on the ceiling above him. "There's nothing that can stop it now, Albert. Your granddaughter *will* take your place on Good Friday—God's new Messenger. I have a beautiful ceremony planned for her ascension. I think you'd approve."

Sara released his arm and turned away, staring into the darkness of the room and listening to the increasingly erratic tone of the heart monitor. The church was hers now. Hers.

She heard a low moan from behind her and turned to see Albert Kneiss struggling to lift his head one last time.

"I prayed for you, Sara. Just like I prayed for all the others." He began to sink back onto the pillow. "But every time must have its Judas."

The pulse of the heart monitor slowed, finally fading to the steady tone that signaled the end of the Messenger's time on earth and a new era for her church.

25

MARK BEAMON TOOK ANOTHER SIP OF HIS coffee and continued to watch the young man through the window of the cafe. He was impeccably dressed—blue topcoat, white shirt, red-and-green-striped tie. And he had the look of clean-cut optimism Beamon had come to expect in the followers of Albert Kneiss. That confident but solicitous carriage that proclaimed, "I know something that you don't."

Beamon scraped up the last of the cream cheese that had dribbled from the bagel he had just wolfed down and popped it in his mouth. It wasn't biscuits and gravy, but he was actually starting to get used to the things.

The young man's pattern hadn't changed since he'd taken his position on the sidewalk across the street almost an hour ago. Eye contact, a confident sentence or two, hand the pedestrian a pamphlet, then attempt to shake hands and engage them in conversation.

From the looks of it, he worked that corner regularly. He'd received and returned at least a hundred silent nods from the early-morning foot commuters, bantering with some he knew well, thanking those who refused a flyer, and giving an occasional impassioned speech to anyone who stopped and expressed interest.

He wasn't doing too badly, either. In the last hour or so, three people had been interested enough to let him lead them through the stained-glass door of the Church of the Evolution bookstore/office behind him. Within a few minutes, he would reappear out front, but without the interested party.

Perhaps they had already been sacrificed in some hedonistic ritual that involved snakes and naked virgins? Only one way to find out. Beamon tossed back the rest of his coffee and went out through the doors of the cafe and into the cold Flagstaff morning. The clouds had parted and the sunlight was beaming through the thin mountain air with an almost tangible force. Beamon slipped on his sunglasses as he jogged across the street and began walking up the sidewalk toward the despicably enthusiastic young man.

"Have you read the latest on human evolution, sir?" he asked, establishing forcible eye contact.

Beamon stopped and took the proffered flyer. The first page was a glossy reproduction of the cover of a recent *National Geographic* containing a story relating to the anthropological discovery that many years ago, various species of humans shared the earth. Across the bottom a quote had been artistically superimposed on the cover:

> *Humanity's path had become confused, with many species competing for the eye of the Lord. But it was only one, Sapiens, that had begun the journey toward enlightenment. God*

sent his Messenger to them, to teach them to see as He did.

NATURE 3:14
THE HOLY BIBLE/KNEISS EDITION

Beamon flipped through the pamphlet's repro-duction of the *National Geographic* article, now modified with occasional italicized passages from Kneiss's Bible corroborating the theories described there.

"People laughed when they first read the New Bible, just like they mocked Jesus and his teachings. But now science is catching up with us, proving that our truth is the universal truth."

The boy's voice carried a deep sincerity, but Bea-mon suspected that if he were at a Kneissian recruit-ing station in New Zealand instead of Flagstaff, he'd be getting precisely the same well-thought-out spiel. It wasn't cocky or condescending, it stayed cozy with the science that people had come to trust and rely on, and finally, it smoothly worked in Jesus so as not to scare off America's devout Christian con-tingent.

"You know, I read something about this awhile back," Beamon said in as earnest a tone as he could conjure up.

"Then you're familiar with our beliefs, sir?"

Beamon shook his head. "Not really. I'm just visiting Flagstaff. I'm from Kansas City. I wish I could remember where I read . . ."

The boy stroked his chin thoughtfully. "There's been a lot of publicity about this lately. Could have been almost anywhere. The fact that science has turned a hundred and eighty degrees to agree with the Bible isn't a common occurrence." He gave a short, self-assured laugh that made Beamon feel like he was in on the joke.

"So, Albert Kneiss wrote this stuff over fifty years ago?" Beamon said, looking down at the pamphlet.

"I'm really not as much of an expert as some of the people inside. If you've got a few minutes for a cup of coffee, I'm sure I can dig up someone who could answer your questions with a lot more authority than I can."

Beamon shrugged. "Sure, I guess I have a minute."

The boy grinned and led Beamon through a set of double doors and into the tastefully decorated outer office. "This gentleman would like to speak with someone about the article," he said to the woman behind the counter and then turned back to Beamon. "I'm sorry, I forgot to ask your name."

"Mark."

He offered his hand. "Todd."

Todd hung around and chatted until a woman came out and politely stood off to the side until Beamon finished what he was saying.

"Mark, this is Cynthia," Todd said. "Cynthia, Mark."

Beamon turned to the woman and took her hand. "Very nice to meet you, Cynthia."

She was quite striking, with a long, straight nose and blonde hair covering her shoulders in a tumble that somehow didn't look random. Just by looking at her, Beamon would have put her in her early thirties, but the way she carried herself made him adjust upward a bit.

She led him through the door of a spacious but cozy room full of antique furniture and pleasantly worn rugs and offered him a chair next to a roaring fire. As he settled into the soft leather, she slid a tray with two steaming mugs on it toward him. He ignored the cream and sugar on the platter as he reached for one of them.

"Me too," she said. "I'd go intravenous if I could."

Beamon smiled and took a sip. He expected it to be good, and it was. He pulled out a cigarette he had rolled at the bagel shop, more to see her reaction than anything else. "Do you mind?"

"Not at all."

As he lit it, she opened a thick leather book and laid it on the table between them. "Would you care to sign our guest book?"

He hesitated, once again to judge her reaction. "I'd rather not. Not just yet."

"That's fine," she said with an easygoing flair, closing the book and sliding it down next to her chair. "So, Mark, how familiar are you with our church?"

"Not very, Cynthia. I mean, I know the basics. That you believe Albert Kneiss is a messenger from God who comes down to earth every couple of thousand years to teach."

"That about covers it. Want to join?"

They both laughed. Beamon was confident that if he had actually been there for the reason she thought, the remark would have done exactly what it had been designed to do—relieve any tension he might have felt.

"Seriously, you're right," she continued. "But in order for someone to teach, he or she has to take into consideration the abilities of the students. You don't try to teach a toddler calculus."

Beamon nodded his understanding, prompting her to go on.

"So when God's word was first written down in a coherent way—in the original Bible—a lot of parables and analogies were used. God revealed of himself only what the people of that time could digest."

The woman was starting to look a little peaked from his smoke, so Beamon tossed the cigarette into the fireplace. "Just can't seem to completely kick the habit."

"We have wonderful programs for that," she said. "I'm told they have the best success rate of any in the world."

Beamon took a sip from his mug, washing the taste of tobacco from his mouth. "So the new Bible—your version—tells the whole truth. Throws out the superstition and cuts right to the chase. The nature of God, what He wants from us, why we're here."

She smiled engagingly and shook her head. "Oh, no. We've come a long way in the last two thousand years, but unfortunately not that far. We still aren't prepared to fully understand God. Albert has simply given us God's teachings in the current context, so that we can understand more about Him. In another two thousand years, Albert will be back, under another name, to explain as much as he can based on what we've learned over the next two thousand years."

She was good. She exuded the calm confidence and sense of belonging that everyone was after. On another level, she was very attractive and roughly the right age for Beamon. He wondered if his spirit guide would have been some dashing hunk if he were a woman.

"I've read a few articles about your church in Germany. That they seem to think you're breaking the law—some kind of threat."

She looked sadly into the fire for a moment. "Obviously, the Germans have a poor history of accepting diverse faiths. Our followers have had to struggle there, it's true. We're giving them all the help we can, but as you know, not all countries put the same premium on freedom that we do."

A perfect answer, Beamon concluded. It attacked the attacker instead of defending the victim and it brought up the rather intangible concept of freedom that was guaranteed to get any American's red blood pumping.

"I have to admit, though," she continued, "we are a pretty close-knit group. The church provides business networking, counseling if you need it, help for the needy, health care, and hundreds of other things. Do you have children?"

Beamon shook his head.

"Too bad. We've built some of the finest schools in the country. We're really dedicated to education—probably more than anything else, we cherish that."

"I hear it's pretty expensive to be a member of the church," Beamon interjected.

A look of mild suspicion crossed her face and

then was gone. "Not particularly. Obviously, with all the services we like to provide and our commitment to charities, we do ask for some support from our members."

"Does Albert Kneiss ever appear in public?"

The look of suspicion stayed a little longer this time. "Are you a reporter?"

Beamon was a little surprised by the abruptness of the question, but then remembered Chet Michaels's difficulty in dredging up press articles on the church.

"A reporter? No. No, I'm not."

There was a long pause and Beamon began to wonder if the interview was over.

"Albert meditates," she said finally. "As I'm sure you've heard, his time with us is nearly over."

Beamon stood and pulled another cigarette from his pocket. "I really appreciate your time, Cynthia. I learned a lot." He pointed to a stack of Kneissian Bibles by her chair. "I'd love to have one of those if you can spare it."

She handed him one, somewhat reluctantly. "I hope it touches you as much as it did me."

Beamon flipped through the book and smiled. "I have no doubt that it will."

26

BEAMON COASTED INTO HIS SPACE, MANAGING for once to avoid sliding into the trees in front of it. He left the car running as he lit a cigarette and pulled his new notepad off the windshield. Turning on the interior light, he began flipping through the pages.

Reluctant to dismiss Hans Volker's views on the church, Beamon had begun to watch for cars that could be tailing him. Every time he saw one that might be popping up behind him more often than probability dictated, he jotted down the color, make, model, license number, time, and approximate location. Then, every night when he arrived home, he'd check to see if there were any matches.

So far there had been nothing exciting—other than the fact that he'd almost run over two pedestrians and a border collie while trying to juggle a cigarette, a cup of coffee, and the pad of paper.

Beamon ran his finger down the list of four cars he'd entered that day, memorizing their make and model, then shuffled back through the prior pages. He stopped at an entry on a red Taurus and flipped back to that day's record.

The license numbers matched, but that didn't mean anything. Could be just a neighbor who left for work at the same time. He compared the time of day. Nine A.M. and 3:45 P.M. Location: One between his home and the office, the other nowhere near either.

Beamon leaned back and blew a smoke ring at his rearview mirror. It could be a coincidence, of course, but that seemed unlikely. The real question was whether or not it was the church and if it was, whether it had anything to do with Jennifer Davis. If Hans Volker was right and the Kneissians were generally paranoid about the government's enforcement machine, it seemed likely that they would keep an eye on the head of the FBI's Flagstaff office on principle alone.

Beamon kicked his feet up onto one arm of his sofa and worked his head into the soft pillow covering the other.

The Kneissian Bible that the church had been kind enough to provide him appeared to be separated into four books—Nature, Old Testament, Jesus, and The Future. Each book had at least twenty subheadings.

Beamon flipped to the last page. Number 1,212. Probably better just to skim.

It took him about an hour to figure out the significance of each book. Nature took the place of Genesis, describing the creation of the universe, as well as the evolution of man and the "lesser species," from a significantly more scientific standpoint than the original Bible. In the universe according to Kneiss, God breathed life into the primordial soup that existed on Earth—as well as on an undisclosed number of other planets in the universe—and then waited to see what happened.

Actually, that wasn't entirely true. He occasionally saw fit to muck around with the evolutionary process, creating the more intricate structures of life such as wings and the complex organs that created a spider's web, among other things that had baffled anthropologists since Darwin.

Of course, he had taken a special interest in humanity, sending the first Messenger many years ago to stack the deck for homo sapiens against the protohumans who had turned out not to be the sharpest knives in His drawer.

The Old Testament section tended to debunk sections of the original Bible more than anything else. It provided insight into the characters of the original Old Testament, making them much more human and therefore much more believable. David became a murderous and somewhat vain man necessary to God's plan. The black-and-white treatment of the Romans melted to a gunmetal gray, and God's motivations became clearer and more ambiguous at the same time.

The Jesus section seemed to serve much the same function as the Old Testament chapters. It covered many of His most pivotal moments on earth, told from His point of view. The squalor and superstition that ruled the lives of the people of that time was rendered so artfully that Beamon could almost feel Jesus's frustration as he tried to impart the mind of God to a population that understood nothing and feared everything.

The section entitled The Future replaced Revelation, and was the book most starkly different from its predecessor. It stated that the end of humanity was not yet etched in stone. God's hope for mankind was that it would evolve to a state of complete enlightenment. That was to be the criteria on which it would be judged. Would humanity be able to leave behind superstition, fear, and hate? To develop fully those things that set it apart from the other species that shared the earth?

Beamon yawned and laid the book down on his chest. Four-thirty in the morning. He looked over at the coffee table and counted the empty beer bottles on it. Eight. Three more than his daily allowance.

He picked up Kneiss's Bible again and stared at the black cover.

As a work of literature, it was truly amazing. The prose style was a seemingly impossible mix of passion and reason, formality and accessibility. It stripped the wings off the angels and the horns and teeth from the devil, offering humanity a glimpse of its potential and a clear path to achieving that potential. It provided answers to a world trying so desperately to find meaning and clinging to gods that had stood still while their flocks had moved on.

27

"IT'S A MIRACLE!"

Beamon surveyed his office with a sense of satisfaction. True, the cables were still hanging from the ceiling and there was still that unavoidable layer of white dust over everything, but by God, the concrete floor had disappeared beneath a layer of utilitarian tan carpet.

His secretary walked up next to him and leaned against the doorjamb as though she hadn't noticed until he pointed it out. "A miracle, huh? From what I hear, you had a conversation with the general contractor about his continued ability to—how did he put it—travel America's highways and byways? I understand his people were in here all night."

"Morning, Mark."

Beamon didn't look out from behind his paper. "Have a seat, Chet. Your shoes aren't dirty, are they?"

"Nope. Nice carpet."

"Clearly a floor covering befitting a man of my stature," Beamon said, finishing the article he was reading and tossing the paper on the desk.

Michaels chuckled quietly. "Clearly."

"What did you think of your friend's theory, Chet?"

Michaels's expression turned serious. "At first, I was really embarrassed to have dragged you out there. But then I couldn't sleep that night, you know? The angle of the bullet, the scratches on his hand. I don't know, Susan's really smart."

"Attractive, too," Beamon said. "How'd you ever let her get away?"

"Lesbian."

"No."

"Yup."

"Well, a good woman's hard to find. Sometimes you just have to overlook their little imperfections." Beamon looked at the blue folders his young protégé never seemed to be without. "So what have you got for me?"

"Wait a minute, Mark. You can't leave me hanging like that. What do *you* think of Susan's theory?"

"We'll get to that, but first things first," Beamon answered, shaking his finger again toward the folders.

Michaels reluctantly tossed one of them onto Beamon's desk. "That's a bunch of articles on the church that have come in from the publishers. Some are pretty old—actually most are. Objective media coverage seems to be less every year."

"I'll read'm tonight. I've got a meeting starting in an hour that's going to take all day. Is there anything in here that I need to know right now?"

"Not really. There's some stuff criticizing the church's business tactics and the fact that they use nuisance suits to beat down their detractors. Some stuff on how it's really expensive to belong . . . oh, and there's a really interesting *Psychology Today* article about the pressure the church puts on its people to recruit new members and the toll it takes on them emotionally. That one was pretty cool. Now, what about Susan's theory?"

"We're going to work on that in a few minutes," Beamon said, pointing to the remaining folder lying in the young agent's lap. "What's that one?"

"Information I put together on your neighbor and Sara Renslier."

Beamon waved him on. "Give me the *Reader's Digest* version."

"Robert T. Andrews. Thirty-five years old, originally from Louisiana—Baton Rouge. Career military: 82nd Airborne. Honorably discharged a sergeant June 1995. As near as I can tell, he's been unemployed since then. I tried to check out his prior address—it's a property up in the mountains. Couldn't get there, though—the road leading to it was snowed in." He looked up at Beamon. "You think this guy's watching you?"

Beamon shrugged. "Probably not. Just a feeling."

"I can dig deeper."

Beamon shook his head. If the church *was* watching him, best not to jump up and down with his pants around his ankles. "Do me this, though. See if you can quietly find out if anyone else is living at his prior address and if so, get me some general information on them, too. Now what about Renslier?"

"Sara Renslier is fifty-one. Lists the church as her employer and Kneiss's compound as her permanent residence. It looks like she was an accountant for a few years after school, then went to work for the church. No criminal record; nothing specific about what she does for the church. Time to talk about the suicide theory yet?"

Beamon stood up from behind his desk. "It's

time. Go get me Theresa and James," he said, naming the two agents in his office, besides Chet, who seemed the most flexible and imaginative. "And let's not mention the church angle, okay?"

Michaels looked confused, but complied. Beamon followed him to the door. "Hey, D., you were a drama major, weren't you?"

"I *do* have a public administration minor," she said a little defensively.

"Don't need an administrator. Need an actress. Are you any good?"

She looked at him suspiciously, obviously waiting for the punch line. When none came, she said, "There are worse."

"Shut the door behind you, Chet," Beamon said as Michaels walked in with the two agents Beamon had sent him for.

"Okay, here's what's happening. Chet and I have a theory about the Davis case and we need some help working it out. Now, what I'm going to tell you doesn't leave this room. I mean that. If I hear anything that leads me to believe it has, I will make it my life's work to track down the leak and see him or her thrown out of the Bureau. Anybody have a problem with that?"

Beamon surveyed the young agents' faces and the face of his secretary as they all mumbled their assent.

"Okay then. We have physical evidence that leads us to believe that Mr. Davis may have shot his wife and then committed suicide."

With the exception of Michaels, the expressions worn by the people in the room turned to shock. There was some low murmuring, but no one spoke up clearly. Probably still intimidated by his little speech.

"Now, my problem is that I can't figure out a motivation for Mr. Davis that fits the rest of the facts. And that's where you all come in."

Beamon grabbed some note cards from his desk drawer and began writing on them. "D., you're Patricia Davis." He handed her a nametag that she taped to her chest.

"Theresa—you're Jennifer, I'm Eric Davis. And Chet and James—you guys are our hypothetical perpetrators." He handed them nametags reading "Thing 1" and "Thing 2," then leaned back to examine his cast. Something was missing. He handed Michaels a stapler and James a ruler. "Those are your guns."

Something was still wrong. He looked at Theresa's neatly trimmed hair and conservative blue business suit, then down at his desk. He unwound a paper clip and broke a third of it off. Fashioning the remaining wire into a loop, he held it out to her. "Put this on your nose."

She looked doubtful.

"Jennifer has a nose ring," he said impatiently. "Come on, let's get with the program."

She reluctantly stuck it to her nose, then looked down at it cross-eyed.

"That's what I was looking for," Beamon said. "Okay. Chet, would you like to give us our first scenario?"

"Wait a minute, Mark," D. broke in. "You know all there is to know about Mr. Davis, and Jennifer's life story has been plastered across the newspapers since she disappeared. But I don't know anything about my character."

Beamon pointed at D. but looked at the others. "Now that's what I'm talking about. A little enthusiasm."

He stood and took a position with his back against the wall, inviting D. to do the same. "Patricia Davis put her husband through college and supported him in his various business ventures, but hasn't worked since adopting Jennifer thirteen years ago. She's active in the PTA, an apparently devoted mother—though Jennifer considers her kind of, uh, square? She's also involved in numerous charities and belongs to a bridge club. Jennifer is her only child. Never had one of her own."

D. held up her hand. "That should do it."

"Okay, then. Chet, I believe you were about to convince me to kill my wife and commit suicide."

Michaels reached out, grabbed Theresa, and held the stapler to her head. "Okay, Mr. Davis. Shoot your wife and kill yourself or your daughter gets it."

Silence.

"Uh, I don't have a gun, son," Beamon said.

Chet turned to James. "Give him your gun."

James looked doubtful. "No way. There's no telling what a guy would do in this situation if he were armed. I'll shoot him for you if you want, though."

"Yeah, you're right," Michaels said, releasing his grip on Theresa.

"That's okay. That's what we're here for. To eliminate possibilities," Beamon said. "How about this. Jennifer never made it home. Her dad went nuts and killed her on the way."

Beamon took Michaels's stapler and aimed it at Jennifer. He was about to pull the "trigger" when his secretary grabbed him from behind and started choking him.

As he peeled her arm from his throat, Theresa ran to the door. Beamon corrected his scenario. "D.'s right on that one, there was evidence of a struggle." He grabbed her and "shot" Jennifer. D. played the distraught mother beautifully, throwing herself to her knees next to her fallen daughter— obviously having the time of her life.

"Okay, okay," Beamon said. "You're right. Super-unlikely that he could have killed Jennifer and then controlled the mother long enough to get her home. Hell, why bring Mom back at all?"

Theresa lifted her head from the carpet. "What if she was in on it and then you—Mr. Davis— started feeling really guilty when you got home?"

Beamon was skeptical. "What do you think, D.? Do you feel like you were in on it?"

She shook her head.

"Me neither. No indication of this type of tendency at all in either of them. And then there's the Big Question—where the hell's the gun?"

They all grumbled as they wrestled with the problem.

"Okay," Beamon said, ignoring the crowd forming on the other side of the window to his office. "Let's try the obvious one on for size. Dad goes nuts, Jennifer gets away."

He turned to D. "Patricia, you've left the cap off the toothpaste one too many times. Bang."

D. fell to the floor and Theresa ran to the edge of the room. Beamon pointed the deadly stapler at himself, "bang," and fell to the floor.

His eyes were closed, but he could hear Theresa walking toward him. "I'm sorry, Mark, but I can't think of any reason in this world why I'd take that gun."

Beamon sat up. "Shit. Me neither. Eliminate that one."

"What if Jennifer was involved?"

Beamon shrugged. "Takes us back to the first scenario. Even if she had an accomplice holding a gun to her head and she was pleading with her father to kill her mom and shoot himself, I don't think he'd have done it. Besides, what would be the point of taking the gun and making it look like murder after going through all that trouble? And why hasn't she reappeared to collect her inheritance? And where the hell is . . . Shit, I don't know . . ."

"What if they walked in on a robbery?" Chet began. "And the robbers take Jennifer and tell the parents that they're going to rape and kill her. That she'll be dead in a half-hour. Dad gets despondent—kills himself and his wife."

Beamon shook his head. "No way. He'd at least call the cops. Try to save his daughter in the next half-hour. And once again, where's the gun?"

"What if Jennifer was killed early on?"

"What, with the robbery scenario? Why the hell would they take the body? Necrophilia? I think we're reaching."

Beamon stood and helped his secretary to her feet. "Okay, guys, thanks. You've helped a lot."

They filed out through the door, discussing further possibilities in quiet whispers. Michaels closed the door behind D. as Beamon sat down at his desk and took a sip of cold coffee from his mug. "What are we going to do about this one, Chet?"

Michaels frowned. "I just can't think of anything we've missed. I mean, there's the church angle, but I sure don't see how that fits in with Eric Davis shooting his wife and killing himself."

Beamon rubbed his temples, feeling the beginnings of a throbbing that was likely to last until this thing was over. "Unfortunately, *I* can."

Michaels looked hopelessly frustrated. "Please, Mark. This thing's killing me."

"I'm gonna say it again, Chet. None of this leaves the room, right?"

Michaels nodded his assent.

"I've talked to a few people about the Church of the Evolution and done a little research myself," Beamon said. "They've created quite a religious machine for themselves—and their followers are incredibly devoted. Let's consider the facts in chronological order." Beamon held up his index finger. "One: Jennifer's real mother changes her name and place of residence numerous times, though for no reason we can find.

"Two: Jennifer's real mother and father are killed in a mysterious fire in the middle of the night, but their two-year-old daughter manages to escape and is found wandering around in the yard.

"Three: The Davises, a couple who moved to Flagstaff around the same time as the church did and who'd never tried to adopt before, pop in and take Jennifer right after she gets to the foster home."

Michaels had a strangely bemused look on his face.

"You okay, Chet?"

"Huh? Yeah. It's just that I do all this work gathering information for you—spend a ton of time writing it out, give it to you every morning, and, well, you always seem to be only half paying attention. I never thought you actually remembered any of it."

Beamon laughed. His mother used to get on him for the same thing. "Where was I?"

"Four."

"Four: Albert Kneiss decides he's going to die this year, leaving a leadership void at the church."

"Five: Kneiss's granddaughter suddenly disappears, and her adoptive parents, in essence, kill themselves."

Beamon stood up and grabbed his mug. "Process those five facts while I get another cup of coffee.

When Beamon sat back down, the young agent was scribbling furiously on a yellow legal pad. He finally laid it down on the desk, and Beamon could see that he'd written down the five points almost verbatim. Michaels looked up at him. "I'm still thinking."

Beamon put his feet on the desk and blew gently across the top of the mug. "Thinking is good. No hurry."

Michaels sat motionless for almost five minutes, elbows on his knees, staring at the pad. Finally his head rose and he leaned back in the chair. "Okay. I've got something, but it doesn't seem right."

"Go ahead."

"Jennifer's biological mother was running from the church. Kneiss wanted Jennifer to eventually succeed him, but his daughter didn't want anything to do with him and his followers. People from the church burned down her house with her and her husband in it, but made sure Jennifer wasn't injured."

He paused, looking a bit uncertain.

"Doing okay so far, keep going," Beamon prodded.

"The church sends two devoted members to adopt her right away. They keep her, pretending not to be part of the church, because they don't want any appearance of wrongdoing that could get into the press that they fear so much, and they wait. Finally, Kneiss announces that it's time for him to ascend. The church takes Jennifer and orders her adoptive parents to commit suicide. Religion is probably as good a motivation for suicide as any— history's proven that."

Beamon nodded thoughtfully.

"There's just one problem, though, Mark. Why the suicide?"

"It would be the only option. Think about it, Chet. They have to get rid of her folks—they'd be the first people I went after when she disappeared. And their backgrounds wouldn't have taken heavy scrutiny with all the church connections."

"Okay, I see your point. But why not just kill them? It's like you always say, the simplest answer is usually the right answer."

"You *could* just kill them, but consider the problems. Jennifer would hate her captors for killing her folks and would probably be reluctant to get involved with the Church. The second, better option would be to take Jennifer and then kill them. The problem there is twofold: Jennifer would think she had a family to get back to, making her conversion even more problematic. And, of course, when she did eventually find out they were dead, the shock could undo all their careful brainwashing."

Beamon sipped at his coffee. "If it were me, I'd

have the Davises commit suicide right in front of her. That would convince her of their devotion to the church and cut her off from any family support. I mean, can you imagine what something like that would do to a fifteen-year-old kid?"

28

JENNIFER DAVIS LOOKED DOWN AT THE dripping faucet and estimated the time at between 2:30 and 3:30 in the afternoon, March 6.

The design was simple. She had counted endlessly—one Mississippi, two Mississippi—while the dripping of the faucet filled the cup she had been provided. Then, by filling the sink with the cup and carefully scratching lines in the porcelain with a fork, she had built a clock.

Regaining her sense of time had gone miles toward helping her get her balance back. She'd used it to establish a routine: go to sleep at ten, wake up around eight. During the day, study the Bible the old man had given her; early afternoon, try to get some exercise. Then more study in the evening.

Her first impression had been right. Her meals were being served at erratic intervals, sometimes as little as an hour apart, sometimes as much as eight hours apart.

She hadn't seen or spoken to anyone in seven days and she'd used that time to think. Sara was a liar. She told herself that at least ten times a day, trying to get the message to penetrate her fear and loneliness.

The old man she had been taken to—her grandfather—knew nothing of how she was being treated.

That she was sure of. Sara was going to try her best to break her, she knew. Sara wasn't going to hand over her position as head of the church easily.

At the sound of the key hitting the lock, Jennifer ran out of the bathroom, afraid that her makeshift timepiece might be discovered. She stood in the middle of the room and watched the door open and Sara walk through.

"I'm so sorry, Jennifer. So sorry to have left you alone for so long."

Jennifer jerked back when Sara brought her hand up to touch her hair. The woman's face transformed into an expression of concern. "Oh, honey. I know how lonely you must be, but you have to trust me. There's no other way."

Jennifer looked past her and saw the man who always seemed to accompany Sara on her visits standing in the doorway. She'd only caught brief glimpses of him before today—identifying him by his thick black mustache. But now she could see the scar running from it to his expressionless right eye and his thin, powerful build.

"What do you want from me?" Jennifer said, having trouble keeping control of the jumble of emotions trying to take hold of her. Sara was the only person who came to see her, the only person who really spoke to her. And while she knew that it was Sara who had imprisoned her, it was so hard to distrust the only voice in her life. Late at night she found herself trying to reinvent Sara as someone who cared about her. To convince herself that the only human being she had any real contact with was good.

"You know what I want, Jennifer. I want to keep you safe from the others. This is very complicated, you—"

"I don't believe you," Jennifer said. She'd rehearsed this conversation at least a hundred times over the past few days, but was still having trouble getting the words out.

"What did you say?"

Jennifer could hear the edge of anger in Sara's voice and felt a sickening twinge in her stomach. She felt her resolve faltering, suddenly feeling like a small child who had angered her mother. She bit the inside of her mouth and concentrated on the pain, a trick she used to focus her mind when she raced. "I don't believe you."

"Jennifer. Listen very carefully. It's important that you fully understand what I'm going to tell you. Are you listening?"

Jennifer nodded.

"You've been alone in here too long and I know that what happened to your parents has affected you very deeply. You're not thinking clearly right now. You have to trust me. I'm going to take you to see your grandfather now, but there will be others there. It's very important that you say absolutely nothing unless it's in answer to a direct question posed by me. Okay?" She reached out again, but Jennifer caught her by the wrist.

"No. It's not okay."

Sara withdrew her hand and looked down at the floor for a moment. When she raised her head again, her eyes had turned cold. Jennifer took an involuntary step backward when she saw the man at the door coming toward her. She dodged right, but wasn't quick enough and felt herself being lifted off the ground and then slammed face first down onto the bed.

"Let me go!" she screamed as the man pinned

her arms behind her. She thrashed wildly, feeling the rage building in her. They had no right! No right to hold her here. No right to have taken her life away. She kicked out hard when the pressure on her back eased for a moment, but only connected with air.

She struggled even harder when she felt the cold metal against the back of her hands and then heard the ratcheting sound as a pair of handcuffs closed around her wrists. She twisted around as Sara came toward her and then fell back onto the mattress, exhausted and helpless. There was nothing she could do.

The man holding her moved away when Sara reached for the chain between the handcuffs binding her wrists. Jennifer cried out in pain when the woman forcefully twisted the chain, but something in her kept her from fighting back.

"Don't make another sound," Sara said quietly. Jennifer complied, lying motionless on the bed as the man returned to his position outside the open door.

Her wrists felt like they were going to break, and the combination of the pain, fear, and frustration was bringing tears to her eyes. She pressed her face into the tangle of sheets beneath her and wiped them away.

"That's better." The pressure on the handcuffs eased. "See what happens? If you do what I tell you, everything will be all right."

Sara didn't speak again for what seemed like forever, and Jennifer just lay motionless on the bed listening to the woman's breathing.

"I told you that I was taking you to see Albert and that some other people were going to be there.

What else did I tell you?" the woman finally said.

Jennifer's throat had gone completely dry and was making it a struggle to speak. "You . . . you told me just to answer your questions," she managed to say in what sounded like a loud whisper.

"That's right, Jennifer." There was another long pause before the woman spoke again. "There's no one else, you know. Your parents gave you to me. I cause your meals to brought to you, provide you with clean clothes, water. You've been orphaned for a second time, Jennifer. There's no one left who cares what happens to you. No one but me."

Jennifer pressed her face into the pillow again and began to sob quietly. Why was this happening to her?

"Don't cry, dear," Sara said, running her fingers gently up the inside of Jennifer's bare leg and over the back of her panties. "Don't cry. Everything's going to be all right."

Jennifer could feel the lines of sweat that Sara's fingers had left on her thigh. It made her feel cold.

The old man's room was different now. The windows seemed to have lost their tint, and the heatless light of the afternoon sun painted the floor in wide strips.

The elaborate array of medical machines was gone and the old man's bed had been moved into the middle of the room. Around it stood five conservatively dressed people. Two women and three men.

Jennifer's breath came out as steam as Sara led her through the frigid room. She pulled back when they came within about fifteen feet of the bed, but Sara put a hand on the back of her neck and forced her forward. As they moved closer, she could see that the old man was completely motionless and that his limbs had been arranged in a configuration too neat to be natural. She felt the tears begin again as she was forced to accept the fact that the old man, whose eyes had carried away some of her loneliness and fear, was gone. And now there really was only Sara.

The people turned slowly from the old man's body and locked their eyes on her as she and Sara stopped a few feet from them. The man who had handcuffed and later released her continued past them and joined the small group.

"Jennifer," Sara said in a clear voice obviously meant for the others in the room. "Your grandfather told you that you were the one that God had named to take his place. Do you remember?"

Jennifer continued to stare down at the old man, the image of his lifeless body filling her mind.

"Jennifer?" Sara prodded in a gentle tone that carried a hint of menace in its timbre. "Do you remember?"

What she remembered was the biting steel of

the handcuffs against the bones of her wrists and Sara's quiet threats.

"Yes."

"Then you accept your place in the church?"

Jennifer took a deep breath and looked away from her grandfather, trying unsuccessfully to clear her head. What else could she do?

"Yes."

The people began walking up to her one at a time, each silently leaning over and kissing her on the cheek with eyes full of awe. All except the man who had come in with them. The man with the mustache. He kissed her as the others had, but his expression was one of quiet triumph.

In a moment they were all gone and she was alone in the room with Sara, her nameless companion, and the shell of what was once her grandfather and God's messenger on earth. Jennifer looked around her and then back down at her grandfather's body, feeling a small glimmer of hope in her chest. Sara didn't want her there, she knew that. And she wanted nothing to do with her church. Jamie's mom would take her in. It would be less than two years until she went to college and then she could build her own life. One that had nothing to do with Albert Kneiss or Sara, or her parents.

"I don't want any of this," Jennifer said. "Bring the others back in and I'll tell them. You can have the church. It's yours."

Sara's mouth curled into a smile devoid of warmth. "I don't think you understand, Jennifer."

"I do understand. My grandfather wanted me to take over for him as the head of the church."

Sara shook her head. "He wanted much more than that for you."

Jennifer was confused for a moment. She knew what he had said.

"Albert has served God for many years," Sara said. "And God has taken him to his reward." She reached out and took Jennifer's hand. "You haven't been chosen to lead the church, Jennifer. You've been chosen as God's new Messenger."

Jennifer tried to step back, but Sara tightened her grip on her hand. She looked down at her grandfather's body, Sara's words penetrating her mind. Good Friday was still a few weeks away. He wasn't supposed to be dead yet.

"It will be time for you to take your place with God soon, Jennifer."

"No!" Jennifer screamed, pulling away and trying to run. The man at Sara's side caught hold of her before she could make it even a few feet. "That's not what he said! It's not and you know it. My grandfather wanted to give the church to me!"

"Your grandfather is dead, Jennifer," Sara said smoothly. "You have no idea what he wanted. How could you?"

Jennifer squeezed her eyes shut and bit the inside of her cheek again, harder this time. How could she have been so stupid? She'd let Sara trick her into telling those people that she wanted to die.

She pushed at the man holding her, knowing that she had no hope of escaping his grip, and then sunk to the floor. There was no one left to help her. No one cared if she lived anymore. And Sara only cared that she died.

29

Beamon took the plastic bag off his frozen doorknob and pushed through the door into his living room. He leaned back outside for a moment to shake the snow off his parka and briefcase, then pulled the door tightly shut.

They were rotating, he thought as he sat down on one of the stools at the edge of his kitchen counter and began to flip through the pad he'd brought with him from the car. And they liked Fords.

He grabbed a Hi-Liter and put a green stripe over his notes relating to a red Taurus that had been popping up behind him more often than it should. That was two cars. It was possible that there were more, but he hadn't been watching long enough to be sure of the pattern. What he was sure of, though, was that he was being followed. And worse, he was about seventy-five percent sure that his new neighbor's decision to rent in that particular location had been influenced by the view. Of his condo.

He reached into the plastic bag that had been hanging on his door and pulled a damp envelope from it. The envelope contained a single yellow Post-it note.

> Never got a chance
> to thank you for
> watching Emory.
> Dinner at seven?
>
> Carrie

Beamon glanced at his watch and then looked at the briefcase bulging with administrative bullshit. It had been backing up for weeks—what harm would one more day do? He walked over and opened the fridge but found nothing more than a few cans of beer. Showing up on Carrie's doorstep with the dregs of a twelve-pack of Busch probably presented a little too realistic an image for this early in their relationship. Probably better to go empty-handed.

But then, what did he know? His history with women was less than impressive. If you didn't count the logistically impossible attraction between him and his old partner, Laura Vilechi, his last date had been almost two years ago. A friend had set it up, describing the woman as intelligent and attractive, but a witch. Beamon hadn't seen any serious problem with that—he himself had been known to be an occasional pain in the ass. What he hadn't understood was that "witch" hadn't been an evaluation of her personality; it had been a statement of religious affiliation.

It had been torture. A black cat had wandered in front of them on the way to the restaurant, then a woman who had something that looked like an enormous wart on her nose sat down in booth next to them. He'd bravely resisted temptation, though, and managed to make not a single comment through the appetizers and most of the main course. Then she had to go and start telling a story that somehow involved a broom. He'd ended up alone with a lap full of red wine.

Since then, there had never seemed to be time. Always some life-or-death case tempting him from the sidelines or some administrative snafu that promised to make his life miserable if he didn't deal with it yesterday.

Until recently, his plan had been to continue with his former lifestyle and drop dead of a heart attack a few years before he reached mandatory retirement. But he finally realized that was stupid. There was more out there than the quickly waning adrenaline rush of a good case.

Beamon went into the bathroom and smoothed down a curl in what was left of his hair. At least the weight he'd lost had thinned out his face. A significant improvement, though he still wasn't in any real danger of being described as good looking. But what the hell—he had other endearing qualities.

Beamon rapped on Carrie's door and glanced at his watch. Only ten minutes late. She came to the door almost immediately, accompanied by her daughter and the smell of garlic.

"Will you accept me empty-handed, Carrie? I just walked in from work."

"Absolutely. Come on in."

Emory attached herself briefly to his leg as he stepped into the house, a credit to her mother's exhaustive training.

"You're dealing with that better and better, Mark," Carrie said as she walked back to the kitchen.

"I think my conditioning experiment is working."

Beamon picked Emory up almost to the ceiling and spun her around. "I remember my first autopsy, Carrie. It's amazing what you can get used to." He swung the little girl back to the floor, ignoring the smirk on Carrie's face. "Right, Emory?"

"Right!" she agreed and threw herself onto the sofa in front of the TV. "Your show's over."

Beamon walked into the kitchen with a questioning look on his face.

"Emory seems to think you have your own show. Every evening at the same time she switches the TV to the local news and watches for you." Carrie poured him a rather full glass of red wine. "She's very impressed."

Beamon smiled and sipped at the wine. He'd never really acquired a taste for it. "It's nice to know I have a fan."

"How are you doing on that case, Mark?" she said as she turned to check the oven. "I saw the thing about the white slavery ring. It's so horrifying."

"There *is* no godda—" Beamon cleared his throat and lowered his voice. "There is no white slavery ring."

"No?"

"No. That came from some psychic. The press printed it like it was gospel 'cause they consider violence without sex kind of dry."

She slid a bubbling casserole out of the oven using a pair of garish oven mitts and then reached back in for a tray of muffins. "I think we're about ready."

The meal was indescribable. Despite the rich garlic smell and the satisfying bubbling of the deep red sauce, Carrie's eggplant parmesan tasted like, well, like his fork. Its blandness was matched only by that of the almost dressing-free salad.

"You know, Mark, someday I'm going to write a cookbook," Carrie said, right on cue. "I swear, the cookbooks you get today are so full of things like sour cream and butter that the dishes could kill you if you just look at them." She pointed at his plate. "I just leave all that stuff out. You can't even tell the difference."

"I sure can't," he lied through a mouthful of muffin that seemed to be soaking up saliva faster than his body could produce it. "How's that thesis you're working on going?"

"Really well, thanks for asking. It's almost done. It looks like it's going to get published next month."

"That's great. Congratulations. I trust you didn't have to crash any more weddings to finish it."

She affected a seductive pout that seemed to transform her into an entirely different woman. "You're not still mad about that, are you? You did get two free dinners out of it, for God's sake."

"No, no. Not mad," Beamon said, laying down his fork and hoping that dessert wasn't on the menu. "Intrigued. I actually find the Kneissians fascinating."

That turn in the conversation was the last straw for Emory, who asked to be excused from the table and rushed off to her room before her mother could answer.

"Me too. You know, it's really the first religion to embrace science. Most faiths in one way or another are at odds with technology. I mean, God has to make statements, and those statements remain static while the world continues to move forward. Causes friction. The other thing I find interesting is that the Kneissians' belief system isn't built around a lot of set-in-stone—if you'll excuse the pun—rules like many other Western religions. Right and wrong is a little more of a gray area. They're more interested in being all they can be."

Beamon nodded thoughtfully and reached over to refill her wineglass. "Does that make them dangerous?"

She thought about that for a moment. "I don't mean to say that they don't have a strong sense of morality—all you have to do is look at them to see that they do. All I'm saying is that their Bible allows for more flexibility. That in turn should keep it from becoming obsolete as we continue rushing toward . . . whatever it is we're rushing toward."

She stood and stacked Beamon's plate on top of hers.

"Let me help you with that," Beamon said.

"Oh, I'm not cleaning up—just getting these out of the way. Back in a sec."

She was wearing a pair of brown wool slacks and a loose-fitting white blouse that, once again, draped along the curves of her body beautifully. Beamon watched her with admiration as she glided off to the kitchen and then reappeared a moment later.

"Let me ask you a related question," he said.

"Am I being interrogated?"

"Absolutely not—I'm just trying to distract you while I get you drunk."

"Oh, that's okay, then," she said, sitting down and picking up her wineglass. "What's your question?"

"From a psychological point of view, why isn't religion as important now as it was, say, a thousand years ago?"

She swirled her glass and stared into the deep red liquid contained there for a few moments. "What you expect me to say is that we just don't need it as much. That we used it to explain things we didn't understand and we understand more now. That we don't suffer as much during our lives now, so we don't need an afterlife as desperately." She took another sip of her wine. "But I don't know if that's it. With the speed that our lives go by now, we don't have as much time for real companionship. We're losing the ability to reach out to people around us. Maybe we need God more now than we ever did."

"God, yes. But religion?"

She shrugged. "I don't think the answer to your question is as psychological as it is political. You're a historian, aren't you?"

Beamon chuckled. "I squeezed in a history degree between benders at Yale, yes. But I don't think anybody would confuse me with a historian."

She looked at him with what might have been affection; his senses in that arena were hopelessly dull. "Somehow I think you're being modest. You tell me, Mark. You don't seem to be in the habit of asking questions you don't know the answers to. Why is religion less dominant today than it was a thousand years ago?"

Beamon took a deep breath and tapped his nail against his glass, producing a clear, unwavering tone. "Maybe it's not the worshipers, but that religions limit themselves."

"How so?"

"It seems to me that all organized religions have some factor that keeps them from gaining power. The most obvious is what we were talking about—

the backward thinking. Some of the older religions of the world have customs and dogma that worked well when they were first implemented, but now, hundreds or thousands of years later, they create barriers to progress—to meeting the needs of today's worshiper. The Catholic church in the United States might be a good example of that. Their views on the marriage of priests, women, abortion, divorce—all reflect a time that's long gone."

He paused for a moment to examine her expression and make sure she wasn't finding this offensive. So far so good. "Another limiting factor, particularly for newer religions, would be a very unusual belief system. The Mormons and Scientologists—right or wrong—run into trouble there. What they have to say is perhaps too new. It doesn't tie back to a concept that people grew up with and therefore don't question."

"What about some of the Eastern religions? What's their 'limiting factor'?"

"A lot of them are more philosophies than religions. They lack a central deity to order them around and really don't seem to have developed political agendas. Too inward-looking."

"Okay, then. Here's one for you. What's the Kneissians' 'limiting factor'?"

Beamon picked up the wine bottle in front of him and poured some into his glass. "That's just it. I can't think of one."

30

THE PATTERN HAD COME CLEAR OVER THE weekend. Three cars. All Ford Tauruses—one blue, one green, and one red—rotating daily.

Beamon had dropped the red one in town almost an hour ago. It really wasn't difficult to lose a tail; the problem was making it look like an accident. They'd find out he knew they were watching eventually, but he preferred to put that off for as long as possible.

Beamon checked his rearview mirror one more time, looking back over the empty road and flat, snow-dusted desert behind him. Satisfied that he was the only thing moving for miles, he decided to cover the last quarter-mile or so on foot and pulled his car to the curb.

Despite the fact that all the houses in this oasis of a neighborhood looked the same, Beamon found the one he was looking for with little difficulty. After almost a minute of pounding on the door, though, there was still no answer. He stepped back and double-checked the numbers between the garage and front door. They were the ones given to him that morning when Ernest Willard's former book agent had called him out of the blue and told him that the man who had written the now-unavailable exposé on the church had agreed to a meeting.

Beamon thought he heard a dull scraping sound coming from inside the house and stepped back onto the porch. "Hello?"

"May I see your ID?" came a muffled voice on the other side of the closed door.

Beamon pulled out his credentials, but the door didn't open. He stepped back and, finding a peephole oddly located about halfway up the door, held them up to it.

A moment later, the door swung open and he was faced with what looked a little like a small tank in a sunflower print muumuu.

The woman backing up to give him a clear path into the house seemed impossibly fat. The garish tent/dress she wore went from her thick neck to her knees in what looked like a perfectly straight line. Her legs, where they appeared under the dress, resembled gigantic sausages in tan nylon casings. What gave her that true tanklike feel, though, was the wheelchair she had, by some strange anomaly of physics, managed to stuff her rear end into.

"I'm sorry, Mr. Beamon. I was in the back." She diverted her gaze to the chair for a moment. "It takes me a little longer to make it across the house than it used to."

"I'm the one who should apologize, I didn't mean to attack your door like that. I thought maybe you couldn't hear me," Beamon said, closing the door and following her as she wheeled through the hallway toward the back of the house. "Is Ernest Willard in?"

She pulled to a stop in a small room overflowing with computer equipment, newsmagazines, and reference books. There wasn't a single surface that hadn't been used to haphazardly route cables or wasn't covered with some piece of high-tech machinery or phone book–thick document.

"About Ernest Willard," Beamon prompted again, "I think he agreed to see me?"

"I did," the woman said, turning her wheelchair to face him. "I'm Ernest Willard. Well, actually I'm Ernestine Waverly. But I wrote the book you're interested in."

"A nom de plume," Beamon said, moving a stack of computer disks from a chair and taking an uninvited seat.

"At the time, it seemed like a good idea."

"Well, I'm glad we have the opportunity to talk. When my associate called your agent a while back, he was told that she hadn't heard from you in years."

She smiled. "I provide her with books—computer tech manuals now—and in turn, she protects me."

"Protects you? From what?"

"The church has . . . held a grudge. They can be very difficult. I don't see anyone anymore."

"You're seeing me."

She used her thick arms to propel herself toward him, stopping a few feet from where he sat. "I dream about you, Mr. Beamon."

Beamon shifted uncomfortably in the chair as the woman stared at him. "I'm not quite sure how to respond to that."

"It started a few months ago," she explained. "I couldn't see you clearly at first, but every night your face became a little sharper. Of course, I didn't know who you were, until I saw you on TV."

"And what am I doing in these dreams?" Beamon asked, not sure he really wanted to know.

"Different things. Tell me, Mr. Beamon, do you believe in God?"

"That's a complicated question."

"No, it's not."

"Let's say I have an open mind."

His answer seemed to satisfy her. "That's more than most people can say. Now what is it I can do for the FBI?"

Beamon let out a quiet sigh of relief. He wasn't really looking to spend the day debating theology with a woman who seemed to have a less than iron grip on reality. "I'm interested in the Church of the Evolution and I'm told you're probably the most knowledgeable resource in the world."

"May I ask what this is about?" she said, though there was something strange in her voice that made Beamon think she already knew.

"Nothing in particular. I'm just looking for general background information."

"I'm sorry, Mr. Beamon," she said, suddenly sounding like a surgeon telling someone that they had a week to live. "I did do a significant amount of research into the church before I wrote *Betrayal*. But that was in 1986—more than a decade ago." She looked down at the floor and shook her head sadly. "I don't know if I can help you anymore . . ."

"Hey, it's okay, Ernie," Beamon said, reaching out and patting her soft shoulder. She looked like she was about to start crying for some reason. "I'm sure you're going to be a lot of help."

Beamon picked up an old copy of the *Wall Street Journal* lying on the table next to him. He recognized the issue as one containing an article on the church's business dealings. "It looks like you still keep up."

"Only superficially. I've let myself get distracted by work." She punched herself in the leg. "And by my own stupid problems. If only I'd known earlier that you were coming . . ."

Beamon looked over at a wood-framed photograph propped on the table next to him. It depicted a pleasantly plump woman with what looked like a touch football team. "You?" he said, trying to distract her before her mind wandered so far it got lost.

"In happier times."

"When you were with the church?"

She nodded slowly. "When I was an official member of the church."

"What was it that drew you in, Ernie?"

She cocked her head for a moment and then waved a thick arm around at the computer systems that surrounded her. "I'm a programmer, Mr. Beamon. A mathematician and formerly a Baptist. Like many people, I suppose, I had a hard time devoting six days a week to the study of science and technology and then forgetting everything I'd learned on the seventh so that I could be with my God."

"So it was the church's mix of science and theology that appealed to you."

"Initially, yes. Then I read Albert's Bible." Beamon noted the reverent drop in her voice at the use of Kneiss's name.

"I've read it," Beamon said. "Brilliant. He even had me going there a couple of times. And that's not easy."

"Have you ever seen him speak, Mr. Beamon?"

"Please call me Mark. On TV."

She shook her head sadly. "It's not the same. I can't imagine anyone seeing him in person and still doubting that he is who he says he is."

"God?"

"God's messenger. But then, you know that."

"So it was seeing him that hooked you."

"There's so much more, Mark," she said, struggling into a more comfortable position. "It's hard to explain to someone who's never been involved. After you show initial interest, they barrage you. Invitations to dinners, picnics, promises of important business connections, as well as more personal introductions. If you have children, they're invited on camping trips and other activities. I guess they gave me a sense of belonging that I wanted but had never had."

Beamon looked down at the picture again and at the other faces staring out of it. They all had that clean-cut look of optimism that stamped them as Kneissians. "How long were you involved with the church?"

"As a member? Four years."

"Really?"

"You sound surprised."

Beamon laid the picture down. "I guess I expected you to say six months or something. I understand that you wrote a pretty scathing exposé. I assumed you joined, hated it, and left."

She shook her head. "As efficient as the Kneissians are at getting you into the church, they're even better at keeping you there. You have to understand that your entire life is wrapped up with them. I worked as a freelance computer consultant at the time. After a few years, probably eighty percent of my customers were members of the church. I met my boyfriend at a church function. You become too intertwined. And then, of course, there are the psychological factors . . ."

"Psychological factors?"

She looked at him with a strange intensity that was really starting to make him feel uncomfortable. "Are you aware that the Kneissian Bible you buy publicly is only a portion of Albert's writings? That more books exist?"

Beamon took off his jacket and pulled a pad and pen from the pocket. "If by more books, you mean other sections to the Bible, no, I'd never heard that. What's in them?"

"I don't know. You see, it's all a matter of levels. When you enter the church you go in as a Novice or Level One. You're encouraged to take classes and go to counseling sessions in order to improve your standing—your level. Of course, they're quite expensive and you rarely pass the first time."

"How many levels are there?" Beamon asked.

"Eleven last time I counted. I was a Three when I left the church."

"So you're learning what's in these secret books in order to move up?"

"Not exactly. Actually, getting to Level Two has nothing to do with God or religion. The class you have to pass is on—how would you describe it? Manners? General conduct?"

Beamon raised his eyebrows. "Come again?"

"You've got to understand the philosophy of the church, Mark. They're very interested in growth, but they're also interested in quality membership. I guess you could call their first class 'communications.' You learn how to dress, firm handshakes, looking people in the eye when you talk, what fork to eat with at a nice restaurant. That kind of thing. I know it sounds ridiculous, but it works. You've probably noticed that Kneissians project a pretty uniform image."

Beamon nodded and she continued.

"So getting to Level Two isn't very hard. Moving up through the later levels involves more theological training and very strenuous counseling sessions. Those are a lot like the Catholic confession. But, of course, there are other factors."

"Other factors?"

"I started getting a bit disillusioned when I was working on my Four. Level Four, that is. I flunked twice. That's twelve thousand dollars' worth of classes for nothing. I should tell you that at the time, I was making about forty-five thousand dollars a year and living in a one-bedroom apartment with two other women because all my money was going to the church. Despite that, though, it wasn't the money or the time that bothered me, it was the people who were passing. Many of them had done much worse than me in the class."

"Politics," Beamon said knowingly. "It always comes down to politics."

"You're exactly right. I found out later that some of these people were doctors and lawyers and politicians. I was just a lowly programming consultant. In the scheme of things, not that useful to the church."

"And for you, moving through the levels was important?"

"Oh, yes. It is to everyone. I really can't stress how important. Your level and how long you've been a church member are public knowledge, so it's really embarrassing if you're not doing well. The flip side of that is, if you are doing well, there are all kinds of bragging rights. There's a pervasive obsession with levels that the church really encourages."

"What about these other books to the Bible?"

"You don't start getting to look at those until you're a Seven. The rumor is that they're sections from the Bible that will be given to humanity when the Messenger returns."

"Two thousand years from now?"

She nodded. "Obviously, you must be very evolved to understand them. People who are Sevens and higher are treated like royalty. Everyone wants to learn what's in those books."

"The meaning of life," Beamon said.

"Perhaps. I've met very few people who have reached above Six. The 'counseling' sessions become increasingly strenuous and expensive. I've even heard rumors of the use of psychoactive drugs in high-level sessions."

"I find it hard to believe that anyone would submit to that."

"I would have."

Beamon leaned back in his chair and chewed the end of his pen for a moment. "I went to one of the recruiting stations a few days ago. The woman they set me up with must have gone through your 'communications' training. She was very good. Not very taken with me, though, I'm afraid."

Ernie smiled and reached into the small fridge she had parked her chair next to. "Diet Coke?"

Beamon held a hand out and caught the ice-cold can.

"I'm sure you're right on both counts," she said, popping the top on her can and taking a quick sip. "You can't work a potential recruit unless you're at least a Two. And I can almost guarantee that she wasn't, as you say, very taken with you."

Beamon held his hands out innocently. "How can you say that? People love me."

The thick folds in Ernie's face rearranged themselves into a nervous smile. "I'm sure they do, but, again, it's all about levels. Let me guess: you didn't want to sign the register—what they call the guest book."

"Uh, I think I did pass on that."

"You just got a One there. Ask a few tough questions? Tell her you'd heard some negative things about the church?"

"Yeah, probably. A few."

"Well, the first negative question you asked got you a Two. The second, a Three. When you hit Four she'd have asked if you were a reporter."

"She did!" Beamon said, impressed. "She did ask me that."

"They hate reporters. Afraid the press might shine too bright a light into their organization."

"You shined a pretty bright light into it, Ernie. What did you find?"

"Paranoia. When I started getting upset about the politics in the levels, I started talking with people—both active members and people who had quit for one reason or another. I started to get a picture of an organization trying to control everything. Its members, its image, and more and more, the secular world." She sighed deeply. "It didn't take long for me to find out that some of the ex-Kneissians I was talking to were plants. Put there to ferret out anyone who wasn't toeing the party line. I had to go before a council of elders from my parish and they stripped me of my levels. Later I was thrown out."

"Then what?"

"I continued to dig. I must have gone through ten thousand pages of documents and talked to two hundred people. I figured they'd already excommunicated me, what more could they do?" She laughed bitterly.

"I take it there was more."

"At first it was just threatening phone calls. I kept changing my number, but it never did any good. Then the lawsuits started. I've been sued for just about everything you can imagine. I was once sued for sexual harassment by a man I had never met."

"But you won the suits."

"Oh, sure, I won. Every one of them. But I had to declare bankruptcy from all the legal bills. They also made available, to anyone who wanted them, some of the more personal aspects of my counseling sessions—confessionals—which are taped as a matter of routine."

"This is all before the book came out, though, right?"

She nodded. "When the book came out, things went crazy. A man came to my door and threatened me with a knife; I was being constantly followed. Later, I found out that a woman who had befriended me while I was at a really low point was a member of the church and had been directed to subtly drive me to suicide. It almost worked."

She took another sip of her Coke. "I've moved twelve times since I wrote that book. I've been here eight months. They'll find me soon. Then it will all start again—the cars driving by the house too slow, the calls . . ." She suddenly looked deflated.

"What happened with the book?"

"It never went anywhere. The initial print run was twenty-five hundred and they were instantly bought up and destroyed by church members. Then the publisher was purchased by a church-owned corporation set up specifically for that purpose. So then they had the rights to the book and they used those rights to keep it out of the stores."

"Do you think that when Albert Kneiss is gone the church will come back in line?"

Her head jerked as though he had struck her. "Why would you say something like that?"

"Well, Albert—"

"Albert doesn't know about any of this! I wrote the book for him. He knows nothing about what's happening, what they're doing."

"But he must know," Beamon said. "It's his church."

"You're wrong," Ernie spat out. "*She* keeps it from him, relies on his goodness to keep him from suspecting what she's done."

"She?"

"Sara. Sara Renslier. She's the one who's twisted the church into what it is now."

"Tell me about her."

"She's evil."

Beamon frowned. "Could you be more specific?"

"She took over the leadership of the Seven Elders probably twenty-five years ago . . ."

"When the church's membership started to take off?"

Ernie reluctantly conceded the point with a short nod. "She's systematically isolated Albert and now hides behind him and uses his name to control everything. Her and a man named Sines."

"Sines? You got a first name?"

She shook her head. "Just Sines. I know he came to the church from the military. He's the head of security." She ran a finger from her lip to her right eye. "He has a scar here. Hides part of it with a mustache. Rumor has it that he's put together a group of ex-policemen and military people fanatically devoted to Albert."

"Meaning they answer to Sara," Beamon said.

She nodded. "Sara uses the fear of this group to keep the high-level members in line."

"Have you ever met one of them?"

"No. There are probably fewer than ten in total." She pointed to her wrist. "I was told by someone who once met one of them that they have an iron bracelet welded to their right arm. A sign of their devotion to Albert—who probably doesn't even know they exist."

Beamon started gnawing on his pen again, replaying in his mind his struggle with David Passal. He remembered the man's fear and how he'd mistaken them for someone else. During the struggle he had grabbed Beamon's right wrist, and suddenly that fear had disappeared. Passal had immediately stopped fighting and demanded to know who he was.

"Mark? Are you all right?"

Beamon looked up. "Sorry, I was just thinking. What was it you were saying?"

"I was saying that the church has become more sophisticated and efficient now. They pay people not to publish books about them. They don't have to buy publishers anymore. Through their members they control companies that you would never expect. They influence politicians with contributions. Companies owned by church members control a huge number of government contracts that the Elders find interesting—they just make the lowest bid or put a minority in as the head of the company."

Beamon glanced at his watch. He had about a hundred more questions that he'd like to ask, but he was running late. Again. "I'd love to read your book, Ernie. Would you have a copy I could borrow?"

He followed her unbidden as she wheeled her chair down the hall to a narrow set of stairs. She unwedged herself from the chair and began struggling down the steps to the basement, scraping both walls as she descended.

Beamon followed, shaking his head in disbelief. She wasn't crippled at all, just a whale. Couldn't entirely support her body weight out of the water.

The basement was stacked with still more documents, books, and old computer equipment. Except for the poor lighting, it didn't look much different from her office. Beamon flipped through a stack of old computer paper almost three feet high. "This stuff's all on the church?"

"Most of it," Ernie said, struggling to reach a high shelf and pull down a dusty book with a dark green jacket.

"I may want to borrow some of it, if you don't mind."

She waddled over and handed him the book. "It's just primary source material. I've summarized pretty much all of it in the book."

He pointed to the teetering stack of paper at his feet. "What's this?"

"It's a list of the church's membership from 1981."

Beamon kicked at it, trying to make a guess at its weight. "Can I borrow it?"

She walked over to an old computer resting on a card table and turned it on. Beamon winced when she sat down in the metal folding chair in front of it, but the chair managed to hold her with only a slight creak.

"I don't think you really want a hard copy, Mark. There are almost a million names on that printout. Let me put it on disk for you."

She punched a few keys as Beamon approached, and he saw the list of names and other personal information come up in alphabetical order.

"Can you search for specific names?" Beamon asked as she slid a new diskette into the computer.

"Of course."

"Could you do a couple for me? Try Jacob Layman."

She typed in the name of his boss and searched the screen. "No match."

"Would members' children be in there?"

"They should be."

"Try Chet Michaels."

She typed in the name. "I've got a hit on that one."

Beamon frowned and looked over her shoulder.

"Born 1943, joined in 1980," she said, running a plump finger along the screen. Beamon let out a sigh of relief. That would put Michaels in his mid-fifties.

It took almost a half-hour to save all of the names to the stack of disks now stuffed in the various pockets of Beamon's coat.

"Thanks, Ernie. I'm sorry to take these and run, but I'm real late."

"So what is your open mind telling you now, Mark?"

He stopped with one foot on the staircase. "Excuse me?"

"You said you had an open mind where God was concerned. What is it telling you?"

"Nothing. I guess I'm still a devoted skeptic."

Her smile held a trace of irony. Beamon was amazed at how subtly expressive her face was, considering the deep folds of fat surrounding it. "What?" he said.

Ernie struggled out of the chair and across the basement, stopping next to him and supporting herself on the banister. "What are you going to do with what you've learned here today, Mark? Do you know?"

Beamon shrugged. "Same thing I always do, I suppose. Try to use it to find the truth."

"The truth about the church?"

"Maybe."

"Have you ever thought you were being directed by God? That your goals are really His goals? Is it a coincidence that you are here talking to me three weeks before Albert is to take his place with the Lord and Sara is to become the unchallenged leader of the church?"

Beamon suddenly understood the strange looks and the stuff about the dreams. He looked down at her and shook his head slowly. "I'll tell you, Ernie, if I'm the Chosen One, we've got problems. God's really scraping the bottom of the barrel."

31

"WHAT'RE YOU LOOKING FOR?" CHET Michaels said.

Beamon pushed the box onto his new carpet in frustration and began digging through the green folders that had been stacked beneath it.

"I'm trying to find the stuff we got out of Eric and Patricia Davis's safe." He pointed down at the haphazardly stacked boxes that were beginning to take over his office. "It's just not here. I don't even know what half this shit is."

Michaels leaned over one of the boxes that Beamon had already searched and carefully emptied its contents. "Voilà," he said, pulling three unmarked manila envelopes from the bottom.

"You know, those kinds of envelopes do take ink. You could label them," Beamon said, stalking back to his chair.

Michaels looked a little hurt when he sat down and began emptying the contents of the envelopes onto Beamon's desk. "You never try to find stuff yourself, Mark. I figured if you wanted anything, you'd ask me or D."

Beamon scowled. Michaels was right, of course, but he was in no mood to have his tendency toward absentmindedness pointed out to him.

"How'd your meeting with Willard go?" Michaels said, wisely changing the subject.

"Fine."

"Productive?"

"Yeah, it was," Beamon said, finding it impossible to stay mad. "We've got confirmation that Sara Renslier runs the church. As far as Ernie's concerned, Kneiss isn't really aware of what's going on anymore. That could be a biased view, though."

"It'd make sense," Michaels said, looking at the calendar on his watch. "The guy's pretty old and he's said in no uncertain terms that he's planning to die in about three weeks. I would think he'd have pretty much turned over the church to someone by now."

"I suppose so," Beamon said.

"What else did he have to say?"

"Who?"

"Willard."

"It's *she*, actually. And it's Waverly. Willard was a pen name. She painted a pretty vivid picture. Not a very attractive one, though."

"How so?"

"In her mind the church is paranoid and bent on control. Of their members, people they perceive to be their enemies, whoever."

"Maybe *she's* the one who's paranoid. She's the only person who's ever written an exposé-type book about the church. Maybe she had an ax to grind. How'd she come off? Did she seem grounded?"

Beamon shrugged. "I don't know if I'd use the word 'grounded.' 'Wacko' might be more descriptive. But I'll tell you, every time I thought what she was saying was getting a little farfetched, she'd come up with something I could corroborate with what we've already dug up. I also skimmed the copy of her book she gave me and it seems well researched and, well, pretty credible. My gut feeling is that she gave it to me straight."

Michaels gave the thumbs up sign. "So we've found a great resource. All right."

"Maybe," Beamon said in a wavering tone.

"What? She doesn't want to talk to us anymore?"

Beamon shook his head. "No, I reckon she'll give us anything we need. I'm just a little concerned about her motivation."

The young agent's eyes widened. "You think she's a church plant? Like they set her up to feed people misinformation? Wow . . ."

"Ho, Chet. Come on back to reality with me here. All I meant was that she's still loyal to Kneiss—I think she believes he's who he says he is. In her mind, it's this Renslier woman who's causing problems."

Beamon leaned forward and began digging through the pile of documents Michaels had spread across his desk. "She also may think that I've been chosen by God to put the church back on track."

Michaels made a sound like a strangling cat as he stifled a laugh.

"Go ahead," Beamon said. "Laugh."

"Sorry, Mark," Michaels said through a loud guffaw. "It's not that I don't think you'd be a good choice, it's just that I think if God needed someone to do his work on Earth, he wouldn't pick a guy who refers to Christ and His disciples as 'JC and the boys.'"

Beamon found what he was looking for and threw it at Michaels, who was wiping a tear from the corner of his eye. "That's pretty much what I told her—though not in so many words."

Michaels looked at the stock certificates that Beamon had thrown at him, still smiling. "What's up with these?"

"I want you to look into those two companies."

"These are just stock certificates from closely held corporations that Davis had bought into. His investment here is really pretty insignificant. Certainly nothing to kill him over."

Beamon began stuffing the rest of the safe's contents back into the manila envelopes lying on his desk. "According to Ernie, one of the things the church has gotten into is buying up companies that might provide them with information or control over areas they think are important. Apparently they don't do this directly, they do it through various members buying stock."

Michaels's eyebrows rose. "So then it looks like a bunch of unrelated people own the company, but it's actually run by the church. Cool."

Beamon pointed to the certificates. "I don't think the Davises were killed or Jennifer was kidnapped over Eric's ownership in those two companies, but let's see if we can learn something about how the church operates. Might be useful."

Michaels laid the certificates out flat on the desk. "Vericomm, I can already tell you, is a long-distance provider and Internet service."

"Maybe you can pull some information from the FCC? Do it quietly, though."

"I can do better than that—and quieter, too. There are at least two annual reports on Vericomm in one of the filing cabinets in Mr. Davis's home office. I'll go grab 'em and see what I can figure out."

"What about TarroSoft?"

Michaels shrugged. "I don't remember seeing anything on them in any of Mr. Davis's stuff."

"Ever hear of them?"

"Nope."

Beamon stood and began walking toward the door to his office. "Okay, Chet. Run with that and get me what you can on a guy named Sines—he's the head of the church's security. I don't have a first name on him, but I think he's ex-military and he's got a mustache and an obvious scar on his face." He paused with his hand on the doorknob. "I don't want it to get back to him that I'm looking. Not quite ready for that headache yet, okay?"

He didn't wait for Michaels's answer, but pulled the door open and began threading himself through the tightly packed desks and construction equipment that filled the office. The workmen seemed to be less obvious now that the heavy work was done. With a little luck they'd be history in a few weeks.

He made his way to a small cubicle along the far wall, pausing to chat briefly with the young agents who inhabited this part of the office and answer the myriad questions that always seemed to be on the tips of their tongues. He hadn't been doing much of a job on the management end of things lately. Once he got on top of this Jennifer Davis thing, he promised himself, he'd turn over a new leaf.

Beamon poked his head into the cubicle next to him and looked at the back of Craig Skinner, the young man who managed the office's information systems.

"Craig! How're you doing with those disks?"

The young man started and swiveled around in his chair to face Beamon.

He didn't look like he belonged in an FBI office. His hair went well past his shoulders and his interpretation of the dress code was that anything was acceptable as long as you wore a tie with it. But the kid knew his way around a computer, and Beamon wasn't about to lose him over the FBI's obsession with throwing a three-piece suit on everything that came through the door.

"Jeez, Mark. What is this? A copy of the D.C. phone book?"

"Don't worry about it. Are you done?"

"Yeah, I've loaded it into a database. What now?"

"How would I go about searching for a name?"

The young man did some magic with his mouse and a prompt appeared on the screen. "You'd just type it in here. Last name, comma, space, then the first name."

"And what if I wanted to check another name when I was done with that one?"

Skinner pointed to the top of the screen. "Just click here and the prompt will come up again."

Beamon motioned for him to stand. "Why don't you go grab yourself a cup of coffee for a minute."

"Uh, sure," Skinner said, looking a little confused.

Once he was gone, Beamon sat down in his chair and typed in "Davis, Eric."

The cursor turned to an hourglass for a moment and then the name appeared with Davis's birthdate and "August 1968" in the field reserved for the date the person joined the church.

Beamon didn't feel the elation that normally

overtook him when one of his off-the-wall theories started to come together. The prospect of going up against the Church of the Evolution and its eleven million followers wasn't a pleasant one. He was getting too old and too wise for this kind of crap.

He cleared the screen the way Skinner had showed him and typed in the name "Davis, Patricia." It, too, was positive, showing a membership date of January 1968.

The dates indicated that both had been children when they joined. Their parents must have been among Kneiss's original followers. Great.

"Can I come in yet?" Skinner's voice called from the other side of the cubicle wall.

"One second," Beamon said, his fingers hovering nervously over the keyboard. He hated himself for being such a suspicious sonofabitch, but he couldn't help it. Beautiful women with advanced degrees just didn't normally knock down his door.

He typed in "Johnstone, Carrie" and held his breath as the computer searched.

NO MATCH FOUND.

PLEASE REVIEW

SEARCH PARAMETERS.

"Come on in, Craig," he said, abandoning the chair and swiveling it toward Skinner, who took a seat.

"Thanks, Mark."

"Okay, here's the deal," Beamon said. "I want you to run this list against the FBI's personnel list. See if you get any matches. Is that possible?"

"Sure, but it might take some time."

"Okay, but let's keep it quiet. Don't tell anyone anything about this."

Skinner grinned. "I couldn't if I wanted to. I don't know anything."

"You'll be happier that way in the end, Craig. Believe me."

"Come on, Mark. Just give me a little hint. You looking for spies?"

32

"THAT CAN'T BE GOOD," BEAMON SAID, stepping to his right and setting a large box of doughnuts on his secretary's desk.

She covered the mouthpiece of the phone she was talking into and said, "Sorry, Mark. I wanted to warn you."

Beamon leaned out so he could see through the window of his office. Jacob Layman had planted himself in his chair and was staring intently into a folder that Beamon had left on his desk.

"What's his mood look like, D.?" Beamon asked as she hung up the phone.

"I don't think it's good, Mark. He didn't even look at me when he came in. Just walked over to your desk and sat down."

Beamon sighed and began slowly walking toward his door. "You know, D., I was reading a play by Shakespeare yesterday . . ."

She shook her head sadly. "It's not Desdemona."

"Okay, I'll leave you in charge of the doughnuts," he said, pointing at the grease-stained box he'd left on her desk. "If I'm not back in an hour, organize a rescue."

"Jake, how're you doing? What brings you to my neck of the woods?"

Layman closed the folder in front of him and laid it down on the desk. He spent a few seconds tapping at the edges so that none of the paper peeked out. "What are you doing, Mark?" he said without looking up.

Beamon rolled his eyes at Layman's tone. That private school headmaster shit hadn't worked on him when he was kid and it hadn't become any more effective over the last thirty-five years. "I'm walking across the office to get a cup of coffee. You want one?"

Layman pushed a stack of computer disks across the desk. "What are these?"

Beamon looked back over his shoulder, recognizing the disks that contained the Kneissian membership list. Getting the morning off to a pleasant start.

He took a chair across from his desk and tried to make eye contact with his boss. Layman, who looked like he was struggling to maintain control, continued to stare at the folder in front of him.

"Look, Jake, we're both busy men," Beamon said. "You know what's on those disks or you wouldn't have hauled your ass up here from Phoenix. What do you want?"

Beamon regretted his word choice the second they were out of his mouth. Layman looked like he was about to explode all over his new carpet.

"Last time we talked, what did we talk about?"

Beamon took a sip of his coffee. "We talked about the Davis case. That you didn't think the church lead was worth pursuing."

"I don't think that's quite what I said. I told you to *stay away* from the Kneissians on this. That the FBI's taken enough flak already over Waco. And you agreed."

"I agreed that the FBI had already taken enough flak over Waco. Not that the church angle wasn't relevant in this situation."

That did it. Layman jumped up from the desk. "I don't give a shit what you did or didn't agree to. I gave you a direct order and I expect you to carry it out!"

Beamon looked at him calmly in the silence following his outburst. "Look, Jake. I've got a missing fifteen-year-old girl and two adults with their brains painting the walls of their house. I've got the press up my ass twenty-four hours a day wondering why I haven't lived up to my reputation and figured this thing out yet. It's easy for you to shut down lines of inquiry, 'cause the buck stops in my office. If I miss something, it's my ass, not yours."

"Who the hell do you think you are, Beamon?" Layman leaned farther over the desk, making sure his voice was loud enough to carry through the open door of the office to the young agents outside. "You know why you're in Flagstaff? The director had to promote you and give you an office so he'd look good in the papers. There were only three open offices small enough that you couldn't do any real damage. Do you know why you ended up in this one?"

Beamon took another sip from his coffee. The cream tasted like it might be going off. "I guess you're going to tell me."

"Shut up!"

Layman's train of thought got lost in his anger for a moment. Unfortunately, it only took him a moment to find it again. "You're here because I was on vacation. That's it—I was on vacation. The other two SACs were around to threaten to quit if they got you. I wasn't."

He sat stiffly back down in Beamon's chair. "And as for your reputation? It's for being a pain-in-the-ass drunk who stumbled over the solutions to a few high-profile cases. I wouldn't worry too much about protecting that image." Layman paused for a moment, but Beamon kept his mouth shut.

"Your career is pretty much finished, Mark. You know that as well as I do—it has been for years," Layman said, the volume of his voice dropping off. "Mine's not. I still have places to go in this organization and I'm not going to let a glorified supervisor dead-ended in Flagstaff fuck that up for me. Do you understand?"

"Okay, I think I'm ready to talk now," Beamon said, slamming his cup down on the edge of his desk hard enough that coffee sloshed over onto the papers strewn across it. "Am I finished at the FBI? Sure, probably. I've been the Bureau's dirty little secret for years. But you can't always get the job done by kissing the right asses and spouting off a bunch of politically correct bullshit. Sometimes you just got to go out there and get the sonofabitch you're after. And I'm sorry if things get a little politically inconvenient for you, but this seems to be one of those times. So why don't you let me do my job, and maybe, with a little luck, I'll stumble over little Jennifer Davis and we'll both be heroes."

Layman stood and grabbed the disks off the desk. "This is your last chance, Mark. If it wouldn't cause too much speculation in the press, you'd be off this case. I suggest you take the rest of the day off and give some serious thought to your future here."

Beamon leaned back in his chair as Layman stormed out, already starting to replay the conversation in his head. He probably could have handled that better. After a few more moments of contemplation, he decided that he couldn't have handled it much worse. So much for the new, improved Mark Beamon.

He sighed loudly, walked across the office, and leaned out the door. Layman was gone, but his presence was still palpable in the hush that had fallen over the office. Beamon waved at Chet Michaels and then turned to his secretary. "D., I've got a job for you, but you're going to hate me for it." He thumbed behind him to the wall of boxes containing the data on the Davis case. "See those boxes?"

She nodded hesitantly.

"I need one copy of everything in there."

"When do you need them by?" she said, wincing slightly.

"Top priority. I want you to lock yourself in the copy room and try to get it done by midday tomorrow. If anyone else needs the copier, tell 'em to go to Kinko's and save the receipts. Okay?"

She nodded. "I'll get started right after lunch."

"Thanks, I appreciate it." He stepped aside and let a nervous-looking Chet Michaels walk by him and into his office. "Get some of the guys to carry the boxes to the copier for you. They're pretty heavy."

Beamon walked back to his desk and settled into his chair. It was still a bit damp from Layman's back. "How're you coming on Vericomm and TarroSoft, Chet?"

"So-so, Mark."

"So-so?"

"I've got some stuff on Vericomm, but I haven't been able to find anything on Tarro."

"Okay, then. Vericomm."

"Like I told you, they're a holding company for long-distance carriers and a few Internet access providers. Their business is concentrated in small long-distance carriers in about twenty states. They're those ones that you call an 800 number and then punch in your personal ID number before you dial and you get a good rate. Kind of like having a really cheap calling card that you use at home, too."

Michaels pulled an envelope and some glossy papers from his coat pocket and laid them on the desk. "This is the Arizona-based Vericomm subsidiary. I got one of their solicitations about a week ago. Fortunately for us, I'm a procrastinator and haven't sent it in yet."

Beamon reached over and picked it up. The cover letter had NICKELINEAZ in glossy red letters across the top.

"It's a really good deal, actually," Michaels continued. "Five cents a minute, twenty-four hours a day, seven days a week. I have no idea how they stay in business, though. I looked at their financial statements. They're kind of strange."

"Strange?" Beamon said, finishing the solicitation letter and flipping through a stack of NICKELINE stickers and application material.

"Well, they're not a very large company—under thirty million in annual sales."

"Is that unusual?"

"Well, considering they cover, like, twenty states. That's not very many customers per state."

Beamon pursed his lips and shrugged. He was the first to admit that this financial stuff just wasn't his bag. Thank God the Bureau was infested with CPAs.

"It gets more interesting," Michaels promised.

"They lose a lot of money—every year I looked at, so the last three. There isn't a lot of financial data on this type of long distance company, but when you compare them to RMA and some other data I was able to dig up, they're really out of whack."

"Huh?"

"RMA gets financial statements from all kinds of companies and creates a database for financial statistics on different types of businesses. So you can take the statements of any given company and compare them to an average for that industry."

"And they don't line up?"

Michaels shook his head. "For one thing, Vericomm has absolutely no debt. They fund everything—including their losses—through the sale of stock."

"I don't know much about this stuff, but it seems like if you lost money every year, people would stop investing."

"Normally they would. The other thing that's funky is that they have too many fixed assets."

"Come again?"

"They have too much, uh, stuff. All companies have a different makeup of assets and liabilities. Take, say, a consulting firm. You wouldn't expect them to have, oh, I don't know, inventory, say, as high as a grocery store's. A grocery store has tens of thousands of dollars' worth of food and a consultant has, like, a computer and some reference materials."

"Makes sense."

"Well, Vericomm has way too many fixed assets. It's like they have enough equipment to run a company five times as big."

"Maybe they're setting up for a growth spurt?"

"Maybe, but I doubt it. It looks like they've had about the same number of customers for the last three years."

"Okay, good job, Chet. I wouldn't have gotten any of that. Do me a favor; put it in writing. Give me the numbers and details—so I can understand them, though, okay?"

Beamon watched Michaels walk from the office and pulled out his wallet. He searched through his credit cards and the other junk that had accumulated, finally coming up with a bright yellow laminated card. His name and a ten-digit number were emblazoned across it, beneath an orange box with bright red letters spelling out "NICKELINEAZ."

33

THE SNOW-COVERED HILLS STRETCHED OUT as far as Beamon could see, broken only occasionally by a thick stand of pines. He eased the car to a stop in front of a tall iron gate, reluctantly rolling down the window and letting the wind whip the inevitable fine mist of snow through the opening.

The guard who stepped from the small wooden booth to greet him was dressed in the standard garb—blue pants with a stripe running down the length of each leg, solid blue tie, and a down parka with an official-looking patch on the shoulder. The man himself, though, was a little less typical. The way the heaviness in his arms and shoulders tapered to a minute waist was obvious even through his bulky coat. He walked with a relaxed, businesslike stride that said he was more than an eight-dollar-an-hour rent-a-cop. A hell of a lot more.

"I'm sorry, sir. Albert is not available to take visitors right now. If you give me your name and e-mail address, I'll be happy to have him contact you as soon as possible," the man said, putting his hands on the car's windowsill and flashing a courteous smile.

Beamon examined the guard's right wrist, wondering if this might be one of the phantom protectors of the faith that Ernie had told him about.

Unfortunately, if there was an iron bracelet welded there, it was hidden by his sleeve.

The guard's polite speech had a practiced air, suggesting he'd repeated it at least a thousand times before. Obviously, there was a problem with Albert Kneiss's awestruck followers coming to his compound to try to get an audience. Beamon had to admit to being a little impressed by the reaction to his uninvited visit. It wasn't every church that offered timely e-mail access to the Messiah.

Beamon reached into his jacket, noting the slight tensing of the guard's body.

"I'm Mark Beamon with the FBI," he said, pulling his credentials from his pocket and flipping them open. "I'd like to speak with Mr. Kneiss on an official matter."

The guard examined Beamon's ID carefully. "Just a moment, please, sir." He walked back to the guardhouse and picked up a phone. Beamon rolled up his window and dusted off the snow that had accumulated on his dashboard while he waited. It didn't take long.

"Sir, if you continue up this road, you'll come to the main house. Just park right under the portico. There'll be someone waiting for you there."

The man stepped away from the car, and Beamon accelerated through the gate. It was almost a half-mile on the narrow road before he crested a hill that afforded a spectacular view of a small valley dominated by an enormous Tudor-style mansion. The house was beautifully constructed and meticulously maintained, but it sprawled out a bit unnaturally, suggesting that the expansive wings on either side had been an afterthought.

The car skidded a bit as Beamon maneuvered it

down the other side of the hill and pulled up beneath the wide portico at the front of the building.

"Mr. Beamon. Please come in," the woman standing at the front door said as he stepped from the car and started up the steps. "My name is Sara Renslier." She walked through the door and motioned to a beautifully wrought antique coat rack. Beamon hung his jacket on one of the brass pegs and stretched out his hand. "Mark Beamon."

The strength of her grip belied her small stature. "Very nice to meet you, Mr. Beamon. Please follow me."

The mansion was spectacular. It was decorated with an unlikely combination of artifacts from all over the world that seemed to melt into an odd harmony. The pieces all looked fantastically expensive, but they were laid out sparsely enough to maintain a vaguely monastic atmosphere.

Beamon followed the woman obediently as they progressed into the heart of the house. There was nothing that looked even remotely suspicious, but he couldn't help wondering what the chances were that he was within two hundred yards of Jennifer Davis. By the time they entered the small room at the end of the hall, he'd decided they were probably better than fifty-fifty.

"Please take a seat," Sara said, pointing to a heavy-looking leather chair in front of a roaring fire. "Warm yourself."

Beamon sat down and looked around him as Sara made coffee in an ornate press. The room was perhaps a bit more opulent, but beyond that, it differed very little from the one he'd been taken to at the recruiting station. Obviously, the church had figured out the formula that worked, and then didn't deviate from it.

Beamon took the offered coffee and watched Sara settle into the chair across from him. Her short dark hair was not unstylish, but screamed utilitarian. She was perfectly groomed and neatly dressed, as he would have expected from the leader of the perfectly groomed and neatly dressed hordes that had taken over Flagstaff. What he hadn't expected was the air of power and self-control she exuded. He'd met more than a handful of the most powerful men in the world, and there weren't many who sucked the air out of a room like she did. Now that he had met her, he didn't find it the least bit surprising that this woman had been able to take an esoteric cult and turn it into the fastest-growing religion in the world.

What did surprise him was the fact that she was there meeting with him. Undoubtedly she was about to provide a perfectly logical reason why it was going to be impossible for him to speak to Kneiss. The question was, why would a woman who controlled debatably the most efficient religious machine in history meet personally with a lowly ASAC?

She seemed to be waiting for him to speak, so he took a sip of his coffee and started. "As I told the man at the gate, I'd like a few minutes of Mr. Kneiss's time."

"May I ask what about?"

"It's a private matter relating to a case I'm working on."

"Jennifer Davis?"

"Excuse me?" Beamon said, slipping into a suitably coy expression.

"The disappearance of that little girl," Sara said. "I read about it in the papers almost every day."

He considered lying—telling her that it was a

different case—but it was obvious that she knew exactly why he was there. And it was even more obvious that she didn't really care. There was something in her posture, the way she sipped at her cup, that was infinitely condescending.

"Jennifer Davis, yes," he said, pulling a pad from his pocket and flipping though it, purely for show. "Sara Renslier. You pretty much run the church. Is that right?"

She smiled at him as though he was a child who had just added two and two and come up with five. "No. No, it's not. Albert is in control of all parts of his church. I just carry out his wishes as best I can."

"And what are those wishes?"

"That's a fairly broad question," she said, laying her cup down on the leather insert in the table next to her. "Albert is obviously very committed to world charities and the purity of the faith he started. I help translate his ideas into reality. I watch after the mundane details."

"And will you take over the church when he dies?"

"Ascends," she corrected.

"Right. Just a little more than two weeks now, isn't it?"

She nodded politely. "He'll rejoin God on Good Friday, as he has in the past. Who will lead the church when he's gone? That's entirely up to him."

It seemed a bit unlikely that she wouldn't have given that matter a little more thought, but Beamon decided not to press the issue. "May I speak to him?"

"I'm afraid not. He's in Turkey meditating."

"Really? Turkey? How long's he been there?"

"He left in January. He has a great deal to prepare for."

"Yeah, I guess so."

Sara crossed her legs and leaned back into the chair. "If you have a message you want to get to him, I will do my best to pass it along. I can't promise anything, though."

Beamon nodded absently, watching the writhing of the flames next to him. It was pretty much the answer he'd expected. "Does Mr. Kneiss have any living relatives?"

"None that I'm aware of. He's certainly never spoken of any." Her answer was too easy. She'd been ready for that question.

It was time to make a decision on how to play this. There was the smart way, of course—stand up, thank her for her time, and leave. But that seemed kind of boring. The other option was to shoot himself in the foot and see if he could make the ice princess sweat a little.

"I'm afraid I have to insist on speaking with Mr. Kneiss," he said, deciding that the low road had always worked for him before.

Sara's eyebrows rose slightly. "I don't know what you want me to do. He's incommunicado. I already told you that."

"Then make him communicado," Beamon said, wondering idly if Jake Layman was going to put him in front of a firing squad for this or opt for the more traditional hanging. "I have to admit I'm finding it a little hard to believe that you've misplaced your messiah. I suggest you take a couple of thousand bucks from the ten billion you make every year and rent a helicopter. Fly it to whatever mountaintop he's sitting on and hand him a cell phone."

He had to give her credit. For a woman who had probably never been spoken to like that, she retained her self-control admirably. The slight quiver in her jaw and a nearly imperceptible crinkling around her eyes, though, told Beamon he'd just crossed the line. There would be no going back now.

"I'll be back to check on your progress in a couple of days," he said, standing and offering his hand.

That same irritating smile he'd seen earlier reappeared on her lips. "Oh, you will, will you?"

"Yeah. I will."

Beamon dialed his cell phone with one hand and tried to maneuver the car around a slick corner with the other, all while trying to calculate how long it would take for his meeting with Sara Renslier to get back to Layman.

"Mark Beamon's office."

"D.! I want you to get Ken Hirayami on the phone for me. He's our guy in Athens."

"Greece?"

"Yeah. You may have to get him on his home number—it's probably the middle of the night there."

"Okay. That's going to take a few minutes, though."

"No problem. Put me through to Chet while you work on it."

The phone went dead for a few seconds.

"Chet Michaels, can I help you?" came the earnest voice.

"Jesus, Chet, you sound like the guy at the McDonald's drive-through."

"Thanks, Mark."

"Here's what I need you to do for me. Check the

passenger manifests on all flights going to Turkey last month. You're looking for the name Albert Kneiss."

"You think he's fled the country?"

"Hardly. Also, find out if the church has a private jet. If they do, call our guys in Oklahoma City and get 'em to find out if they registered a flight plan for Turkey—you'll need the numbers off the plane's tail."

"How do you suggest I find out if they have a plane?"

"I don't know, be resourceful. Tell them you're from *Corporate Jet* magazine and you heard they've got the biggest cockpit in town. I don't care—"

"Hey, Mark," Michaels said, cutting him off. "D.'s waving at me. I think I have to transfer you back."

"Drop everything and get on this, Chet. I want it tomorrow morning. Understand?"

The phone clicked again and his secretary's voice came on. "Mark. I've got Ken."

"Great. Hey, D.—How're you coming on those copies?"

"You'll have them, Mark."

"You're a goddess."

"Uh-huh. Here he is."

"Ken!" Nothing. "Hey, Ken!"

"Mark? Yeah, I'm here. Do you know what time it is?"

Beamon looked at his watch. "Four-thirty in the afternoon."

"—hole." There was a slight delay on the line that cut off the first part of Hirayami's reply, but Beamon could guess at it.

"Ken, I need a favor. Actually, I need two."

"What?"

"I need you to get the cops in Turkey to find out if there's any record of Albert Kneiss coming in there in January."

"You got a date?"

"Nope."

"Shouldn't be a problem. Everyone has to get a visa when they come in. They either get it here or at one of the consulates. When do you need it by?"

"Yesterday."

"Why did I ask?"

"Look, this is important, Ken. Get me this by tomorrow and I will literally get down on my knees and kiss your ass next time I see you."

"I'll have to give that offer some thought. What's the second favor?"

"I'll get back to you on that."

"Uh-uh. I'm going back to bed, Mark. I'll call you tomorrow."

34

MARK BEAMON PUT HIS HANDS ON HIS LOWER
back and bent backward, trying to stretch the muscles that were twisting his spine. Feeling guilty about
blowing off his new personal trainer last week, he'd
unwisely decided to haul the mountain of boxes containing the Davis file copies to his car by himself.

Satisfied that he wasn't permanently crippled,
Beamon began threading his way through the sea of
desks toward Craig Skinner's cubicle. His young
computer clerk saw him coming, though, and made
a dash for the bathroom.

"Freeze, Skinner."

The young man stopped a few feet short of the
men's room. Beamon grabbed him by the collar and
led him back to his cubicle. "Sit. What the hell happened, Craig? Do you not understand the word 'quietly'? Let me translate: The use of subtlety. Wanton
sneaking. The overzealous practice of stealth. What
did you do, call personnel and ask them if you could
download their files?"

Skinner twisted a lock of his hair around his
index finger. "Well, do you know how long it would
take me to scan in the entire FBI personnel list? I figured it would be easier that way."

Beamon pushed his glasses up and pinched the
bridge of his nose between his thumb and index fin-

ger. "Okay, I've got something else for you, Craig. But this time we're going to keep it between us. And by us, I mean just you and me, right?"

Skinner looked doubtful. "They thought I was a spy or something, man. I got in a lot of trouble, you know? Layman made me delete the whole file."

Beamon ignored his protest. "There's a software company—TarroSoft. I want you to find out what you can about them."

Skinner thought about it for a moment. Finally he turned toward his computer and began working with his mouse. At a screen with Yahoo! written across it, he typed in the word TarroSoft.

"That's weird."

"What?"

"No hits. You sure it's a software company?"

Beamon shrugged. "Not dead sure. But with a name like that I figure it's either software or toilet paper—and I'm guessing it's not toilet paper."

Skinner chewed the end of his pencil, obviously intrigued by the problem. "Let me do some digging and I'll let you know."

Beamon looked at him sternly.

"Subtle digging," Skinner corrected.

Satisfied, Beamon turned, walked to the middle of the office, and jumped up on a chair, opting for a less subtle approach to solving his next problem. "May I have everybody's attention, please? Hello?"

The low buzz of voices that made up the background noise in the office faded and the agents all looked up from what they were doing.

"Thank you. I'd like everyone here—everyone— to write down on a piece of paper what long-distance company they use." He pointed to Michaels. "Then bring them to me at Chet's desk."

Beamon jumped down, feeling another twinge in his back, and then dragged the chair over to Michaels's desk. "Where have you been all day, Chet?" The young agent still had snowflakes clinging to his red hair.

"Workin' for you, Mark."

Beamon dumped out Michaels's inbox and pointed to the empty container as the first people began walking up with scraps of paper in hand. "And what is it you've been doing for me?"

"Freezing to death at a private airport before six this morning."

Beamon didn't let the fact that he was impressed show. He hadn't been at all sure that Michaels could run down the church's plane this fast. "Kind of waited till the last minute, didn't you? What did you find?"

"They do have one private jet capable of making it to Turkey. I got the numbers and called them into the Oklahoma office this morning. They're checking with the FAA."

"What's the time frame?"

"Real fast. I told them it was top priority," Michaels said, taking a manila envelope off the edge of his desk and handing it to Beamon. "I ran some computer checks on the previous address of your new neighbor—Robert Andrews. Kind of interesting. There are seven other people who list that address as their permanent residence. All men. All between the ages of thirty and forty. All ex-military or ex-cops, now self-employed. But then you knew what I'd find, didn't you?"

Beamon looked over his shoulder. The inbox was full of paper, and everyone appeared to have sat back down and gone back to work. "I didn't *know*—it was just a hunch. Ernie told me that Sara Renslier had put together a specialized security group at the church. Fanatics who'll do anything she says. I think you found them."

Michaels looked a little worried. "Based on the records I was able to pull, Mark, these aren't people you want to mess with . . ."

"And you should remember that. What about Sines?"

"Sines sounds like he's probably part of this group. Ex-military—resigned for no apparent reason shortly after being promoted to major. He's forty-one. Lists the church as his employer and Kneiss's compound as his permanent residence. No criminal record. I couldn't find anything relating to what he does for the church—just that he works there. Same as Renslier."

Beamon opened the manila envelope in front of him and wrote each of the names it contained on a piece of legal paper, adding the name of the man watching his condo to the bottom. "I'll be back in a second."

He walked across the office and stuck his head into Skinner's cubicle. "Hey, Craig."

"It's only been a few minutes, Mark!"

"Calm down, son," Beamon said, holding out the paper in his hand. "I just want you to run these names against that list I gave you."

"I told you, Mark. Layman made me delete that file."

Beamon rolled his eyes. Skinner had a hacker's heart. There was just no goddamn way he'd deleted that file. "Run the fucking names, Craig."

"Well, uh, maybe there is a way to reconstruct the file," Skinner said, reaching hesitantly for the sheet.

"Uh-huh," Beamon said, starting back toward Michaels's desk.

"What else you got, Chet?"

Michaels turned his palms upward. "I'm sorry, Mark. Nothing. David Passal's known acquaintances are a dead end—and I don't mean that I couldn't find anybody he knew who might fit the profile—I mean I can't find anybody he knew. The guy was a freaking hermit. Otherwise, there are no local sex offenders with MOs even close, or for that matter the opportunity. Our national search of people who have been involved in this kind of thing so far is a big zero. Recent parolees? Another big fat zero. And we've got nothing on the physical evidence side."

Beamon looked blankly at the young agent. "That's quite a laundry list of things you don't know. So what do you think happened here?"

Michaels let out a loud breath. "Maybe it does have something to do with the church. Or maybe the whole thing was a big coincidence. A fluke."

"How so?"

"What if Jennifer's dad just went nuts? Killed her mom, then himself? Jennifer saw it all. She panics. Runs out into the street where she flags down a passing car. Turns out that the guy who picks her up is a bad seed. Things get out of hand and he kills her. I'm starting to think that one way or another, we're gonna find her when the snow thaws."

"Why didn't she just use the phone? Call for an ambulance?"

"Couldn't stay in the same house with what was left of her folks."

"Reasonable. Why'd she take the gun?"

Michaels shrugged. "I've been thinking about that. She's completely freaked out. She falls to her knees and cries for a while beside her parents' bodies. She's got no relatives living, so she's totally alone. She can't take it. Picks up the gun, puts it to her head, then chickens out. Forgets to drop it when she runs out of the house."

"Why wouldn't she just go to a neighbor's?"

"Maybe the guy in the car saw her running without a jacket toward a neighbor's house and offered her a ride. She'd have probably taken it."

The phone on the desk started to ring, but Michaels ignored it.

"I don't think so, Chet," Beamon said, speaking slowly. "It's good piece of reasoning, but my gut just says its wrong."

"Mine too, actually. That leaves us with the church, but Layman's pretty much shut us down there."

Beamon had purposely kept many of the individual components of the investigation—his visit to Sara, much of the information he'd gotten from Ernestine Waverly—from the young agent. He had a feeling that the less Michaels knew, the better off he'd be in the end.

"Chet!" D. yelled, holding her phone in one hand and waving with the other. "There's a guy from the Oklahoma City office on the line. Says you'll want to take the call."

"Could you put it through, please?" He picked it up on the first ring.

"Hi, Terry. Nothing, huh? Nothing on the commercial flights, either? Hey, thanks for doing this so quick. Yeah, I'll tell him . . ."

Beamon reached out and plucked the phone

from Michaels's hand. "Terry. Mark Beamon."

"Mr. Beamon. How are you, sir?"

"I'm good. Hey, I just wanted to tell you myself how much I appreciate you jumping on this like you did."

"If there's anything else I can do, Mr. Beamon, please let me know."

"Actually, there is, Terry. Tomorrow afternoon I want you to try to pull that flight plan again."

"We've never had problems with the FAA before, Mr. Beamon. I think the information is accurate . . ."

"I'm going to have to ask you to humor me on this one. It's important."

"Of course. I'll call you tomorrow evening."

"Thanks, Terry. I owe you one."

Beamon replaced the handset and looked into the confused face of Chet Michaels. "Another hunch," he explained. "Chet, keep going where you're going on this case. Make sure we didn't miss anything and I'll concentrate on the church. Stay away from that. Okay?"

Beamon grabbed the scraps of papers that had accumulated in Michaels's IN box and walked back to his office.

After going through them, all but two were in his garbage can. He took out a Post-it, wrote his name on it and put it in between the one with his secretary's and Michaels's names.

"D.!" he yelled at the open door to his office. She leaned around the corner.

"When did you sign up for NickeLine?"

"I don't know exactly. It was probably around the same time I took this job. So about a year and a half ago." Beamon heard the phone on her desk start to ring and she disappeared to answer it. Her head reappeared in his doorway a moment later. "It's Ken Hirayami from Athens."

"Put him through, please," Beamon said, picking up his phone.

"Ken! What'd you find out?"

"No record, Mark. As far as Turkey's concerned, he's not in the country." There was a pause over the phone. "Now are you going to tell me what the second favor is?"

"Yup," Beamon said. "Tomorrow afternoon I want you to run the same check again."

"The same check?"

"Yeah."

"I don't know if I want to do that, Mark. I think the Turks would find it a little insulting. It'd look like I was saying they didn't know how to do their jobs. And they do."

"Ken, I got fifty bucks that says they find a record of Kneiss's visa this time through."

"What've you got cooking over there, Mark?"

"Will you do it?"

"I guess I can find someone else to run the search and hope it doesn't get back to the first guy. Yeah, I'll do it."

"Thanks, Ken. Oh, and Ken?"

"Yeah."

"I want my fifty in American." Beamon pushed the lever on the phone down with his index finder and stared at it like it was the enemy. He had to do it, he knew. He had to make the call. But he knew he was going to live to regret it.

He pawed through his Rolodex and dialed one of the numbers he found there, grimacing as it started to ring.

"You've reached Goldman Communications Consultants, leave a message at the beep," a mechanical voice told him.

Goldman Communications Consultants. It sounded so benign. The Goldman part was Jack Goldman. They had worked together years ago when Beamon was just starting with the Bureau and Goldman was just getting ready to retire.

Goldman had started as a telephone repairman when he was still in his early teens and when phones in private homes were probably more the exception than the rule. After he got busted placing bugs for Al Capone's organization, J. Edgar Hoover had taken him under his wing and Goldman had become the king of the FBI's "black bag men."

When Beamon first met him, Goldman was already older than God. And about as cantankerous a sonofabitch as had ever walked the earth. That little personality flaw aside, though, he was the best. Always had been, always would be. The man could bug the incisor teeth of a rabid Doberman.

Despite his undeniable skill, the government wouldn't work with him anymore. His corporate clients, though, were more than happy to put up with his colorful demeanor in return for his ruthless efficiency at finding—and most likely placing—any eavesdropping device ever invented.

"Mr. Goldman, this is Mark Beamon. I have a question that might be up your—"

There was a momentary screech of feedback and then, "Mark! Goddamn, boy, I can't remember the last time I heard from you. Someone told me that you'd screwed the pooch one too many times at headquarters and they sent you off to pasture!" His voice shook with age.

"Uh, hello, Mr. Goldman," Beamon said slowly into the phone, already starting to regret the call. "I'm in Flagstaff now."

"Jesus, son. They did put you in a one-horse town. What do you do there, investigate shoplifting?"

"It's actually a pretty good size—"

"Uh-huh. So what do you want? I'm a busy man, you know."

"Yes, sir. I have a theoretical question. If I bought one of those phone companies where you dial an 800 number and enter your PIN before you call long distance, could I listen in on all the calls that went over those lines?"

"No."

Beamon was momentarily confused by Goldman's answer. Could he have been wrong? "You couldn't? It's impossible?"

"Shit, I don't know if it's possible or not. But why the hell would you want to? Think for once in your life, boy! Why buy a goddamn phone company for millions of dollars when you could hire one of my more unscrupulous colleagues for a few thousand? And then you'd get the goddamn local calls, too."

"But what if you wanted to spy on a group, Mr. Goldman? Let's say you hated, I don't know, Jews. You could offer a great long-distance rate to influential Jews through the mail and get a feel for what they were doing though their long-distance conversa—"

"You saying that we kikes'll do anything to save a few cents a minute on long distance?"

"No, sir. I was just using it as an example—"

"Think we're stupid?"

"No, I—"

"That's an interesting theory you got there, Marko. It's clean—almost no chance of detection. Elegant—except for the part about not getting local calls. I'd have to research it, but off the top of my head I can't think of a reason it wouldn't be technologically possible. Of course, you'd have to have serious computer power to monitor the number of lines you're probably talking about. And a hell of a lot of storage space, too, it wouldn't be practical to have people listening in real-time."

"So, it's possible?"

"What did I tell you? I'm going to have to look into it. It's an interesting concept, though. Interesting. Maybe I should come out there. Get the lay of the land. Yeah, get a feel for what you're into."

Beamon bolted upright in his chair. "No! Uh, thanks anyway, Mr. Goldman, but there's no way I can get authorization for your fee . . ."

"We could work that out, Mark. I'll tell you that I'm getting good and goddamn sick of sweeping the offices of a bunch of fatcats for bugs. Not one of them's got a damn thing to say that anybody would want to listen to, let alone record. Yeah. Maybe I'll come out and give you a hand . . ."

Beamon desperately switched gears and tried another approach. "You know, Mr. Goldman, it's really not much of a case. Embezzlement. I've spent the last three weeks reading through a ten-foot-high stack of paper filled with about a million numbers. Starting to go blind." He paused to see if his words had any effect and then added, "It's not even about that much money," for good measure.

Goldman didn't seem to have even been listening. "Yep. Sounds like you're in over your head again." The phone went dead.

Beamon began banging his head slowly and repeatedly on the blotter that covered his desk. How could this day get any worse?

When he sat back up and looked through the window into the outer office, he saw Jake Layman, flanked by two rather serious-looking men in dark suits. The speed at which they were moving his way seemed to answer his question.

"That's them over there," Layman said, pointing to the boxes stacked along the wall. He looked up at Beamon. "Are those all the Davis files?"

"Afternoon, Jake. I'd ask you to sit down, but my chair is otherwise occupied."

"Are those all the files?" he repeated angrily.

Beamon watched the two men who'd burst through his door alongside his boss struggling to lift the overflowing boxes. "That's all of them."

Layman balled his fists and pressed them against Beamon's desk as he leaned toward him. "I got a call from Travis Macon today." Beamon recognized the name of one of Arizona's senators. "You know what he said?"

Beamon shrugged.

"He said that he got a call from one of his constituents at the Church of the Evolution yesterday. That you went to one of their most sacred buildings and started throwing around threats."

Beamon smiled weakly. He didn't regret the way he'd handled his meeting with Sara Renslier—he needed to shake this case loose. What he *was* starting to regret was the way he'd handled Layman. His boss probably wasn't a bad guy. Just trying to play it smart and not suffer the repeated screwings that Beamon had brought upon himself. That was fair.

"Look, Jake. I'm sorry. I shouldn't have gone in there without talking to you first; sometimes I can be kind of an . . . asshole. Tell your guys to go get a cup of coffee and we'll shut the door and I'll lay out what I've got on this case. I think once you've heard—"

"I didn't ask you what you think," Layman yelled. "I just spent two hours on the phone getting a lecture on the meaning of religious freedom from one of the most powerful senators in the country! You are off this case, Beamon. I told you twice— clear enough for even you to understand—to back off. I've written a full report to headquarters about your conduct and I'm telling you that you don't have many fuckups left. You're lucky to still have a job."

Beamon suddenly came to the realization that every time he tried to be reasonable and maybe even lightly kiss an ass or two, it was like throwing gas on a wildfire. It was time to face the fact that he just didn't have the gift.

"I don't feel lucky, Jake."

Layman stormed over to the remaining boxes, picked up one that was too heavy for him, and refused to put it back down. He looked a little like a penguin as he teetered out of the office toward the elevator.

35

BEAMON HAMMERED ON THE DOOR OF THE small house again, this time harder. "Ernie! It's Mark! Open up."

He knew she was home. There were no tire marks in the driveway and little chance that she could negotiate the snow-covered walk on foot or in her thin-tired wheelchair.

Beamon bent at the waist and put his face close to the peephole so that she could see him. A moment later he heard a chain rattling on the other side of the door.

"Ernie! Damn, I was starting to get worried."

"I'm sorry. I was downstairs," she said, backing her wheelchair away from the door.

He followed her as she glided down the hallway, trying to decide what he was going to do. "I lied to you, Ernie."

She stopped for a moment but didn't turn around. "The difference between a saint and a hypocrite is that one lies for his religion, the other by it." She gave the wheels another push and they passed through the door to the cluttered office at the back of the house.

"Albert Kneiss?"

"Minna Antrim. But it was one of Albert's favorite quotes." She picked up a piece of pizza from her desk and slid the steaming end of it into her mouth.

"I told you that the questions I was asking about the church didn't relate to the Jennifer Davis case. That isn't entirely true."

She peered out at him through the folds of flesh on her forehead but seemed to be seeing something else. "I know," she said finally.

There was a casual thoughtfulness in her voice that for some reason made Beamon believe her. "How did you know?"

"Because I dream about *her*, too."

Beamon questioned his strategy for the fiftieth time since leaving the office. Spilling everything he'd learned and suspected about Jennifer and the church to a morbidly obese woman prone to ecstatic visions seemed a little stupid. But what choice did he have? Layman would make damn sure he wouldn't have access to the Bureau's resources to run down the church. And he wasn't going to get this done alone.

He took a deep breath, forcing his doubts from his mind. At this point there were no other options. But if she started showing any signs of stigmata, he was history. "Do you understand the connection between Jennifer and the church, Ernie?"

She shook her head. "God hasn't seen fit to reveal that to me. I assume that's why He sent you."

"This is just between us, right, Ernie? You, me, and God. I'm about to tell you some things even the guys at my office don't know."

"Of course."

Beamon hesitated. Getting her involved in this wasn't fair. It wasn't her job. What the hell was he doing here?

"Are you all right, Mark?"

"Look, Ernie. You've come up against the church before and look what happened. Maybe this isn't such a good idea." He started to stand. "I've changed my mind. You don't need to be involved in this."

"Please sit down, Mark." Ernie said. "I already am involved in this. I have been for years. I thought that God had directed me to write my book—to warn Albert about what was happening to his church—and for all these years I thought I'd failed Him. Now I know that my real purpose was to be here for you."

Beamon hesitated and finally sat back down. He was feeling increasingly uncomfortable and dishonest—like he was a fraud playing to this woman's faith.

"Okay, Ernie," he said slowly. "You're in, but I feel like I should tell you again that I don't for one minute believe that I'm being directed by God. I just want to find this girl so I can look like a hero and twist the knife in my boss. If, as a by-product, Sara Renslier takes a beating and your church gets the overhaul you think it needs, then fine—but in the end, I don't really care. It's not my job to save people from themselves."

She smiled. "It doesn't really matter what you believe. What either one of us believes. God will do what He will do."

Beamon took off his parka and threw it on the floor after extracting his copy of the Kneissian bible. He pulled a couple of legal-sized sheets of yellow paper from the book and smoothed them out on his lap. On the sheets, he'd sketched out the theory that had woken him up at 2:00 A.M. that morning. What he needed from Ernie was for her to tell him he was wrong.

"What's that?" Ernie asked, wheeling her chair around and handing Beamon a slice of pizza. He accepted it gratefully.

"It's something I want you to help me think about."

She craned her thick neck and looked at the unintelligible writing connected by undecipherable arrows and grids.

"I think better in pictures," Beamon explained. "Let me translate." He took a bite of pizza and slurred through a mouth full of cheese and dough. "Fact number one: Jennifer is Albert Kneiss's granddaughter."

Ernie shook her head. "Carol Kneiss died childless."

"Actually, your research wasn't entirely accurate with regard to her death. Carol Kneiss died Carol Passal in a fire in the early eighties after changing her name and moving a number of times. I'm guessing that she knew she was being watched by the church and that she was afraid for her daughter."

"I didn't know . . ." Ernie said sadly.

"Fact two. Well, actually, this is more of a strongly supported hypothesis, but let's raise it to the exalted status of fact. Eric Davis killed his wife and committed suicide. Both had been members of the Church of the Evolution since the late sixties."

"What? Why?" Ernie stuttered.

"They adopted Jennifer shortly after her biological parents' death—I'm guessing at the direction of the church."

"But why would they . . ."

Beamon held his hand up and silenced her. "I thought it was to cut Jennifer off from her support system. The church couldn't kill them without alienating Jennifer and they couldn't leave them alive because she'd have a home and family to get back to. And what better way to show Jennifer their strong belief and dedication to the church?"

"So you think they're trying to brainwash her to replace Albert?"

"I did. Until last night, I was convinced that when Kneiss died, the church would tell the world they had her. They'd have her say that she knew Albert was her grandfather all along. That her father went nuts, killed her mother and himself, and she ran to granddad—her only living relative. The church elders would swear they didn't know anything about it till Albert told them on his deathbed." Beamon took another bite of the quickly cooling pizza. "Then Jennifer is inserted as head of the church. Easy as pie."

Ernie shook her head. "Except one thing. Sara Renslier will never give up her power over the church. She gives God and Albert almost no credit in building it—she believes that it's hers." The hatred in her voice cut through the air.

"I met Sara," Beamon said. "And I got the same feeling. That, combined with the fact that Albert's already dead, is what woke me up last night."

Ernie jerked back in her wheelchair so hard that it drifted back a foot. "Albert isn't dead. He can't be. Not until Good Friday."

"I know this is hard for you, Ernie, but let me finish. I tried to get in to see Albert the day before yesterday. Sara told me he was in Turkey meditating."

Ernie looked like she was about to say something, but Beamon ignored her and continued. "There's no record of him entering Turkey, nor is there a record of him taking a commercial or private flight to Turkey. Why would Sara keep me from talking to him? The best reason I can come up with is that he's dead. He must have ordered Jennifer's retrieval before he died. Sara wouldn't have wanted to, but she would have had to obey. So we can hypothesize he was still alive as of the day Jennifer was kidnapped—give or take. Then, at some point since then, he's died. I mean, the guy was pushing ninety and hadn't been seen in public for years. He had to have been on his last legs."

"But he can't die until Good Friday. That's God's will!" Ernie repeated in a voice tinged with desperation. "What if Sara has isolated him completely? Taken over . . ."

Beamon shrugged. "Maybe, but we know he wasn't isolated before Jennifer was kidnapped—he must have given Sara the order in front of a group of people, probably the Elders, or else she could have just ignored it. And I think it would have been difficult for Sara to suddenly isolate him in his final days when everyone is wondering what exactly to do with their new leader, don't you? No, the simplest answer is the best in most cases. He's dead."

Beamon doubted he was ever going to win Ernie over with the dazzling logic of his argument. Logic was oil to religion's water—always had been. She'd need more.

He opened his copy of the Kneissian Bible to a page marked with a Post-it note. "There is a way that he could be dead, Ernie."

She looked at him blankly, obviously still struggling with what he'd told her and the credibility she thought God had bestowed on him.

"It says here that Kneiss hasn't always been the Messenger, right?" Beamon said, trying to coax her out of her stupor. She didn't respond.

"Right?" he prompted.

"Yes. Yes, that's right. Our Bible specifically names three of his incarnations. Kneiss, Jesus, and before that Persiah. Eventually God will take him to his reward and he'll be replaced by another, like he replaced the one before him."

Beamon flipped to another marked page and began reading. "I was once flesh like you . . ."

Ernie finished the passage in a voice so quiet that Beamon had to lean closer to hear. ". . . full of fear, doubt, and hatred . . ." She looked up at him. "It's central to our belief. That the Messenger was once human and became more. An example to all of us."

Beamon closed the book slowly, feeling the tightness at the bottom of his stomach cinch down a bit more. He *was* right. Somehow he'd known he would be. "Follow me now, Ernie. Kneiss is dead, but he didn't ascend on Good Friday. That can only mean one thing, right? That he's served God long enough. That he has been accepted into heaven."

She still didn't seem to be fully tracking on what he was saying, but she nodded with enough authority for him to continue. "To replace Albert, God will choose a worthy human being, right?"

Ernie nodded again.

"We know that Sara isn't going to be happy about turning over the church she spent a quarter of a century building to an adolescent girl with a ring in her nose, so she needs to get rid of her,"

Beamon paused. "The question is, how far would Sara go?"

He could see from Ernie's expression that his words were beginning to sink in. She reached out and grabbed his arm in her soft hand. "Of course, it's the only way she can protect her position. If Albert is dead, she could tell the other elders anything. And if she told them that Jennifer had been chosen . . ."

Her voice faded away and Beamon finished her thought. "Then Jennifer has to ascend on Good Friday."

Ernie's hand tightened around his arm. "And then there will be no one. No one but her!"

Beamon chewed on his lip, wishing for once that his instincts had failed him. He'd come hoping that he'd missed something. Hoping that Ernie's intimate knowledge of the church would point him in another direction. He looked at the calendar on his watch. Fifteen days until Good Friday. If he was right, and his gut told him he was, he had to find Jennifer in the next two weeks or he never would.

Beamon stood and patted Ernie on the back, trying to comfort her as her sniffling turned into sobbing. He wondered if it was for Jennifer or if it was the final realization that the church she loved had turned so far from God.

"Ernie. Ernie? Come back to me now. We can still turn this thing around if we work together." She sobbed louder. "Come on, Ernie. The Bureau's left me hanging on this one. You and I are all Jennifer's got. We're all the church has."

She wiped at her eyes with her sleeve and her sobbing faded back into sniffles.

"I want you to do something for me, Ernie. I

want you to run your old Kneissian membership list against lists of influential people. Give me an idea of who we might be coming up against."

She looked up at him. "What . . . what kind of lists?"

"I don't know exactly. Politicians. *Who's Who.* World's richest people. That kind of thing. Whatever you can think of. Are you up to it?"

She nodded. "But I want you to do something for me in return."

"Sure."

"Pray with me."

She pulled at his sleeve and he sank to his knees next to her wheelchair. She squeezed her eyes shut and began moving her lips soundlessly. Not really knowing what to do, he bowed his head and waited for her to snap out of it.

36

BEAMON ADJUSTED HIS READING GLASSES TO a more comfortable position on his nose and slid a withdrawal slip and his driver's license through the teller window. "I'd like to get five thousand dollars from my savings account, please."

The teller looked the two documents over briefly and then punched a few keys on the terminal next to her. "Just a moment, please, sir."

Beamon felt a nervous twinge as the young woman hurried off and disappeared through a door at the back of the teller line. His fears were dispelled, though, when she reappeared a few moments later and started counting hundreds onto the counter. When she was finished she slid an envelope to him and he stuffed the cash into it.

"Come and see us again, sir."

Beamon smiled and walked back out onto the sidewalk, pausing to watch the flare of orange on the horizon slowly deepen and cast a red glow over the mountains. He stood there for a few minutes, filling his lungs with the cold dry air and trying to focus his mind on the most urgent problems facing him. There were so many to choose from—the fight he'd purposefully started with the eleven million members of the Church of the Evolution, the tenuous grip he had on his job, the fact that there was a good chance that Jennifer Davis had only two weeks before Sara sacrificed her on the altar of power and influence.

Beamon sunk his hands into the deep pockets of his parka and jogged down the sidewalk toward a dully flickering PACKAGE LIQUOR sign a block and a half away.

In his two months in Flagstaff, he'd been into that particular liquor store more times than he'd like to admit, but this was the first time he'd set foot in the attached bar. It was about what he imagined. Dark and worn, with the strangely comforting smell of age and countless spilled drinks.

It was almost completely empty, he saw as his eyes adjusted to the gloom. There was a woman in a dark coat to his right, speaking to the bartender as though she knew him well. Across the room, in the booth next to a dead jukebox, he could see the thick brown hair of his favorite computer nerd, Craig Skinner.

Skinner had become a little paranoid after the unfortunate incident with the Kneissian membership list and Jake Layman. He'd taken Beamon's lecture on keeping things quiet a little too seriously, insisting that they meet away from the office in order to give him what would undoubtedly be a rather mundane report on TarroSoft.

Beamon had picked the place. Figured he might as well kill two birds with one stone—his beer inventory was getting dangerously low.

Beamon sneaked up behind the young man and leaned in close to his ear. "The blue moose howls at the moon," he whispered.

Skinner jumped and almost spilled his drink. He was still clutching at his chest as Beamon slid onto the bench across from him.

"Jesus, Mark! You almost gave me a heart attack!"

"If you don't give the countersign, I'm going to have to kill you."

"You said be subtle!"

Beamon nodded and lit a pre-rolled cigarette. He had said subtle.

"So what have you got for me, Craig?"

"I talked to some friends . . ."

Beamon stopped in mid-drag and raised his eyebrows.

The young man held his hands out. "Subtly. I talked to them subtly. TarroSoft is a holding company—they don't actually produce software themselves. They own BiblioNet and apparently do software design work for the telecommunications industry. Mostly for a company called Vericomm."

"Vericomm I've heard of, but what's BiblioNet?"

"You know, the company that created the software for the national interlibrary loan system?"

Beamon looked at him blankly.

"You know. Have you ever tried to check out a library book and they didn't have it, so they ordered it from another library?"

"Yeah, I guess."

"That's the interlibrary loan system. It used to be state by state, but now it's nationwide. BiblioNet created the software for the system and now they manage it under a government contract."

Beamon took another deep drag on his cigarette and blew the smoke out through a thin smile, appreciating the irony of Skinner's report. The FBI had tried for years to get the right to track what books people were buying and checking out. There was a pretty strong argument that keeping tabs on books relating to poisoning, bombs, murder, and so on could be a powerful tool in the right hands.

Unfortunately, there was just no way that kind of a Big Brother tactic was going to fly in the U.S. of A. Not for a government agency, anyway. But what about a private organization? Chet Michaels had received his NickeLine solicitation about a week after Beamon had sent him crawling through the local libraries looking for information on the church. He'd assumed that Michaels had simply run into an astute Kneissian librarian. He took another drag on his cigarette. It was that kind of small thinking that was going to make Jennifer Davis dead.

"I can probably get more, if you need it," Skinner continued. "But I won't be able to be as quiet about it . . . I don't need any more trouble from Layman, Mark. I don't know if you noticed, but I don't really fit in at the Bureau. You're, like, my only ally."

"No, that's what I needed, Craig. Thanks." Beamon tossed a few bills on the table for Skinner's drink and slid out of the booth.

"What about the names I asked you to run against that database?"

"All positive but one."

"Okay, thanks. I'll see you at the office tomorrow."

Beamon walked through a door next to the bar and into the attached liquor store. He grabbed a twelve-pack of Pabst Blue Ribbon out of the cooler, then walked along the rack of red wine against the wall. He examined a few labels, but they meant nothing to him. Finally, he decided to follow the theory of "you get what you pay for." He pulled the most expensive bottle out of the rack and took a place in line behind a man in a tall cowboy hat who was making a less than persuasive argument about the Communists' and Democrats' involvement in raising the price of chewing tobacco. Losing interest in the debate, Beamon let his mind wander back to Sara Renslier and her church.

He'd underestimated her, he knew now. He'd read Ernie's book and talked to Volker at the German Embassy, but in the back of his mind he'd considered both of their reports a bit suspect. Some people just had conspiracy on the brain—anyone who'd been with the Bureau for as long as him knew that. How many times had he been surrounded at a party by people wanting the inside scoop on the space aliens that had really killed Kennedy or the CIA/KGB team that had developed the AIDS virus?

But now here he was, tilting at an organization with millions of followers and a yearly income that would give it a respectable position on the Fortune 500 if it were a corporation. They were watching what people read and—though he hadn't gotten Goldman's confirmation yet—they were probably listening in on the long-distance phone conversations of some of the country's most influential people. And then there was the small matter of that group of ex-military nutcases fanatical enough to weld bracelets to their wrists.

Beamon pulled his credit card from his wallet and laid the beer and wine on the counter as the cowboy walked away, still grumbling.

"How are you today, Mr. Beamon?" the man at the register said.

"I've been better, Barry. You?" He was in this store regularly enough to have become a favored customer. He would probably put braces on Barry's kids' teeth before he got transferred out or canned.

"I'm good, Mr. Beamon. Thanks for asking."

"The kids?"

Barry frowned and ran Beamon's credit card through the machine again. "They're good, too. Taking them to their mother's house for the weekend."

The skin above Barry's nose creased as he looked down at the little black keypad next to the cash register.

"Problem?" Beamon said.

"It doesn't seem to want to accept your card. Could you be maxed out?"

Beamon shook his head and handed the man his other card, though he didn't have much hope for it.

"How you doing on that little Jennifer Davis girl?" Barry asked as the machine decided how it felt about Beamon's second credit card.

"Working on it. See what happens."

The man nodded knowingly and looked down at the keypad again, obviously a little embarrassed. "It doesn't like this one either, Mr. Beamon. There must be something wrong with the machine. Let me put it on your account."

Beamon took a deep breath and let it out slowly. "Thanks, Barry. And while you're at it, could you throw in a carton of Marlboros?"

"I thought you rolled your own," he said, pulling down the carton and laying it on top of the beers.

"Oh, I did. But I think I might be needing them faster than I can roll 'em for a while."

Beamon sat in his car and ceremoniously bent his credit cards back and forth until the pieces littered the floorboard. He stared at the brightly colored shards of plastic lying at his feet and thought about what they represented.

What could the church hope to gain by getting their lackeys to screw with the credit of an FBI executive? In the long run, nothing but trouble. So why expose themselves and their tactics so blatantly? He could only come up with one answer—that he was right about their plans for Jennifer.

They just needed to distract him for the next two weeks. At the end of that time, when Jennifer's body was being used to help prop up one of their new cathedrals, the church would use its money and influence to silence any report of their attacks on him. At worst they would make a quiet statement apologizing for their overzealous members' treatment of him, knowing full well that at that point he wouldn't have a prayer of connecting them to Jennifer or her parents.

37

BEAMON STOOD OUTSIDE THE DOOR OF HIS condo and gently twisted the doorknob again. He vividly remembered locking it when he'd left that morning and now there it was, unlocked.

He looked over his shoulder at the front windows of the condo occupied by the guardian angel the church had so thoughtfully provided him. As usual, it was dark. There was just enough light reflecting off the snow, though, to see that the curtain was propped back enough for someone to see out. He could almost feel the crosshairs tickling his forehead.

Beamon pulled his gun from its holster and slipped into his living room as quietly as the ice-encrusted door would allow. The battalions of well-armed Holy Rollers that he expected to find weren't there. The room was empty.

As he worked his way across the living room, he noticed a strange hum coming from his bedroom and froze. The sound was undoubtedly mechanical in origin. Some kind of a booby trap?

He considered backing his way out of the condo and calling for backup, but decided against it. What if it was nothing? He didn't need to give Layman any more ammunition regarding his alleged paranoia.

He paused for a moment with his back a couple of inches from the wall next to the door to his bedroom and then spun smoothly into the opening.

The man standing by his bed didn't seem to notice Beamon's arrival and continued examining pieces of his disassembled phone, looking up at the screen of an open laptop computer every few seconds.

"You're clear here, Mark," the man said as Beamon holstered his sidearm.

He hadn't laid eyes on Jack Goldman in more than five years. The decade hadn't been kind to the old man. His white hair had thinned considerably, revealing wrinkles across his scalp that made it look like it was a size too big for his skull. The thickness of his glasses seemed to have more than doubled and now looked too heavy to be propped up by the gnarled nose beneath them. The lenses distorted light so badly that the middle of Goldman's head seemed to flow like liquid when he moved.

"Mr. Goldman," Beamon groaned. "What're you doing here?"

The old man turned away and began collecting the parts of the phone scattered across the bed. "What the hell's it look like I'm doing, boy? I'm sweeping your house. And I'd thank you to use a more grateful tone with me. I normally charge two thousand dollars." He paused. "Plus expenses."

The phone was about ninety percent reassembled when it started to ring, but Goldman was having trouble timing the tremors in his hands efficiently enough to plug the cord back in. Beamon walked over to him and tried to offer a hand, but was stopped short when Goldman grabbed his cane and hit him across the shins with it.

"Jesus Christ," Beamon howled, bending over and grabbing the leg that had taken the brunt of the impact. "What the hell did you do that for?"

"Don't think I can put a phone back together? I've been taking phones apart and putting them back together since . . ."

Beamon hobbled back out into the living room and out of range of Goldman's voice in time to grab the phone in the kitchen. "Yeah, hello," he said, sitting down on a stool and continuing to rub his shin.

"Is this Mark Beamon?" The voice was lightly accented. "This is Hans Volker at the German Embassy."

"Hans! An unexpected pleasure. How are you?"

"Mark. Thank God. I'm fine, but how are you? I've been hearing some very disturbing things."

"I've been getting a lot of that lately. What exactly are you hearing?"

Volker's voice was a bit hesitant. "I have to have your word that what I'm about to tell you is just between us, Mark."

"Sure, Hans. Just between us."

"We have a few well-placed . . . informants inside the Church of the Evolution. You suspected as much, I'm sure, but you can see how this kind of, uh, monitoring, if it became public, could be very embarrassing to us."

"Like I said, Hans. Just between us."

"Your investigation of the church is generating quite a lot of interest, Mark. Quite a lot. My sources tell me that the church is convinced that you believe they're involved in the kidnapping of Jennifer Davis. They are very concerned about this, and about your continued efforts to penetrate the outer layers of their organization."

Beamon grunted into the phone. He wasn't

happy about how public this all seemed to be getting, but there wasn't a hell of a lot he could do about it now.

"Frankly, Mark, I'm becoming concerned about your safety."

"How so? "

Volker cleared his throat nervously. "The church has a significant number of weapons in its arsenal to deter this kind of inquiry. They've made quite an art of keeping their business private. But you probably already know that."

"Sticks and stones, Hans."

"It goes further than that, Mark. It's come to our attention that the church may have formed a security force that could be used for violence against people who aren't persuaded by their normal methods."

"Are you sure about that?"

"I'm not," Volker admitted. "It's hearsay, really. I'm concerned that if they've already guessed that you won't succumb to their normal techniques, and if this group actually exists, you could be in physical danger."

Beamon walked over to the refrigerator and pulled out a beer. "I appreciate the warning, Hans. Believe me, I'm doing everything I can to protect myself . . ."

"One more thing, Mark. I believe you know a man named Jacob Layman?"

"He's my boss. The SAC Phoenix."

"There's some very circumstantial evidence that the church may have influenced Mr. Layman's appointment to that position."

Beamon gave the beer bottle's cap a hard twist and tossed it in the sink. He'd already considered that possibility. Layman had final authority over the office covering the Kneissians' back yard. And it was Layman who was so desperately against the investigation into the church.

"I appreciate the heads-up, Hans. Anything else you can tell me?" Beamon said, watching the stooped form of his latest problem as it hobbled into the living room.

"To get out of town for a while?"

"Can't do that."

"Well, then I'll tell you to be careful. And that I'll do whatever I can for you. Do you still have my number?"

"I keep it right here, close to my heart."

"Good luck, Mark."

Beamon caught him before he hung up. "Hey! Hans!"

"Yes?"

"Answer a question for me. What long-distance service do you use?"

There was a pause over the phone. "Um, AT&T, I think. I'm honestly not sure."

"So you just pick up the phone and dial—no codes or anything."

"I just pick up the phone and dial. Why do you ask?"

"Just something I've been working on. Nothing important. Thanks again, Hans."

Beamon hung up the phone and chewed at his lower lip. This was going to get ugly. He could feel it coming.

"What's with the cane, Mr. Goldman? You actually need it or is it just a weapon?"

"Sprained my ankle skydiving," the old man grumbled.

Beamon laughed. As best as he could remember, he'd never heard Goldman say something funny. At least not on purpose.

"What're you laughing about, boy?"

Beamon looked down at the old man's ankle and then at his cold expression. "You're serious? What the hell were you doing skydiving?"

Goldman shrugged, causing the hump growing between his shoulders to rise and fall. "Never did it before. It was stupid, though."

"Stupid?"

"They jump right on either side of you," Goldman said in a disgusted tone. "Don't let you make your own decisions."

"When to pull the cord?"

Goldman shook his head. "I just turned ninety, Mark. It's whether to pull the cord now."

Beamon almost laughed again, but something told him that the old man was serious. He decided to change the subject. "What'd you come up with on Vericomm?"

"Is that the long-distance company you were asking about? Never heard of them."

"It's a holding company. They're called Nicke-LineAZ around here."

Goldman hobbled over to the sofa and leaned against the arm. "Okay, sure. They're NickeLineNY in New York."

"Do you use them?" Beamon asked. He'd never really considered it, but Goldman—the top man in corporate eavesdropping countermeasures—would be an obvious target.

"I get offers every now and again, but I ain't never found a good reason to actually *pay* for long-distance service."

"So have you had time to research my question? Is it possible?"

"For a small carrier to listen in on long distance? Probably not for a standard company. They rent phone lines from the big boys, like AT&T, but calls just go through whatever line is available at the time. But the kind of company you describe is IP based—IP stands for Internet Protocol. That type of system compresses analog signals and routes them through the Internet. It'd be expensive and hardware-intensive as all hell, but a company like that *could* listen in on calls."

Beamon remembered the devastating losses taken by NickeLine and the fact that they owned far more equipment than they should. It looked like he was right again, but he was having a hard time getting his arm around exactly what that meant.

What did Sara know? Goddamn near everything about everything, he guessed. And another interesting question—who could he trust? Even if Jake Layman wasn't a Kneissian, what had he said over a long-distance line that they could use to persuade him of the righteousness of Kneiss's God? He *was* starting to get a clearer picture of the Church's vaunted investment record, though. Half the corporate executives in the U.S. were probably NickeLine patrons.

Beamon looked down at the old man and took another pull from the beer bottle. What was he going to do with him? Trying to cut loose from him was pointless. Jack Goldman did whatever the hell he wanted. And right now, he wanted to be involved in this case.

"Who we after, anyway?" Goldman said.

Beamon figured there was no way he was going to get rid of him, so he might as well make the best of it. He really *was* the best in the world. "The Church of the Evolution, Mr. Goldman. I think they're involved in the Jennifer Davis kidnapping."

"The Kneissians? Those goddamn weirdos? Christ. I say we return the favor."

"The favor?" Beamon said.

"I'll show those assholes a thing or two about bugging phones. We'll be able to hear 'em taking a dump when I get through with 'em."

Beamon held his hand up. "There's no way I'm going to get a court order for a tap, Mr. Goldman. So we're gonna have to forget that."

"Court order? What the hell's wrong with you? Show a little initiative."

There was a knock at the door, and Beamon slid off the stool and started across the living room. "I'm still an FBI agent, sir. No illegal wiretaps."

Beamon started opening the door but stopped halfway and squeezed through the opening. "Carrie!" he said loudly, trying to drown out Goldman's voice.

"If Hoover was still alive, I'd have wires so far up those guys' asses, they'd chip a tooth on 'em when they ate!"

"How are you?"

She looked at the door. "What was that?"

"What? Oh, my uncle. He's up for a visit. A brief visit. He's a little crazy—excuse me, I didn't mean to say 'crazy.' Older'n God, you know? Worked on the construction of the Roman aqueducts."

She smiled. Beautifully. "Can I meet him?"

Beamon shook his head a little too violently.

"Not decent. Never wears pants. Something about letting his legs breathe."

She smirked and took one last suspicious look at the door. "I haven't seen you since we had dinner. Are you avoiding me?"

"No," Beamon said firmly. "I am definitely not avoiding you. In fact, I was planning on coming over to see you tonight, but . . ." He thumbed at the door. "Hadn't really expected company."

He reached behind him for the knob. "I'm going to take Uncle Jack to where he's staying and then I'll be back. You'll be up for a few hours, won't you?"

"He's not staying with you?"

"Uh, doesn't want to. Hates my place. And he's not really that crazy about me, either."

She turned and began walking toward the stairs. "If it's past eight, don't ring the bell. Emory'll be asleep."

38

THAT HAD BEEN UNPLEASANT.

For a few minutes there, Beamon had thought he was going to have to pry those bony old fingers off his sofa with a crowbar. But if it had come to that, he would have. He had enough problems without that crotchety old SOB limping around his apartment. There was just so much he could take.

Goldman had given him the silent treatment through their entire search for an apartment complex that offered furnished units by the day. He hadn't spoken a single word when Beamon had lugged his equipment into the dingy interior of the only place they could find. Goldman had barely perked up when Beamon, overwhelmed by guilt, had invited him to be in on his meeting with Ernie Waverly tomorrow.

Beamon hung his parka next to the door and walked across the living room to his answering machine. He grabbed the bottle of wine he'd purchased earlier that evening while the tape rewound.

"Mr. Beamon. This is Terry Bland calling from the Oklahoma office." The hiss of the tape couldn't disguise the nervousness in Bland's voice. "I checked on that flight plan to Turkey again like you asked. There is, I repeat, *is* a record of that flight plan being filed last month—for January fifteenth . . . I'm really sorry, Mr. Beamon. I don't know how we made that error. Normally we get it right the first time. Let me know if you need anything else . . . Again, I apologize for the error and hope it doesn't cause you any problems."

Beamon made a mental note to call that kid when all this was over and tell him it wasn't his fault.

The machine beeped loudly and a somewhat garbled voice faded in. "Mark! Ken Hirayami here. I don't know how you called it, but you were right, goddamn you. There *is* a record of Albert Kneiss's visa in Turkey. He arrived January sixteenth and is apparently still there. I'll send you your fifty goddamn bucks when you call me and tell me what's going on. I've got some Turkish friends who would love to know how you found a glitch in what they thought was a pretty good system."

Beamon sighed loudly and headed for the front door, bottle of wine tucked securely under his arm. In forty-eight hours, the church was two for two on Kneiss's imaginary trip to Turkey. Beamon had hoped they wouldn't have the juice to falsify the records at all, but had reasonably expected they'd get to the FAA and fail in Turkey. The arms of the church seemed to be looking longer and longer, he reflected as he walked down the stairs outside his condo and rapped quietly on Carrie Johnstone's door.

She opened it a crack and then slipped outside. "Emory fell asleep on the couch," she explained.

Beamon handed her the wine, and she looked at the label with an expression somewhere between gratitude and surprise. Obviously, she'd expected less from a Pabst Blue Ribbon drinker.

"How about Tuesday?" Beamon said, realizing

that the question didn't make much sense after it had already escaped from his mouth.

"Tuesday, what?"

"Dinner. I thought we could go out."

Beamon felt the knot in his stomach, started by his theory on Jennifer Davis's impending doom, tighten at the thought of his dinner with Carrie. He had to distance himself from her until he got this church thing straightened out—there was just no other way. The tough part was doing it without: A) making it sound like a blowoff, B) making it sound like he was the kind of guy who couldn't commit to a goldfish, or C) making it seem that FBI agents were just too much trouble to seriously consider having a relationship with.

"Sounds great. Pick me up at seven." She leaned forward and kissed him lightly on the mouth, then disappeared back into her apartment.

Beamon stood there for a moment, stunned by the kiss. The clean, vaguely tropical scent of her hair still hung in the air, cinching down the knot a little tighter.

He cursed the church under his breath for their timing as he started back to his apartment. Couldn't Kneiss have done his messiah act and died last year? Before he'd moved in above the most spectacular woman he'd ever met?

Spectacular or not, though, he had to figure out a way to get rid of her for a while and hope she'd come back to him when all this was over. That is, if Sara Renslier saw fit to leave anything for her to come back to.

39

Making it look like an accident when he dropped the church's tails was getting more and more complicated. The blue Taurus had been a little more tenacious today, forcing Beamon into a combination car wash/playacted road rage scenario that probably looked pretty thin.

He slowed a bit as he passed Ernestine Waverly's house, noting the unfamiliar car parked in the driveway, and then eased to a stop against the curb about a block away.

The muffled shouting from inside her house was audible by the time Beamon made it halfway up the walk. He slid his hand around the handle of his revolver and put his ear against the door.

"Don't do it, for Christ's sake! Put that pizza down!"

"You have no right to judge me! That's for God to do."

"A few more slices and He's going to be the only one that's going to be able to haul your ass out of that chair!"

Beamon peeled his ear off the door and opened it. The car in the driveway and the voice inside belonged to Jack Goldman. He'd apparently arrived early—before Beamon had had a chance to prepare Ernie for his colorful disposition.

"Decided to sleep in? Whole morning's gone," Goldman said as Beamon walked into the cluttered room.

Ernie glared at Goldman as he struggled over to a small table and leaned against it, breathing sporadically. She looked like she was trying to stroke him out by sheer force of will as she tore into a piece of cold pizza with spiteful abandon.

"Morning, Ernie," Beamon said. "Am I in time for breakfast?

"Don't encourage her, Mark," Goldman croaked.

"You be quiet," Ernie shot back through a half-full mouth of pizza.

This was just perfect. He was up against an organization with millions of fanatical followers, nearly unlimited capital, and apparently unparalleled information-gathering capabilities. Even with the FBI behind him, he'd probably lose this one. But he didn't have the FBI behind him. What he had was a man who had bought a Model T new from the showroom and a morbidly obese shut-in who thought he was some kind of avenging angel.

Ernie shoved the rest of the pizza into her mouth with a final Herculean push and reached over to pull a piece of paper from under her keyboard. She wadded it up and threw it at Beamon. Hard. "That's what you asked for. I ran the church's old membership list against every database I could find."

"Hmmff," Goldman let out as Beamon unraveled the paper. He ignored the old man and ran a finger down the list of names. It was about what he'd expected. The presidents of two mortgage companies—one of which was probably getting ready to foreclose on his condo—the head of a medium-sized health/life insurance company, the heads of Vericomm and its sister company, Verinet. On the political side, three senators—one of whom chaired Ways and Means—and eleven representatives, not to mention more than a handful of high-level bureaucrats. Interestingly, though, no credit card companies. Of course, any lowly clerk probably had the juice to completely unravel his credit for all time.

"You done screwing around yet?" Goldman said.

"Look, *Jack*," Ernie said. "Mark is looking at the information *I* got for him. Maybe you should be quiet for once."

Goldman glared back at her and pulled a stack of papers out of a briefcase that looked as old as he was. He caned his way across the room and spread them out on the table next to Beamon. They seemed to consist of wiring schematics and maps, though Beamon could only guess at their significance.

"The church's compound, where that Kneiss guy lives, is here," Goldman said, jabbing a gnarled finger at a colorful map. "They've got eight phone lines running out to an aboveground pedestal, here." He flipped to a wiring schematic. "And then into a cross-connect box about a mile away. We can hit 'em at the box. There are four lines coming into Ernie's house, so we can terminate the taps here— use cell phone service. Then we can run a redundant site into the apartment I'm staying in. I've got three additional lines being installed this afternoon."

"Where the hell do you get this stuff, Mr. Goldman?" Beamon said, shaking his head. "You just got here yesterday, for God's sake."

"You don't think I have contacts?"

Beamon rolled up the maps and handed them back to Goldman. "Contacts or not. I may not have the support of my organization, but I'm still an FBI agent. No illegal wiretaps. That's the final word."

"Jesus Christ, boy! You know what you're up against here? They aren't playing by your rules—"

Ernie cut off his tirade before it gained too much momentum. "As much as I hate to say it, Mark, he's right. God doesn't follow man's law. We have to ask ourselves what He wants of us. The Lord gave us the ability to see beyond black and white."

Beamon leaned his head forward and rubbed his temples. "Ernie, darlin', you've got to give me a break on the religious stuff. I'm just an FBI agent, not Martin Luther."

Goldman looked smug. "Well, for whatever the reason, I'd say it's two against one."

Beamon looked up at him. "Fortunately, my decision is the only one that counts."

40

JENNIFER DAVIS LAY MOTIONLESS ON THE COLD floor with her heels resting on the bed that had become the focus of her life over the past month. The burning in her stomach had just about subsided, so she lifted her back up off the floor and began a second set of situps.

After forty repetitions, her muscles felt like they'd caught fire, but she just pushed herself harder, trying to burn her anger, loneliness, and fear in the flame spreading across her abdomen. After fifty-five, the fuel for the fire was gone and she struggled to her feet and walked over to the remains of her breakfast lying on a plastic tray by the door.

She took the spoon off the plate and turned it over and over again in her fingers. Always a spoon now. The knife and fork had never reappeared since the day she had been taken to see her grandfather's body. That pale bitch Sara must think she was going to kill herself and rob her of the pleasure.

Jennifer stuffed the spoon in the waistband of her underpants and lifted the heavy bed away from the wall. Using the end of the utensil, she scraped a small line in the plaster next to a group of similar lines. March 15. She moved the bed back, trying to force herself not to calculate how much time she had left. She was unsuccessful, though, just like she was every morning. Twelve days, her mind told her as she dropped the spoon back onto the tray. The metallic clang seemed to echo through the room before being swallowed up by the silence that had swallowed her up. Two weeks.

"It doesn't matter," she said aloud.

She was going to get out of here. She'd done the hardest part, gotten control of her fear and managed to turn her loneliness and the memory of her parents' death into a fierce sense of self-reliance. She'd figure out a way to get out of here. She had to.

And when she finally did escape, she *would* have a place to go. Sara wanted her to think she was alone, but she wasn't. Jamie and his mother would take her in until it was time for her to go to college. With the money her parents must have left her, she could buy them a new house. Mrs. Rodrigues didn't deserve to be stuck in that horrible trailer park.

The key hitting the lock startled her, as it always did, but she managed to fight the urge to back against the wall, instead standing in the middle of the room and facing the door defiantly.

Sara came in alone, but Jennifer could see the man who always accompanied her as he took a position outside the door. She'd never get past him. She had to think of another way.

"The elders would like to see you again, Jennifer," Sara said, stopping a few feet away from where she stood. "You're very important to them now."

Jennifer struggled to control her rage. She couldn't tear her eyes away from the woman's throat and couldn't stop wondering if she could choke the life out of her before Mustache Man made it through the door and dragged her off.

"You tricked them. They don't know what my grandfather really wanted," Jennifer said.

Sara made a move toward her but then stopped when Jennifer didn't shrink away. The woman glanced behind her at the open door, confirming her companion's presence, and then turned back. "Think, Jennifer. If you do, I think you'll remember things differently. You'll understand what you are and what you'll become."

"You're a liar," Jennifer said. "He gave the church to me. He wanted *me* to have it."

Sara smiled. "There's nothing you can do to stop this, Jennifer, it's God's will. Deep down you know that's true, don't you? Your parents believed—enough to die for you."

"It's not true!" Jennifer said. Sara was just trying to confuse her.

An expression of anger crossed Sara's face and then disappeared. "I thought you might like to leave this room one more time. But now I see that it's impossible." She walked out into the hallway and began pulling the door closed behind her. "Good-bye, Jennifer."

"No! Wait!" Jennifer heard herself say. But Sara was gone.

She stood alone in the middle of the room for a long time, quivering with rage and frustration. She had to get out. In less than two weeks they were going to kill her. This wasn't a game—it was real. She fell onto the bed and pulled her knees to her chest, feeling the tears well up in her eyes for the first time in a week.

She stared at the heavy wood door for a long time and thought back over the month she'd been there. There wasn't any reason for them to let her out again. And even if they did, what could she do? The strength and will she'd managed to piece together over the last few weeks wouldn't do anything against the Mustache Man.

She was lying to herself. They would never let her escape. In twelve days Sara and the Mustache Man would come through the door for the last time. She'd struggle uselessly as they plunged the syringe into her. And that would be the end.

41

A HUNDRED AND FIFTY MILES BETWEEN THEIR offices and he just couldn't keep that man's ass out of his chair.

Beamon looked through the window to his office at Jake Layman, who was, once again, flipping though the paperwork he'd found on Beamon's desk. He didn't look as angry as he had the last time Beamon had seen him, but he wasn't sure if that was good or bad.

"Morning, Jake," Beamon said, opting to skip the trip to the coffee pot in an effort to get Layman back on the road ASAP. "To what do I owe this visit?"

Layman looked almost happy as he slid a two-page fax across the desk.

It was copied from a newspaper article, Beamon saw when he picked it up. The headline, in bold capital letters, read: MARK BEAMON—FIT FOR DUTY?

"I have a friend at the *Chronicle*," Layman explained. "He was courteous enough to send this to me before it hits the paper tomorrow."

Beamon scanned the article, hoping that the headline was just a teaser and that the rest would get better.

It didn't. The focus of the piece seemed to be his drinking habits and was heavily slanted toward the negative. It failed to mention his uncanny conviction rate and what a fun guy he was at parties, instead using a collage of unrelated anecdotes spread out over many years to portray him as a pathetic, decaying drunk.

He had to give the author credit, though, the piece was beautifully written and exceptionally well researched. A chronology of undeniable facts taken completely out of context.

Following a brief introduction of the unfortunate theme, the article began with Beamon's fraternity days at Yale, giving a detailed description of his invention of the Hop Hose.

Beamon almost managed a bitter smile as he remembered piecing the Hose together out of an old cooler and a bilge pump during exams his junior year. It had been a simple yet inspired device. You filled the cooler to the top with beer from a keg, stuck the hose emanating from the front into your mouth, and pushed the doorbell on the side. The bilge pump would fire up, a siren on top would start, and, well, you'd get filled full of beer in about a second and a half. As far as he knew, the original Hop Hose was still enshrined in a specially constructed glass case at his old fraternity house.

The article moved on to outline his inauspicious first meeting with the born-again director of the FBI, which, in hindsight, probably *had* involved about ten ounces too much bourbon and about a pound too much sarcasm.

The rest was more mundane, but equally damaging. Anonymous, but despicably accurate, stories of late-night party excesses and bloodshot mornings. It concluded with the same tired old crap about the vaunted FBI old-boy network protecting his "secret," yada, yada, yada.

Beamon threw the fax back onto the desk. "Interesting timing."

"Excuse me?"

"Nothing."

Beamon sat silently, eyes locked on Layman, waiting to hear exactly what his boss was planning to do about this unfortunate little essay. He didn't have to wait long.

"I've tried to protect you, Mark. But I just can't anymore."

Beamon would have liked to know exactly how Layman had tried to protect him, but decided this probably wasn't the time to ask.

"What they don't have here, thank God," Layman said, stabbing a finger at the fax, "is the report that you'd been drinking when you examined the scene of the Jennifer Davis kidnapping, and the fact that you were drunk when your primary suspect was somehow killed."

Beamon couldn't seem to work up anything that felt even remotely like anger. He just felt tired. He should have seen this coming, and now he was getting exactly what he deserved for not staying awake. "Come on, Jake. I had a few beers while we were playing golf—you were there, for God's sake."

Layman opened his arms and shrugged. "I wasn't watching. I have no idea how much you drank that day. But I do have a report from two cops who were at the scene that you smelled like a brewery when you arrived."

Beamon seriously doubted that, since, as he recalled, he had about six pieces of gum in his mouth by the time he got out of the car. "I don't suppose it matters that David Passal fell down a ladder while I was twenty miles away, trying to mend some fences with the local cops . . ." He let his voice trail off. Of course it didn't matter. He could see from his boss's expression that he was wasting his breath. No point in making this any more fun for Layman than it had to be. "Okay, Jake. Cut to the chase. What's this to me?"

"I spoke at length with the director this morning."

Beamon closed his eyes and took a deep breath. That couldn't be good.

"We went over the issues I just spoke about, and your recent lapses in judgment . . ."

"Lapses in judgment?" Beamon said, opening his eyes.

"Your investigation of the Church of the Evolution. The fact that you've become obsessed with the Kneissians and that you've ignored my repeated attempts to put you back on track."

"Come on, Jake, you weren't even keeping up with the facts of the case. Who are you to question my investigative judgment?"

Layman just smiled calmly. "I'm your boss, Mark. Maybe if you could remember that, you wouldn't be in the position you're in today."

Beamon grabbed the fax and held it up. "Hasn't it occurred to you that this is pretty typical for the church? They probably own the fucking *Flagstaff Chronicle*."

"Typical? Are you talking about the organization that's built hospitals and schools all over Arizona, and feeds the homeless during the holidays? The organization that gives hundreds of millions of dollars to charity every year? This is what I'm talking about, Mark. You've become paranoid. And we think it's from the drinking."

He leaned back in Beamon's chair and began picking at one of his nails. "You're a competent agent, Mark, and we don't want to lose you. Whatever help you need, you're going to get. You might even be able to come back from this if you really focus on getting your problems ironed out."

Beamon looked up at the ceiling and took a deep breath, fighting to keep some kind of emotional distance between himself and what was happening.

"You're being put on immediate paid leave until we can get this straightened out."

Portraying as much outward calm as he could, Beamon reached into his pocket and pulled out his FBI credentials. To Layman's credit, he was almost successful in suppressing his smile when Beamon handed them over.

"We've scheduled a physical for you on March twenty-fifth. You're to report to headquarters on that date. Any questions?"

Beamon managed to push his suspension and the irreparable damage that was going to be done to his reputation tomorrow to an unused corner of his mind. Sara Renslier was going to find that he wasn't as easily handled as some others.

"What long-distance carrier do you use?"

Layman looked at him strangely and shook his head as he walked around the desk to leave. Beamon grabbed his arm. "You asked if I had any questions. That's my question. What long-distance carrier do you use?"

"What the hell are you talking about, Mark? Are you drunk now?" Layman said, trying to pull free. Beamon squeezed harder, sinking his fingers into the flesh of Layman's forearm.

"I don't know," Layman said finally. "You dial a code. It's five cents a minute."

"Mark, have you seen this?" Chet Michaels said, running into the office without his customary nervous pause at the door. "A friend of mine just sent it to me." He slapped a bad fax copy of the offending article on the desk.

Beamon nodded and continued picking through his drawers, occasionally dropping an item or two into the box at his feet. He hadn't been there long enough to accumulate much junk. Usually this operation took days.

"It's the church, isn't it? What do you want to bet the guy who wrote that article is a member?"

Beamon shrugged.

"So what are we going to do about it?"

Beamon looked up from the drawer and into the innocent face of Chet Michaels. "Nothing. I've been suspended. It's over."

"Suspended? No way! They can't do that! You're the best we've got. Everybody knows that."

"Thanks, Chet. I appreciate that. I really do," Beamon said, standing and pulling his coat off the back of his chair. "I guess I'll see you around."

"Come on, Mark, you know the church is involved. We can't give up now."

"Finding Jennifer isn't my job anymore, Chet. And it's not yours, either—Layman's going to take this one."

"But he won't—"

"Chet! Let it go. There'll be other cases. If you don't screw up here, you'll still be around to solve them."

"It's not just a case, Mark. Have you forgotten Jennifer? What about her?"

Beamon shrugged and picked the box up off the floor. "What about her? Wake up, Chet. I'm just in this for the game. And I lost."

42

BEAMON PINNED THE BOX FULL OF HIS PER-
sonal effects against the wall and struggled to get
his keys out of his pocket. He glanced back over his
shoulder at the condo inhabited by Robert Andrews,
his church-appointed spy. The window looked the
same as it always did, curtains pulled to within a
couple of inches of being fully closed, interior dark.

There *was* one change worth noting, however.
Andrews was standing on the walkway that ran
along the front of his building, leaning casually
against the railing and staring right at him.

Beamon was too far away to read the man's
expression, but his stance spoke volumes. The
church was letting him know that they were responsible for his current situation. That they had filed
down his teeth to the point that they didn't even
need to hide their presence anymore.

Beamon turned his key in the lock and threw
the door open, sending a shower of snow and ice
onto his carpet when it slammed against the wall.
He dropped the box on top of the Davis case files
covering his sofa and pulled an unopened bottle of
bourbon from the top of it.

The familiar weight of it wasn't as comforting as
he thought it would be, but he still pulled what was
left of his beer stash from his refrigerator and

dumped it ceremoniously into the trash.

He grabbed the carton of cigarettes lying on the counter and dropped into a chair, unscrewing the top of the bottle with one hand and punching the remote next to him with the other. The church's channel came to life on the screen with a young woman professing how Kneiss's bible had changed her life. He lit the first of what he hoped would be many cigarettes and watched the smoke curl through the virgin air of his condo.

It had changed his life, too.

He'd always pushed the envelope at work and it had hurt him—personally and professionally. But that had been his choice—to never move very far up in the ranks, to work for men and women whose abilities were inferior to his, to be bounced around from office to office, state to state.

He'd managed to find a delicate but generally durable balance between his often self-destructive impulses and his ability to get the job done faster and more efficiently than anyone else. It was that balance that had allowed him to keep his job. And it was that balance that Sara Renslier had managed to disrupt.

She'd done a hell of a job, too. Not only was he most likely facing early retirement, but he was going to leave the Bureau under a black cloud that would follow him for the rest of his life. It seemed reasonable to expect that the lucrative private-sector job he'd need to feed himself in retirement wouldn't be forthcoming.

"You want fries with that?" he said to the empty room, raising his glass in salute to nothing in particular. Never too early to start training for a new career.

His thoughts turned to Jennifer Davis as he took his first slug of bourbon since arriving in Arizona. He was dead sure now that the theory that had seemed so farfetched to him at first was correct. Sara Renslier was not going to allow a fifteen-year-old orphan to take her church from her, to strip her of the power that she had spent twenty-five years acquiring and seemed to wield so effortlessly. And if he accepted that fact, then Jennifer had a real problem. Either she was already dead—the granddaddy of all problems, and one historically difficult to fix—or Sara had managed to convince the Elders of the church that Jennifer was the next Messenger. If that was the case, she was going to get rid of the kid in some kind of bullshit religious ceremony that would assure Sara continued control over the church for life.

Beamon downed another slug, feeling the alcohol begin to work its way into his mind. The beer-only diet he'd been adhering to seemed to have wreaked havoc on his tolerance. But then, it was probably good to be a cheap drunk when your career prospects were looking this bleak.

He decided that if Jennifer was already dead, the church would have stuffed her body in a chuckhole somewhere in Outer Mongolia by now and Sara would be making a real show of cooperating with him, knowing that without a body, he couldn't do shit.

But she wasn't cooperating. She was aiming the church's entire arsenal at him—a senior FBI man—and in doing that, taking a hell of a risk. No, they were playing for time. He looked at the calendar on his watch. Eleven more days.

And that brought up another interesting, but ultimately depressing point. When Good Friday—

and Jennifer—had come and gone, Sara sure as hell wasn't going to wait around for him to gather his notes and write a book. No, once that little girl's body was safely stowed, it would be time for him to slip on the ice and crack his skull or to have some equally mundane, yet fatal, accident.

There was a knock at the door, but Beamon ignored it and worked on the solution to his problem. How the hell was he going to find Jennifer in the next eleven days? He took another gulp from his glass and felt the liquid burn down to his stomach, then reverse its course and go straight to his head.

His front door opened a crack, creating a bright swath of light that illuminated the curling smoke drifting through the gloom.

"Mark?" Carrie's reddish-brown head snaked into the room. "There you are. Why didn't you answer?"

Beamon lit another cigarette with the embers of the old one. "What're you doing home in the middle of the day, Carrie?"

He turned back to the TV as Carrie closed the door quietly behind her. A well-dressed young man was asking for donations to buy food for the starving children from one of those starving-children countries.

"Chet called me and told me what happened. He's really worried about you, Mark."

Beamon let his head loll back on the chair as he remembered the look on Michaels's face when he'd left him standing in his office. What he'd said to him about only being in it for the game had been pretty harsh, but what choice did he have? The kid was too damned ready to get dragged down with him.

"Are you all right?"

"It's not as grim as it sounds, Carrie," he lied. "Just politics, you know."

She moved the box containing most of his life and sat down on the arm of the sofa. "Switching from beer to liquor isn't going to help your case any," she said, nodding toward the bottle in his hand.

He laughed bitterly. "My strict program of self-improvement doesn't seem to have done a whole hell of a lot of good. I figure, why close the gate after the horse has bolted?"

She was silent for a moment and then said, "You didn't answer my question."

"I don't remember you asking one."

"Are you *all right*?"

"Sure. I'm fine. Things like this happen."

She looked at him compassionately. "You've never married, have you, Mark?"

"Excuse me?"

"Married. You never married. Why?"

Beamon shrugged, wondering if that was kind of a bizarre change of subject or if he was just more buzzed than he thought. "I guess I never found the right woman. I've had a career that's pretty much been one crisis after the other. There just hasn't been much time."

"You've given a lot to the Bureau. What is it now? Fifteen or twenty years of putting it before everything else. And now the Bureau's turned its back on you. That must be hard."

Beamon grinned and shook his head. "Jesus, Carrie. Now I *am* depressed, do you have a rope on you? I thought psychiatrists were supposed to make you feel better."

"That's a myth, I'm afraid. We help people

identify their problems and then we force them to confront them."

Beamon's slightly fogged mind conjured up the pale, expressionless face of Sara Renslier. "Oh, I've identified my problem, Carrie. I just haven't figured out a way to confront it and come away with my skin."

She walked over and knelt by his chair. "Do you want to tell me about it?"

He put down the bottle and ran his hand gently through her hair. "Not right now. I just need to sit here and think for a while. We're still going out tomorrow, though, right? We definitely need to talk."

She pressed his hand against her cheek. "I guess you're going to want me to pay for dinner now, huh?"

43

"WE'RE GOING TO GET THOSE SONSOFBITCHES for you, boy," Jack Goldman shouted, swinging his cane wildly to punctuate his point and inadvertently knocking over a stack of books next to him.

"Would you be careful with that thing! I've got expensive equipment here!" Ernie hollered back at him.

"Come on, guys. Calm down," Beamon said, trying to bring the noise in the room to a level that wouldn't split his head open. He adjusted his sunglasses on his nose and began restacking the books at Goldman's feet, trying to ignore the nausea gripping him and the fact that he was the only member of his "team" who was capable of completing this simple task.

"If this is your new FBI," Goldman continued in a quieter voice, "you can have it. When Hoover was alive, they wouldn't begrudge a man a drink! Now all they want to do is hire a bunch of pansies who aren't afraid to cry and then send 'em to sensitivity training. No one would've dared—"

"Where's your bathroom?" Beamon asked, cutting Goldman off before he got too warmed up to his subject.

Ernie pointed behind him. "Down there, your first right."

She looked a bit confused as he sat down and dug a handful of Advils from his pocket. His stomach rolled over at the prospect of sending anything down to it, but he forced a couple of tablets anyway. "Don't need it now," Beamon explained to her. "Just wanted to get a fix on it."

"Drinking never solved anything, Mark."

Beamon let out a short, painful laugh. "I said the same thing to Mr. Goldman here nearly twenty years ago." He looked up at the old man. "You remember what you told me?"

"I told you that sobriety never solved anything, either."

"That's right."

Goldman waved his cane around again, but this time in a more controlled pattern. "It's time to get off our asses, Mark. We're letting ourselves get screwed here."

"The suspension's done," Beamon said. "It is what it is. They're trying to get me to take my eye off the ball."

"Jennifer," Ernie said.

Beamon nodded. "The FBI won't be pursuing the church angle, so they have no chance of getting her back before her time's up. We've got to do it. I'm open to suggestions as to how."

Ernie leaned forward in her wheelchair as far as her bulk and the straining banana-print fabric containing it would allow. "The church doesn't have that many places where they could be holding someone against their will, Mark. Maybe you could search them."

Beamon shook his head. "I can pretty much guarantee you that Jennifer's being held at Kneiss's ompound, Ernie. I don't think we need to look any further than that."

"Then why don't we—"

"How?" Goldman cut in. "I looked at that place. It'd take an army to get in there with all that security."

"Mr. Goldman's right, Ernie. There's no way in there. Do you think they might move her? If we're right, don't you think Sara would have to invent some kind of ceremony for her death? Where would they do something like that?"

Ernie shook her head. "There's no one place, Mark. The chapel in the compound would be as good a place as any."

"I doubt they'd dispose of the body on Kneiss's property," Goldman said. "Ground's frozen anyway. Maybe we could get them red-handed when they bring her body out Easter weekend?"

Beamon stood and began pacing back and forth across the room, the motion settling his stomach a bit. "No. No way. I refuse to be responsible for this girl's death. We're going to get her before anything happens to her."

"Then we're back to Jack's wiretap," Ernie said.

That was exactly where they were, Beamon knew. He'd spent most of his career at the FBI being a pain in the ass, completely unconventional, and occasionally even sneaky. But he'd never done anything illegal. "How long, Mr. Goldman?"

"Now you're talkin', son. You and me, tomorrow night. It'll be fun."

Beamon unbuckled his seatbelt and leaned out the car window to get a better look at the screen of the cash machine. It was heavily overcast, but he was still unwilling to take off his sunglasses and that was making it even more difficult to read the small letters.

UNABLE TO PROCESS TRANSACTION

He tried again, with the same result.

Beamon pulled his car into a space close to the door of the bank and went inside. He walked down the long line of teller windows and slid his ATM card to a young girl with bright pink barrettes in her hair. "I seem to be having some trouble making a withdrawal from your machine. Could you check my account for me?"

"Of course." She held the card up and examined it carefully. "Sometimes the magnetic strip on the back of these things gets messed up. Do you keep it in the little sleeve?"

He shook his head as she punched his account number into her terminal. An expression of mild confusion spread across her face as she looked at the screen, giving Beamon a not-so-unexpected sinking feeling.

"This is kind of weird," she explained. "You're showing a zero balance. Could you hold on a second?"

She hopped off her stool and hurried to an older woman standing at the end of the counter. The woman returned with her and, with a brief smile acknowledging Beamon's presence, began punching buttons on the keyboard.

"Could I speak to you over here, please, sir?" she said after less than a minute. Beamon followed her to a deserted area at the edge of counter.

"Mr. Beamon, your accounts have been liened by the IRS. They've ordered us not to accept any further transactions on any of your accounts."

Beamon felt his jaw tighten and he closed his eyes for a moment. When he opened them again, the woman had stepped back a couple of feet.

"I'm afraid there's nothing I can do," she said nervously. "Except give you the number of the local IRS office so you can get this straightened out."

Beamon walked out of the building to his car, looking carefully around him at the people in the parking lot. He was sure he hadn't been followed to Ernie's house, but now, in this busy part of town, it was possible that they could have reacquired him.

Satisfied that he wasn't the subject of any undue attention, he reached under the seat and ran his fingers along the envelope containing the five thousand dollars he'd withdrawn last week. All the money he had in the world now.

He wondered if he'd get a chance to spend it.

44

BEAMON STRAIGHTENED HIS TIE NERVOUSLY and then forced his hands to his sides and tried to look casual. If someone had bet him that he'd one day dread a date with Carrie Johnstone more than any he'd ever had, he'd have lost a lot of money.

Despite a substantial effort on his part, Beamon hadn't been able to come up with a single credible lie as to why he had to stop seeing her for a while. It looked like he was going to have to fall back on a rough approximation of the truth and hope he didn't scare her off. That is, if this morning's newspaper article hadn't already done that for him.

Beamon knocked again, this time a bit harder. Emory wouldn't be asleep this early—Carrie was probably in the back with a blow dryer running or something.

"Come on, Carrie," he said to himself. It was starting to get cold, and he was getting more nervous by the minute.

Carrie finally answered the door dressed in an old pair of jeans and a sweatshirt, just as he raised his hand to knock again.

Beamon pointed to a splotch of faded paint on the sweatshirt. "I was suspended *with* pay, Carrie. I was actually planning on springing for a nice restaurant."

She remained silent and took a step back in a way that was clearly not an invitation.

Beamon noticed that her eyes were tinged slightly pink. The aftermath of tears that had recently dried up. "Carrie. Are you all right? Did something happen to Emory?"

His words seemed to sting her. More than that, actually. They seemed to stagger her. She reached down to the small table next to the door and picked up something that looked like a business card.

"Carrie, what's wrong with you?"

In answer to his question, she held the card out to him at arm's length, tensing visibly when he reached for it.

"What is this?" Beamon asked, looking down at the clean white card with the words *Child Safety Administration* printed on it in authoritative black letters.

"Two men came here today," she said in a voice so strange that Beamon had to look up to make sure she was actually the one speaking. "They told me that you're being investigated for child molestation."

Beamon felt his heart twitch as a quick burst of adrenaline surged through him. He started to take a step toward her, but stopped when she moved back again. "Carrie, this is bullshit. Look, I'm investigating a very powerful organization and they're doing everything they can to discredit me. I was going to tell you about it tonight." He held up the card. "I mean, Jesus Christ, there's not even a phone number on this . . ." He let his voice trail off. She wasn't listening. The tears he had thought were exhausted earlier started to shimmer in her eyes again and he remembered. *She'd left her daughter with him.*

He looked into her face and saw horror, guilt,

and betrayal there. For a moment he was enraged. That the church would stoop to something like this. That Carrie would believe it. But then he remembered Jennifer's uncle. David Passal had been run out of Oregon for similar unsubstantiated charges. And Beamon hadn't for a moment questioned his guilt, only his motivation and ability to get at Jennifer.

What was it that Passal had said when Beamon had last seen him alive? Something about there being a plot of land down the hill—that he'd save it for him.

Beamon closed his eyes to block out Carrie's face and the card that seemed to be burning in his hand. Passal had probably been a good guy. More than likely, he'd tried to help out his brother and sister-in-law, and for that he'd been condemned to dying alone in the bitter cold of the Utah mountains.

Beamon opened his eyes again, realizing there was nothing left to be said. He slipped the card into his pocket and turned away without looking up. "Good-bye, Carrie." He walked slowly out onto the snow-covered walk and across the courtyard. Halfway to the parking area, he finally heard Carrie's door push shut. A moment later, the laughing started.

Beamon stopped and watched Robert Andrews lean over the rail outside his second-floor condo for a moment and then walk inside his unit, still laughing. The small gap in the drapes, there since Andrews had moved in, disappeared. A clear message that the church no longer saw him as a threat.

Beamon felt the anger build in him until it was at the edge of his control. He'd spent the last month screwing around, treating this like any other kidnapping case. And that had kept him from seeing the big picture—from believing that the church could actually mount an effective attack on him. He'd concentrated everything on offense, ignoring defense. And now Carrie, his job, his reputation were all gone—probably never to be recovered. He had no family to stand behind him and most of his friends would run hard and fast at this kind of trouble. They had their own lives and careers to worry about.

Beamon jumped over a small hedge and ran up the steps toward Andrews's apartment, taking them two at a time. When he burst through the man's front door, he was sitting calmly on his sofa. Waiting.

"What a surprise," Andrews said, not rising from his position on the couch.

Beamon yanked his pistol from its holster and aimed it at the man's face. He could feel the blood throbbing from his heart to his head to his gun hand.

"Oh, my!" Andrew said, mocking Beamon by throwing his hands up in a cartoonish display of terror. "A desperate man with a gun."

"Shut the fuck up!" Beamon screamed, rushing forward and stopping with the barrel of the pistol only a few inches from the man's nose. In his mind, he saw Andrews walking up to Carrie's door and handing her that business card. He could see the expression on her face as she went back inside her home, knelt down, and looked into the eyes of her daughter.

"What is it you want exactly?" Andrews said, casually lowering his hands. Beamon followed their progress with his eyes, focusing on the band around the man's wrist. It was made of black iron, probably three-quarters of an inch wide and a quarter of an inch thick. A deep white scar had been carved into the man's skin beneath the heavy bracelet. A souvenir from the torch that had been used to weld it in place.

Andrews moved his arm to better display the symbol of his devotion. "Well? What do you want?"

"I want to cut your heart out with a fucking spoon," Beamon said through clenched teeth. "That's what I want."

Andrews rolled his eyes. "I'd heard that you were given to fits of melodrama. Now why don't you run on home before you get yourself in any more trouble."

Beamon pushed the gun closer until it was almost brushing the skin of the man's forehead. "Get Sara Renslier on the phone. Now!"

Andrews ran his tongue slowly over the front of his teeth. "I'm not sure why she'd want to talk to you."

Beamon flicked his wrist and caught Andrews in the mouth with the barrel of his pistol. The blow split the man's lower lip and at the sight of the blood, Beamon's control slipped a little farther away from him. He grabbed the handset of the phone from the table next to the sofa and slammed it into the side of the man's head. "Do it now!"

Andrews's mouth tightened into a thin slit, increasing the flow of blood from his lip. He began to rise, but when Beamon cocked the hammer on his pistol back, he sank back into the cushions and sat motionless.

"You better start dialing that phone, boy."

Andrews thought about it for a few seconds and then picked up the handset and began punching angrily at the buttons.

"Ms. Renslier? This is Robert Andrews." Pause. "He's standing right here pointing a gun at me . . ." He looked directly into Beamon's eyes. "No, I'm in no danger. I don't think he can do much harm to anyone anymore."

Beamon snatched the phone from Andrews's hand and raised it to his ear. "What the fuck do you think you're doing?"

Silence.

"Answer me!"

"I'm not sure I understand your question, Mr. Beamon," Sara Renslier said, speaking slowly and clipping her words as though Beamon was a child who had difficulty understanding adult speech.

"I'm not through with you, *Sara*. Do a little research. I always get who I'm after."

"Oh, yes. Special Agent Beamon *was* impressive. But you're not Special Agent Beamon anymore, are you? You're just a drunk, out-of-work pedophile."

"Fuck you!"

He couldn't tell if the mechanical edge to the laughter coming over the phone was the result of the line or the woman. Beamon suddenly realized that she was enjoying this immensely.

He let the phone drop a few inches and looked around him. At Andrews sitting on the couch, at the sparsely furnished condominium that was a mirror reflection of his own. The pounding in his head was starting to subside, leaving him feeling disoriented—like he'd just woken up from an intense dream.

What the hell was he doing? Running up there all rage and no reason. Throwing around a bunch of threats that everyone knew had no teeth. He was looking like a complete idiot, even to himself.

"Do you have anything of interest to say, Mr. Beamon?" he heard Sara say. "I'm rather busy."

The pathetic thing was, he really didn't. Suddenly he just wanted to be out of there.

"Your God must be very proud, Sara—" He almost finished the sentence with, "plotting the death of Kneiss's granddaughter so soon after his death," but he realized that it would have been his bruised ego talking. Tipping his hand like that would be stupid. There might still be time to do something. That is, if he could manage to pull his head out of his ass.

"Did you ever consider, Mr. Beamon, that if you had accepted God and followed His path, you wouldn't have been so easy to break?"

Beamon looked up at Andrews, who was still sitting calmly on the couch, and holstered his gun. "Oh, I'm not broken yet. I'm just really bent out of shape."

The liquor store was nearly deserted when Beamon walked in. He went straight to the back, picked up a half-gallon of bourbon, and returned to the counter.

"Better throw in a carton of Marlboros, too. I'm having a really bad day."

The girl smiled and grabbed a carton off the wall behind her.

"Put it on my account. The name's Mark Beamon."

At the mention of his name, she started to look a little nervous.

Beamon rolled his eyes and sighed. What now? Had the church bought the fucking liquor store and cut off his credit? He figured they'd want him drunk.

"Could you hold on a second?" she said and then scurried out from behind the counter, returning shortly with the store's manager.

"Barry. What's the problem?" Beamon said.

The man held out a white business card, but Beamon didn't bother taking it. He knew what it was.

"Some men came around today asking questions about you," Barry said angrily.

Beamon remembered that he always made a point of asking after the man's seven-year-old daughter when he came in.

"I'd appreciate it if you didn't come in here anymore, Mr. Beamon. We don't need your kind of business."

Beamon tapped the top of the bourbon bottle on the counter. "Let me pass along a piece of advice my dad gave me years ago, Barry. Never refuse a bottle and cigarettes to a heavily armed out-of-work child molester."

Barry took a step back but managed to regain his composure quickly. Apparently seeing the wisdom in Beamon's words, he walked behind the counter and pulled out an index card that Beamon assumed was his tab.

Barry nodded toward the items on the counter as he ripped up the card. "They're on the house. So's your account. Now there's no reason for you to ever come back."

Beamon slammed his hands against the steering wheel of his car. It felt good, so he did it again. And then again.

If the church's lackeys had gone so far as to visit his liquor store of choice, they'd probably talked to every goddamn person he'd ever known. He was screwed. Thoroughly and completely screwed.

It was unlikely now that he'd ever get his job back. And he probably had a better chance of marrying Christie Brinkley than getting Carrie to speak to him again. Or for that matter, getting any of the few friends he had to speak to him again.

Not that it really mattered, he reminded himself. When Sara had completed her little plot, she'd turn her attention back to him. Most likely, he and Jennifer would be sharing that chuckhole in Outer Mongolia.

He slammed his hand into the steering wheel one last time and felt the pain vibrate up his arms.

Enough. He had ten days and very little left to lose—nothing but his life, really. And from where he was sitting, that just didn't seem all that valuable anymore.

Beamon started the car and pointed it toward Jack Goldman's apartment. After making an ass out of himself in front of Andrews and with Carrie thinking he'd felt up her daughter, home just didn't seem that inviting.

45

"SLOW DOWN, BOY. CAN'T SEE A GODDAMN thing if you drive like a bat out of hell."

Beamon let his foot off the gas and flipped on the high beams. When the speedometer had drifted down to twenty miles an hour, he returned his foot to the accelerator.

Back at Goldman's apartment, there were only a few sad inches left in the bottle of bourbon Beamon had taken over last night. As for what was left in the carton of cigarettes, he was trying not to think about that. It was hard not to, though, with his lungs feeling like someone had poured a quart of motor oil into them right after they'd emptied their old car battery into his stomach. And then, of course, there was the crowbar prying apart his skull.

"I think you should talk to her," Goldman repeated for what must have been the hundredth time. Despite the fact that the old man had kept up with him shot for shot, smoke for smoke all night, he seemed miraculously unaffected. It must be the excitement—that or all of the old SOB's nerve endings had preceded him into the grave.

Beamon groaned. The bourbon had loosened him up enough to mention his unfortunate position with Carrie last night. "Let's concentrate on what we're doing, okay, Mr. Goldman?"

The old man looked over at him. "Son, I don't need you to tell me how much to concentrate to set a phone tap."

Beamon backpedaled. In his current condition there was no way he could take one of Goldman's tirades. "*I* need to concentrate. I've never done this before."

"And you're not going to do it today. You're just going to stand there and let me do my job." Goldman gazed out the window. "Yeah, I'd march right over there and talk to her. Make her listen. Get this thing straightened out once and for all."

The pounding in Beamon's head rose in tempo from a polka to more of a disco beat. "I appreciate the advice, Mr. Goldman, but you've never even been married. So—"

"Not because there weren't plenty of women willing, that I didn't get married. Hell, when I first started in this business, I could just walk into people's houses in the middle of the day and wire their phones while I ate lunch. That's before women got all hot and bothered about careers and trying to compete with men. No, those little housewives used to be damned happy to see me . . ."

"So why didn't you ever make an honest woman out of one of them?" Beamon said, hoping desperately to change the subject before Goldman started relating details of his sexual prowess. His stomach was just barely hanging on as it was.

"Why buy the cow when you can get the milk for free? Turn left here." He looked over at Beamon. "But son, you aren't me. Let's face it, you ain't the best-looking guy in the world. You're a sloppy dresser, and, well, you're a little obnoxious. No offense."

"None taken."

Goldman reached over and smacked Beamon on the stomach. "Hey, at least you took care of that weight problem. Now what was I saying . . ."

"That I'm not you," Beamon sighed

"You're not me, right. Son, if you've got an intelligent, attractive woman interested in you, I say you should get your ass in gear before she changes her mind. May not be anybody around the next corner, you know?"

"I think she already has changed her mind, Mr. Goldman."

"Boy, you just don't know anything about women, do you? They change their minds like the weather."

Beamon wasn't sure, but he suspected Goldman hadn't ever been in quite his situation. A woman who initially thought you dressed funny and watched too much football might come around, it was true. A woman who thought you were keeping compromising Polaroids of her four-year-old daughter in your wallet would probably be a little more difficult to win over.

"I'll try flowers," Beamon said.

"That's the spirit, boy. Broads love flow—There it is! The cross-connect box is right there."

Beamon tapped the brake and started easing the car toward the curb. "Jesus, son, don't slow down! Drive past it and park around the corner there."

Goldman was out of the car before it had completely stopped, walking without his cane and with very little difficulty. In the harsh glare of headlights reflecting off the snow, he still looked like he'd been dead for a couple of days, but when he turned his back and began digging in the back seat for his gear, he could have been forty years younger. His movements were decisive, quick, and smooth. He was back in his element.

Beamon took a position behind Goldman, hefting the large duffel the old man passed back and following him as he hurried up the sidewalk with a bright red toolbox dangling from his hand.

Beamon didn't see the large metal cabinet half-buried in the snow until Goldman slipped a headlamp over his thick knit cap and shined it off to their right. It was about ten feet back from the road amidst a widely spaced stand of pines that were casting long shadows across it, blending it into its background.

"You're going to have to dig, Mark," Goldman said, struggling through the snow toward the box.

Beamon sighed, pulled a collapsible Army-issue shovel out of the duffel, and started to work on the snow blocking the doors.

The nausea hit him full force on about the fifth shovelfull of icy snow. He did his best to ignore it but ended up having to stop. He unzipped the vaguely official-looking overalls Goldman had provided him and felt the cold wind dry the sweat covering his chest.

"No time for a coffee break, boy."

Beamon looked down at the shovel and then at the old man's head, then went back to chopping at the ice blocking the doors. Ten miserable minutes later, they were clear.

Goldman inserted a key into the box and opened it as Beamon stepped back into the shadows and fell onto a snowbank. The cold against his back felt like it might bring him back to life, given enough time.

The old man looked like a surgeon as his twisted

fingers danced over the bundles of wires with dexterity that should have been impossible. He stopped his work every ten seconds or so to look at a complex schematic that he had stuck to the inside of one of the open doors.

A car's headlights suddenly illuminated them as it turned the corner and started down the street in their direction. Beamon tensed and sat up, but Goldman seemed to read his mind.

"Relax, son. Just a couple of repairmen working late. Everyone expects their phones to work perfectly but they don't give a second thought to the people who keep them working. In five minutes, the guy in that car won't even remember he saw us."

Beamon had no reason to think Goldman was wrong, so he settled back into the snowbank and breathed in the scent of the pine tree behind him. He tried to let his mind go blank, to focus only on the quiet rustling as Goldman did his magic and the sweet smell of frozen pine needles, but it didn't work. Thoughts of the women in his life kept pushing out any momentary peace he might be able to steal.

The women in his life.

His mother had been dead for years and his sister pretty much hated him, leaving only three women of any importance. Jennifer Davis, a fifteen-year-old girl whom he'd never met and who he would probably get to remember as the other girl he couldn't save. Carrie Johnstone, a woman who now saw him as a psychotic pervert with eyes for her daughter. And Sara Renslier, who would do everything in her considerable power to destroy his life, and who, when he was rendered completely helpless, would undoubtedly swoop in for the kill.

God. How sad was that?

"Drill, Mark! Quit daydreaming and give me the drill!"

Beamon fished around in the duffel lying next to him and pulled out a beefy-looking battery-operated model, which Goldman used to cut a small hole in the side of the metal cabinet. He ran a wire through it and then went back to whatever it was he'd been doing before.

"Mark, there's a white fiberglass box in that duffel. About a foot square." He pointed in the general direction of a crooked pine tree behind the cross-connect box. "Bury it in the snow over there somewhere. One side of the box has two cables coming out of it. That's the top. Make sure the shorter of the two cables is sticking out of the snow so I can get at it."

"What about the long one?"

"Run it under the snow to the base of the tree behind you."

Beamon grabbed the box and the shovel and walked over to the spot Goldman had pointed to. "How deep?"

"Deep as you can. But make it look natural."

Beamon was just finishing—smoothing out the surface to match the unturned snow around it—when he heard the cabinet close. Goldman took the shovel from him and began digging a trench between the box Beamon had just buried and the cross-connect box, then spliced the wires together and buried them neatly in the trench.

"Is that it?" Beamon asked.

Goldman turned off his headlamp. "Nope." He reached into the duffel and pulled out another fiberglass device, this one smaller than the one Beamon just buried and painted in a brown and gray camouflage.

Goldman connected a thin brown cable to it and handed it to Beamon along with a pair of bungee cords colored in a similar camouflage. "Climb as high in that tree as you can and tie this to the trunk."

Beamon looked at the snow-covered tree behind him. "You've got to be kidding."

"You want it to work, don't you, boy?" Goldman pointed at the ground where Beamon had buried the other box. "Whenever a call comes into or goes out of the church's compound, that box will dial us on a cell and we'll get the call real-time. It'll run into Ernie's computer and a computer at my apartment, in case of a problem." He pointed at the unit in Beamon's hand. "That's the booster."

Beamon sighed and pushed his way through the lower branches of the tree, feeling snow invade every unsealed opening in his suit. He put a foot up on a sturdy-looking limb and turned to Goldman. "Who's paying for all this cell service?"

Goldman rolled his eyes. Kind of a surreal gesture given the uneven magnification of his glasses and the moonlight.

Beamon started his struggle up the tree. "I know, I know. What kind of idiot pays for cell phone service?"

46

BEAMON STEPPED FROM HIS CAR AND TRIED unsuccessfully to ignore the sad drama playing out before him in the courtyard in front of his condo.

A woman and her young son were having a playful snowball fight in the intermittent glare provided by the common area floodlights. When she saw Beamon, she jogged through the snow to the boy and began speaking quietly into his ear. Beamon couldn't help watching as the boy's attention turned from the snowball in his hands to him.

The scene confirmed what he already knew. He had to get the hell out of there before the home-owners' association started burning crosses on his lawn. He'd just draw too much attention if he stayed.

Beamon moved quickly across the courtyard and stepped up his pace even more as he walked past Carrie Johnstone's front door. Murphy's Law stated clearly that she would pick that precise moment to go to the store, take out the garbage, or whatever. He just couldn't take another confrontation right now.

For the first time in weeks, Murphy wasn't in control of his life and he reached the relative safety of his living room unscathed.

The warmth of his condo started to make him

sweat almost immediately, amplifying the hangover that was showing no sign of weakening in its twelfth hour. Remembering the beer he'd thrown away, he flipped the top of the garbage can open and dug around until he came up with a couple of bottles.

He felt pretty pathetic as he washed a now-unidentifiable leafy vegetable off them, but drastic hangovers called for drastic remedies. He slid one bottle into the freezer, punched the play button on his answering machine, and unscrewed the cap from the bottle in his hand.

"Mark, it's Chet. Pick up if you're there." Pause. "Look, I don't know what you're doing, but it's really starting to hit the fan here. I just spent most of my day getting grilled by Jake Layman and a couple of his ASACs. I knew you wouldn't give up on this thing. Call me. I want to help."

Beamon reached out for the phone, hesitated, and erased the message instead. He had to keep Chet out of this. At least for now.

After a warm beer and a cold shower, he was feeling marginally better. The shakes that had come close to knocking him out of that goddamn pine tree had subsided and his mind was starting to flash pictures of Denny's breakfast menu. A sure sign that the healing process had begun.

The phone rang as Beamon was toweling himself off. Probably Goldman, hopefully calling to tell him that the taps he'd wired were receiving five by five.

"Mark. Jake Layman."

Great.

"What can I do for you, Jake?" Beamon said as he finished drying himself and began rummaging though his drawers for a pair of jeans.

"I'd like you to come down to Phoenix. Tonight. We need to talk."

Beamon cradled the phone in the crook of his shoulder as he pulled on his pants. "I'd love to, Jake, but I'm afraid I just don't have the time right now."

"Look, Mark, I've been hearing rumors. About you. We—"

"Rumors about what, Jake? I'm already on suspension, why don't you just call the Office of Professional Responsibility and add whatever it is that's bothering you to their laundry list."

"Look, Mark. The FBI doesn't need—"

"What, Jake? Another black eye? Someone said that to me once and I stuck my ass out about a mile for the 'good of the organization.' Look where it got me."

"I know you're upset, Mark, but try to look at the big picture—"

Beamon cut him off again as he zipped his pants. "With all due respect, Jake—fuck you. I've got enough problems right now. I just don't have time to solve yours."

He leaned over the bed and replaced the phone's handset. The doorbell rang less than a minute later.

"If you work for the FBI, come on in," he yelled. "If not, I'll be right there."

He heard the door open and leaned out into the living room, still bare-chested. The two young agents self-consciously wiping their feet were from his office. Fucking Layman didn't even have the decency to send up a couple of his boys.

"What took you guys so long?" Beamon kept his tone light, but in reality he had no idea what he was going to do. "I'm still getting dressed. Hold on for a second."

Poor kids looked like they were about to die of embarrassment.

"Mr. Layman asked us to, uh, give you a ride down to Phoenix," Kate Spelling said. Her cohort pretended to be fascinated by a poorly framed print hanging on the wall.

Beamon disappeared back into his bedroom but left the door open. "I just got off the phone with him, Kate. Let me get my stuff."

"Sure. Take your time." He could hear the relief in her voice as he walked into the bathroom and began throwing toiletries with unerring accuracy into an open suitcase on the bed.

After stuffing a week's worth of clothes into the same suitcase, he got down on his knees and poked his head into the mess that was his closet. It took some digging, but he finally found the shoebox where he kept memorabilia from the cases he'd worked over the years. He dug through the old newspaper clipping and photographs, finally finding a fake driver's license he had used on an undercover assignment a few years back. He stuffed it in his pocket, then slid a shirt off a hanger and pulled it over his head.

The shotgun wasn't as easy—he had to pry it out from under a stack of unpacked boxes. He peeked out of the closet for a moment to make sure he wasn't drawing undue attention and then slowly pulled back the slide to make sure the gun wasn't loaded.

It took another minute to find the box of shells. He tossed them over his shoulder, hitting the suitcase dead center, and then crawled back out of the closet, leaving the shotgun just out of sight.

He closed up the suitcase and once again donned his bright red parka. Looking at himself in the mirror across the room, he took a deep breath. There wasn't going to be any turning back after this. If he didn't come up with the goods—Jennifer—he might as well just walk up to Sara Renslier and hand her a loaded gun.

Beamon grabbed the suitcase in one hand and the shotgun in the other and walked out into the living room. The two young agents' eyes widened when they saw the gun.

"It just occurred to me that I have a prior engagement. Tell Jake I'll have to catch up with him later."

They watched him as he walked into the kitchen and grabbed a steak knife.

"Uh, Mark. Mr. Layman was pretty clear about this. You really have to come with us."

Beamon started across the living room. "No, I don't, Kate. I'm the one with the shotgun." He opened the door and looked back at the two kids standing hapless in his living room. "Look, Layman isn't going to blame you for losing me. Tell him I went nuts. Pulled a gun. What were you supposed to do, shoot it out with me in a heavily populated condo complex?" He stepped outside. "You guys stay in here for about five minutes, okay? There's a beer in the freezer. Split it."

He closed the door behind him, knowing from their expressions that they'd do exactly what he'd told them. In hindsight, he'd have to thank Layman for not sending his own people. He'd have never gotten away with that bullshit if they'd been a couple of experienced agents Beamon didn't know.

He'd have had to crawl out of the goddamned window or something equally undignified.

He spotted their Bureau car and shoved the
steak knife in the passenger-side tires before jumping in his car and spinning out of the parking lot. He
adjusted his mirror and watched his home for the
last two months recede into the distance. Another
minor adjustment brought into focus the church's
increasingly tenacious chase car. It was going to take
some fancy driving, but it was time for him to permanently disappear.

His cell phone started to ring as he sped around
the corner and toward the highway. As soon as he
regained control of the car, he reached over and
turned it off.

47

"YOU'RE SURE THERE'S NOTHING," BEAMON said, continuing to scan the nearly empty parking lot.

Jack Goldman shoved yet another piece of mysterious equipment into the back seat of his car. "Damn right I'm sure. I've checked the entire spectrum—twice. Your car ain't transmitting. It's clean."

They were alone, then. With the insane driving he'd done getting there, it was inconceivable that anyone could have followed him without his knowing it. Even multiple cars with drivers connected by cell phone couldn't have stayed with him.

Beamon looked up at the sky and felt the heavy snowflakes falling against his skin. Visibility was horrible. No way to track him by air.

"Okay, then, Mr. Goldman. We abandon it here." He opened the passenger side door and pulled what was left of his five thousand dollars from the glove box and his suitcase off the seat. "I'll need you to rent me a car."

"Where's your coffee pot? I'm fading fast," Beamon said, straightening a precarious stack of dishes before they teetered into the sink.

Ernestine Waverly wheeled to the edge of the kitchen. "I don't drink coffee, Mark. Bothers my stomach. There are Cokes in the fridge."

Beamon ducked his head into the refrigerator and grabbed one. His first swig emptied half the can. It wasn't exactly what the doctor ordered, but it was better than nothing. His return to binge drinking had had the desired effect—made it almost impossible for his mind to focus on the fact that he'd lost everything meaningful in his life in the course of seventy-two hours. The problem was that it was making it impossible to focus on anything else, either.

"You okay, Mark?"

"I'm better, thanks," he said as he followed her back to the office, where Jack Goldman was doing his best to pace back and forth. "I think it's safe to run that by me again. If the phone taps are working like a dream, what's the problem?"

"E-mail," Goldman said, continuing to shuffle back and forth.

"Never had much use for it."

"You know how it works though, right?" Ernie said.

"I guess. You type something into your computer and send it to someone else's computer. It's just a fax without the paper."

"Essentially, that's right. We're picking up phone conversations clear as a bell on all six lines coming out of the compound." She nodded a brief acknowledgment toward Goldman.

"I thought you said there were eight lines."

"There are. One is dedicated to the security system, so there're no calls coming through on it. The other is dedicated to a computer. E-mail is going out over that one."

"So?"

"So, it's encrypted. We can't read it."

"Encrypted? You mean in code?" Beamon fell onto a chair and set his half-empty Coke can on the table next to him. "What the hell are they up to?"

"It doesn't really mean anything," Ernie said. "Encryption's not that uncommon. In fact, the program they're using is very common—it actually comes with the e-mail software when you buy it. I use the same system."

"Why?"

"I don't want half the people on the Internet to be able to read my letters."

Beamon chewed at his lower lip for a moment. "I've got a friend at the NSA. We go pretty far back. He might still be willing to help me. I don't know."

Ernie adjusted her muumuu nervously. Apples and pears today. "I don't think that would do us any good, Mark. Even with their resources it would take them years to crack the Church's encryption code . . ."

"What are you telling me, Ernie? That the National Security Agency can't crack an encryption program that I can buy at Toys "R" Us? They—"

Goldman stopped pacing. "Forget it. We're talking about an encryption code that encompasses thousands of characters. Literally trillions of possible combinations. There's no way."

Ernie nodded her agreement and looked hopefully at Beamon. Waiting for divine inspiration to strike, no doubt. Unfortunately, he wasn't feeling very inspired.

"Come on, Mr. Goldman," Beamon said. "You could record a conversation between dead people."

Goldman started his pacing again. "You get me in there and give me some time with their computer, maybe I could do something . . ."

Beamon let his head loll onto the back of the chair and stared at the ceiling. "You mean I almost got myself killed climbing a goddamn ice-covered tree in a blizzard and it isn't going to do me any good?"

"Blizzard, my ass," Goldman said. "And we got the phones."

"Screw the phones! I doubt they use them for anything more sensitive than ordering takeout. Whatever they have to say that's of interest to us is going to go out over that e-mail system. Shit . . ."

What the hell was he going to do now? Rent a tank and drive it through the front gate of Kneiss's compound? Shit, they'd probably have a newer, faster tank with more firepower waiting for him on the other side.

"There is something we could try," Ernie started.

"Oh, come on, woman!" Goldman said. "Don't waste my time!" He turned to Beamon. "Vericomm's the answer, son. That's where we need to concentrate our resources."

Beamon ignored him. "Go ahead, Ernie. What're you thinking."

"We could send the church an encryption software update."

"Come again?"

"I used to play a game with a friend of mine— he's a programmer, too. We'd try to break into each other's computers. Leave messages, move files around, that kind of thing. Well, once I had the idea of breaking the encryption to his e-mail—the same system the church is using."

"But you said that it would take years."

"If you took a conventional approach, it would. What I did was went out and bought a copy of the encryption software and reprogrammed it a bit."

"Reprogrammed it?"

She nodded. "I rewrote it so that when he sent an encrypted e-mail, he sent his encryption key along with it. Then I printed a big official-looking sticker that said there was a bug in the version he had purchased that was causing computer crashes. I re-shrink-wrapped the whole thing so it would look official and then mailed it to him."

"And it worked?"

"Uh, no."

Beamon sighed and crushed the Coke can in his hand. "It didn't work."

"Uh-uh. But I know why. Like I said, Rick—my friend—is a programmer. Even though I put on the sticker that there was an encryption problem with his version, he wanted to know the details of what was wrong. He called the software company and, you know, found out that there was no glitch."

Beamon thought about that for a moment and then turned to Goldman. "Couldn't you set up an eight-hundred line and run it in here? We could just put that number on the label—a special help line dedicated to this little problem."

The old man was looking more and more irritated. "I could, if it wasn't a complete waste of time. What did you tell us when we came in this morning? We've only got a week left! Even if the church bought this bullshit, it would probably take them a couple of weeks to get around to installing the goddamn update. By then the girl's dead, and you're not far behind."

"They've been pretty efficient at completely screwing up my life," Beamon said. "No reason to think they don't maintain their computers with the same diligence. Go ahead, Ernie. Nothing to lose."

"Jesus Christ, Mark! Wake up!" Goldman shouted. "We have to concentrate on Vericomm. Get something we can use against them."

Beamon shrugged. "I'm with you, Mr. Goldman, but I'm not hearing you give me a realistic course of action. You told me yourself that it'd take an army of people like you to figure out how they're doing it. And I doubt they're going to invite us over to their headquarters and show us their tapes. No, unless you can give me a concrete action plan, we're going to go with Ernie's suggestion. Set up the eight hundred line. Ernie, can you get that thing out in the mail tomorrow?"

"I've still got it. I can get it out today if you can take it to town and get it shrink-wrapped."

Goldman grabbed a half-full drinking glass from the table next to him and threw it across the room. Beamon ducked involuntarily as it smashed against the wall. "We can't afford to waste time like this! That little girl is going to die while you two are screwing around! We've got to get to Vericomm!"

"What the hell, Mr. Goldman! What do you want me to do? Blow the place up? I would, but it wouldn't even do us any good!"

Goldman grabbed his coat and headed for the door. "Somebody's got to get off their ass and do something," Beamon heard him grumble as he passed by.

"Jack, wait," Ernie said, but Goldman had already disappeared down the hall.

"Jesus," Beamon said when he heard the front door slam. Ernie wheeled her chair to face him and looked at him sternly

"What?"

"Don't you think you're being a little hard on him, Mark?"

"Don't bust my ass, Ernie. The guy was throwing shit around the room and cussing us out for no reason."

"He's having a tough time, Mark. I think you could try to be a little more compassionate."

Beamon couldn't believe what he was hearing. He was the one whose life had been completely trashed. It'd be dumb luck if he didn't find himself in jail or lining a shallow grave somewhere by this time next month. And now, on top of all that, now he was expected to coddle Jack Goldman, one of the most difficult SOBs to ever take a breath.

"Mark, you've got to understand that for the first time in his life, Jack's being beaten at his own game. The church has created a bugging system that he can't dismantle, expose, or subvert. He's feeling old."

"He *is* old," Beamon said, completely exasperated now.

"He's doing the best he can, Mark, but he's feeling like a dinosaur. He wants so desperately to do one more thing that really matters. And he wants to protect you. I don't think you realize how much he admires you. How much he cares about you."

Beamon was about to come to his own defense, but she held her hand up before he could open his mouth. "He can also save Jennifer. It's hard to explain. He didn't have children and he almost feels like if he can save the two of you, that you'll be a little piece of immortality for him."

"Where do you get this stuff, Ernie?"

"He tells me things."

Beamon had never heard Jack Goldman tell anybody anything other than how incompetent they were. "Look, in my own way, I love the old guy. I really do. But I don't know what he wants from me."

"Not that much, Mark. Your respect. Maybe a little friendship."

48

VERICOMM'S HEADQUARTERS BUILDING LOOKED like a ghost. Most of the lights in its glass facade had gone out over the last hour and now it just reflected the darkness and the swirling of snow though the thin mountain air.

Jack Goldman adjusted himself into a more comfortable position in the cramped car seat and let his mind wander into the past, as it seemed to want to do more and more every day. Back to the simple elegance of analog phone lines. Before digital transfer, encryption, and computer systems that were a thousand times as fast as he was and ten times as smart. Back to the time of closet-sized listening posts that reeked of coffee, tobacco, and sweat, and the reel-to-reel tapes filled with voices of glamorous hoods bragging endlessly about women, money, and death.

The building in front of him was a testament to the new age that he didn't want to be part of. It housed a system so grand in its scale that his ancient mind could have never dreamed it up. A system that stole the art from his vocation and turned it into pure digital science.

He was buried too deep in his own thoughts to notice the security guard's approach, but wasn't startled when he heard a knock on the window. He rolled it down about halfway and treated the guard to his most grandfatherly smile. "Hello, young man."

He saw the man's expression change from stoicism to mild concern. Goldman's age had turned into an increasingly effective tool over the last twenty years, but it was one he detested using.

"Uh, this is reserved parking, sir. You'll need to move your car."

"I'm so sorry. I was driving by and started feeling a bit ill. I just pulled in to rest for a few minutes." He reached for the key dangling from the ignition. "I didn't realize I was illegally parked."

"You're not really illegally parked," the guard said, starting to sound a little uncertain. "It's just that it's reserved. It's actually not a problem if you stay for a while. The guy who's assigned this space won't be back till tomorrow."

"I don't want to cause you any problems," Goldman said, holding his hand far enough from the keys so that the guard could see it shake.

"Not a problem. Really. Is there someone I could call? Maybe you'd like someone to pick you up? You're welcome to leave your car overnight in one of the unassigned spaces."

Goldman shook his head. "That's kind of you, but I'll be fine. At my age, you just have to rest every now and again."

The guard straightened and tapped the top of the car. "Okay, then. If you change your mind or if you need any help, I'll be just inside the front doors."

Goldman watched the man walk back toward the building as a wave of pain and nausea seized him. He leaned forward onto the wheel, his breath coming in short gasps. The attacks were getting longer and the time between them shorter as the cancer digested what was left of his stomach and continued its march through his other vital organs.

Two years ago, he'd ignored his doctor's gloomy six-month prediction, but now he felt it coming in the brief flashes of peace and numbness that overwhelmed him after the pain had, for the moment, stopped. He couldn't be sure, but he guessed that was death working to get a grip that he wouldn't be able to break.

There wasn't much time now. Just long enough to get Mark out of the quicksand he'd trapped himself in. And to save the girl.

Goldman smiled as he remembered Beamon as a first office agent. Smart. Jesus, he'd been smart. But even back then he'd had a gift for taking careful aim at his foot and shooting himself in it. Goddamned miracle he could still walk.

Goldman snapped himself back into the present and focused on a small man with a briefcase walking from the glass doors at the front of the building. He'd never laid eyes on Eugene Marino, Vericomm's tech manager, but this could be him.

Goldman had parked next to one of the few remaining cars in Vericomm's expansive parking area. The curb in front of it had "MARINO" stenciled in bright yellow letters, partially obscured by the snow.

"Mr. Marino?" Goldman said, opening his door and relying heavily on his cane as he eased himself out into the cold.

The man looked up and pulled his keys from his pocket as Goldman struggled across the icy asphalt toward him. "Yes, I'm Eugene Marino. Can I help you?"

Goldman stopped three feet from the man, ignoring the pain in his legs and another attack building in his stomach. "Yes, I think you can." He pulled a gun from his jacket and, holding it low enough that it couldn't be seen from a distance, aimed it at the man's stomach.

Marino's eyes widened, but it was clear that he didn't know what to make of the situation. "Is this . . . is this a mugging?" he said in a disbelieving voice.

Goldman could barely keep himself from laughing. He hadn't mugged anyone in over seventy years.

49

JENNIFER DAVIS LOOKED DOWN AT THE plate of food in her lap and forced herself to take another bite. She chewed purposefully, but had to concentrate not to gag when she swallowed. It had been getting harder and harder to eat. Harder and harder to sleep. To exercise. To do anything.

Her entire body quivered now, from the time she woke up to the time she finally turned out the lights and prayed for sleep to overtake her. It seemed like her brain was slowly leaking adrenaline—just enough to keep her constantly on edge but not enough to give her any strength.

Days and nights came and went—she knew that only because of her makeshift clock in the sink. As Good Friday got closer and closer, her own internal clock—the intuition that told her when she was tired, when she was hungry—had failed her.

Only seven days left.

The hope of escape that had kept her going had slowly died in her. She had seen no one since that day Sara had come and asked her to meet with the Elders. The plate of food appeared only once every twenty-four hours now—every night when she was asleep.

She fell back onto the bed and closed her eyes, trying to quiet the butterflies that flew tirelessly in her stomach all the time now. How could this be happening to her? She was only fifteen and she'd never done anything to hurt anyone.

In the last week, she'd spent her waking hours trying to live an entire life in the time she had left. She created elaborate fantasies about a future she would never see, infusing them with such intricate detail that sometimes they almost seemed real. She imagined her high school graduation: the sound of the principal's voice as it echoed across the auditorium, the bright pink high-top tennis shoes peeking out from beneath her black gown. She could feel the late-summer sun on her face as she watched herself packing her car and driving to college. She saw what her dorm room would look like. The silly arguments she'd have with her roommates. What it would be like the first time she made love.

Then her mind would wander forward. To her wedding. The pain of the birth of her first child. Finding her first gray hairs.

And one night, far in the future, she would walk, slightly stooped, to her bed. She would have just talked to her daughter and son-in-law on the phone. Their son—her grandson—was expecting his first child. She'd turn off the light that night and lie down. Then, smiling into the dark, she would close her eyes for the last time.

50

"YOU'RE DRIVING ME CRAZY WITH THAT thing, Mark," Ernie said, turning her chair away from him and covering her ears.

Beamon pulled his cell phone from his pocket. He'd finally turned it back on a few hours ago—worried that he'd miss something important. It had been pretty much ringing off the hook ever since.

"You're either going to have to answer it or turn it back off," Ernie said, hands still over her ears.

Beamon sighed and punched the button to pick up. "Yeah."

"What the fuck are you doing!"

He moved the phone to a more reasonable distance from his ear. "Jake. What can I do for you?"

"Kate Spelling told me you pulled a gun on them!"

"Melodramatic, but accurate."

"Look, Mark—I know you like to play the maverick, but you've gone too far this time. We're not just talking about your job now. We're talking about putting out an APB and making this thing public. The director's getting fucking hourly reports on this, and I'm not going to be able to keep him out of it for much longer. Let me help you."

Beamon rolled his eyes. "You want to help me."

"Okay, Mark. You say you like plain talk, so I'm

going to give it to you. I could give a shit about you. The thought of you getting run over by a bus gives me a hard-on. But despite all that, I'm probably the best friend you've got."

Sad, but possibly true, Beamon knew.

"Look, neither one of us wants this thing with you to blow up in the papers. Me because I've got a shot at an assistant directorship and this isn't going to help me; you because it's your life. Now, get your ass in here, and let's try to get control of this thing before it goes too far."

"I appreciate the honesty, Jake, but it's already gone too far."

"No it hasn't, Mark. Just—"

"Relax, Jake. Life as a fugitive doesn't suit me."

"When are you coming in?"

"I don't know yet. Soon. I've got some loose ends that need to be tied up."

"That's not good enough, Mark. The director is flying in to meet with me on the first, and you can be goddamn sure I'm going to have something for him. The gloves are coming off."

"You do what you've gotta do, Jake. I understand. The gloves are off."

Beamon pushed the button cutting off the connection and looked down at Ernie. "This just keeps getting worse, hon. I think it's time for you and me to part ways."

She looked horrified. "No! How can you say that? I'm as much a part of this as you are—you can't do it without me. I *have* to stay with you."

"Because God told you to?"

"You laugh at me behind my back, I know it. You and Jack both. But it's what I believe. How can you be sure there's no God? And that He hasn't brought us together to save His church? How can you?"

"I can't," Beamon said honestly. "I'm not sure. I'm never sure about anything. Look, I appreciate everything you've done for me and I admit that I wouldn't be anywhere with this investigation if it weren't for you. But things are going to start to escalate and I don't want to put you in harm's way." Beamon pointed at the computers behind her. "We've got a phone feed going into Mr. Goldman's apartment where I'm staying. We can monitor things from there—"

She shook her head violently and pushed her wheelchair forward until they were as close together as they could be, considering her chosen mode of transportation. "What more can they do to me, Mark? Look at me! Look around you! I haven't left this house since I moved in. And look what I've done to myself—I can barely walk. You and Jack are probably the best friends I have in the world—and I just met you. What more can they do?"

"They could kill you, Ernie. As long as you're breathing, you can change things. Take back what they took from you."

"You think I'm afraid to die?" she said indignantly.

"I hope you are, Ernie. I am."

Her face broke into a slow smile. "Thank you. Thank you for caring about what happens to me. But you really shouldn't worry. That dream I keep having, the one I told you about in the beginning. It goes on a little longer every night. Albert's in it now. He's waiting for me."

Beamon's eyes widened. "Ernie, you're starting to scare me now. You're not going to die."

She seemed so serene, sitting there in her chair.

"It doesn't matter. I know what I have to do, and I know why. For the first time, really. You can't imagine what it feels like to know—to be absolutely sure—that there is a God. And to know that you're important to Him. That you've been chosen by Him." She pointed at Beamon. "He's chosen you, too, Mark. But you'll never believe it, will you?"

"I guess I've never had much use for God, Ernie."

"But he's got use for you."

She turned her chair and wheeled it to a table that had been recently cleared of its normal complement of computer-related debris and pointed to a new blue phone. "The eight-hundred number comes in here."

"The bogus helpline on that e-mail update you sent?" Beamon said, consciously letting her change the subject.

She nodded. "They haven't called yet. But I've been praying."

Beamon smiled politely. What the hell was he going to do with her? He'd always made a practice of trying to do what he thought was right—no matter how much of an ass it made him look like or how disastrous the consequences. But what was the right thing here? He could walk out right now, have Goldman cut off the phone patch to her and never see her again. She'd probably be safe then, but without her help would he be able to find Jennifer? And how much danger was Ernie really in? He'd been so careful to keep her involvement from the church . . .

A phone started ringing, and Beamon's eyes darted to the blue one on the table.

"Sorry, Mark," Ernie said, picking up the green one next to her computer. "Hello? Oh, hold on, let me put you on speaker."

She laid the handset down on the table and punched at her keyboard. "Jack, can you hear me? Mark's here."

"Loud and clear, Ernie. How you doing, Mark?"

He sounded very strange—happy. Giddy might be a better word. Maybe it was just the reverberation of the computer's speakers.

"I'm okay, Mr. Goldman. How about you? You sound a little funny."

"I'm great. Having a wonderful evening. Ernie, I'm downloading something into your system on the seven-three-four-two number. Could you confirm that you're receiving?"

Ernie wheeled to another computer and tapped the mouse with her index finger, lighting up the monitor. "Yes, I'm receiving."

"FAN-tastic."

Beamon shifted uncomfortably in his chair. He'd never heard Goldman sound anything like this. Could he be finally losing it? At his age, senility was definitely starting to look overdue. "What is it you're sending, Mr. Goldman?"

"We were right about Vericomm, boy. I'm sending audio files of some of their more interesting tapes."

Beamon stood and walked hesitantly to Ernie's side. Leaning close in to the microphone next to her computer, he said, "Come again?"

"Vericomm *has* been taping the NickeLine long-distance calls—we were right. I'm dumping their archive to Ernie's computer."

"Are you screwing with me?"

"Of course not."

Beamon grabbed one of the speakers on the table and spoke directly at it. "You are a fucking genius, Mr. Goldman. I always knew you were. The best there ever was."

"I'm starting with the One-A-A stuff," Goldman said. "If I can get it all sent, I'll work on the lower-priority tapes."

"One-A-A?"

"Oh, Mark, this system is a thing of beauty. You wouldn't believe it." His tone had changed from giddiness to something between admiration and awe. "All calls made on NickeLine come through the computer system here at the central office. They're instantly given a number code based on who's calling. They know 'cause of the PIN you dial. Priority one means the person is important. You, for instance, as the head of the Flagstaff office, would be a priority one. A senator might be another example."

"What are the letters for?"

"The first one relates to keywords. The computer has some really spectacular voice recognition software. It listens for interesting words. *Bribe, sex, kill, Kneiss, Evolution*, and *money* are a few. Various swear words, too. It also measures volume, on the premise that if people are shouting, they're probably saying something interesting. If an important person hits on the right keywords, the conversation is given the code of one-A and it's sent down to a group of listeners who get right on it."

"Have I mentioned that you're a genius?" Beamon said, feeling for the first time in a week that he might just weasel his way out of this thing with his skin still wrapped around him. "What's the last letter for?"

"Oh, that signifies that it's been listened to and tells you how interesting it actually turned out to be."

"So we're getting the good stuff."

"Oh, yeah. I think you'll find it to be interesting listening. Could you hold on for a second?"

Beamon and Ernie both jumped at the loud crack that came over the speakers. It was followed by a muffled whimpering.

"Would you please shut up already? Try to be a man, for God's sake." Goldman's voice, but it was clear that he wasn't speaking to them.

"Mr. Goldman! Hello? Mr. Goldman? What the hell was that?"

"Huh? Oh, sorry, Mark. Just giving 'em something to think about."

Beamon realized that he'd been so elated by Goldman's coup that he hadn't really considered how he'd pulled it off. "Where are you, exactly?"

"Vericomm's tech center. Hold on for just one more second."

There was another crack that Beamon now knew was a gunshot.

"Yeah, you want some of that? Put your head out there again!" Goldman's voice taunted over the speakers.

"What's happening, Mark?" Ernie said, an expression of fear and confusion playing across her distorted features.

He held up his hand as Goldman's voice started, giddy again. "Their security boys are looking pretty upset, I'll tell you. Don't think it's going to be long before they figure out how to get that door the rest of the way open, though."

"Jesus Christ, Jack, get the hell out of there," Beamon said.

"Only one door out, Mark, and you can believe me when I tell you that they've got it covered."

The gunfire that sounded over the speakers this time was fully automatic.

"Damn!" he heard Goldman shout. There was rustling and the sound of things being knocked over as the old man took cover.

"What the fuck, Jack! You must have had a plan when you went in there," Beamon shouted desperately.

"I did. I planned on it being a one-way trip. I'll keep the feed going as long as I can. Been good knowing you, boy. Good-bye, Ernie. Oh, and Ernie? Lose some weight and find a man, for God's sake."

The phone went dead and Ernie wheeled to the screen behind her. Tears began running down her round face as she stared at it.

After a little less than a minute she made a quiet choking sound. "The feed's down."

51

SARA RENSLIER DIDN'T TURN WHEN THE footsteps began echoing off the walls behind her, but continued to concentrate on the large cross hanging above the altar on invisible wires. A symbol of everything she had built. "Was there any . . . damage?" she said when the footsteps stopped.

"Yes. A substantial amount of audio material was transmitted. All recent. All highly sensitive."

Sara took a deep breath and felt the burn of bile rise in her throat. "Were you able to trace the phone number it went to?"

Silence.

She turned and faced Gregory Sines, the head of the church's security force. His face was sunken and pale, accentuating the narrow pink scar that ran from his mustache to his right eye.

"Did you trace it?" she repeated.

"The call went to a hotel room, where it was connected to another number."

"What number?"

"There's no way to tell. Whoever set up the transfer knew what he was doing."

"Who was he?" she said.

"The man who got into Vericomm? We don't know yet. White male. Probably well into his eighties . . ."

"His eighties!" Her breath was coming short now. She closed her eyes and forced herself to calm down.

"He wasn't carrying any identification. We found the car he was driving, but it had been rented under an alias. We've fingerprinted his body and sent copies to one of our people at the FBI. We should know more soon."

"It doesn't matter," she said. "Beamon's behind this. That man was working for him."

Their private investigators hadn't been able to dig up anything substantial to use against Beamon—he was unmarried so no affairs, he wasn't a closet homosexual, no history of drug use or any other illegal activity. What they did find, though, was his drinking, his self-destructive behavior, and his lack of close friends or family—suggesting that he was a weak man with no foundation. A man the church's psychologists insisted would be easily diverted.

It was clear now that they had underestimated him. And she knew that she had accepted their analysis too easily, considering Beamon a relatively small player in another one of the government's hopeless bureaucracies.

Over the last decade, as the church's power had grown, she had begun to discount the power of the world's governments. Organizations led by men and women of shockingly limited intelligence who could be bought and sold with little more than glass beads. Beamon didn't seem to fit into that category.

She backed away from Sines and sat down on the steps leading to the altar. There was no turning back. She had created a nearly perfect plan to maintain her power over the church. But the plan didn't include a way out. When she had spoken her version of Kneiss's dying wishes to the Elders, she had set something in motion that couldn't be stopped. Jennifer had to die on the appointed date with all the Elders present. If she died before her time, the Elders—many of whom were already silently suspicious of her—would begin to put things together.

Until now, she had kept them weak by creating conflicts and jealousy between them—showing occasional favor toward one or another in Kneiss's name, passing out generous monetary rewards and severe penalties. But if they began to suspect what she had done, they would band together. Even Sines and his Guardians would be powerless in the face of that.

She considered for a moment the possibility of keeping Jennifer alive, telling the Elders that she had misinterpreted Kneiss's words. Isolating his granddaughter as she had him.

But that was impossible. Eventually they would gain access to her. And then they would learn the truth. No. There was only one way.

"We can't afford the luxury of keeping Mark Beamon alive anymore. We'll deal with whatever problems his death causes when they arise."

Sines remained silent.

"That's all, Gregory," she said, waving him away. "See to it. Now."

"We don't know where he is."

"What are you talking about?" she said, rising slowly to her feet. "He was being watched . . ."

"Our people lost him in the storm yesterday. He hasn't returned to his apartment and I don't think he will." Sines's expression turned indignant. "You've left him very little to come back to."

Sara swung an arm across the altar, sending a crystal urn and a set of elegant candlesticks crashing to the floor. "Don't you dare speak to me like that! I assumed that you would be competent enough to watch one broken man. Perhaps it was my fault for trusting in your abilities."

"It was a mistake to have him suspended. It freed him. Before, he was easy to watch and bound by the rules of the Bureau. Now—"

"I didn't ask for your analysis!" she shouted. "I only asked that you follow my instructions."

She stepped back and tried to calm down. This was not going to fall apart now. It couldn't. Not because of an overweight low-level bureaucrat.

"He's alone now," she said aloud. "The man who helped him is dead. He's alone. Homeless. He's lost everything. He can't possibly care about the girl anymore."

Beamon was controllable, she told herself. He had to be.

52

FIVE SHOTS OF BOURBON HAD SLOWED THE shaking in Beamon's hands enough for him to hold a lighter to the tip of his cigarette. He took a deep drag and felt the smoke fill his lungs. The instant lightheadedness and heaviness in his chest that he had been experiencing since he abandoned his new health regime seemed to be gone. A sign that the healing process, started when he moved to Arizona, had been completely reversed. Hallelujah.

A cockroach scurrying across the linoleum floor caught Beamon's eye. He followed it as it found its way through the maze of boxes, cables, and computer equipment that were strewn across the room, finally disappearing beneath the overalls Goldman had worn when he'd wired the church's phones. Draped over the empty box in front of Beamon, they looked like the old man's goddamned ghost.

Relying heavily on the worn arm of the chair he was sitting in, Beamon pushed himself to his feet and stuffed the still-damp overalls into the box. He began to close the cardboard flaps but stopped himself midway, realizing that this was the closest thing Goldman would ever get to a burial.

He had known the man for almost twenty years. He'd never counted it up before, but that was how long it had been.

Goldman's hair had been a little darker and fuller when they'd first met, and his skin had fit him a little better, but overall he'd been pretty much the same. People who had worked with him since the beginning—all dead now—swore he'd been a cantankerous old bastard at the tender age of nineteen.

Beamon wanted to call someone, but who? Goldman's family was long gone. As far as he knew, the old man didn't even have a secretary—having given up on them when they started objecting to being patted on the ass and called honey, and insisting that his battery of answering machines and mountains of software were more efficient and less flighty. But whenever he made that familiar speech, it was always with a tinge of loneliness in his voice.

Goldman had probably called him four or five times in the last three years. Beamon would pick up the phone and the old man would start into a tirade about something or other—the FBI, the CIA, politics, television. That was just the old man's way— he'd always known it. Goldman didn't know what else to say. But he had used Goldman's harmless badgering as an excuse to avoid him. Avoid the man who had just given his life to save a little girl and to get him out of the trap he'd sprung on himself.

Closing the flaps on the box was like throwing dirt on a coffin. Beamon raised his glass in salute, sloshing about a quarter of it down his arm. "You were right, Jack. I am a worthless sonofabitch." Words he'd have to remember for his own tombstone.

He scooted a chair up to the nearest computer terminal and unwrapped the computer disks containing the Vericomm audio from a piece of legal-sized paper that contained the instructions on how to listen to them.

He was having a little trouble bringing the instructions into full focus, but after a few minor wrong turns, he was faced with a screen full of file names. Each started with the surnames of the people on the line, then gave a date and time.

He slipped a pair of headphones over his ears and clicked twice on the first file. He recognized the name of one of the callers, but he couldn't place it exactly. A governor or senator or something.

Two hours later, halfway through the last file on the list, he tore the headphones from his ears and threw them to the floor in disgust.

"Jesus Christ!" he said to the empty room.

He'd always been a pretty hard-boiled cynic when it came to the people who chose to crawl around in the muck of politics, but never in his darkest alcohol-induced imaginings would he have ever come up with the contents of those tapes. Prepubescent prostitutes, bribes, blackmail, unholy alliances, and borderline treason. And all in glorious digital stereo.

The really worrisome thing, though, wasn't that the men running the government were into things that would make Caligula blush, it was that they weren't bright enough not to talk about those things over the phone. No, Beamon reminded himself, actually, that wasn't the most worrisome thing. The worst part of the whole thing was that the people whose voices were immortalized on his hard drive would slit their own mothers' throats to keep their extracurricular activities quiet.

As he leaned back and lit another cigarette, the cell phone in his pocket started up again. He flipped it open and put it up to his ear. "Hello, Sara."

The caller on the other end was silent for a moment. "Mr. Beamon."

"Somehow I knew you'd reconsider," Beamon said. "Real Christian of you."

"I assume that you're still interested in a meeting," Sara said.

The fury and frustration clogging her throat would normally have given Beamon at least a little bit of satisfaction. But sitting there in Goldman's empty apartment, he just felt numb. "Love one."

"Where?"

"There's a little restaurant called Antonio's. It's—"

"I know where it is."

"There, then. I'll let you buy me dinner. Tomorrow night. Seven o'clock."

Beamon flipped the phone shut and let out a long breath. Antonio's would be crowded. He'd be safe. Probably.

He looked at the calendar on his watch. He—Jennifer—had six days. Sara would try to play him for time. He was going to have to make this bargaining chip count.

The phone rang again and he picked it up on its third ring. "Let me guess. You don't like Italian."

"Mark?"

The accent was a little thicker and the voice a little higher-pitched than he remembered it, but there was still no mistaking who it was.

"Hans? It's good to hear your voice. How are you?"

"I am not well, Mark. Not well at all." He spoke quickly. "I have word from our people in the church."

"Yeah?"

"The church's leadership has recognized that you cannot be deterred by the normal means. Mark, I believe they mean to kill you."

Beamon lit another cigarette and blew the smoke into the phone. "I think you may be right, Hans."

"You must get out of there! I assure you that they not only have the will but also the means. Come here, to the embassy. I can offer you protection while we talk. Perhaps together we have enough information to expose them for what they are."

The offer was tempting. There was only one little problem. "What are your sources telling you about Jennifer Davis?"

"Nothing, I'm afraid. If the church does have her—and I know you believe that they do—they're keeping it very quiet. Knowledge at the highest levels only."

Beamon nodded and stared at the file names on the computer screen. "Well, when it's all over, if I'm still standing, I'll have an interesting story to tell you."

"Make sure you're still standing, then, Mark. A man with your reputation coming out against the church could do much to end the friction between our two governments."

"And I want to help you do that, Hans. But the girl's what I'm after. If I can do both, I will. If not, I'll have to leave politics to the politicians."

"Fair enough. But, Mark . . ."

"Yeah?"

"You must be careful. *Very* careful."

53

"DO YOU KNOW WHAT YOU'VE DONE?" Sara screamed as the door flew open and slammed into the wall.

Jennifer rolled off the bed, where she'd been lying in the half-sleep that seemed to have overtaken her in the last few days. The jolt of the cold floor cleared away some of the cobwebs, but she was still too groggy to dodge when Sara ran at her and pushed her back onto the bed.

Jennifer raised her hands too late to deflect a vicious open-handed slap that hit her full in the face. The stinging pain in her cheek cleared her mind a little more as Sara jerked her head back. The face she found herself staring into was unfamiliar—it was Sara, but the woman's eyes had gone wild and her pale complexion had turned bright red with rage.

"You think I'm going to lose everything because of you?"

She heard more than felt Sara's second strike across her face.

"Albert would still be preaching on a street corner if it weren't for me."

Jennifer tried to push her away, but she was too weak. Sara brought her face close and tightened her grip on Jennifer's hair. "No one's coming for you, Jennifer. No one."

"Why are you doing this to me?" Jennifer felt the tears coming and choked off a sob. "I just want to go home! I just want to go home."

The desperation and hate in Sara's face began to fade into the now-familiar expression of cruel superiority. "You'll never go home, Jennifer. You know that, don't you? You should have never come here."

"I didn't come here," Jennifer said, letting her body relax and her mind begin to drift away again. "You took me."

Sara was talking in a voice so low that she could almost feel it in her chest, but the words were meaningless to her. She looked away and let her eyes wander across the blank wall, trying desperately to return to the make-believe world that had taken away some of her loneliness and fear. Her gaze lingered for a moment on the door to the room. It was still open, and the poorly lit hallway was visible through it. For a moment the image confused her. Something was different. It took a few seconds for her to grasp why she could see straight through to the far wall of the hallway. The man who always stood silently at the door wasn't there.

He wasn't there.

Jennifer could feel her heart rate slowly increasing. After a few more seconds, she could almost hear it. The blood began to push through to her limbs, clearing away the lethargy that had overwhelmed her as she'd slowly lost hope.

The meaningless drone coming from Sara stopped short when Jennifer turned back to face the woman.

Closing her mouth was probably the only thing that saved Sara's front teeth.

None of the elaborate fantasies Jennifer had constructed over the last week could compare to the feeling of her fist connecting with the face that had tormented her and twisted everything in her life around. The face that had caused her father to go crazy and her mother to die. The face that she saw in the dark when she bolted awake at night.

Sara's hand fell from her hair and she watched the woman stumble backward, finally falling hard in the middle of the room. She was on all fours trying to get back to her feet when Jennifer reached her at as full a run as the short distance between them would allow.

Sara tried to cry out, but it was strangled in her throat when she was nearly lifted off the ground by Jennifer's bare foot.

A second kick, aimed at her head, glanced off her jaw.

Jennifer started to line up for another blow, feeling an indescribable sense of release as the burning in her stomach and the shaking in her limbs stopped. She wanted to kill this woman. She'd never wanted to hurt anyone before in her life, but now all she wanted was to feel this woman's skull cave in beneath her foot.

There wasn't time, though.

Instead of continuing the attack, Jennifer forced herself to use the momentum in her leg to jump over the woman and run from the room, slamming the door behind her and hoping desperately that it locked. Or, better yet, that she'd done too much damage for Sara to get up.

Which way?

To her left, the hall seemed to get darker, to her right, brighter. She picked right and began sprinting down the corridor, hoping the light was coming from the sun. She had to get out.

When the hall came to a T, she had to make another decision. *Come on, Jennifer,* she thought. *This is your chance. Don't go off half-cocked. What are you going to do?*

The possibility of her walking out of there was most likely less than zero, she realized. She had no idea where she was, it was the dead of winter, and she was in her underwear. A phone. She had to find a phone.

She moved as quietly as she could to the first door she saw, trying to get control of her breathing before someone heard her. It was a bathroom. She ducked back out of it and padded down the hall to the next door.

An office.

She went in and closed the door quietly behind her. The phone was on an antique desk, neatly stacked with official-looking papers. She picked it up and dialed 911.

A recording started, prompting her to stay on the line.

"No," she said quietly, hanging up the phone. She could already hear people in the hall.

She tried her boyfriend's number. He had an answering machine—so even if no one was home, she could tell him enough for the police to find her.

A voice over the phone told her that she had to dial a one to reach that number.

The noises in the hall were getting louder as she depressed the hang-up button on the phone and redialed Jamie's number as a long-distance call.

"Please enter your access code," came a mechanical-sounding voice.

"Oh, God, please, no." Tears began to run down her face as she punched in numbers at random.

"I don't recognize that code. Please reenter it now."

She depressed the hang-up button again, finding it impossible to catch her breath. The sounds in the hall were close now, clearly audible over her own panting.

She looked out the window. The brightness in the hall had been artificial—it was dark outside and she could hear the quiet whine of the wind. She leaned closer to the glass, reducing the glare, and saw that there was nothing out there, only low snow-covered hills and a pine forest in the distance. She'd freeze for sure. Probably in only a few minutes.

Jennifer looked over her shoulder at the closed door behind her and then back at the window. She couldn't go back to that room. She couldn't.

She was about to replace the handset and unlock the window when one last idea came to her. She crossed her fingers for a moment and then dialed another number, trying to ignore the increasing commotion outside.

It started to ring and was almost immediately picked up by a recording.

"Thank you for calling the Colorado Cyclist. If you have a touch tone phone, press one for sales, catalog requests, or product registration . . ."

It was the only eight hundred number she knew by heart. There was an access code for long distance, but why would there be one for toll-free calls? She pressed the key for the sales department just as the door flew open.

Holding the phone with both hands, she backed

against the wall and screamed as the Mustache Man ran at her. When he got hold of her, she let her knees go limp and sank to the ground, protecting the phone with her body. He tried to reach around her and pry it from her hand, but there was no way for him to get a grip.

She felt his weight come off her for a moment and she twisted around, trying to grab him as he went for the cord.

It was too late. She saw the wire ripped from the wall and heard the connection go dead, but couldn't bring herself to release the phone. It had been her only hope.

She struggled violently as he pulled her arms out from under her and pinned them behind her back, knowing that it was her last chance to fight before they threw her back into that empty room.

Jennifer heard the uneven clatter of running footsteps and craned her neck to try to see the person approaching, but she knew who it was. A splatter of blood hit the carpet in front of her as Sara dropped to her knees and swung a clawlike hand at her face. Jennifer braced for the blow, but the man holding her caught Sara's hand before it connected.

"Sara, stop! She can't be marked," Jennifer heard him say.

Sara's breath was coming in short gasps as she pulled away from the man and raised her hand again.

"Sara!"

Reason began to creep back into her eyes and she reached down and dug her fingers into Jennifer's cheeks, pulling her head up farther. "You don't ever touch me! Ever!"

Jennifer jerked her head to the left and got her teeth around Sara's thumb. She felt the warm blood starting to flow into her mouth and heard Sara scream before everything went black.

54

"TURN HERE," BEAMON SAID, LEANING OVER the front seat and pointing out the windshield.

"It'd be a lot faster to go up a couple of blocks. Your way would take us through a neighborhood."

"It's my dime."

The cab driver apparently saw that as sound reasoning and swung the cab right. He slowed to under twenty-five miles an hour as the commercial area they had been driving through gave way to a quiet neighborhood of small, well-kept homes.

Beamon twisted around in his seat and stared out the back window. Other than the occasional middle-aged man turning his snowblower for another pass at his driveway, the street was pretty much deserted. Not that he really thought he was being followed. What would be the point? The church knew where he was going. Of course, they would do everything they could to reacquire him when he left the restaurant, but better to worry about that later.

When his cell phone started ringing, he sank back into the seat and dug it out of his pocket. "Hello?"

"Mark! It's me!"

Ernie's voice. She sounded like she'd shaken off the depression that had gripped her since Goldman's death.

"If I didn't know better, I'd say you had some good news for me. Tell me I'm right."

"You're right! In fact, not only do I have good news, but I have good news and better news. Which do you want first?"

"Give me the good."

"The eight hundred number rang today."

"You're kidding," Beamon said, jolting upright in the seat. He had pretty much agreed with Goldman that the chances of her software-update scheme working were about the same as G. Gordon Liddy voting Democrat. "What did they say?"

"They wanted to confirm that there were no problems with the actual encryption."

"I trust you were very reassuring."

"Very. They're loading tonight!"

Beamon pumped a fist in the air, startling the cab driver, who had been looking in the rearview mirror. "That's gonna be hard to beat, Ernie. What's the better news?"

"I've got a recording of a call that went out from Albert's compound. I think you'll be interested. Let me try to patch it through."

There was some clicking on the line, and then a woman's voice announcing that he had reached the Colorado Cyclist and had some options. A tone sounded, then there was a loud crash, a scream that sounded like it came from a young girl, and an abrupt end to the call.

Beamon sat silently for a moment listening to his heartbeat. "That had to be her, Ernie. It had to be."

"I read in the papers that Jennifer was a mountain bike racer. I called the Colorado Cyclist. They sell mountain bike accessories."

"Fifty bucks says that if I hadn't left all the files

on this case in my condo, I could find all kinds of charges from that place on Jennifer's credit card."

"I don't think I'd take that bet," Ernie said excitedly.

"One thing bothers me, though . . ."

"Why would she call them?"

"Yeah."

"I've been thinking about that and I'm pretty sure I have an answer. If that is her, we know they're holding her at the compound, right?"

"Right." Beamon saw that they were only a few blocks from the restaurant. He put his hand over the mouthpiece of the phone and told the driver to circle the block.

"The compound is a long-distance call from where Jennifer lived," Ernie continued.

"So?"

"The place I used to work at had a phone system that made you dial a code before you could call long distance—that way they knew if you were charging personal calls to the company. What if the church has a similar system?"

"So she called an eight hundred number," Beamon said. "Clever girl. But why not just call nine-one-one?"

"I tried. Kept getting a recording. When I called the Colorado Cyclist, though, they got right on the line."

It made sense. She somehow got past Sara and her lackeys and made it to a phone. She'd have limited time before they found her. She'd try 911 first and get a recording. She'd probably call a family friend next—maybe that lady with the beehive. But she'd find out that she needed a code. Then it would occur to her that she probably wouldn't need one for an eight hundred number and she'd call the only one she could remember. Or if she knew a few, the one that had the fastest patch through to a human.

"It's like I told you, Mark. God is on our side."

"If that's true, I hope He comes up with something a little better."

"What? Better than this?"

"I already assumed that Jennifer was being held at the compound, Ernie. I just didn't know what to do with the information. If the call was more concrete, I'd send it to someone I trust at the Bureau." He paused for a moment, trying to think if there was anyone anymore. "But as it is, they'd never get a warrant—even if they bought into the theory."

Beamon tapped the driver on the shoulder and waved his hand in the general direction of the restaurant.

"Then this is all for nothing," Ernie said, sounding a little dejected again

"Hell no, Ernie! Things are starting to go our way. Shit, God's probably just warming up."

"Do you think so?"

"Sure. It's been my experience that investigations are all about momentum, and we're finally starting to get some. The only problem is, we don't have much time to let it build."

"Were you able to play the audio I sent you?"

"Yeah."

"What did you think?"

"It was something, that's for sure. We'll know if it's gonna do us any good within the hour."

"I listened to it. I can't believe the godless whores we've chosen to run this country."

"Who'd you think ran it?" Beamon said as the cab eased to a stop in front of the brightly lit façade of Antonio's Italian Ristorante.

"Look, I gotta go, Ernie," Beamon said, digging in his pocket for the quickly thinning envelope of cash. "Great work, hon. We're gonna win this thing. Don't worry."

"How are you, sir," the host said, holding a hand out for Beamon's coat. "Do you have a reservation?"

"I'm meeting someone. Last name's Renslier."

He ran his finger down the book in front of him for a moment. "Ms. Renslier arrived a few minutes ago. If you'll wait for just one moment, I'll take you to her table."

Beamon watched him as he opened a closet and picked out a hanger for the red parka that had been serving him so well. "There aren't any private parties or anything going on tonight, are there?"

The host looked a bit confused. "Private parties?"

Beamon knew he was being paranoid, but he couldn't help himself. "Yeah. Like, no one called and rented the whole place out for tonight, did they?"

"No, not tonight. We do parties like that occasionally. We also have private rooms available. Make sure you give us a call at least a week ahead of time if you want one, though."

Despite the host's assurances, Beamon couldn't help studying the faces of the diners as he weaved through them on the way to the back of the restaurant.

There were definitely Kneissians there. The annoying, fresh-scrubbed optimism that oozed from every pore all over their well-coordinated outfits gave them away. Most were couples, though, and many had tediously well-behaved children with them.

Beamon nodded his thanks to the host and slid into the booth across from Sara Renslier and a man he'd never seen before. The scar emanating from his mustache was exactly as Ernie had described it, though. Beamon reached across the table. "Greg Sines, isn't it? I don't think we've met."

The man's eyes bored into him as he put a death grip on Beamon's hand. He'd seen that look more than a few times before. It said, "One day I'm going to tear your heart out with whatever blunt instrument happens to be handy." With few exceptions, every man who had ever looked at him that way was either dead or in jail. Hopefully that record would continue with this asshole.

Sines tucked some kind of hand-held device— probably a rig that checked for wires—into his pocket and left without a word. Beamon looked around him and, confirming that he was in the smoking section, lit a cigarette. "Nice to see you again, Sara."

She looked different. The light in this part of the restaurant was set at a level more conducive to mood than discerning detail, but the heavy makeup was an obvious departure from the look required of Kneiss's minions. The other thing, less apparent and possibly a trick of shadow, was the slightly lopsided look to her face.

"Hurt your hand?" Beamon said, leaning a bit to the side to get a better angle on the line of her jaw. If he didn't know better, he'd say she had been punched in the mouth.

Sara looked down at the new white bandage wound around her thumb. "An accident."

Beamon tried unsuccessfully to stifle a smile. Now he knew how Jennifer had made it to the phone. He really *had* to meet that girl one day.

"So, Sara," he said, letting cigarette smoke roll from his mouth as he spoke. "What do we talk about?"

"We could start with the fact that we both have something the other wants."

Beamon was surprised at her directness. "I know what I have that you want, but what do you have to give me?"

"Your life back."

He'd hoped for a different answer. "My life?"

She nodded and took a piece of bread from the basket on the table. "I've heard rumors that the molestation allegations against you may be false, and I could probably find proof of that if I were to put some of my people to work on it. I also may have access to information regarding your credit and some friends at the IRS who could be helpful to you."

"And my job?"

She took a small bite of the bread, more as a nervous gesture than from hunger. "Of course that's in the FBI's hands now. I do have friends who might be able to help. Friends who have some weight."

Beamon nodded but didn't say anything.

"I would also be happy to make a donation to your legal defense fund—you may need attorneys, and they can be expensive. Of course, if you were to simply choose to take early retirement, whatever was left in that fund would be yours."

He couldn't resist. "How much are we talking about?"

"What do you think you would need to mount an adequate defense?"

"Uh, five million," he said, pulling a number out of the air.

To his surprise, nothing at all registered on her face. "I think that sounds reasonable."

Beamon leaned back in his chair and waved down a waiter. "Jim Beam on the rocks, please." He pointed to Sara, but she just shook her head.

He had to admit, the woman knew how to put a tempting offer on the table. Of course, it would take him a while to adjust to retirement, but he figured he could get used to being a wealthy man of leisure. And with his reputation dusted off a bit, Carrie would probably be back in the picture. Maybe he could try his hand at being a househusband/full-time stepfather? Learn to bake.

Nah.

"I want the girl."

"The girl?" Sara looked mildly amused. "Oh, yes. Jennifer Davis. The girl you think Albert for some reason kidnapped and is holding in his dungeon."

"Kneiss is dead."

"Excuse me?"

"Don't talk to me like I'm an idiot, Sara. It pisses me off. Kneiss is dead. We both know it. Obviously, it's not in the best interests of the church—that is, your best interests—to let that little tidbit leak until Good Friday. Got to keep that collection plate full."

"I understand now," Sara said, starting a smile but stopping its progress across her face with a slight wince. "You believe that Albert died and I needed a new messenger. I've heard that you believe that Jennifer Davis is Albert's granddaughter. If that's true, she'd be the perfect replacement, wouldn't she?"

Sara shook her head. "I'm disappointed, Mr.

Beamon. I would have thought you'd understand us better by now. There's no need for a new messenger. And for that matter, no expectation that there would be one for another two thousand years."

"I know that. I was thinking more along the lines that Kneiss wanted someone to replace him as head of the church instead of putting you in the job. I think Albert understood what you were doing and didn't like it."

"What I was doing?" she said, suddenly angry. "What do you think it is that Albert doesn't like? The fact that I've devoted my entire life to spreading his message and building his church?"

"I don't think it was your results, Sara. I think it was your methods." Beamon jerked his head toward the bar. "Men like Gregory Sines don't exactly fit into most people's idea of a church elder."

"What I've done, I've done for God."

Beamon smiled. "I believe that most of the war, torture, and cruelty in our history were started by men with those same words on their lips."

"I don't think you have any idea what it is to have faith, Mr. Beamon. God directs me in all things. He tells me what is right and wrong. He has given me the strength to accomplish what I have."

"And the strength to protect the church when it's threatened."

"That too," she said, looking directly at him.

"And Jennifer's a threat now, isn't she? You built the church, not Albert. He had the message, but you had the means." Beamon took a sip of his drink. "And then, right before he dies—the old sonofabitch gives it away. Gives away *your* church. To a fifteen-year-old girl with dyed blonde hair and a ring in her nose, no less. That had to be a kick in the ass."

"I have no idea—"

Beamon cut her off. "But then Albert goes and dies—not ascends, just dies like the rest of us. Or maybe you helped him along? Either way, it would leave you in quite a pickle, wouldn't it? The only way you'd be able to explain it is that his time as the Messenger was over. That someone is being chosen to take his place."

Sara sat perfectly still. The heavy makeup and dim lighting would have made her look like a mannequin if it hadn't been for the reflection of her eyes.

"Seems to me that Jennifer would be a good choice," Beamon continued. "Fixes your little theological glitch and has the added benefit of getting her out of your way."

Beamon put his cigarette out in the ashtray on the table. "Because somebody has to take Kneiss's place next week. Don't they?"

Sara's eyes darted left. Toward Sines, Beamon guessed.

"That's quite a theory, Mr. Beamon. I'm not sure how to respond."

"Then let me make a suggestion. Give me Jennifer. You religious leaders are masters at dredging up obscure Bible passages to justify whatever it is you want to do. Hell, tell your people that God appeared to you in a box of Cracker Jacks and told you that it was Jennifer's destiny to be a Protestant. I don't really give a shit."

"Do you think your position is strong enough to be making threats, Mr. Beamon? What do you have? A few illegally obtained recordings of conver-

sations between—who? Can you prove these people's identities? I doubt it. And I doubt even more
that you can prove how the recordings were originally obtained."

"Oh, I think you're probably right. From a
letter-of-the-law standpoint, I'd have a real uphill
battle. But if those recordings were sent to the FBI
anonymously—or maybe better, to some of my
contacts in the press—with a detailed explanation
of what they were and how they were obtained, I
imagine that I could generate some real interest in
the way you operate your church. Hell, I probably
wouldn't even have to go through all that trouble. I
could just give them to your biggest fan—the German government—and trust them to use them to
do the absolute maximum damage."

Gregory Sines slid silently into the booth next
to Sara, prompting Beamon to move his hand a little closer to his gun. "Look, Sara. I don't care about
the people on the tapes. And I care even less about
the people who vote those idiots in. It's not my job
to save the public from themselves. But the girl,
well, as I see it, she's gotten a raw deal."

"I don't understand you, Mr. Beamon. You've
lost nearly everything of value to you in the span of
a few weeks. And for what? If I had the girl, I certainly wouldn't let you find her." She shook her
head in sadly. "Take what I'm offering you. Marry
that psychiatrist. Move away from Flagstaff."

Beamon grimaced and finished his drink. "Can
you imagine what it would be like being married to
a psychiatrist? Her always knowing what you're
thinking? Besides, I'm considering learning to ski."

"Is this just stupid male pride? No matter what
happens, you lose." Her voice lowered. "If you

think what you've suffered so far has been difficult, I can assure you that you won't like what your future holds. God will not let you stand in the way of His work."

Beamon smiled. "God's work." He reached out and squeezed her hand, coming suggestively close to her injured thumb. "My guess is that you're about as religious as I am. But if I'm wrong and there is a God, I'm starting to think He's on my side."

55

"ARE YOU OKAY?" ERNIE SAID, A LOOK OF concern spreading across her face.

Beamon hung up his cell phone in disgust, promising himself that that was the last time he was going to succumb to curiosity and retrieve his phone messages. "What? Oh, yeah, fine."

"Anything interesting?"

He shook his head. "A kind of nasty call from the IRS and some woman from an AIDS counseling outfit who wants to discuss my recent diagnosis."

Ernie's hands went to her cheeks. "I'm so sorry, Mark, I had no idea . . . But I've read that there are some new medical—"

Beamon laughed easily. "Relax, Ernie. I don't have AIDS. Sadly, I can't even remember the last time I had sex."

"The church?"

He nodded. "I guess I won't be applying for a new life insurance policy anytime soon. So what's so important that I had to haul my butt down here like it was on fire?"

Ernie grabbed a few sheets of paper from her desk and held them up proudly. "E-mail."

"You actually got it working?"

She handed him the papers. "The Lord provides. We've received six e-mails in total, but most of them relate to financial matters, things I don't think you'd be interested in."

"And the others?"

She nodded toward the papers in his lap. "Read the top two."

To: tara@retreat5346.com
From: ak@compound6758.com

Members currently studying are absolved. Clear all students and personnel from the Retreat by midnight tonight.
God Bless

"The Retreat?" Beamon said

"It's a ranch in eastern Oregon. Kneissians who've done something to anger the church go there."

"Oh, yeah, right. There was something about that in your book. It's the place they go and pay an arm and a leg to eat bread and water and get marched around in the mountains till they drop."

"Till they're forgiven," Ernie corrected.

Beamon flipped to the second page.

To: Nolan@Guardians5278.com
From: ak@compound6758.com

Sara will arrive at the retreat by
seven a.m. tomorrow morning. You
and two of your men will be waiting
for her there. She will instruct when
she arrives.
God Bless

Beamon rubbed at the bottom of his jaw and
read the two e-mails again.

"What do you think, Mark?"

"I forgot to tell you that I figured out how Jennifer made it to the phone."

"Really? How?"

"Sara's mouth was swelled up pretty good. In an area about the size of a fist." He pointed to his right hand. "And she had a fresh bandage on her thumb."

Beamon watched Ernie's eyes turn distant for a moment as she imagined what it would feel like to beat the crap out of Sara Renslier.

"This is it, Ernie," Beamon said, bringing her back from her ecstatic vision before he lost her entirely. "Sara is injured right around the same time as Jennifer makes it to a phone and damn near gets a call out. Suddenly they're clearing out the closest thing the church has to a prison and sending three of the wristband brigade there to meet Sara."

"I think they're going to move her, Mark."

Beamon nodded. "The question is, how? If they've left already, they could maybe drive straight through, but that would be tough. Timing-wise and risk-wise. They'd have to drug her and put her in the back of a van or something . . ."

"They're not going to drive."

"They're not?"

"No. There's no road leading to the Retreat. They have a landing strip that's kept open year-round."

56

BEAMON EASED HIS CAR THROUGH THE OPEN chain-link fence and rolled to a stop in the middle of a random grouping of vehicles near the tower building. The lights from the runway were just an undefined halo, not really penetrating the dark, just changing its color. Even the light seeping from the windows of the building next to him barely managed to filter through to his car. According to the disembodied voice coming over the radio, a warm front had crashed into a mass of cold air above Flagstaff, resulting in the torrential rain that was flowing across his windshield and over the backs of the overwhelmed wipers.

Beamon stepped out of the car and began across the tarmac, hunched uselessly against the rain. His jeans and sweatshirt were completely soaked through in less than a minute, and the clammy material against his skin reminded him that in Flagstaff, "warm front" meant low forties.

He straightened up and slowed to a normal pace as the glow from the buildings behind him faded to nothing and a light source, roughly in front of him, strengthened. He adjusted his course slightly and headed straight for it.

Two red dots seemed to float in space for a while, but as he moved closer, the unbroken white of a plane's wings began to appear, illuminated by light pouring through its open door and the small windows in its side.

Beamon circled to his right and stopped near the tail. He pulled a damp piece of paper from his back pocket and read the numbers off it before the rain smeared them into an illegible blob.

They matched. This was the plane. Thank God for Chet Michaels.

He could barely see through the haze created by the heavy raindrops exploding against the stairs leading into the plane, but as he edged closer, he could see that there was no movement inside.

Sliding his gun from the holster beneath his sweatshirt, he put his foot on the first step and gently weighted it. He'd never been on an aircraft this small and wasn't sure if his weight would rock it and telegraph his approach.

Whether it was the mass of the plane or his recent diet, the steps didn't budge under his feet, and he crept slowly up them and into the dry cabin.

The pilot in the cockpit to his left seemed to be engrossed in whatever was contained on the clipboard in his hand. He seemed completely oblivious to the sound of water dripping from Beamon onto the thick carpet, and continued running his finger down a column of switches in front of him.

There were nine seats in all, each half again as wide as the ones in an airliner's first-class cabin and each lovingly covered in soft tan leather. At the back, there was a small storage area that Beamon could see was empty.

"Excuse me," Beamon said, taking a step toward the cockpit.

The pilot tensed, bouncing a few inches out of

his chair, and then twisted around to look behind him. He gasped quietly when he saw Beamon. Or, more precisely, when he saw down the barrel of Beamon's gun.

Unbidden, the pilot raised his hands above his head. "What do you want? This is a small plane—Mexico's as far as I could get you."

Beamon wrung out the bottom of his sweatshirt and smiled. He'd never considered hijacking as a career choice, but in the current context it was looking pretty attractive. Fly down south of the border, sell the plane for a few mill to a drug runner, and spend the rest of his life on the beach with a drink in one hand and a taco in the other.

"Take it easy," Beamon said. "I was told to meet some people from the church here—that there might be some trouble . . ."

The pilot relaxed a bit. "Look, man. I just fly this thing, you know? Nobody ever tells me what's going on—I just get people where they're going."

He was a rather puffy-looking man, Beamon noted. Not really fat, just kind of formless, with a round face that was strangely pale and hairless in a way that made it difficult to guess his age.

"Okay, then. Why don't you step out of there—without touching any more of those buttons and switches, please—and have a seat back here."

The pilot looked more than happy to oblige and moved slowly but efficiently from the cramped space of the cockpit and past Beamon, all the while keeping his hands as high as the low ceiling would allow. He took a seat in one of the plush leather seats facing Beamon and looked up to see if there were any more instructions for him to follow.

Beamon couldn't think of any, unless there was

a coffee pot somewhere, and there didn't seem to be. He leaned his back against the uncomfortably curved wall next to the door leading outside and looked down at his hands. They'd turned bright white from the cold and felt completely lifeless. He pressed his index finger gently against the trigger of his revolver. The finger still worked, but the frozen skin covering it didn't register the increased pressure. He'd have to be careful of that.

"Isn't there a heater in here?"

The pilot shook his head. "Not until I start the plane."

Beamon frowned and tucked his left hand into his armpit, accomplishing nothing but to wring a little more water from the sweatshirt and start it running down his side.

The rain had died down a bit, but the wind was still gusting through the door and sending a cold mist washing over him every few seconds. He struggled to keep his teeth from chattering and hoped things would move quickly. Of course, they didn't.

He ended up spending the next hour trying to fight off the effects of the cold and wondering what the hell he was going to do if he was wrong and a bunch of church executives showed up with their wives and kids for a quick beach trip.

Beamon pressed himself a little closer to the wall when the dim red glow coming through the door wavered and then began to fade into a set of approaching headlights. He gave the pilot a quick glance that said "stay quiet" and poked his head around the corner of the door. Another Taurus. The church must get a bulk discount on those things.

The car stopped maybe twenty feet from the plane and both driver and passenger immediately jumped out. They had their backs to him, so he stepped fully into the doorway and watched as they opened the back door of the Ford and began to pull something out.

Even from behind, they were both easily recognizable. The small woman by her severe haircut and the bandage wound around her right thumb, and the man by the thick mustache, the tips of which were visible when his head moved. Beamon had hoped Gregory Sines wouldn't make an appearance tonight. He looked like the kind of man who would be hard to control in a situation like this.

Beamon smiled and let out a long, quiet breath as the headlights reflecting off the plane illuminated a white-blonde head of hair.

He realized that he really hadn't expected this moment to ever come. The slow burn he'd been feeling in his stomach had been the unfamiliar sensation of defeat, and he recognized now that his recent actions had been governed more by the desire to go down swinging than anything else. He had to admit, though, that it made this moment that much sweeter.

Sara and Sines draped the arms of their cargo across their necks and turned toward the plane heads down, searching for any remaining patches of ice on the asphalt.

From where he was standing, Jennifer looked to be completely unconscious; her body was limp and the toes of her bare feet dragged across the tarmac as she was carried across it. He couldn't see her face, but the skin on her arms looked as white as his—no trace remained of the athletic glow so evident in her photographs.

"Shit!" Beamon said in surprise as he threw a

hand out to keep himself from rolling down the stairs. He twisted hard to the right, keeping his eyes on Sines, who had looked up just as Beamon was hit from behind by the pilot.

The man managed to get an arm around Beamon's neck but wasn't able to lock it off. Beamon twisted again and threw an elbow as Sines reached behind him for what no doubt was going to be a really big gun.

The pilot's arm slid off the wet skin of his neck and he stuck a foot out just in time to trip the man and send him pitching out the door head first.

"Stop!" Beamon yelled over the sound of the rain and the pilot's head connecting with the ground.

Despite his warning and the fact that his gun was already at waist-level, Sines's hand disappeared beneath his jacket and was now starting to come back out. Fast.

Beamon waited as long as he dared, but when the butt of Sines's gun became visible, he squeezed the trigger.

The round hit Sines dead center, as Beamon knew it would—hell, there was probably only fifteen feet between them. Sines jerked back and fell, but somehow managed to land in a sitting position and retain control of his gun hand. Sara dove to the ground, leaving Jennifer to fall face first to the asphalt.

Beamon fired another round, this time without giving it much thought. Sines was already dead. It just hadn't registered with him yet.

Beamon ran down the stairs as Sines fell to his back for the last time and caught Sara by the collar before she could make it to her feet.

"Let go of me, you sonofabitch!" she screamed as he dragged her toward the plane and handcuffed her to the bar that supported the stairs.

Beamon stepped away from her and looked down at the pilot's motionless body. "Stupid asshole," he said, quietly reprimanding himself. Watching his life come crashing down around his ears was fucking up his judgment. Eleven million members and what, the church is going to use a Mormon to transport a kidnapped girl?

The pilot looked like he'd probably wake up with nothing more than a baseball-sized knot on his head, but he couldn't say the same for Sines—he was just going to lie there staring up into the rain. Beamon didn't feel a great deal of remorse over Sines's demise; what concerned him was *why* the man was dead. It was because he was allowing lapses in his concentration and getting sloppy.

Sara lunged at him, her unwounded hand twisting into something that resembled a claw. The motion brought Beamon back to the present and he watched her body jerk to a stop as the handcuff around her wrist went taut.

"Be careful you don't hurt yourself now," Beamon said, scooping Jennifer up from the puddle she'd landed in and cradling her in his arms. He could feel the warmth of her body seeping into his chest as he pulled her to him.

"Take these off me!" Sara screamed. "You *will not* do this!"

"Looks like I already did."

She grabbed the chain between the handcuffs and pulled mightily but pointlessly against them. Blood had started to flow from her wrist and was mixing with the rain to run pale pink down her hand.

"It's just you and me now, Sara. None of your lackeys are around to accuse me of child molestation or alcoholism. No computers to fuck up my credit cards. It looks like your God's abandoned you and come over to my side, doesn't it?"

She suddenly froze and looked up at him, a forced calm registering on her face. "Put her down, Mr. Beamon. It isn't worth it. If you take her I'll destroy you and everyone you've ever known."

Beamon flipped Jennifer over his shoulder, drew his gun, and aimed it at Sara's head.

"No!" she cried, throwing her hands in front of her face and shrinking back as far as the handcuffs would allow. Beamon kept the gun trained on her as she crouched down and averted her eyes toward the pavement, stoking his anger until he couldn't feel anything else—not the cold, not the weight of Jennifer on his shoulder. Nothing.

He knew he should do it—she would come after him and the girl with everything she had. He should do it for Jennifer, for Goldman, for himself.

But he'd already gone far enough across the line. He took a deep breath and holstered his gun. "You don't look like much when you're not surrounded by your church." Beamon patted the unconscious girl on the backs of her legs. "Thanks for screwing up and letting me get Jennifer back. I reckon she'll go a long way to straightening out my life."

The desperation in Sara's voice warmed Beamon's heart as he started walking back to his car. "You talked about five million dollars last time we met, Mr. Beamon. What if it was ten? Twenty?"

Beamon paused and turned around so he could enjoy the full effect of Sara's panic.

"Twenty million? Is that the number?" She pointed to Sines's body. "No one has to ever know about this."

She smoothed the damp folds in her dark suit and raised herself to her full height. "You don't have anywhere to take her anyway, do you? Who can you trust? The FBI? I think you know better than that."

He took a backward step away from her.

"Wait," she said in a tone that would have been appropriate for talking a jumper out of leaping from a tall building. "You've proven what you can do—I have a hundred times the resources you do and you beat me. You beat me. Now put her down and unlock these handcuffs. Do that, and whatever you want is yours."

Flattery, no less. He really would have liked to stick around and let her kiss his ass some more, but it was about time to get the hell out of there. The pilot was starting to twitch and somebody at the tower had to have heard the shots. They were probably up there trying to decide which one of them would get to brave the rain.

Beamon turned and started for his car.

"Stop! Wait!"

He quickened his pace.

"You'll never get out of this," Sara screamed. The calm, persuasive tone she'd been trying to ply him with was gone. "You're alone now—we put the old man out of his misery and that little fanatic can't help you anymore."

Beamon slowed and finally stopped, still within earshot.

"How could you have left her alone like that? A helpless woman in a wheelchair. How was she supposed to defend herself?"

57

THERE WAS NOTHING THE FIREFIGHTERS could do at this point—other than make sure the blaze didn't spread to the other homes in the neighborhood. Even the sheets of rain lashing the house could do little to contain the jets of flame gusting from the broken windows and into the dark night.

Beamon parked almost a block and a half away from the bonfire that a few hours ago had been Ernestine Waverly's house, not wanting to be spotted by the men who had set it. He looked over at Jennifer, whose only movement for the last hour had been prompted by the rocking of the car. Her head was propped against the window and her mouth was open, though Beamon had to concentrate to hear her breathe.

He checked her seatbelt again for no particular reason, then leaned forward and rested his head against the steering wheel. "We got her, Ernie," he said quietly. "We won."

When he looked out the windshield again, the chance of the fire spreading seemed pretty remote. The firefighters had abandoned their vigil over the other houses in the neighborhood and were moving through the small knot of rain-slickered people who had braved the elements to see the little house consumed.

He flipped his headlights back on—not that they were necessary, the glow from the fire had lit up the entire neighborhood—and put the car in reverse.

She was dead, he knew; all he could hope for now was that it had been quick. He tried to convince himself of it, but he knew that he was lying to himself. Sara's Guardians would have undoubtedly wanted to know were he was and what he was up to.

Either she hadn't told them at all or she'd held out long enough that they hadn't had time to make it to the airport. Thank God there had never been a reason to tell her where Goldman's apartment was.

That was it. The last of his patched-together team was dead. And once again, it was his fault. He'd been able to stave off the feeling of guilt about Goldman—at least temporarily. The old man had known what he was doing. Hell, he'd probably been breathing longer than he should have or wanted to.

Ernie was another story. He should have cut loose from her a long time ago. But he hadn't. He'd been blinded, as he had been a hundred times before, by the problem. Solving it, beating his opponent, proving management wrong. Those things had become everything to him. He'd used her and left her to the wolves.

As the glow in his rearview mirror faded, Beamon couldn't help thinking about Ernie's God and her unshakable faith. He'd never believed. He'd never really wanted to. There was something about the concept of a Supreme Being that made him uncomfortable. It robbed the universe of the free will and chaos that made it so interesting. And for that, all you got was an eternity of peace and tranquility. He'd always thought it was a bad trade, making life just a pointless, painful blink of an eye in an eternity of bliss.

For the first time, though, he actually hoped he was wrong and Ernie and the others like her were right. He hoped that in death Ernie would find what she had been looking for in life.

58

BEAMON PULLED HIS SHOTGUN OUT OF THE back seat and leaned it against the side of the car. He looked around him at the rundown apartment complex that had become his new home, but didn't see any movement. Other than the muffled sound of yet another pre-coitus spat coming from the apartment next to his, the complex was silent.

Fortunately, it was also pretty dark. Most of the bulbs in the parking area's floodlights were burned out and none of the residents seemed interested in paying for the power necessary to keep their carriage lights on.

Beamon pulled Jennifer's limp body from the car and slung her over his shoulder. He looked around him one more time before picking up the shotgun and beginning across the icy walkway toward Goldman's apartment.

The snow in front of his door had been washed away by the rain, making it impossible to look for telltale footprints. The curtains were still closed and it looked to be dark inside the apartment, but that didn't mean a hell of a lot. He unlocked the door, took a deep breath, and pushed it open with the barrel of the shotgun.

Empty.

No doubt thanks to the seemingly endless supply of phony IDs under which Jack Goldman had transacted nearly all his business.

Beamon kicked a couple of boxes off the sofa and dropped Jennifer onto it, then fell into a chair and turned on the TV. Unscrewing the cap from what was left of the bottle of bourbon next to him with one hand, he flipped to a local station with the other. Ten more minutes until the eleven o'clock news.

He'd gotten what he wanted so badly, he reflected, taking a long pull directly from the bottle. The infamous Jennifer Davis was now gracing his sofa at the low, low cost of three lives. Three and a half, if he counted what was left of his own.

Beamon took another shot from the bottle and then screwed the cap back on. It wasn't over yet. Four more days until Jennifer was scheduled for her promotion to godhood. Four days for Sara to correct her mistake. And with the FBI after him and Ernie and Goldman dead, holding onto the girl might prove more challenging than finding her had been. By now there were probably a thousand Kneissians scouring every apartment complex and hotel for three hundred miles looking for him. Not good.

He looked over at Jennifer. Except for the bare feet, she was dressed in the same clothes that she was reported last seen in—the pair of shorts and sweatshirt she'd donned after her fourth-place finish in Phoenix. She looked thinner than she had in her photographs and the calculatedly obvious dye job that kids seemed to favor these days had grown out a bit, revealing an infinitely prettier natural brown. The ring was gone from her slightly swollen nose, and dark circles had painted themselves under her eyes. All in all, she looked like the only person on earth who had had a worse month than him.

The local news opened with dramatic scenes of the blaze at Ernie's house. Interviews with firefighters suggested that they hadn't yet investigated the cause of the fire or whether anyone was inside when it started. They said they were just going to let it burn out and would know more tomorrow.

Beamon watched the rest of the program, his eyes darting nervously to the door every few seconds. There was still no mention of Goldman's death and nothing on the shooting at the air terminal. He suspected there never would be.

When the weather came on, Beamon turned the old TV off and lit a cigarette.

What now?

If he could keep Jennifer alive for the next four days and get her story on record, she should be safe. Sara struck him as vindictive but certainly not stupid.

Staying at the apartment was out of the question. It was possible that the church's people would never find this place—the threads leading to it were pretty thin—but he couldn't risk it. And that left very few options.

One: Dump the car and hole up in a motel somewhere.

Not exactly ideal. It still left him alone against the combined forces of the church and the way his luck was running, he'd end up in a Kneissian-owned hotel. But even if he didn't, they'd sure as hell be looking for him at all the hotels in the area and would be watching all the roads out of town.

Two: Take her to the press.

But who in the press? Obviously, the church

had contacts there or he'd still have a job. Besides, they'd be watching for him there, too. And that didn't solve his problem of keeping Jennifer's head off the chopping block until the Easter season was safely over.

Three: Take her to the FBI.

Probably his best option, but still less than ideal. He wasn't really ready to go in yet—there were some loose ends that he wanted to tie up before he condemned himself to six months in endless conduct hearings, and probably three to five in any number of conveniently located local penitentiaries.

Chet Michaels was the answer. Or at least the lesser of the evils. They could meet somewhere a few miles from the Phoenix office and Michaels could drive them in, with Jennifer, Beamon, and his shotgun keeping out of sight.

Even if Layman was involved with, or being blackmailed by, the church, what could he do? Jennifer would be standing in the middle of a crowded office and would become public property. From then on, the whole thing would be someone else's responsibility.

59

BEAMON JERKED AWAKE AT THE QUIET creak of the sofa. He was confused for a few moments—by the weight of the shotgun lying across his lap, by the young girl unconscious on the couch.

The events of the prior week started replaying themselves before his mind was completely back on line. His suspension, Carrie, Jack's and Ernie's deaths, and finally, the girl he'd taken possession of last night. Along with a whole host of other problems.

Jennifer was still more or less in the position he'd left her in, Beamon noted as he stood and stretched his back. The apartment was silent, except for the low drone of the computers that surrounded him. The only thing that had changed was the sun filtering through the dusty blinds.

Beamon leaned the shotgun against his chair and walked over to the sofa. He reached down and gave Jennifer a gentle shake. Her muscles tensed for an instant and then went slack again. Faker.

He shook her again, this time a bit harder. "Come on, Jennifer. Rise and shine. I know you're awake."

No reaction at all this time.

He went into the kitchen and filled a rusty pan halfway with ice from the freezer. "Wake up, Jennifer. Last chance," he warned as he filled the pan the rest of the way with water.

Humming quietly, he put a lid over the pan and walked back to the sofa, slowly swirling the mixture. He could see Jennifer's neck stiffen almost imperceptibly as she tried to decipher the unfamiliar sound of ice rolling against metal. Beamon moved the lid so that there was about a three-quarters-inch gap and began pouring the contents of the pan on her face.

The first splash of water had barely reached her before she was off the couch and diving over the old coffee table toward the chair Beamon had slept in that night.

It was quite a show, really. By the time Beamon had tilted the pan back up to check the water's flow onto the now-empty sofa, he had a very scared-looking fifteen-year-old girl pointing a loaded shotgun at him.

Beamon screwed up his face and closed his eyes hard. Nearly two decades of putting some of the most notorious criminals in the world behind bars and an adolescent girl was the first person to ever get ahold of his gun. In the unlikely event he survived long enough to write a report on this investigation, he'd probably leave this part out.

Beamon slowly opened one eye. "Looks like you got the drop on me, Tex." He opened the other. "Jesus, I don't remember ever being young enough to move that fast."

"Freeze!"

"How 'bout I sit instead?" He placed the pan on the coffee table and plopped down on the sofa.

"I'll shoot!" Jennifer said as Beamon reached into his pocket. He slowed the motion of his hand

and pulled out a pack of cigarettes. Tapping one out into his hand, he said, "I believe you, kid. But let's make sure that if you *do* shoot me, it's because you want to." He held his lighter to the end of the cigarette. "What would you say about moving your finger off that trigger a little bit?"

He patted what remained of the stubborn roll of fat that wouldn't release his waistline. "I think you'll agree that I'm in no condition to get all the way across the room before you can move your finger half an inch."

She looked at him suspiciously but finally moved her quivering finger off the trigger. "Who . . . who are you?"

"Mark Beamon. I'm with the FBI."

"You don't look like an FBI agent."

He assumed she meant his casual clothing. People seemed to think FBI agents slept in their suits. "Thank you."

"Let me see your ID."

Beamon frowned. "Actually, saying that I'm with the FBI is a bit of an exaggeration. I *was* with the FBI until I got suspended last week. That's your fault, actually."

"I don't believe you."

Beamon shrugged. "What're you going to do, then?"

Jennifer chewed her lip for a moment, then moved toward a haggard-looking sideboard and began pulling open the drawers. She found a phone book in the third one she looked in and flipped through the first few pages, keeping one eye trained on him.

"Oh. I'd rather you didn't do that," Beamon said as she reached for the phone on the sideboard.

"Could be traced here. Use this one." He slid his cell phone off the coffee table and rolled it across the floor to her.

She looked at it like it might explode but eventually picked it up and dialed.

"Hello? Hi. Uh, I'd like to speak to Mark Beamon, please." She looked him up and down while she waited to be connected. The gun was shaking less now and the barrel had dipped a bit from its previous position pointing directly at his face. Not that it really mattered.

"Hello? I'm trying to reach Mark Beamon . . . No, I don't want to leave a message, it's pretty important . . . Oh. Really? Could you hold on for a second?"

Beamon caught the phone she tossed him and put it to his ear. "Hello? You still there?"

"Mark! I've been trying to reach you! Where have you been? And who was that?"

"I've been around, D. Enjoying my time off, you know?"

"Have you heard what's been happening here?" she said. Her voice echoed slightly. Because she had cupped a hand around the mouthpiece of her phone, Beamon guessed.

"No, what?"

Jennifer looked like she was getting impatient and Beamon flashed her a quick smile.

"Mark, they're talking about going public with the fact that they're looking for you. We're talking APB. The director's flying down personally to meet with Layman."

D. really was the ultimate secretary. If a clerk at headquarters got a paper cut, she knew about it the same day.

"When?"

"The APB? There's no decision yet, just talk. The director's coming in on the first, though. I think if Layman doesn't have something by then, you can count on this thing going public that day. What did you do? You wouldn't believe some of the things I've been hearing."

"Oh, I probably would. What time are Layman and the director meeting?"

"I don't know. Morning. Mark, what's going on? Are you all right?"

"Sure, fine. Hang on a sec, would you? Someone wants to talk to you."

Beamon tossed the cell phone back to Jennifer.

"Hello? Yes, ma'am. I just wanted to ask you, is that Mark Beamon? Uh-huh. You're sure. Okay. And what's his job there exactly? He is? Thanks. 'Bye."

She turned off the phone and slumped into the chair behind her, laying the gun carefully on the floor.

Beamon leaned forward. "Smart, Jennifer. Very smart. I take it I've checked out to your satisfaction?"

She seemed to have used up the last of her strength and bravery to grab the gun and confirm his identity. Her head went forward to her knees and her entire body shook as she began quietly sobbing.

Beamon wasn't sure what to do. He got up and knelt down in front of her. "It's okay, Jen. You're okay now. You're out of there."

She threw her arms around his neck and pulled him to her.

"Uh, hey, come on. Don't cry. I'm depressed

enough already," he said, patting her on the back tentatively.

"They were going to kill me, Mr. Beamon!" The words came out in jumbles when she momentarily caught her breath. "They kept me in this room, and I was all alone and they wouldn't let me out. They were going to kill me!"

She used the sleeve of her sweatshirt to wipe at her running nose and then suddenly jerked back from him. "What day is it?"

"Tuesday. Tuesday the twenty-fifth."

She pushed him away, jumped out of the chair, and slammed her back against the far wall. "Oh, my God. Oh, my God."

"Jennifer, calm down. What's wrong?"

"It isn't over. She won't stop. It's not time yet."

Beamon stood and led her to the couch. "Good Friday?"

She nodded. "My grandfather, he . . . he wanted me to be in charge of the church. But she lied to them. She wants to kill me so it . . . it's hers."

"Who's 'she'? Sara?"

Jennifer nodded again.

"It was a religious thing, though, wasn't it?" Beamon said. "Albert—your grandfather—died too soon and she was able to use that to justify killing you. She said that you were the new Messenger and had to ascend in his place, right?"

She didn't seem to be paying attention to what he was saying. Her head was moving from side to side as though the church's forces were going to materialize from the walls at any minute. Hell, maybe they were.

"Jennifer, is what I just said right?"

"Yeah."

He reached out and gripped her shoulders. "Okay, then. Cheer up. All we have to do is keep you safe till midnight Friday; then you'll be useless to them, right? That's only a couple of days—no problem."

He tried to keep his tone light and to make sure none of his doubts shone through.

"Promise?" Jennifer said.

"Promise. You want something to eat? I've got Cocoa Puffs."

"That stuff's just a bunch of sugar," she said, her eyes moving from the door to the window and back again.

He opened the refrigerator. "Well, I've got hot dogs. But no buns."

"I guess I'll have the cereal."

"I love this stuff," Beamon said as he grabbed the box out of a cabinet. "Cuckoo for it." She actually almost smiled at that.

"Do you know anything about computers, Jen?" She nodded.

"Why don't you see what you can do with the one over there while I whip this up."

"What do you want me to do?" she said, sitting down in front of the screen and tapping the mouse.

"Check for voice messages and e-mail."

"Why don't I just make the cereal? You know where everything is in here."

"Actually, I barely even know how to turn the thing on. It's not mine. I was kind of hoping you could figure out how to work it."

"Whose computer is it?" she said, looking a bit nervous again.

"A friend's."

"Where is he?"

"He had to go home. His father's been sick for

years and he took a turn for the worse a couple of days ago," Beamon lied.

She looked up at him for a moment and then turned back to the screen. A few moments later, recorded phone conversations were playing over the speakers.

"Hey! That's me!" Jennifer said when the recording of her call to the Colorado Cyclist came on. Her smile faltered when she heard herself scream and the sound of the brief struggle before the phone went dead.

Beamon laid the bowl of cereal down next to the computer and pulled up a box to sit on. The messages—recordings of the church's phone tap, actually—were still playing, but he wasn't really expecting anything interesting. They seemed to be pretty careful about using the phone.

"What about the e-mail?"

Jennifer clicked on a mailbox icon and the sound of dialing momentarily drowned out the conversation playing over the speakers.

"Seven messages," she said, clicking on the first.

It came up a jumble of letters and characters.

"It's encrypted, Mr. Beamon."

"Call me Mark."

She looked over at him, a dribble of chocolaty milk running down her chin. "You don't look like a Mark. You look like a Mr. Beamon."

He shrugged. "Suit yourself. WrathofGod."

"What?"

"The encryption key. WrathofGod. One word, the 'W' and the 'G' are capitalized."

A moment later the e-mails began rolling off the printer.

The first six were pretty mundane—financial directives, mostly. The last was a rather innocuous-looking note including Ernestine Waverly's address. He wondered if she'd seen it. If she'd known they were coming. His cell phone had rung just before he arrived at the airport. Had it been her calling for help? And if he'd picked up, what would he have done?

"Are you all right, Mr. Beamon?"

"Sorry, I'm fine. Here's the deal, Jennifer. We need to get you to the FBI. I think you'll be better off with a hundred people watching you than just one." He smiled. "Even one as gifted and handsome as myself."

"But you're going to go too, right? I mean, a hundred people didn't find me—you did."

She really was a clever kid. If they were all like her, he'd have actually considered having children. "I'll be right there. I'm going to call a friend to help us and this afternoon you'll have the whole FBI to keep an eye on you till Saturday. You won't have a thing to worry about."

She looked around her at the dingy apartment, gripping the table in front of her so tightly her knuckles turned white. "Maybe we should just stay here. Maybe that would be better."

"You've already been here too long, Jennifer," Beamon said, dialing his cell phone. "There are a lot of people looking for you and eventually they're going to find this place—"

"Hello?"

"Chet! Is that you?"

Michaels's voice lowered into the same whisper D. had employed to talk to him. "Jesus, Mark. Where the hell are you? We got guys from Phoenix crawling all over the office trying to figure out how to find you."

"I'll bet. Listen up, Chet. Do you remember the time you and I went to talk to the guy about that embezzlement case you were working on?"

"Yeah, sure."

"You remember where we ate?"

"Uh-huh. Mark, what the hell's—"

"Meet me there at three. Leave like you always do for lunch. Drive around a little, get a bite, and make goddamn sure no one is following you."

"But you—"

Beamon looked at his watch. "Why are you still talking? I've got eleven-fifty-six."

He heard Michaels sigh over the phone. "I'm walking out the door."

"Oh, and Chet?"

"Yeah?"

"There are three people who have helped me with the Jennifer Davis case. You're the only one still breathing. You still want to come?"

There was a long pause over the phone. "You're going to tell me what's going on when I get there, right?"

"Yup."

"I'll see you in a few hours."

Beamon turned off the phone and looked into Jennifer's worried face. "If you want to get cleaned up or anything, you'd better get going. We've gotta get out of here."

She stood and started for the bathroom.

"Hold on a sec," Beamon said, picking up the shotgun and holding it up so that she could see it. He pointed to the slide under the barrel. "It's really unlikely, but if anything should happen to me and you would have to actually fire this thing, remember that you need to pull this back or it won't shoot."

A look of horror spread across her face. "You mean all that time I was pointing it at you, it wouldn't have even worked?"

"Strictly speaking? No. But it *was* a hell of an effort."

60

IN THE TWO AND A HALF HOURS IT TOOK TO drive from Flagstaff to Phoenix, the outside temperature had risen nearly thirty degrees. The sun that Jennifer hadn't seen in over a month was beating relentlessly on them through the car's windshield, finally prompting her to pull Beamon's parka off her bare legs and toss it into the back seat.

"Can we turn down the heat a little now, Jen?" he asked, wiping a bead of sweat from his upper lip.

"Okay."

She leaned her head against the window and fixed her gaze on the desert landscape as it sped by, but didn't really seem to see it. After perking up a bit at the apartment when she'd first discovered she was free, Jennifer seemed to have withdrawn into herself.

She probably wanted to talk, Beamon knew. About her parents, her treatment at Sara's hands, her future. But he just didn't know how to get things going. He sighed quietly and thought about Carrie. She'd know what to do. How to help.

"You'll like Chet, Jen. He's a lot younger and hipper than me. Just don't mention his resemblance to Howdy Doody."

She remained so still and silent that he wondered if she'd even heard him. Call that a swing and a miss.

Perhaps the direct approach might prove more effective. "Is there something out there that's more interesting than me, or are you just contemplating life?"

He glanced away from the road for a moment and saw that she had turned from the window and was staring right at him. Her face had fallen into an expression of pain and sadness that someone her age shouldn't have been able to produce.

"I was thinking about Eric and Patty."

"Who?" Beamon said, and then remembered. "You mean your parents."

She turned back toward the window. "I mean my keepers."

Beamon wasn't sure how to respond to that. He did have an unasked question that had been killing him since she'd regained consciousness, though. "What really happened that night?"

"He killed her," she said simply.

"Who?"

"Eric."

"Your father," Beamon corrected again.

"He wasn't my father. My father's been dead for years. He was just some guy the church hired to watch me until it was time to kill me."

Beamon wanted to just let the subject drop—he felt like he was forcing her to dredge up memories best left buried. Deep down, though, he knew it was probably better for her to let them out. "So your—I mean Eric—killed Patricia. And then he killed himself, didn't he?"

She nodded.

"Damn," Beamon muttered. There had always been a trace of doubt in his mind about that. He'd have to give that cute little lesbian coroner a firm pat on the back, if he lived to see her again.

"She just stood there, and he killed her," Jennifer continued. "They didn't care what happened to me. Neither of them."

Beamon looked over at her again, amazed at how well she was holding up. He tried to put himself in her place, to imagine what it would be like to be fifteen years old and see something like that. "I don't think that's true, Jennifer."

"You weren't there. They gave him a gun. He could have stopped them, but he didn't." She turned back to the window. "He didn't."

"You're angry right now. And you've got a right to be. But given some time, I think you'll understand that there was more going on there than maybe you see right now."

A bitter smile compounded the pain etched across her young features. "Patty used to use that on me. 'You'll understand when you're older.'"

"I'm sorry to say, I've found that to be a myth. The years come and go and your perspective changes, but I'm not sure you really ever understand more."

Beamon slowed the car and eased onto an off-ramp. "Your—sorry, Eric and Patricia—believed very strongly in God. They didn't show you that part of their lives, but it was incredibly important to them. They believed that you were, well, almost divine. When they did what they did, in a way, they did it for you. They wanted you to leave them behind. To become more than they could ever be. I know it's weird, but really it's what all parents want for their children."

"For some psycho bitch to kill them so she can keep her job?"

Beamon slowed the car a bit more and tugged on her arm so that she would meet his eyes. "I've spent the last month or so doing nothing but working on this case, Jennifer—I know more about it than anyone in the world, and I'll tell you right now that your parents had no idea what Sara was planning. No idea."

"Maybe they should have stuck around and tried to find out."

The restaurant where Michaels was waiting, thankfully, was just ahead. His first foray into adolescent counseling seemed to have been an unsurprising bust. Probably better to change the subject before he did irreversible damage. "That's it. The reinforcements should be just ahead."

Jennifer started to look nervous. Panicked, almost. "Let's forget this, Mr. Beamon." She twisted around and looked through the rear window. "Please, let's just turn around and keep driving."

Beamon suddenly realized what was probably going through her head. Her parents had pawned her off on the church, and now he was going to pawn her off on the Bureau. "Jennifer, we're less than three miles from one of the largest FBI offices in the country. I'm not just throwing you to the wolves here. They can protect you better than I can. And when you're safe, I'm going to stick a knife so deep into Sara Renslier and her church that they'll never be able to hurt you again. I'm doing the best I can."

She grabbed his arm. "I want to stay with you. You can't even run a computer. I could help."

Beamon eased into the parking lot and spotted Michaels standing in the open door of his car. He pulled into the empty space next to the young agent and looked carefully around him. The lot was nearly full of cars but almost devoid of people. The restaurant's lunch rush was probably pretty much over and dinner hadn't yet begun. Most of the cars probably belonged to the patrons of the shops that were lined up neatly across the street.

Michaels's eyes jerked to the left as Beamon stepped from the car.

Shit.

Beamon fell back into the driver's seat, reached behind him and pulled his gun from the exposed holster in the small of his back, but it was too late. Two men with compact machine pistols held low had already stepped from opposite sides of an old panel van.

He looked behind him. Jennifer had slid from the seat and crammed herself in the small floor space in front of it. She was clutching at the armrest on the door, trying to hold it shut as a similarly armed man tried to open it. Beamon grabbed Jennifer under the arm and dragged her over the seats and out the driver's-side door with him.

"I swear they didn't follow me, Mark. They were already here when I got here."

"Shut up," the man Beamon's gun was aimed at said.

"You shut up, fuckhead," Michaels said angrily.

Beamon winced. That wasn't productive. He felt Jennifer's arms wrap around him. "Take it easy, Jen. We're okay."

That wasn't entirely true, of course. The man who had been trying to get at Jennifer though the passenger-side door had circled around and now there were three men, spaced at about five-foot intervals, facing him. Michaels was between them, looking fantastically pissed off.

Beamon looked around him. There was one other person in the parking lot about fifty yards away, but she was oblivious to what was happening, more interested in getting her key into her trunk without having to put her packages down. If they had to, these guys could shoot him and Michaels, throw the girl in the van, and be two blocks away before anyone knew what had happened.

"You're to come with us," one of the men said.

Beamon adjusted his aim toward the man's chest. He looked a couple of years older than the other two, but he probably still hadn't seen his thirty-fifth birthday.

"Yeah? Screw you!" Michaels said.

"Jesus, Chet," Beamon said quietly. "Could you maybe try and be a little more constructive?"

Michaels frowned and bobbed his head as if he'd just been scolded for not taking out the trash.

Beamon looked around him again. The woman with the packages was driving away. The lot was now empty except for them and a bunch of owner-less cars. The man who had spoken a moment before had his firearm aimed at Michaels. The other two guns were on him.

They wouldn't kill her—Beamon was sure of that. Without the religious mumbo jumbo Sara had attached to Jennifer's death, she would just be murdering her messiah's only living relative. A poor career move, particularly with her main enforcer's recent decision to stop a couple of Beamon's bullets with his chest.

Interestingly, he himself was safe from immediate execution, too. Sara wanted the Vericomm tapes and undoubtedly planned on making his life unpleasant enough to get him to tell her where they were.

Now, Michaels had problems. His life expectancy had just gone from fifty years to less than an hour.

"Let's go," the man said. Ignoring the fact that Beamon had a gun trained on him, he reached out and grabbed Jennifer's arm, pulling her to him.

"No!" she whimpered, tightening her grip around Beamon's waist until it actually made it hard for him to breathe.

Beamon grabbed her hand and peeled her off him, letting the man drag her away with a satisfied smirk. "Not quite the man I'd heard you were, Beamon. I expected some theatrics, at least."

"You sonofabitch," Jennifer said, glaring at him. "You promised."

Beamon didn't see that he had many options. Desperate times demanded desperate measures. In one smooth motion, he cocked back the hammer on his revolver and adjusted his aim to center Jennifer in his sights.

The eyes of the man holding Jennifer widened, but not as much as hers did.

"I got it figured this way," Beamon said calmly. "You've been told not to hurt the girl and to bring me back in one or two pieces—but alive." He looked over at Michaels. "Him, well, you'll probably just kill him the minute we get in your van."

"Great," Michaels said in a mildly irritated tone. He sounded like he'd come out of the restaurant to find that someone had scratched his car.

Beamon ignored the interruption and continued. "I know what you've got planned for her. She'll be dead on Friday morning and in the days until then, you'll have her drugged in some room, alone and scared." He shook his head. "If I let you guys take her, I doubt I'll live to find her again. Maybe it's better that we just end it here. Quick."

He turned his head away from the increasingly confused-looking man and locked eyes with Jennifer. "What do you think, Jen? Out here in the sunshine, or on some altar with Sara hovering over you?"

She looked to be completely frozen. The two men who had their guns trained on Beamon looked at each other, then back at him.

"Here," Jennifer said weakly. Her voice seemed to jolt the man holding her and he took a step backward, but he didn't release her arm.

Beamon was dumbfounded by her answer and struggled to keep his face impassive. He'd asked the question just to add a little more drama to his bluff. He was prepared to go down shooting, yes, but sure as hell not shooting at her.

"You—there's no way," the man said. "You're bluffing." The slight stammer told Beamon that he'd won.

"What would make you say that, son? If we go with you we're all dead—and you make the last few hours of my life real unpleasant. And what if I were to survive? I'm out of a job, broke, and branded a child molester. I'd call my prospects limited, wouldn't you?"

The man looked behind him, but his compatriots weren't offering any help. "Look into my eyes," Beamon said. "What do you see?"

The man fidgeted for a few moments and then released his hold on Jennifer's arm.

She seemed uncertain of what to do, so Beamon grabbed her and pulled her to him. She was probably having a hard time accepting the guy pointing a loaded gun at her as her savior.

"Chet," Beamon said, dragging Jennifer around the car and stuffing her into the passenger door. "Get in your car and get out of here. Jennifer, slide over. You drive."

She quickly negotiated the armrest and had started the car before her butt hit the driver's seat.

Beamon kept the gun pointed toward her and his eyes on the three men standing in the parking lot. He leaned in close to Jennifer and said, "Let's get out of here before they figure out I'm full of crap." She looked over at him, her lower lip quivering slightly, and threw the car into reverse.

One of the men was already talking into a cell phone as Jennifer cautiously negotiated the exit to the parking lot and turned out onto the street.

"Let's pick it up a little, Jen," Beamon said, watching the men disappear into the distance a little too slowly. "Get back out onto the highway and head south."

Satisfied that they weren't being followed, Beamon pulled his address book out of his pocket and found the number for Delta Airlines.

61

"But you're not going to leave me, right?"

Beamon rubbed his eyes with his knuckles as the cab pulled away from them and back into the dark of pre-dawn Washington, D.C.

"Right?" Jennifer repeated, wrapping her arms around herself against the cold and uncertainty.

Beamon put a hand on her back and started toward the dimly lit entrance of the German embassy. She was still in the shorts he'd found her in, though they'd managed to find her a jacket with "Phoenix" stenciled across it in the airport.

"I think we've established that, Jennifer—try to relax. You and I are going to sit in this embassy 'til I can gather together some people I trust. We'll be safe here. You know how the Germans feel about the church."

Beamon banged on the front door as Jennifer pressed up against him for warmth. She was starting to shiver, but Beamon didn't know if it was from the cold or just the stress of the last forty-eight hours. The last month, actually. It was amazing she was still walking and talking.

A dark shape appeared on the other side of the glass, moving quickly toward them. A moment later, Hans Volker pushed the door open.

"Come in. Quickly."

The German looked a little more haggard than he had the last time they'd met. His meticulously pressed double-breasted jacket and expensive-looking tie were nowhere in sight, and he wasn't wearing any shoes. But then, it was four in the morning.

Beamon stepped through the door with Jennifer still attached to his hip. She eyed Volker suspiciously.

"Jennifer. This is Hans. It's his job to watch the church for the German government."

"So this is Jennifer Davis," Volker said. He reached out and took Jennifer's hand. "Goodness. Your skin feels like ice. We'll go up to my office. You can wash up there and you'll also be happy to know that I have two big sofas. I've availed myself of them a number of times and can vouch for their softness."

"Is anyone in yet this morning?" Beamon asked as they began to climb a staircase to the second floor.

"Not yet. I've called our security people. They should arrive any moment. There's an office and bathroom that we aren't using in the basement. You can stay there until you're able to marshal your forces. While you're here we'll have round-the-clock security in the building."

"I really appreciate this, Hans. I'm going to put some stuff together that you're going to love."

"I have every confidence," Volker said, pushing through a set of double doors and pointing down a short hall that terminated in his office. "After you."

"Hey, Hans," Beamon said as he followed Jennifer down the hall. "Could you possibly find Jennifer some long pants—actually, a couple of changes of clothes would be even better."

"Of course."

Jennifer went through the door to the office, but only made it about two feet before she began backing out of it.

"What're you doing, Jen?" Beamon said when she bumped into him.

There was something unmistakable about the feeling of a gun barrel being pressed into one's back, Beamon reflected as he felt a cold cylinder bump his spine. Somehow it was easily discernible from any other object—be it pipe, wooden dowel, whatever.

"Please keep moving forward, Mark," Volker said, giving him a gentle nudge with the gun he must have had lying on his secretary's desk out front.

Jennifer pushed back against him. "No," she whimpered.

He didn't know for sure what was waiting for them in Volker's office, but a theory was forming in his mind. One that he should have come up with weeks ago.

Beamon wrapped his arms around Jennifer and whispered in her ear, "I'm sorry, this is my fault," then used his superior weight to force her forward.

To their left, two men stood in the corners of the office. To their right, Sara Renslier was sitting behind Volker's large desk, flanked by another man Beamon didn't recognize.

"Good morning, Mr. Beamon," she said, standing up from behind the desk. "Hello, Jennifer."

Jennifer stepped back as if the words had struck her a physical blow. She continued to press against Beamon for comfort, though he didn't have any idea why. She probably would have been better off on her own. He'd made more bad decisions in the last week than he had in the last ten years. The church had his life so fucked up, he didn't know what the hell he was doing anymore. "Stupid," he said quietly to himself.

"Excuse me?" Sara said, holding her hand up to her ear. The bandage on her thumb had been joined by one on her wrist. Undoubtedly from her struggling against the cuffs he had used to secure her to her airplane. Beyond that, there was no trace of the woman who had cowered in front of him that night. The armed men surrounding him had revitalized her air of superiority and her condescending tone.

Beamon took a deep breath to try to clear the anger overtaking him. Not at Sara, but at himself. "I said I'm stupid. Your fight with the German government. It's just a publicity stunt."

"A bit late, but of course you're right," Sara said as one of the men behind Beamon stepped forward to take his gun. "We discovered early on that Germany wasn't very fertile ground for our recruiting efforts. It just was costing us money, really— churches, recruiting stations, advertising, et cetera. We did bring in a few influential people." She nodded toward Volker. "But on the whole, there seemed to be something in the German psyche that just wasn't compatible with the Church on the scale we were looking for."

"So you changed your tack," Beamon said. "You used the contacts you'd made to focus your efforts on something you knew would be compatible with the German psyche. The fear of the rise of any insular group to power."

Sara smiled. "It wasn't difficult and cost almost nothing."

Beamon slid his arm around Jennifer's shoulders. "You knew that there'd be a violent reaction in the U.S. The fear of religious persecution has been bred into Americans for over two hundred years."

Jennifer shrank away as Sara approached, trying to get behind Beamon.

"I think it's been my greatest success. We've seen a twenty-two percent increase in inquiries from the American public and a fourteen percent increase in new membership. The outcry against Germany and its persecution of the Church has been over-whelming. The media coverage has been far beyond what we projected."

Beamon was only half-listening to what Sara was saying, instead concentrating on analyzing his situation. It was his considered opinion that he— and more importantly, Jennifer—were screwed. He was outnumbered, didn't have so much as a paper clip to fight with, and had been hopelessly outma-neuvered. It was that last one that really hurt.

"Come over here, Jennifer," Sara said. "We won't hurt you. You're more important to us than you could possibly know."

"Don't let them take me, Mr. Beamon!"

Beamon looked at the faces of the men around him and wondered if they knew that Sara had sold their messiah out. "Now that's not entirely true, is it, Sara? Jennifer's Albert Kneiss's granddaughter and a threat to your power. That's all you really care about anymore, isn't it? Your power? This doesn't have anything to do with God or the future of the church anymore. The truth is, it just has to do with you holding onto the little kingdom you've built for yourself."

Sara looked away from Jennifer and directly at

him for a moment. "You just have no understanding of the meaning of faith, do you, Mr. Beamon?"

The pain in the back of his head flared for a moment and he heard Jennifer scream. Then nothing.

62

THE CARTOONS WERE RIGHT—HE REALLY could see stars. They weren't quite as well defined as the ones on TV, though; more like fuzzy balls of light darting erratically in the darkness.

Beamon moved his fingers and heard a quiet rustling over the hum of the car's engine. The entire left side of his body was numb and he couldn't feel his hands, but it sounded like they still worked. Not that it probably mattered much, given his current situation.

The nauseating stop-and-start rocking, the confined space, and the vibration and smell of gas fumes left little doubt that he was in the trunk of a car. On the bright side, though, it seemed to be a spacious Detroit trunk and not one of those cramped little import jobs. The Japanese had just never gotten a handle on how to make a trunk that a kidnap victim could get comfortable in.

His feet were tied with what felt like rope, which was, in turn, looped through the chain between the handcuffs binding his wrists. Hog-tied, they'd have said where he'd grown up.

And then there was Jennifer. The little girl who had held herself together through so much, but now was going to die because he was a fucking moron. Beamon laid his head down on something hard, ignoring the warmth spreading across the back of his head as the gun butt wound reopened.

He'd lost.

By now, Jennifer was probably in the Church's private jet on her way to the Retreat—an inaccessible piece of land in the vast nothing of eastern Oregon. Even if he were walking into the J. Edgar Hoover Building instead of lying around in a trunk with his thumb up his ass, there would be nothing he could do. By the time he convinced the powers that be not to throw him in jail and, even less likely, convinced them of the church's involvement, Jennifer would be long gone.

And the Vericomm audio? As good as gone, too.

He was confident that the church would "question" him with the same efficiency and thoroughness that they did everything else. Not that they would have to. At this point, he might as well do himself a favor and make it quick. Tell them about Goldman's apartment—if they hadn't found it already themselves—and about where he'd stowed the Vericomm disks.

It was probably better this way, he told himself, rocking over to try to jump-start the blood flow to his side. He hadn't been looking forward to his new career as the night clerk at some roadside 7-Eleven—a job he'd only be able to keep until the church got around to informing the store's management about his new history of pedophilia.

He thought about Ernie, transposing his face with hers and imagining himself as a morbidly obese computer programmer trapped in his home by fear and embarrassment. Or maybe holed up in a trailer in the middle of nowhere, hunting what he needed to eat during the day and huddling next to an old wood stove at night, like Jennifer's uncle.

Beamon adjusted his position again and tried to ignore the inevitable headache that was starting to form as his mind cleared. He closed his eyes, but it didn't make any difference in the blackness of the trunk.

The stars that had been swirling in front of him were starting to fade and finally burn out as he tried to let his grogginess take him back into unconsciousness. Better to just admit defeat right now and let them put him out of his misery.

"Goddammit," he slurred through the gag in his mouth when the car lurched to a stop and sent him skidding face first into the spare tire.

The brief stab of pain in his nose pulled him from his self-induced daze. What the hell was wrong with him? This was no way to die. He shook his head violently, amplifying the throbbing that had taken hold there. He might not be able to save her, but at the very least he owed Jennifer his best effort at throwing a big wrench into gears of Sara's church.

Beamon took a deep breath that did little but feed his various aches and pains, and moved his hands toward his pocket. He had to navigate more by sound and resistance than sensation—his fingers felt dead.

The lighter sparked to life and maintained its flame on his third try at spinning the small wheel. Now if he could just keep from setting himself on fire, he might be able to say someday that being a smoker had saved his life.

The red parka that had served him so well for the last month and a half was lying in front of him. Other than that, there were a few books and the spare tire and tools that were fixtures in most trunks.

Beamon tried to pull off the gag secured around his head using the rubber of the tire, but it had been tied too tightly and shoved too deep into his mouth. He twisted to his right until his knees hit the top of the trunk and slid his arms painfully under him. When he heard his fingers rustle against the nylon of the parka, he started the long process of pulling the coat under him. He didn't know how long it took but he finally succeeded, getting the jacket to where he could access the pockets.

Surprisingly, his cell phone was still in the inside pocket. His captors either hadn't counted on his hard head, or hadn't expected the traffic jam they seemed to be mired in.

He passed over the phone, knowing it wouldn't be much use with the gag. Finally he found what he was looking for: his pen. He unscrewed it and pulled it apart, taking the thin metal tube that held the ink and ballpoint from the cheap plastic cover.

It took another five minutes, but he managed to pinch the tube flat and work it into the simple latching mechanism of the handcuffs. How to get out of your own cuffs was one of the first things they taught you at Quantico. He didn't remember all the nuances, but after a few false starts he felt the satisfying pain of the blood rushing back into his hands. Another push freed his wrists completely.

Beamon pulled the gag from his mouth and took a gulp of the cold, exhaust-tasting air. He tried to bring his feet up close enough to untie them, but it was impossible in the cramped confines of the trunk. Whatever he was going to do, it was going to have to be without them.

He pulled his parka in front of him again and felt around until he found his cell phone. He wasn't sure who he was going to call or exactly how he was going to describe the predicament he'd found himself in, but at least he could tell someone what the hell was going on.

He flipped it open with his still-numb fingers, not noticing that the battery pack was gone until the numbers on the keypad didn't light up. They obviously planned to bury him with it. Made sense—it'd be kind of embarrassing if his phone turned up for auction at some church bake sale. Beamon zipped the useless phone back into his parka and flipped the lighter back on for a moment.

Options?

The easy answer was to start kicking and screaming and hope someone noticed and called the cops. The drawback there was that it was freezing cold outside, so none of the cars within theoretical earshot would have their windows down. No, most likely his captors would be the only people who heard him and they'd pull off the next ramp and use the opportunity to test out their tire iron on the back of his head.

Option two would be to escape on his own. That was his favorite, but it begged the question of how.

Beamon moved the lighter to the back of the trunk and examined the inside of the lock. Nothing he'd be able to figure out. The handcuffs had been his best—and only—lock trick.

He ran the lighter along the edges of the trunk as best he could, finally stopping at a black plastic tube housing a group of brightly colored wires. That might be something. He grabbed the tube and pulled hard, breaking the wires free with a small, but satisfying, shower of sparks.

The sound of a faltering engine and the feeling

of the car coasting to a stop didn't materialize. Instead, the car jerked a bit to the right as it changed lanes and accelerated, the engine purring smoothly.

"Goddammit," Beamon swore quietly. The wires probably ran the fucking air conditioning.

He held the lighter in front of him and examined the contents of the trunk more closely. There were six books, all relating to the church in some way and all decorated with similarly inspirational pictures of Albert Kneiss. The spare tire looked brand new, as did the jack. And that was it, except for a dirty rag and an old McDonald's wrapper. No sense in complaining—if that was what he had to work with, that was what he had.

Beamon picked up the books and piled them neatly behind him. They stacked to be about eight inches high. No way of knowing if that was going to be good enough.

The lighter began to dim ominously as he unscrewed the wing nut holding the jack in place. Once it was free, he put the jack on top of the books and inserted the lug wrench that doubled as its handle—a tricky and completely blind procedure.

Now if Ernie's God would just cut him one little break here, the jack would reach the underside of the trunk and force it open.

Working the lever, which was behind him, was a slow and painful procedure, but the quiet clicking told him that he was making progress.

He'd been working it for about fifteen minutes when he had to stop and rest. The contorted position of his arms had constricted the blood flow, and it felt like there were knives in his shoulders and about a thousand needles in his arms.

He flicked the lighter again. The flame shuddered and glowed a dim blue, but it was still enough to see. Only about a half-inch to go before the jack made contact.

He shook out his arms as best he could and started in on the jack again as the car started a slow deceleration. He'd gotten off about ten more clicks when the lever stopped. He pushed harder, twisting his body to put a little weight behind it. "Oh, come on. Don't do this to me," he said quietly.

That was it. The jack was fully extended.

"One stupid goddamn break, that's all I as—"

Beamon's words caught in his throat when he was thrown forward into the spare tire again and the jack slammed into the back of his head. His ears were ringing loudly as he tried to scoot back into the middle of the trunk, but he wasn't sure if it was from the impact of the jack or the deafening crash that had preceded it.

"What the fuck!" came a muffled voice flowing into the trunk on a blast of cold air.

Beamon shook his head as a car door outside slammed. "You ever hear of taillights, you assholes? It's fucking pitch dark out here!"

Beamon managed a weak smile when he realized that the wires he'd pulled out must have belonged to the car's brake lights. He rolled onto his back and saw the slow-moving glow of headlights, clearly visible through the gaps between the severely bent trunk and the body of the car.

"Get back here, you sonsofbitches!" he heard as the car started to move again.

Beamon kicked hard with his still tied feet, trying to get the stubborn latch on the trunk to completely break free. Nothing. He took a deep breath, pressed his hands against the inside of the trunk, and kicked again.

The trunk flew open just as the car cut hard onto the shoulder and began to accelerate. He could see the man who had hit them running back to his truck to give chase.

Beamon grabbed his parka and struggled out of the trunk, hitting the pavement hard and beginning to roll backward across the asphalt. The truck screeched to a halt as Beamon staggered to his feet.

"What the fuck!" the man said, jumping from the cab.

Beamon tried to focus on the front of the old pickup. One of the headlights was shattered, and the bug guard engraved with "Pearson Drywall" was hanging precariously from the hood.

"What the hell were you doing in there? Look at my truck!" the man shouted, grabbing him by the shirt. That, combined with the fact that Beamon's feet were still roped together, knocked him onto his back.

He sat up and reached back to brush his hand against the base of his skull. It came back covered in blood.

"Hey, you all right?"

Beamon looked up into the man's craggy face and at the traffic that was quickly bogging down around them. "Can I borrow your knife?"

The man pulled it from a leather case attached to his belt and flipped it open. Beamon took it and cut the rope binding his legs.

"You don't want to mess with those guys," Beamon said, trying to get up but falling back to the ground. He felt like one big bruise.

The man held his hand out and Beamon gratefully accepted the help. "Tell you what. Mr. Pearson, is it?"

He shook his head and looked at Beamon suspiciously. "Name's Caleb. I just work for Pearson Drywall."

Beamon looked again at the truck. It was still running, though the vibration of the engine looked like it was going to knock what was left of the front grille off at any moment.

"Tell you what, Caleb," Beamon said, picking up the parka at his feet and confirming that the inside pocket still contained the envelope with what was left of his money. "You take me to the airport and I'll pay for the damages to your truck in cash."

63

BEAMON HAD EXPECTED TO FIND THE PLACE a pile of ashes, but nothing had changed.

Goldman's overalls were still in the box he'd stuffed them in, the computers were still humming away, and the half-full bottle of bourbon was still where he'd left it.

Beamon limped across the silent apartment and sat down in front of a computer, leaning his shotgun against a chair. He jabbed at the space bar and lit a cigarette, watching the screen slowly come to life.

He felt like someone had put him in a clothes dryer with a couple of bowling balls. The gash in the back of his head had continued to seep blood for hours, forcing him to keep a handkerchief pressed against it for most of the plane ride back to Flagstaff. That, combined with the black eyes and swollen nose, had attracted enough attention that he could be relatively certain that the church was aware that he was back in town.

He took a slug of bourbon directly from the bottle next to him and winced as the alcohol went to work on the cuts inside his mouth. How he'd gotten those, he wasn't sure, but there didn't seem to be a single square inch of his body that the church hadn't left its mark on.

He double-clicked on the mailbox icon on the screen and pulled up the church's hijacked e-mail. The feed was still working.

It took Beamon a good five minutes to figure out how to decrypt the e-mail but in the end he was rewarded with six completely useless communications from the late Albert Kneiss.

And that was the ball game. At midnight tomorrow, Jennifer Davis's life would come to an end—a well-deserved punishment for trusting in him to save her.

She'd be twenty-four days from her sixteenth birthday.

Beamon leaned back and took a slightly more cautious sip from the bottle, hoping that it would start to go to work on his headache.

Even if he knew precisely where the Retreat was, what could he do? Fly to Portland, rent a car, then a snowmobile, and ride across God knew how many miles of frozen tundra like James-fucking-Bond? Or maybe a dog-sled team would be more in keeping with his technophobe image.

He reached into his pocket and pulled his cell phone out as it began to ring, but couldn't decide if he really wanted to answer it. It was probably just Sara. Wanting to gloat a bit and to make a substantially reduced offer on the Vericomm disks.

What the hell, he decided, flipping the phone open. He'd spent damn near the last of his money on the new battery, he might as well get some use out of it.

"Hello."

"Mark! Oh my God, Mark. I've been so worried. I've been trying to get in touch with you for days!"

Beamon stopped the bottle about six inches from his mouth. "Carrie?"

"Mark, are you okay? You sound strange."

"That's probably because I don't know why we're talking. I thought we said everything we had to say last week."

There was silence over the line for a moment. "I'm calling to say I'm sorry."

Beamon set the bottle on the table but said nothing.

"What's going on, Mark?"

"What do you mean?"

"I talked to a friend of mine—a psychiatrist who specializes in child abuse. She'd never heard of the Child Safety Administration. In fact, no one has."

"No big surprise there, Carrie," Beamon said, finding it impossible to hide his anger. "Their god-damned business card didn't even have a phone number on it. A little unusual, don't you think?"

"Yes. I . . . Emory means everything to me, Mark. You know that."

He did know. It wasn't her fault.

"I talked with Emory and I had my friend talk to her. There was nothing. I knew there wouldn't be, but I had to be sure. I trust you, Mark, but . . ."

"Look, I understand, Carrie. I would have done the same thing."

She sighed over the phone and Beamon fought to erase the image of her that was starting to paint itself into his mind.

"I hoped you would, Mark. Can we start over?"

Beamon watched the computer screen in front of him as it turned from a block of text to a simulation of flying through space. "No. We can't. Stay away from me, Carrie. You don't want to be part of what's left of my life."

"What's left of your li—"

He turned off the phone and laid it gently down on the table. The computer picked up the vibration and the screen turned back to the last e-mail from the church, as if it were mocking him.

There wasn't much left for him now but revenge. He'd play the tapes for whoever would listen and try to tell his story, but the church had left him with no credibility, no money, and no allies. He had a feeling that there wouldn't be anyone listening.

Beamon looked at the text of the e-mail on the computer, trying to find some hidden meaning in the financial report printed there, but there was none. His eyes wandered across the colorful buttons at the top of the screen, finally fixing on the light gray lettering in the button on the far right.

SEND.

Beamon wrapped his hand around the bottle of bourbon on the table but didn't pick it up. He leaned forward, bringing himself closer to the screen.

SEND.

64

HER BREATHING WAS ALMOST INAUDIBLE. THE white sheets, into which her pale skin blended so seamlessly, barely moved as her chest rose, faltered, and fell in a stilted rhythm.

Sara ran the back of her hand down Jennifer Davis's unconscious body. She'd never wake again. When the others arrived, they'd see her lying there peacefully, preparing to become humanity's teacher for the next ten thousand years.

Then another dose of the sedative just before midnight, combining with what she already had coursing through her veins, and the life would fade out of her. Sara's control of the church would be nearly unshakable then, and she would use that power to continue her work. To increase the church's wealth and influence, and with it her own.

Sara looked away from the girl and considered the problem of Mark Beamon, the only thing standing in the way of the future that she envisioned for herself and the church.

He was broken. She'd seen the pain and guilt in his eyes when she had taken Jennifer and reduced to nothing his desperate struggle and his sacrifice of everything meaningful in his life.

She recognized his subsequent escape as a fluke, but was becoming concerned that despite her resources, he was still missing. If he hadn't been located by tomorrow morning, she would call him and make a meager offer for the Vericomm tapes. With nothing else left, he'd jump at whatever bone she saw fit to throw.

And then, when he was at his weakest, she'd have him brought to her and end it once and for all.

The men who had let him escape—both in Phoenix and in Washington—had been severely censured, but had kept their positions. She needed the Guardians to complete the consolidation of her power and to keep the rest of the Elders docile. A replacement for Sines would have to be chosen. And soon.

Sara walked to the frost-covered window and looked out at the empty expanse that surrounded the Retreat. She didn't turn when she heard the door open. "I said I didn't want to be disturbed."

There was no answer.

She turned to face a man wearing a thick black jacket standing just inside the doorway. His name was Thomas. Thomas Nolan. He was only thirty-two, but intelligent and strong beyond his years. His parents had been members of the church since almost the beginning. She'd recognized him for his fanatical devotion to Albert when he was still very young and had personally attended the ceremony marking his entrance to the Guardians.

Now the devotion he had shown Albert would be hers. When this was over, he would be the one to step into Sines's position.

"What is it, Thomas?" she said as the other two Guardians staying at the Retreat walked in behind him and took positions at the edges of the room.

"Get out of here," Sara said, letting the anger

creep into her voice. "I told you that no one but Thomas and myself are to enter this room without my permission."

"No. Stay," Nolan said.

The two men held their ground, their expressions undecipherable.

"What did you say?" Sara said, stepping closer to Nolan and looking directly into his eyes. The reverence that she had always seen there had disappeared. Instead of averting his gaze, he glared back at her. "Tell them to leave, Thomas."

"No."

"What's wrong with you?" She took a step back, confused.

She looked around her at the men standing silently along the wall, concentrating on maintaining her outward calm. None of the Guardians had ever disobeyed her before. She was suddenly very aware of the young girl lying on the bed behind her and the precarious position that Jennifer put her in. Had something happened that she wasn't aware of? No, that was impossible.

"I thought that you would be the one to take Gregory's place, Thomas. Perhaps I was wrong. Perhaps you don't have the devotion to Albert that he thinks you do."

She jerked back when his hand shot out, but not fast enough. He caught her by the back of the neck and pulled her toward him.

"What . . . what are you doing?" she yelled, struggling to break free. "Let me go!"

The two other men followed along slowly as he dragged her through the door and out into the hall.

"Stop him. He's gone insane!" she shouted at them.

They didn't seem to hear, so she turned back to Nolan. "Albert will—"

At the mention of Kneiss's name, Nolan threw his weight back and pulled her head into the wall.

She slid to the floor dazed, blood from a gash in her forehead flowing into her eyes. She wiped at it with her sleeve, still trying to understand what was happening. Thomas Nolan was the most devoted of all the Guardians.

She didn't stand, but held her hand out, trying to calm down and to give herself time to think. Something had happened. What?

The cold rage was clearly visible on Nolan's face as he moved toward her.

"Wait," she said, holding her hands out in front of her.

He hesitated.

"Just wait. There is some misunderstanding here and there's no need for Albert to ever hear about it. It's okay. It's okay. Just tell me why you're doing this. We'll straighten it out."

Nolan didn't answer, but instead grabbed her by the hair again and dragged her through the grand entry hall of the old building and out into the snow. Sara felt the sharpness of the cold in her lungs as she tried to regain her footing on the icy ground beneath her.

"Stop!" she screamed, digging her nails into the arm pulling her along.

The cold was beginning to penetrate her skin as Nolan released her and she dropped to her knees in the snow. She looked up through the blood that was beginning to freeze to her face and focused on the two silent men standing a few feet behind Nolan. "Whichever one of you stops this will take

Gregory's place and will have whatever he wants. Do you understand? Tomorrow I will be the final authority of the church. *I* will."

One of them stepped toward her. She pulled away from Nolan and crawled to the man. She held a hand out to him, but he stopped a few feet away and threw a single piece of computer paper onto the snow in front of her.

To: Nolan@Guardians5278.com
From: ak@compound6758.com

Sara has betrayed me.

I have allowed her attacks on my
granddaughter and Mark Beamon, as
well as the death of my most
devoted follower, Ernestine Waverly.
I did this clinging to the hope that
she would look into herself and find
the strength of her faith. That she
would come back to me.

As the day of my ascension
approaches, I must accept that all
she has found is a consuming
jealousy and greed, and that
mankind has not come as far as I
had hoped. It seems that every time
has its Judas.

If allowed to, Sara will destroy the
church and with it, humanity's
hopes and dreams. It is her time to
stand before God and be judged, as it
is mine.

God Bless.

AK

Sara struggled to keep her breathing normal as
the shadow of a pistol crossed in front of her on the
snow.

"This is wrong," she said, turning toward Nolan
and the barrel of the gun. "It's not from Albert. I'm
telling you it's not from Albert. Mark Beamon has
broken the codes we use. He sent this."

Nolan shook his head sadly, but kept the gun
steady. "Those codes have never been broken. We
checked the encryption signature you gave us. It is
from Albert."

"No! Don't you see? That's how Beamon found
her at the airport. He wasn't watching the plane
like we thought. He read the e-mail!"

"No," Nolan, said, reaching out and pulling the
slide back on the pistol. "Albert told him. He was
giving you a chance to repent."

This couldn't be happening. She would not
allow her life to be ended by Mark Beamon, a
drunken nobody whose pathetic life she'd had the
power to destroy with a few words.

"None of this would be here if it weren't for

me, and none of it will survive without me! I *am*
Albert Kneiss!"

Nolan pressed the gun against her temple, grabbing her by the collar as she tried to back away. "That's for God to decide."

65

BEAMON PULLED HIS FEET UP ON THE BUMPER of the car and struggled to light another cigarette in the wind. The hood was quickly losing its warmth as the engine cooled, but it was still better than the alternative. The interior of the car had been closing in on him.

The fate of the two e-mails he'd sent was a complete mystery to him. What the hell did he know about computers? It was entirely possible that the little zeros and ones that the e-mails were constructed from had just been dispersed to the digital void of the Internet. If that was the case, Jennifer was dead and he was waiting for no one.

More likely, the e-mails had been received and immediately reported to Sara, who wouldn't have had much trouble figuring out who wrote them. In that case, he was waiting for a church hit squad.

He'd FedExed the Vericomm audio disks to an attorney who had kicked his ass in court about five years ago. Meanest, most ruthless sonofabitch he'd ever met—a man who clearly could be trusted to carry out his instructions. Upon hearing reports of Beamon's death, he was to distribute copies of the disks—and the handwritten explanation of how Beamon had come to possess them—to twenty-five major newspapers. And with that final act, Beamon's hat was officially out of rabbits.

He took a deep drag on the cigarette and moved to a warmer part of the hood, thinking about the contents of the e-mails he'd sent. The ironic thing was, what he'd written in them was true. Or at least as close to the truth as he could get. After spending the last month studying Albert Kneiss through reading just about everything ever written by or about him, it had been surprisingly easy to get into the old man's head and create a message in an electronic hand that would be indistinguishable from his. A message that Albert might have composed himself if he'd been able to.

Except for the last part, perhaps—the purposefully ambiguous sentence that Beamon knew the Guardians would interpret as a death sentence for Sara.

And that was the drawback to his plan. In the unlikely event that it worked, he was a murderer. But what choice had he been left with? A breathing Sara Renslier couldn't be trusted to stay away from the girl. And she sure as hell wasn't going to let him stroke out playing bridge in an old folks' home. Or was that just a rationalization that freed him to take his revenge?

Beamon spotted the gray panel van slowly approaching from the other side of the parking lot and slid his hand around the butt of the shotgun lying under a towel on the hood next to him. Those assholes who had shoved him in that trunk in D.C. still had his pistol. If he was still alive five minutes from now, he'd have to see if he could get that back. It had been a good friend.

"Mr. Beamon!"

The van hadn't yet come to a complete stop when Jennifer burst from the passenger door and ran to him. She almost knocked him off the slick hood when she grabbed hold of him.

"I knew you wouldn't let them kill me."

"A promise is a promise," he said, stroking her hair with one hand but keeping the other under the towel.

"She's gone," Jennifer said, beginning to sob. "She was in the snow! There was—" her voice caught for a moment. "There was so much blood. It was just like Mom."

Beamon was only about half-listening, concentrating on the van as a young man he hadn't seen before stepped from it and walked around to face him. He patted her on the rear and peeled her arms from around him. "Go sit in the car, okay? I'll be there in a second."

She pulled away from him, and a moment later Beamon heard the door slam shut behind him.

"Mr. Beamon. I wanted to tell you—" the man in front of him started.

Beamon cut him off, speaking authoritatively. "It's okay. We understand. You were only doing what you thought Albert wanted. He holds Sara solely responsible."

"I only wanted to do what was right," he said looking at his feet. "I contacted the others and told them what happened."

Beamon nodded sagely. "Albert wanted me to tell you he was sorry to put you through what he did—to ask of you what he did. But that he knew you were strong enough to handle it." Beamon slid from the hood. "He loved Sara so much. I think he believed that she would come back to him until the very end."

The man turned and began walking slowly back to the van. Beamon thought he said, "He always saw the good in people," but couldn't be sure. The wind had picked up and carried the man's words away.

Beamon adjusted himself in the sofa and looked down at Jennifer, who was lying on the floor in front of the television. "I find it kind of disturbing the way you stare at things but don't really see them, Jennifer."

"Sorry . . . I was thinking."

"Too much reflection can be bad for you. Why don't you come sit up here and have some ice cream?"

She slowly peeled herself off the linoleum and fell onto the couch next to him.

"Oh, by the way, the place looks great."

She'd spent the last four hours scrubbing and straightening the worn-out little apartment they were holed up in, glancing at the clock on the desk every five minutes or so.

He'd tried to convince her that she was no longer in danger, but the fact that his record was a little spotty on that subject, and the loaded shotgun resting on the sofa next to him, made his argument less than convincing.

They both watched as the numbers on the clock flipped over to twelve o'clock. Jennifer sat completely still, ignoring the dented spoon Beamon was holding out to her. It looked as if she was waiting for something. The sound of the church's enforcers rushing the apartment? A lightning bolt from heaven?

"Midnight, Jen. They don't want you as their new messiah. I hear they're looking for someone with a college degree and some practical experience."

Dumb humor didn't seem to be working, so he tried the ice cream again. Women weren't supposed to be able to resist the stuff. "It's Ben and Jerry's.

Cherry Garcia." He stuck the extra spoon in the carton and wiggled it seductively. "Won't last much longer."

She looked like she was going to crumble into another crying fit, and Beamon felt his stomach tense. He just wasn't built for this kind of thing. He hoped to hell that he could get his job back so he could return to the good old days of finding 'em and instantly turning 'em over to the Bureau's shrink.

Fortunately, the spell passed with only a hint of a tear visible in the corner of her right eye. Beamon shook the carton again.

This time she took the spoon. "Thanks. For everything."

66

"WON'T THE FBI BE LOOKING FOR YOU here, Mr. Beamon?" Jennifer asked, lifting herself off the car seat and yanking at one of her pantlegs. The jeans he'd purchased for her were apparently less than a perfect fit.

Beamon looked up at the front door of his condo. "Doubt it. FBI'd probably assume I wouldn't be stupid enough to come back here while they were looking for me."

"So you're a lot stupider than they think."

He pointed to her wide grin as he stepped from the car. "That looks good on you, smartass."

Beamon pulled off his sunglasses and squinted against the bright mid-morning sun. "Can you see my gun?" he said, turning his back to Jennifer and adjusting his sweater.

"No. But this is a problem." She reached over and buttoned his collar. "There. You look good."

He gave a short nod and started up the walkway.

"You all right?" Jennifer asked, following alongside him.

"Why?"

"I don't know, you look a little nervous. You really like her, don't you?"

Beamon rolled his eyes.

"You should tell her you're sorry."

"I think we may be beyond that, Jen."

"Nah. Women go in for apologies in a big way. Trust me on this."

Beamon took a deep breath and knocked on Carrie Johnstone's door. It opened a moment later.

"Mark!" Carrie threw her arms around him and kissed him hard on the mouth.

"Probably don't need to bother with that apology," he heard Jennifer mumble as he tried to keep from stumbling.

Carrie pulled back and turned toward her. "Oh my God. You're Jennifer Davis, aren't you?"

"Uh-huh. It's nice to meet you, Ms. Johnstone. You're all Mr. Beamon talks about."

"I don't think that's really true," Beamon stammered as Carrie put her arm around Jennifer and guided her in the door.

"Are you all right, honey? Maybe you'd like to talk?"

"Mr. Beamon!" Emory squealed as she ran around her mother and attached herself to his leg. He peeled her off and picked her up. "How are you, honey? The Easter bunny didn't bring you healthy candy, did he?"

She bobbed her head as he produced a chocolate moose from the pocket of his jacket and kicked the door closed behind him. "Don't tell your mother."

"Mark, I want to hear everything. Are you hungry?"

Beamon looked skeptically at the casserole cooling on the stove. It looked normal, but he knew that it was a trick. "Uh, sure, Carrie, thanks."

"Jennifer, hand me that spatula over there,

please," Carrie said, pointing to a copper bucket full of cooking utensils.

She scooped a large piece onto a plate and handed it to Beamon. "This is a great recipe. I just make a few substitutions and it turns out perfect."

Beamon smiled weakly and shoveled a forkful into his mouth. "Can't tell a bit," he said through a glob of something that tasted a little like an empty styrofoam cup.

"Mark's such a liar," Carrie said to Jennifer. "He hates my cooking, but doesn't have the guts to tell me. I admire that kind of cowardice in a man."

Jennifer accepted an even larger piece and retreated with Emory to the small table in the kitchen.

Carrie laid her plate on the counter and began speaking in a voice low enough that the girls couldn't hear. "Where did you find her, Mark? I haven't seen anything on the news about it. Are you back with the FBI?"

"You're the only person who knows. And no, I'm not back with the FBI. I may never be."

"You found her on your own?"

Beamon thought of Ernie and Jack Goldman. "I had some help."

She looked over at Jennifer, who was helping Emory cut up the food on her plate. "Is she okay, Mark? Did she actually see her parents murdered? Was she abused?"

Beamon took another bite of the casserole and chewed slowly. "Her parents weren't murdered— her father shot her mother and then himself right in front of her, and yes, she was physically and mentally abused. Not sexually, though." He leaned a little closer to her. "I have no idea what to say to her, Carrie. I've tried, but you've got to help me here."

Carrie waved at Jennifer. "Finished? Why don't you help me with the dishes while Mark takes Emory for a walk and explains why it would be wrong for her to eat that chocolate moose he gave her?"

"You told?" Beamon said as Emory flew off the chair and disappeared down the hall to bundle up. Beamon stepped aside as Jennifer carried the dishes into the kitchen. "There's one more thing I'm going to need your help with, Carrie. Maybe we can talk about it when I get back."

67

THE SUNLIGHT WAS BARELY STARTING TO appear over the mountains as Beamon pulled a Post-it note out of his pocket and slipped his glasses onto his nose. He read the address written on it and checked it against the one stenciled on the neatly kept house in front of him. This was it.

He knocked on the door and waited impatiently as muffled footsteps became audible on the other side. The man who answered was dressed in a meticulously pressed white shirt and gray wool slacks. An unimaginatively tasteful maroon tie was hanging untied around his neck.

It took a few moments—probably because Beamon was backlit by the rising sun—but recognition began to slowly register on the man's face. He tried to back away, but Beamon reached out and grabbed him by the collar, just as a woman wearing a long green robe appeared in the hallway. "Who is it, honey?"

"Excuse me, ma'am," Beamon said, dragging the man through the door. "I just want a quick word with your husband."

"Gary," she called in a worried voice, "is everything all right? Should I call someone?"

"Just finish getting the kids ready for school. It's okay."

Beamon smiled and waved at her, then pulled the door shut.

"You just aren't real bright, are you, Beamon," the man said, trying to jerk away. There was a quiet ripping sound, but Beamon easily kept hold of his shirt. "You still have no idea what you're dealing with, do you?"

Beamon didn't say anything, but dragged him across the driveway and shoved his face into the passenger window of the car idling there, resisting the urge to break the glass with the man's nose.

"You haven't been informed as to the new world order, I take it," Beamon said, looking through the windshield at Carrie. She nodded nervously.

He pulled the man away from the car and released him. Instead of backing away, he stepped forward, bringing his face to within inches of Beamon's. "What're you going to do, Beamon? Arrest me? Oh, no, wait. You can't do that anymore, can you?"

Beamon smiled engagingly and stomped hard on the man's foot. He howled in pain and surprise and limped back a few paces. Beamon turned back to the car and shrugged. Carrie looked horrified.

There had been no prints on the Child Safety Administration's business card other than his and Carrie's, but the eighth stationery store Beamon called had had a record of printing the offending card. "Guess you shouldn't have had the printer mail those cards directly to your home, huh, dumbshit."

The man looked like he was going to charge, but Beamon stopped him by sliding a hand suggestively beneath his parka. The gesture seemed to have the desired effect.

"I have to admit to being a little impressed," Beamon said. "For fifty dollars in business cards and a few hours' work, you could irretrievably fuck up hundreds of people's lives. How many times have you used this little trick?"

The man straightened up and looked Beamon directly in the eye. "As many as we wanted to."

68

"MARGIE! HOW YOU DOIN', HON?" BEAMON said jovially.

Jake Layman's secretary bolted upright at her desk and then jumped to her feet. "Oh my God. Mark! What are you doing here? I mean, they've been looking everywhere for you!"

Beamon put his hand on Jennifer's back. "Margie, I'd like you to meet the girl everyone's been talking about—Jennifer Davis."

The woman's eyes widened as Jennifer fidgeted uncomfortably and tried to get behind Beamon. "Don't stare," he said. "I think she's a little uncomfortable that I bought her clothes in the Junior Miss section of Kmart."

"And . . . and who's this?" Margie stammered, looking at the man standing next to Beamon.

"This is my friend from the Child Safety Administration. He has a story he wants to tell—"

Beamon suddenly noticed that the dull roar of the FBI's Phoenix office had gone dead, replaced by the quiet hush of intermittent whispers. When he turned around, all motion had stopped. It looked like he was viewing the office on a VCR with a stuck Pause button.

"Uh, I hear that the director's here talking about me," he said, turning back to her. "Where?"

"I'll tell them you're here."

"Don't bother," he said. "Just point."

"They're in Conference Room Two."

He stepped back and motioned to Jennifer and the increasingly nervous-looking man who had accused him of child molestation. They started down the hall ahead of him.

"Gentlemen," Beamon said as he walked through the conference room door without knocking. "And Chet."

"Beamon!" Layman said, standing abruptly and almost upsetting the coffee mug on the table. Chet Michaels pumped a fist in the air and silently mouthed, "Yes!" The director just stared.

"Don't look so surprised, Jake. I told you I'd come in when I tied up a few loose ends." He looked out the open door. "Don't be shy."

When Jennifer self-consciously shuffled in, Layman fell back into his chair.

"The first of my loose ends. Jennifer, I'd like you to meet Jake Layman and William Calahan. You probably remember Chet Michaels."

She smiled politely.

His other guest hovered outside the door, forcing Beamon to reach out and haul him into the room. "Sit," he ordered. The man complied silently.

"That's my other loose end, but I'll explain later." Beamon patted the chair next to him. Jennifer sat down and placed the computer disks she'd been carrying on the table in front of her. Beamon nodded toward them, and she slid them across the table.

"What are these?" Layman said quietly.

"Audio from an interesting little setup the Church of the Evolution had going. I figure it's enough to keep your whole office busy for about five years."

"The Kneissians?" Calahan said, speaking for the first time. "What the hell's going on here? And where did she come from?"

"Director Calahan, I—" Layman started.

"Shut up, Jake. I didn't ask you. Beamon's talking now."

AFTERWORD

In writing this novel I had the arduous but fascinating task of creating my own religion. To accomplish this, I borrowed snippets from many faiths and added a healthy dose of my own imagination and the spirit of George Orwell.

Because all faiths have certain common threads, it might be possible to see parallels to any number of present-day belief systems. Let me assure you that if these parallels do indeed exist, they were completely unintentional.

Look for KYLE MILLS' thriller

FREE FALL

Available now wherever books are sold

The sun had long since passed over the bright red fin of the rock Darby Moore was lying on, but its heat still radiated into her chest and stomach. She couldn't bring herself to move. Somehow that fading warmth softened the image of Tristan's lifeless foot hanging from the open door of her van and drained some of the color from the pool of blood in Maryland where she'd left that man lying.

The thirty-hour drive to Utah had been agonizing. Near panic had hit her every time she passed a police car. She'd been too scared to stop anywhere familiar, thinking that someone would be waiting for her. As the little truck had turned into a self-imposed prison, she'd become more and more certain that the file Tristan mentioned was the answer—the only answer. She had to get to it first, then she could use it. How, exactly, she didn't know. To expose the men who'd killed her friend? To bargain for her life? To clear her name? It didn't matter—what was important now is that she get it. Then she'd have time to think. The one thing she was certain of was that without some leverage, those men would kill her without any more thought or remorse than they'd give to swatting a fly.

Darby tried to relax and let the knots in her back loosen as she surveyed the landscape below her. From where she lay, she could see the brown/green of the canyon floor some three hundred feet below, the reddish-orange rock surrounding it, and the distant sandstone arches that leaked the sunset through them. She scooted forward a few feet and hung her head fully over the cliff, examining the way it fell away to the canyon below.

They were getting closer.

There were three of them—she was sure of that now. It was a long way down, but she could make out that two were rather heavyset, with short, dark hair and wearing bright blue jackets, jeans, and what looked like hiking boots or heavy trail shoes. Both seemed to be having a difficult time negotiating the broken rock, deep sand, and jagged plants typical to this part of Utah. They may not have been the same men who had kidnapped her and murdered Tristan, but they certainly looked like they were cut from the same generic cloth.

The third man was more of a mystery. He was wearing shorts, sandals, and a light jacket with a patch across the shoulder that reflected with the familiar color and intensity of duct tape. Unlike his more conservative companions, his hair was a colorless blond and tied back in a ponytail. More interestingly, though, his gait seemed effortless and natural as he hopped from boulder to boulder, diverting gracefully up a sandstone ramp or ledge every few minutes to get a fresh perspective on the terrain.

The small cave where Tristan had hidden the file he'd stolen was about two hundred and fifty feet below her and some fifty feet above the canyon floor. He'd obviously told them where the file was before he'd died. She tried not to think what they had done to coerce him.

Fortunately for her, the men below were discovering something she'd learned long ago—everything looks the same in this part of the world. She'd been watching them for almost two hours now as they moved methodically along the desert floor, agonizing over what she should do and hoping that they would abandon their search as the setting sun threw the canyon into shadow. No such luck.

Darby propped herself up on her elbows and looked down at herself. She'd tracked down a sweatshirt at a Goodwill store somewhere in Kansas, but now regretted the green color, which would stand out against the dusty red of the cliff face. At the same Goodwill she'd purchased, for $1.50, the threadbare pack that was strapped to her back.

The climbing shoes she so desperately needed to get down to the cave had been impossible to obtain. The chance of her walking into a climbing shop without being recognized was about zero, and that left her with nothing but her sandals.

Though better than tennis shoes, climbing in sandals was roughly the athletic equivalent of running hurdles in heels—though the penalty wasn't a twisted ankle. It was, in the colorful slang of climbing, decking. She tried not to, but couldn't help speculating as to the size and shape of the stain she'd likely leave if she cratered from this height. The image of her body spread-eagled on the desert floor in the middle of a red spiderweb pattern of her own blood was actually vivid enough to briefly supplant everything else cluttering her mind. She'd been left with no alternative that she could see, though. No use in whining about it now.

Darby looked over the edge of the cliff again and decided that the timing was as good as it was going to get. The sheer sandstone wall was shadowed enough that she wouldn't stand out too much, but not so dark that she wouldn't be able to find handholds. Unless, of course, therewere none.

Darby took a deep breath, did her best to empty her mind, and swung around so that her legs hung over the precipice. After a few more unintentionally short breaths, she slowly let her body slide off the edge, leaving her dangling straight-armed from the overhanging tongue of rock she'd been laying on top of moments before.

The wind buffeted her gently as she looked down past the brown of her legs and the bloodstains still clinging to her sandals, through three hundred feet of empty air, to the green juniper trees that looked like tiny bushes on the canyon floor. She could feel the blood starting to flow into her forearms and the sweat that would soon become slick, leaking from her palms. She focused all her concentration on a six-inch ledge a few feet in front of her, trying to stay completely focused. Fear was a very real danger in climbing—it wreaked havoc on judgment and balance, and caused premature exhaustion.

She swung her legs at the ledge, feeling her hands slip slightly when she missed by a solid inch. The adrenaline that she was trying so hard to keep under control surged wildly as her forward momentum petered out and her body weight started to carry her into a backward swing that had the very real potential to pull her off and send her into space. She curled her knees to her chest to try to deaden the motion and strained with her fingers to hold the sloping edge of the cliff. Her hands started to slide back, out of control, but at the last moment found a tiny indentation in the rock. It turned out to be just enough to save her.

The blood pulsing through her forearms was starting to give her the familiar feeling of her skin being too tight. She knew from experience that she had only a few more seconds before the lactic acid started building up in her muscles and she began to lose her contact strength.

She kicked out again, harder this time, knowing that if she missed, she wouldn't be able to control the increased force of her back swing. At the last possible moment, she pulled in hard with her stomach muscles and felt the edge of her sandal catch on the ledge. She used it to pull herself in a little and let her leg take as much weight off her hands as possible—but there was no way to know if it would be enough. She closed her eyes for a moment and then let go with her left hand, bringing it slowly down in front of her as her right hand started to slip again. She managed to lodge it in a fist-sized crack at chest level just as her right hand cut loose.

It held.

She quickly swung her entire body to the right and wedged herself into a wide groove in the rock, her breath coming way too fast. Fear again, she told herself—but knew it was something more. She felt strangely at odds with nature—something she'd never experienced before. The rock was too sharp under her hands and the wind was gusting too cold against the sweat dripping down her back. She felt . . .

Darby wiggled into a slightly more secure position, reminding herself that this probably wasn't an ideal time for philosophizing. The three men below her had gathered around something that might have been a backpack, and the blond one seemed to be passing something out to the others. A moment later she saw the individual beams of light leap magically from their hands and cut through the approaching darkness. Flashlights.

Darby started down the chimney-sized groove in the rock, staying as far back in it as possible in an effort to remain invisible, but soon found that the plan had a substantial drawback. The darkness in the small fissure was deepening more each minute, making it increasingly difficult to find the small hand and footholds that were the only things keeping her from falling the remaining two hundred and fifty feet to the ground. She was being forced to rely almost completely on the friction she could generate by pressing her hands and feet on one side of the groove and her back on the other.

Her progress was painfully slow and so much harder than it should have been. If the lack of a rope and harness was eating at her concentration, the lack of the sure-footedness of climbing shoes was destroying it.

No whining, she reminded herself. The situation was what it was.

It took over an hour for her to work her way to a small alcove ten feet above the cave that contained Tristan's file. There had been two very close calls on her way down—one when she'd briefly run out of holds and friction, and the other when she'd knocked off a sizeable rock that had, thanks to a soft sand landing, gone unnoticed.

The men scouring the canyon floor were close now. She couldn't see them from her position, but she could hear the crunch of their footsteps and an occasional eruption of a voice. When she finally worked herself into a position where she could spy on them, she saw that they were nearly invisible. Shadows behind the powerful beams of their flashlights, just like . . .

She waited until their search pattern had focused them in another direction and swung quickly over the lip of the cave. Her luck had finally run out, though, and she felt her hands slide from an unexpectedly polished surface on the rock and then the sudden weightlessness of falling.

It had been years since she and Tristan had stashed their gear in this cave, but she seemed to remember that its floor extended out further than its roof. In most cases she had a good memory for that kind of thing. But if this was one of those rare occasions that she'd confused one cliff with another, her fall would be broken by a pile of jagged rocks fifty feet below. And then all her problems would be solved.

She hit the floor of the cave hard. Unconsciously she had pitched her weight forward, away from the precipice, and she went face-first into the rock. Dazed, she laid there for a few moments and listened to the voices of the men outside grow loud.

They'd heard her.

She struggled into a crouch but then froze, not sure what to do. There was no time.

"What about over there?"

It was the first full sentence she'd been able to make out, no doubt thanks to the acoustics of the cave. The deep, masculine voice had a complete lack of urgency to it. She moved back to the mouth of the cave and saw the flashlights still moving in a more or less random pattern a hundred meters away. The voices hadn't turned to shouts, she realized; it was just acoustics.

She took a moment to collect herself, then crawled to the back of the cave, feeling around her in the darkness for anything that didn't belong. After a few moments the voices started to grow again in volume. This time it wasn't an audio illusion, though; the men had redirected their search and were getting closer.

When Darby reached the back wall, she turned left and started along it in a straight line, trying to conduct as methodical a search as possible under the circumstances. There were broken rocks strewn everywhere, and she could already feel the blood flowing from her bare knees and shins. But that didn't bother her as much as the realization that Tristan would have most likely buried the file with the loose rocks scattered around the floor of the cave. And there was no way to feel the difference between a natural and man-made formation.

"What's up there?"

She froze at the sound of the man's voice as it echoed around her.

The crack of sandstone on sandstone was unmistakable as someone started up the talus field below.

You're still okay, she told herself. *You're still okay*

The fifty-foot climb up to the cave was difficult—solid 5.10. Anyone who would try that in this light, without the protection of a rope, was probably a friend or at least acquaintance of hers. And if they took the time to set up a rope belay, she could be long gone by the time one of them made it all the way up. But not without the file.

She pulled the backpack off her shoulders and fished around in it until she found the lighter at the bottom. The desperate shouts started below the moment she lit it and the cave came flickering to life around her.

She ran around the cave throwing rocks off any formation that looked like it might not have occurred naturally, the sound mimicking the clatter rising from below as the three men scurried to the base of the cliff.

"Fuck the shoes! Go! Go!"

Darby froze for a moment and listened.

"Move, goddamnit!"

The voice was deafening, as though it was aimed directly up at the cave. Or perhaps at someone climbing toward her. She went back to her search, frantically kicking and throwing rocks at the back of the cave until she started to hear the labored breathing and occasional grunts of a climber moving toward her. She picked up a rock and considered rolling it off the edge, but couldn't bring herself to do it. What if it was just a local guide they'd hired? Maybe someone she knew?

A gust of wind blew the lighter out as she started back the way she'd come. She flicked it again and the intensity of the flame as it exploded to life created a dull glitter beneath the sand at her feet.

She dropped to her knees and brushed it away, feeling the unmistakable cold smoothness of plastic. She shoved a large rock aside and started to dig as the sound of the mysterious climber continued to close in on her.

Whatever it was, it had been encased in at least a half-inch of shrink-wrap. She held it up for a moment, but the glare from the flame was too intermittent to see anything but its shape and deep brown color.

Darby shoved it in her backpack and slung the pack over her shoulders just as a loud grunt echoed through the cave and the blond head of the man she'd seen from the cliff top appeared at the mouth. She ran within three feet of him as he struggled to pull himself over the lip, dropping the lighter and lunging at a line of softball-sized holes gouged in the rock by a million years of water flow.

She forced herself not to look back again—there was nothing she could do but go straight up. Moving right would bring her into view of the men on the ground and left would take her back into the cave. Desperation gripped her as she threw herself recklessly at each hand and foothold, forgetting how high she was off the ground, forgetting everything but the man behind her.

She remembered the huge hold at the base of the little alcove above the cave and launched herself at it. She felt her feet and hands leave the wall and her body arc through the night air as a gunshot sounded and a bullet skittered off the rock close enough to kick dust into her eyes. She latched the hold with her right hand and used the powerful muscles in her arm to continue her upward momentum. She rolled into the alcove and hit the back of it hard, then froze and listened for the sound of pursuit.

Nothing—only the sound of her own breathing. Then, a moment later, a quiet, heavily accented voice. "Darby?"

She leaned forward out of reflex. The voice was familiar.

"Darby, come down."

That was enough to put a nationality to the man. Slovenian. She scooted forward a few inches. "Vili?"

"Come down now, Darby."

She almost leaned her head over the edge to see if there was enough light to make out his features, but then remembered the gunshot that couldn't have come from anyone but him.

"You shot at me, Vili."

"Just to scare you." His voice was calm and even, but obviously forced. "The men I am with hired me to help them find you. To bring you to the police for what you did to Tristan."

"I didn't do anything to Tristan. You know that."

"Of course I do. Come down, we will take you to your police. You can tell them."

Whoever the people after her were, they were smart. It had only been three days since she'd escaped from the old farmhouse and they'd already found the perfect person to track her. Vili had been a professional climber for years—he knew the ins and outs of her lifestyle and probably most of her friends. But more, he hated her with a burning passion that she would never understand.

It had been three years ago on Gasherbrum IV in the Himalaya. She'd gone there to attempt a solo ascent of a new route on the west face of the mountain. But he'd sneaked in a week before, with a map she'd drawn, to try to steal the ascent out from under her.

She'd found him about halfway up it, his leg broken and half frozen. She'd almost died about ten times getting him down. He hadn't even tried to help; he'd just lain there and whimpered while she dragged him along the steep slopes in subzero temperatures and blinding snow. A week after he'd been evacuated by helicopter, she'd completed the route, and worse, made the cover of *Climbing* magazine.

She hadn't really been looking for gratitude and she hadn't gotten any. Apparently embarrassed by his behavior and for being saved by a woman, he'd somehow managed to convince himself that his accident had been her fault and that she'd stolen the climb from him.

"Why are you doing this, Vili?"

A shout from below floated up, but he didn't answer it. "To show the world who you really are, Darby. What you did to me."

"You would have died up there."

"You say!" His voice suddenly went from a whisper to a scream. "You forced me down. You took that climb from me!"

It occurred to her again just how pointless Tristan's death had been. He was the victim of the stunted, adolescent egos of supposedly full-grown men. Politicians searched for power, captains of industry pursued for money. For climbers, it was glory. But it was all an illusion. No matter how much they amassed, they would still grow old and weak and die. Tristan should have known better.

Darby stood and looked up the pitch-black chimney cut into the rock behind her. She closed her eyes and tried to remember the most difficult sections that she had passed on her way down and project how hard they'd be in the dark and with the extra weight in her pack.

She calculated a one-in-three chance of making it to the top alive. That could be improved to fifty–fifty if she took her time, but the men below would undoubtedly take the same dirt road up the back that she had and try to be there to meet her.

"Wait!" Vili yelled when he heard Darby start up the chimney. "Darby! Wait!"

She continued on, picking up her pace when she heard him step around the edge of the cave and start the climb to the alcove. She found a spot that she could comfortably stand for a moment and looked down into the blackness. "There's a lot of loose rock up here, Vili."

She heard his progress come to a sudden halt. The meaning of her statement was clear—if he continued up behind her, she'd kick off enough debris to ensure that he took the express to the ground.

"Wait, Darby! Wait!" He switched to his native language, speaking slowly and deliberately, enunciating every word very carefully. Her Slovenian was horrible—self-taught during a six-month climbing trip there a few years back.

He repeated himself, even slower this time, and she struggled to translate. She couldn't nail every word, but the gist was that if she threw the file down he'd let her go and lead the men who had hired him away from her.

Darby reached up and tested a small flake in the rock that was just big enough for her to get her fingers behind. "Don't follow me, Vili. You won't make it," she said, pulling herself up a few more feet. He screamed something she couldn't translate and she heard the crack of another gunshot. She continued on, satisfied that there was no way he could hit her from where he was standing, and that he wouldn't follow. In the end, Vili Marcek was a coward.

KYLE MILLS

Rising Phoenix

Special agent Mark Beamon is a maverick. His open disdain for the FBI's rules – and directors – has exiled him to a no-hope post. But when a shadowy right-wing group starts flooding America's emergency rooms with dead and dying, Beamon is summoned back to Washington. Teamed with an icily efficient female field agent, he is given the thankless task of stopping the slaughter.

As the body count rises, Beamon realises there is something eerily familiar about his adversary, reminding him of the coldest killer he ever encountered. Not a criminal, but a law enforcement colleague. And for the first time, Mark Beamon wonders why he was chosen for this assignment. Was it his expertise? Or his expendability?

'A seductive action novel . . . here's one slick page turner that makes readers think' *San Francisco Chronicle*

CORONET BOOKS
Hodder & Stoughton

KYLE MILLS

Sphere of Influence

Mark Beamon has always been an unconventional FBI agent.

Years of putting the truth ahead of political expediency have resulted in a dead-end job in the Phoenix office. Until a new threat brings him back from the wilderness.

A video tape proves that a terrorist cell in the United States has access to modern missile technology, and Beamon is sent undercover. When his fellow agent is brutally murdered, Beamon's attempts to trace the man who betrayed them lead him into an international criminal conspiracy that may have roots in the American government.

As events plunge him into a river of deceit he is forced to address the most important question of his life . . .

What makes a crime a crime?

'Mills has won praise from some of the top thriller writers around. It's deserved.' *Houston Chronicle*

CORONET BOOKS
Hodder & Stoughton

KYLE MILLS

Free Fall

A top-secret FBI file – buried in an anonymous government warehouse since J Edgar Hoover's death – is missing. The unlucky student who uncovered it is dead, and now his ex-girlfriend is on the run, accused of murder. The only man everyone agrees can find her and turn up the explosive document is 'off-duty', suspended and under the threat of prosecution by the bureau itself.

Mark Beamon knows better than anyone that this is his last shot to save his career – and his country. Tracking the young woman down, though, will be the hardest assignment he's ever tackled, for she's a world-class rock-climber who can drop out of sight anywhere in the globe. And even if he finds her and the file, who can he trust when the FBI itself is under suspicion? Beamon has no room for wrong guesses or moves, if he is to avoid free falling out of the bureau and straight into prison – or worse.

'[A] treacherous, fast-moving yarn full of crumbling footholds, close shaves, narrow escapes, slippery slopes and daredevil risk takers.' *Los Angeles Times*

CORONET BOOKS
Hodder & Stoughton

KYLE MILLS

Smoke Screen

Thirty-two-year-old Trevor Barnett has inadvertently become the lead spokesman for the tobacco industry just as it's on the verge of extinction, facing a $200 billion lawsuit that it will be unable to appeal. America's tobacco companies react by doing the unthinkable – closing the plants and recalling their products.

The message is clear: no more cigarettes until the industry is given iron-clad protection from the courts.

As the economy falters and chaos takes hold, Trevor finds himself the target of enraged smokers, gun-toting smugglers, and a government that has been cut off from one of its largest sources of revenue. Soon it becomes apparent that this had always been his function – to take the brunt of the backlash and shield the men in power from the maelstrom they'd created. As he is slowly abandoned by an industry that his own ancestors helped to create, Trevor begins to fight back.

'Mills is definitely someone to watch' *Publishers Weekly*

Hodder & Stoughton

BRAD MELTZER

The Zero Game

'About as Grisham as you can get without having his name on the cover' *The Times*

Matthew Mercer and Harris Sandler are best friends who have plum jobs as senior staffers to well-respected congressmen. But after a decade in Washington, idealism has faded to disillusionment, and they're bored. Then one of them finds out about the clandestine Zero Game.

It starts out as good fun – a simple wager between friends. But when someone close to them ends up dead, Harris and Matthew realise the game is far more sinister than they ever imagined – and that they're about to be the game's next victims.

On the run, they turn to the only person they can trust: a sixteen-year-old Senate page who can move around the Capitol undetected. As a ruthless killer creeps closer, this idealistic page not only holds the key to saving their lives, but is also determined to redeem them in the process.

Brad Meltzer's super-charged new thriller will take you on a white-knuckle rollercoaster of a read, and confirms him as the most dazzling suspense writer of his generation.

Hodder & Stoughton

STEPHEN LEATHER

Hard Landing

Dan 'Spider' Shepherd is used to putting his life on the line. As a detective working for an elite undercover squad he has lied, cheated and conned in order to bring Britain's most wanted criminals to justice.

But when a powerful drugs baron starts to kill off witnesses to his crimes, Shepherd is given his most dangerous assignment yet. He has to go undercover in a top security prison, a world where one wrong move will mean certain death.

Corrupt prison officers, lifers with nothing to lose, and hard men with something to prove are all gunning for Shepherd. The only way for him to survive is to play his role to perfection, twenty-four hours a day, among criminals for whom violence is a way of life.

But as Shepherd gambles everything to move in on his quarry, he soon realises that the man he is hunting is even more dangerous than the police realise.

And that he is capable of striking outside the prison walls and hitting Shepherd where it hurts most.

'As high-tech and as world-class as the thriller genre gets'
Express

Hodder & Stoughton

JON EVANS

Trail of the Dead

Off the beaten track.

On the trail of a killer.

Paul Wood is trekking with another backpacker in the Annapurna Range of the Himalayas when they find the still-warm body of a Canadian with his skull smashed in and a Swiss Army knife plunged into each eye. An extraordinarily brutal and unusual crime.

And, extraordinarily, Paul has seen such a death before. His girlfriend was murdered in Cameroon two years before, her eyes mutilated identically.

Another terrible similarity: the local authorities are not interested in investigating a murder of and by travelling foreigners. And if Paul has been a witness to two murders, how many more victims are lying in the developing world who have not been discovered? Using every means he can, Paul tries to uncover the killer. But it may be someone he knows. And that means the killer could find him first . . .

Jon Evans' first breathtaking novel is published
on 5 July 2004

CORONET BOOKS
Hodder & Stoughton